"I Did Not Invite You In."

" 'Tisn't your chamber," Raven retorted. "You're naught but a guest, and an unwelcome one at that."

"Then you must be naught but a guest yourself." Roxanne sneered in return. "I don't recall you being Earl of Fortengall."

Raven paused and inhaled deeply. He'd lost control of the conversation already. But he'd had a purpose in coming here to face her alone. "You failed in your plan," he explained in a low voice, "and you'll be a menace no more."

"How dare you!" Roxanne's eyes, dark as purple pansies, flashed. She brought her hands up to her waist and clenched them into fists.

But instead of her threatening stance, Raven noticed the way the light caught her eyes, the way her breasts plumped above the scooped neckline of her tunic. Then his eyes flicked upward, and he considered her hair. Wild, it was, a disheveled mass of thick, soft, blue-black curls. He longed to run his fingers through the ebony vines cascading from her crown to her hips, but instead he clenched his fists as he crossed his arms over his chest.

"I would have you gone," he announced.

"Would you?" Roxanne asked. When he nodded, she reminded him saucily, " 'Tis not your concern. It is Peter I'm to wed, not you."

Dear Romance Reader,

In July, we launched the Ballad line with four new series, and each month now we offer you both new and continuing stories set everywhere from medieval England to the American West—the kind of passionate, romantic stories you love best, written by the most gifted authors. At the back of each book, we'll tell you when you can find subsequent books in the series that have captured your heart.

Rising star Joy Reed continues her charming Wishing Well trilogy with *Emily's Wish* as a spirited young woman fleeing her past stumbles into a celebrated author . . . and a chance at a love story of her own. Next Candice Kohl sweeps us back to the medieval splendor of The Kinsmen as *A Knight's Passion* becomes a breathtaking romance . . . with a Welsh heiress the king intends for his brother.

New this month is veteran author Linda Lea Castle's Bogus Brides series. The Green sisters must invent "husbands" to remain in the charter town of McTavish Plain, Nebraska—and love is an unexpected complication in *Addie and the Laird*. Finally, we return to the bayous of the Louisiana Territory as Cherie Claire offers the second book of the The Acadians. *Rose* dreams of romance . . . but loses her heart to the one man her family has forbidden. Enjoy!

Kate Duffy
Editorial Director

THE KINSMEN

A KNIGHT'S PASSION

CANDICE KOHL

ZEBRA BOOKS
KENSINGTON PUBLISHING CORP.

http://www.zebrabooks.com

ZEBRA BOOKS are published by

Kensington Publishing Corp.
850 Third Avenue
New York, NY 10022

All Kensington titles, imprints and distributed lines are available at special quantity discounts for bulk purchases for sales promotion, premiums, fund raising, educational or institutional use.

Special book excerpts or customized printings can also be created to fit specific needs. For details, write or phone the office of the Kensington Special Sales Manager: Kensington Publishing Corp., 850 Third Avenue, New York, NY, Attn. Special Sales Department. Phone: 1-800-221-2647.

Zebra and the Z logo Reg. U.S. Pat. & TM Off.

First Printing: November, 2000
10 9 8 7 6 5 4 3 2 1

Printed in the United States of America

To the brothers Kohl, Christopher and Dustin,
and the women who are destined to make husbands of them

CHAPTER 1

"Lucien! God's tears, but it's good to see you again after all this time!"

Henry II, still youthful, redheaded, and freckle-faced, greeted Lucien of Eynsham as he entered the king's private rooms. Rising from his chair on his slightly bowed legs, he embraced the young lord like a brother.

"How fare you, Your Majesty?" Lucien inquired, sitting down opposite the king.

"Well, indeed. And how is your family?"

"Adrienne and Lilith are both delightful beauties. My wife," Lucien explained, "is expecting our second child any time now. My mother predicts she will bear twins. Which prompts me, sire, to ask what business has brought me here to you. Whatever it is, I should like to attend to it quickly, if I may. I've no wish to be away from Adrienne any longer than necessary."

"Don't worry about her, Lucien." Henry waved a bejeweled hand dismissively through the air. "Women have been bearing babes throughout the ages without any help from men—at least, not during those moments the whelps are, in fact, making their first appearance. But you speak of the prospect of twins, and that leads us straight to the heart of the matter that's brought you here: your younger brothers, Lords Peter and Raven."

"Oh?"

"Yes. I see them frequently when I am this side of the Channel, though I admit Raven finds his way to court more often than Peter. Though he has no wife or children, Peter—like you—apparently finds his time well spent administering his estate. Raven, methinks, is more easily bored being a landed nobleman. He likes to amuse himself with the beauties who wait upon my royal wife. As I am prone to do myself," Henry added with a wink.

Lucien nodded noncommittally. And waited.

Henry continued. "Having given it much thought, Lucien, I think it high time your brothers wed. 'Tis my wish that they marry two young damsels who have come under my protection."

Jesu! Lucien controlled a noticeable start and merely nodded his head again. That any monarch, least of all His Majesty Henry II, was compelled by custom to assume guardianship for his subjects' fatherless daughters, well ... to Lucien, it seemed extremely foolish. But Henry hadn't enough to do, apparently, not even with his forays into Wales, to prevent him from putting his royal finger in the pudding.

Aloud, he finally said, "My brothers may be twins, sire, but they are not so very much alike. I think Peter may be agreeable to your proposal, but Raven is without a doubt a knave. To date, not a single woman, be she lady or serving wench, has managed to capture his attention for more than a sennight."

"Marriage does not necessarily preclude affairs of the heart, nor even a casual tryst or two. Except, of course, in rare marriages like your own and Adrienne's." Henry slanted his gaze to peer at Lucien contemplatively. "When have you last been in Raven's company?"

"Not since Yuletide. But I do believe he has no intention of taking a wife 'til he's too old to satisfy the endless procession of women who snag his attention day to day."

"Raven of Stonelee has no choice."

The king's clipped words conveyed to Lucien the fact that this matter was not under consideration; Henry had made his decision.

"Nay, I can tell that he hasn't." Lucien paused before asking curiously, "Your Highness, who are these damsels you've chosen to be my sisters-by-marriage? Are they familiar faces at court?"

"Nay. Their sires' keeps were, shall we say, on roads rarely traveled."

Idly, Lucien reached for a flagon of wine on the table nearest his own chair and began pouring himself a cup.

"The girls are cousins," Henry went on. "Their mothers were the princesses Ceridwen and Rhiannon."

"Welsh?" In his surprise, Lucien missed the rim of his cup and sloshed the dark red liquid onto the table.

"Aye. The girls' fathers, Arthur and Cedric, descended from lesser lords from Warwick who were sent out to conquer the borderlands. The baronies that Arthur and Cedric ruled 'til their deaths were neighboring estates a bit west of Offa's Dyke."

"Offa's Dyke!" Ignoring the spilled wine, Lucien tipped the flagon again, half filled his cup, and took a hearty gulp. These wards, he now understood, were heiresses to mighty strongholds, which the king considered critical as he sought to bring all of Wales under his rule. "Arthur and Cedric," Lucien surmised, "were Marcher Earls."

"Aye." As though the information Henry had just confirmed was trivial, he casually reached down to pat one of his spaniels, which presently lolled with its head upon its master's shoe. "Arthur's barony is called Angleford, Cedric's Bittenshire."

The king looked up again at Lucien. "Arthur and Ceridwen had no sons and only one daughter. Lady Pamela was born long years into their union. She had hardly entered her second decade of life when she was orphaned. I made no objection when Cedric and Rhiannon took her in. Rhiannon, her mother's sister, was Pamela's blood kin, and Cedric easily managed Angleford by protecting it with his own men."

"But now Lord Cedric and his lady wife are gone as well?"

"Aye."

"And their daughter? Your other ward?"

"She's the youngest of their far larger, feminine brood. God's blood, Lucien!" Chuckling, Henry sat back in his chair and shook his head. " 'Twould seem these two hulking knights who took Welsh princesses for brides could sire naught but girl children! Lady Rhiannon birthed fully ten, all beauties. I know, for I've seen them with my own eyes. Save for their last born, Roxanne, all have married well."

"Mayhap the Welsh princesses cursed their Norman husbands, denying them male progeny," Lucien suggested.

"I doubt that. Most Norman-English in Wales have mixed their blood with the natives. Lady Pamela, who is still three years short of a score, was certainly her parents' best, if belated, blessing. And Lady Roxanne"—Henry cleared his throat and took a sudden, renewed interest in his hound—"she appears to have been indulged, as she's well past the age most young ladies are wed. She's two years Pamela's senior. Yet, her father did not force her into holy wedlock."

Lucien nodded, stifling his more skeptical observations.

"I need the damsels wed, Lucien, and damned quickly! Arthur and Cedric were both my loyal vassals. When the lord of Angleford died, Ceridwen held his keep secure. When she passed as well, Cedric of Bittenshire managed Angleford's demesne and people, holding it in trust as Pamela's dower. But the time has come for a lord in residence to protect Angleford from the Welsh. If there's any delay, one of the girls' wretched Welsh uncles could coerce Lady Pamela into wedding a Welshman—a Welshman who does not, shall we say, hold your king in high esteem.

"I can ill afford such a loss, Lucien," he added, shaking his head. "As I'm attempting to extend my rule in Wales, 'twould be fruitless to acquire more land there while losing that which had been held for decades by a Marcher Lord whose fealty had been pledged to England's king."

Lucien digested all that Henry had confided to him. "I understand Arthur's daughter needs a husband to rule her sire's estate. But that cannot be the situation with the other maid."

"Lady Roxanne."

"Aye, Roxanne. She has nine married sisters, you say."

"That's true." Henry fingered his neat, red beard. "One of them, Cedric's eldest, already resides at Bittenshire with her husband and children. But do not concern yourself, Lucien. Roxanne is well-dowered. The brother who gains no land through his bride shall obtain other valuables, through me."

Holding his cup just beneath his chin, Lucien peered speculatively over the rim. "My lord, I can well understand why you wish to marry off these ripe maidens who are your wards. But why to my brothers? Both knights are content with the fees you awarded them some years ago. Neither shall welcome becoming entangled with an estate in the Welsh borderlands."

"Because 'tis my decision!" the king snapped, leaping up. Inadvertently, he displaced the hound, which looked up and whined lamentingly before circling his tail and settling down again.

Lucien felt like doing much the same as the dog had done, for he realized he'd presumed too much. Though he and Henry had long been friends, they were far from equals.

"Pray forgive me, Your Highness. 'Twas not my intention to question the soundness of your decision. I was only curious."

With a shrug that implied forgiveness, the king sat down again. "Pray continue, Lucien. What else has you curious?"

He hesitated but then pressed on. "Sire, why am I here and not my brothers? This matter concerns them directly."

Henry had resumed stroking his neatly clipped beard, but now his fingers stilled. "Ah, Lucien. 'Tis this way. One or both of your brothers is going to resent my edict. Neither has any choice in the matter, but knowing those two—especially the one who now calls himself Raven—they may object rather strenuously. I thought to protect them from themselves."

Lucien cocked an eyebrow, and Henry explained, "You see, if I gave them my directive in person, one or both might object and, in the heat of anger, offend me. If either offended me, the consequences could be dire. So to avoid such a possibility, I would have you convey the news to them. If they choose to shout and protest, 'twill be only you who'll hear."

"You are," Lucien muttered softly, "a wise and thoughtful king, Your Grace."

Henry flashed a smile. Crossing his legs, he rested one ankle on his other knee. "I also want you to protect the ladies themselves, Lucien. They are here in this very palace and ready to travel. I charge you, now, with seeing them delivered safely into your brothers' care."

"Which?"

"Which?"

"Which damsel is to be delivered to which brother?"

"Ah, that." The king's eyebrows arched as he threaded his fingers together over his knee. "Knowing Raven as I do, I believe it best he assume leadership of Angleford and mastery of its lady."

Now, Lucien of Eynsham rode through the cold and colorless countryside, two missives from King Henry in his pack, two ladies from Wales in his wake. He felt uneasy as he reined in his mount and gazed up at his brothers' keeps, which had appeared on the horizon.

They were two of the last keeps Henry had licensed, and they looked unusual. Not in style of architecture, but because the structures had been erected so close together, nearly back to back upon a pair of craggy, natural rises nature had cut from the hard earth. Peter's stronghold faced into the wind that whipped around the hills; Raven's faced away. Thus, the former was known as Stoneweather and the latter as Stonelee.

Once, these adjoining fees had been a single barony called Eye. King Henry had offered Lucien and his brothers the land in reward for the assistance they'd given him. But only the twins had accepted, since Lucien, as eldest, had been intent on ruling Eynsham, his own heritable lands. Peter and Raven had divided the property and built their keeps side by side.

The stone structures appeared as identical as Lucien's brothers. But each keep faced in the opposite direction, and that, Lucien mused, reflected their personalities as well.

With a tired sigh, he twisted around in his saddle. Leaning on the cantle, he addressed the women who'd halted behind him. "We are here." He gestured, pointing. "Behold, Stonelee and Stoneweather."

Neither commented. Pamela eyed the strongholds thoughtfully. Roxanne shrugged with indifference. Righting himself in his saddle, Lucien determined to get this ticklish business behind him so that he could return to Adrienne at Eynsham Keep. When he kicked his steed into a trot, the ladies followed apace.

CHAPTER 2

"Lord Lucien!" Stonelee's head steward called in greeting when the trio entered the inner bailey of Raven's barony. The man, Niles, stood atop the wide, stone steps that led to the keep's main portal. "I didn't know you were expected."

"I wasn't. And as you can see, I've brought guests." Lucien halted a little distance from the stairs and dismounted, handing his destrier's reins to a stable boy. Glancing at the riders who'd followed behind him, he saw that other hands assisted the women. "These are the Ladies Pamela of Angleford and Roxanne of Bittenshire."

"Welcome, my ladies," Niles said, rushing down the steps to greet each of the visitors with a courteous bow.

"We encountered one of Stoneweather's servants on the road, so I sent him to alert my brother, Peter, that I'd arrived. The watch guard informed me Lord Raven is in residence."

"Aye. He's home, my lord."

Lucien ushered the ladies toward the door before striding past the steward and into the keep. Niles followed, and inside the great hall, Lucien turned to him. ''Mayhap I'd best seek him out myself. Where might I find him, Niles?''

The steward ducked his chin. ''Ah . . . Lord Raven's in . . . his bedchamber.''

''At this hour of the day?''

''Ah—''

Lucien gave Niles no time for an explanation. Impatiently, he strode away and took the stairs two at a time. ''Get up. You have visitors!'' he informed Raven through his chamber door. Knocking hard with his knuckles, he demanded, ''Why the devil are you abed? Were you drinking and wenching 'til the sun came up this morn?''

Lucien was startled into silence upon opening the door and finding not Raven, but an exceptionally striking young woman with flaming, tousled hair sitting in the rumpled bed. The fur rugs barely covered her hips, but she seemed not at all distressed that a strange man had burst in upon her and settled his gaze upon her voluptuous, pink-tipped breasts.

''Who are you?'' she asked curiously.

''Lucien.''

''And who is it you be looking for?''

''Percival,'' he muttered, so taken aback by the vision before him that he used his brother's birth name.

''Percival?''

''Aye.'' Lucien nodded and raised his gaze to her face again. ''The lord of this keep. The man whose bed you're in.''

''Percival, is it?'' The wench laughed delightedly, a deep, throaty giggle. The sound was so sensuous that even the happily wed Lucien felt the skin on his scrotum tighten. Then she craned her neck, peering around him, and shouted, ''Raven! Have you emptied your bladder yet? You've a visitor here who calls himself Lucien!''

''Lucien.'' From behind him, Raven tapped his brother on the shoulder. ''Let me by, will you? It's good to see you, but as you'll note, I'm naked as a newborn. I haven't a stitch of clothes, except in my room.''

He stepped aside to let his unclad brother enter. Leaning against the door frame, Lucien waited restlessly for his younger sibling to pull on his braies and his leggings. ''I cannot believe the state I find you in,'' he complained. ''Why in damnation are you''—he gestured emphatically toward the woman in his brother's bed—''in the middle of the day?''

Raven grinned as he retrieved a discarded tunic from the floor and pulled it on. ''It's not the middle of the day by any means. In truth, some would say it's evening. What better time to—?'' Mockingly, he also gestured expansively toward the wench. But then he frowned at her and ordered, ''Out of bed now, Lydia. My brother demands my attention.''

''Your brother?'' Lydia's eyebrows arched in surprise as she considered Lucien's russet hair and green eyes. She also slipped one long leg over the edge of the mattress, searching for the floor with her toes. ''You don't look like Raven's brother.''

''They are only twins,'' Lucien advised her, referring to Raven and Peter. ''We are not triplets.''

With more interest than he'd watched his brother dressing, Lucien eyed Lydia as she stretched and pulled on her shift and tunics.

''Put your eyes back in your head, Lucien,'' Raven admonished him. ''You're a married man, and a father in the bargain.''

Turning his attention to Lydia again, he said, ''Give me a kiss that'll hold me.'' The young woman promptly obliged.

''Enough, already!'' Lucien barked when the kiss seemed unlikely to end. After the couple broke their embrace and Raven slapped the girl's round behind, urging her out the door, he added, ''I hope that kiss holds you the rest of your days. There'll be no more from her for the likes of you.''

''What are you mumbling about?'' Raven scowled.

''I'm not mumbling, but I am short on time, so I suggest you heed what I say.''

"Important business, is it?"

"Aye, Raven. The king's business."

Peeved that his brother showed little interest and no concern, but instead merely rummaged about for his shoes, Lucien exclaimed, "God's tears, man! Will you pay attention?"

"You have my entire attention," Raven assured him as he took a step toward a chair.

"Don't get comfortable," Lucien warned. "I've sent for Peter to join us shortly, and as well, you have guests whom I escorted here at the king's behest. We should go down to them immediately." Lucien stepped through the doorway.

Raven followed behind, hopping on one foot as he tugged a shoe on the other. "Who are these men Henry's sent here?"

"They are not men at all," Lucien explained as they headed down the stairs. "The rest you'll understand soon enough."

When they reached the bottom step, Peter was just handing off his heavy, fur-trimmed mantle to one of the Stonelee servants. "Lucien!" He smiled, seeing his elder brother. But abruptly, his grin faded. "There's no trouble, is there? At Eynsham or with Adrienne?"

"Nay. Everything's fine."

"Then, what brings you here?"

"King Henry sent for me, to escort a pair of ladies here."

"Ladies? Here? Why?"

"That's what I should like to know," Raven announced.

"You're to wed us, by your king's decree."

All three men turned toward the lady who had spoken. None had heard her approach, for the great hall was noisy with servants setting up tables for the evening's repast. Though her presence surprised the twin lords of Stonelee and Stoneweather, even Lucien was startled by Lady Roxanne. Like her cousin, she had been presented to him dressed for travel. He had only seen her wrapped in a voluminous, hooded fur cloak.

He had known she stood fairly tall. Because she rode her horse—a stallion—astride, he'd caught a glimpse or two of well-shaped calves encased in men's leggings. But only now, along with his brothers, was Lucien keenly aware of the damsel's awesome figure. She was shapely and buxom, ripe as a juicy melon. And her hair! It looked as black as both Raven's and Peter's. Freed from the confines of a deep hood, Lucien saw she wore it unbound, a riot of loose curls tumbling over her shoulders. Her wide, arched brows and thick, curled lashes were sooty, too. They shaded luminous eyes that he'd first presumed were blue, but which he now saw looked nearer the color of the violet-hued tunics she wore.

It seemed impossible that none of them had noticed her waiting, impatiently, for an introduction. Her presence was astounding even when she wasn't riding her huge horse, skirts hiked up over her knees.

"We're to wed you?" Raven repeated querulously.

"Only one of you is to wed me," Roxanne explained, as though the lord of Stonelee were a dullard. "The one called Peter."

Peter's own black eyebrows arched; his dark eyes raked the lady up and down another time. "I'm the one they call Peter," he informed her before casting a quick glance at his twin. "And today I am glad of it."

"Please, allow me to introduce Lady Roxanne of Bittenshire," Lucien offered a trifle belatedly.

"If Henry's decided Lady Roxanne is to be Peter's wife, then who is my supposed bride to be?"

"Me, milord." Lady Pamela came scurrying from the far end of the hall. "I—I am Lady Pamela of Angleford." Grabbing her bliaut skirt, she executed a formal curtsy.

Raven studied this second female, while his brothers openly stared. Lucien found himself unprepared again for this damsel's beauty. No longer covered head to toe in cape and cowl, she seemed like a butterfly just out of her cocoon.

Lady Pamela looked as young as her years, with her narrow shoulders, tiny waist, and slim hips. Even her bosom was diminutive. Yet, she fit together nicely, and she claimed gorgeous eyes, the color of Fortengall Castle's best brew—a light amber hue. Which was also the color of her shining hair, still bound into two thick braids.

"You're to be *my* wife?" Raven inquired.

"Aye." Pamela nodded, lowering her gaze demurely. "At least, I presume so. King Henry explained to me that my dowerlands require a—a"—she broke off as she raised her eyes to peek timidly through her lashes at Raven—"a hotheaded, hardhanded master to keep the peace there. He said the knight most suitable would be Lord—Lord—"

She turned to Roxanne, who helpfully supplied the name, "Percival."

"Percival!" Raven exploded.

"Aye. Isn't that your name?"

"It is. But no one has called me that in years. I'm known as Raven."

"A wise decision," Roxanne declared with mock sincerity. "A name like Percival doesn't command much respect, does it? I suspect 'tis a name given a younger son destined to join the Church and spend his days in the company of other younger sons, all of them wearing coarse gowns dragging behind their sandaled feet. Was that what your parents expected for you?"

Jet eyes glared at violet ones. "God's blood, but I was ne'er expected to be some genderless, scholarly monk, you—!"

"Raven!" Growling, Lucien silenced his brother before he could call Peter's betrothed a nasty name or worse.

Raven glowered at the black-haired damsel. "You may call me *Lord* Raven."

"Oh?" She smiled tauntingly and arched an eyebrow. "As we shall soon be related, I'd think to call you 'brother.' "

Raven made an unintelligible sound that was clearly understandable to one and all. Managing to pull his gaze from Roxanne, his black eyes burned like coals when he turned to Lucien.

"God's wounds, what in the name of all things holy is going on here?"

"Don't you understand the king's French?" Roxanne drawled. She crossed her arms over her ample bosom, arching a winged brow, and looking decidedly bored. "The Angevin who reigns over England has determined that you're to wed my cousin, Pamela. Your brother"—her eyes flicked briefly toward Peter—"is to marry me. Of course, we both come fully dowered. As an only child, Pamela's sire's keep will go to the man she weds to rule as his own. My dower amounts to little, considering I have a slew of older sisters, so your king is providing lucre of a more portable nature to enhance it."

"Lucien?" Raven uttered the name as a frustrated question. His elder brother nodded in mute response. "How can this be? Why would Henry decide to force these two—"

"Raven." Peter spoke softly but sternly when he interrupted. "Mayhap the ladies would like to refresh themselves before we partake of supper."

"What?" Raven blinked. "Oh, aye. Of course." Distractedly, he strode farther into the great hall and grabbed one of his servants by the sleeve. Tersely, he muttered some directives in the man's ear.

"This way, m'ladies," the servant directed, heading to the stairs and gesturing for the ladies to follow. "There be a chamber what's always ready fer guests. It won't be long now, though, 'til Cook sends out the victuals."

Obediently, Pamela followed the manservant until she disappeared from view. But Roxanne paused on the stairs and looked down at the trio of knights who remained in the hall. "Lord Lucien," she said silkily, "though a brief respite and a hot meal is most appreciated, I do hope wherever it is we are going this eve, the journey shan't be long."

"Pardon?" He felt like she'd pinched his cheek, hard.

Roxanne batted her lashes. "You can't mean to leave us

with these men who are not yet our husbands. Especially as there seem to be no other ladies in residence.''

With a smile as insincere as the light in her eyes, Roxanne finally turned to follow her cousin and the Stonelee servant.

"Jesu!" Lucien muttered. ''I've been so anxious to settle this business and return to Adrienne, the proprieties of the situation never once occurred to me.''

''She's a bitch!'' Raven hissed.

''I remind you you're speaking of my future wife.''

''You can't be serious, Peter. You'll bend to Henry?''

''He's my king.''

Raven snorted and stomped angrily toward the center of his great hall. ''Lucien, tell us all of it. Now. Why did Henry do this to us? And why didn't he send for us directly? Sweet *Jesu,* but I was just in his company a short month ago. Why—''

''I'll tell you all I know, if you'll give me a moment.'' Lucien raked his fingers through his hair. ''First, I need a rider sent to Fortengall Castle. The night is clear, so there should be enough moonlight for Mother to travel here this eve.''

''Mother? You're sending for Mother?''

''Who better than Lucinda of Fortengall, lady wife of the earl, to ensure the damsels' virtue until you two marry them?''

''I refuse to marry them!''

''You only have to wed Lady Pamela,'' Peter pointed out.

''I shan't be wedding Lady Pamela,'' Raven vowed. ''Mark my word, brother. I shan't be wedding her.''

''Roxanne, you were horrid!''

''I wasn't.'' Indignantly, she plopped onto the room's only chair and propped her feet on the room's only stool, effectively denying Pamela a proper place to sit. ''I simply answered the cockshead's questions.''

''Roxy! Your betrothed is no fool.''

''I spoke not of my betrothed, I spoke of yours.''

Pamela gasped before clamping her lips together tightly. As she washed the day's grime from her hands and face, her mind whirled with thoughts of the two lords, one of whom would become her husband. She pictured their wavy hair, their thick, neatly trimmed beards, and their sharp, intelligent eyes, all of which were as black as a rook's wing. But their teeth, she recalled, were even and white, and their bodies not fleshy or formidable, but lean and well-muscled.

Peter and Raven, Lords of Stoneweather and Stonelee, were certainly a handsome pair. She and Roxanne could have done no better had they been given leave to search the kingdom for husbands on their own. Yet, she suspected Roxanne would refuse to be satisfied with the match King Henry had settled upon her.

"Why did you do it?" Pamela asked softly as she patted her cheeks dry with a cloth.

Roxanne's indigo eyes slanted toward her. "Why did I do what?"

"Act as though we've need of a chaperone. We've had none since we left Wales with the king's men."

"It's a question of principle." Roxanne shrugged. "We're ladies, Pamela. Fatherless and husbandless at the moment, aye. But we're not cheap slatterns to be dumped off on these lords' doorsteps as though we had no worth at all."

Shaking her head, Pamela looked down at her skirts. "You can't fight this," she warned. "Lord Peter will be your husband. The king himself's decided."

"He's not my king!"

"He is. Sweet *Jesu*, Roxy, not only that, but he stood as godparent to you at your christening!"

"You lie!" Roxanne's eyes were huge, round, and accusing.

Pamela shook her head determinedly. "I do not. You must know it. Your own mother, Lady Rhiannon, told me so."

"You heard her wrong, then."

"Even if I did," she conceded, "you are descended from a

long line of Normans, English subjects all. You are bound to show your allegiance to the English king.''

''But my mother, like yours, was a Cymry princess! And I, like you, was born in Cymru! Besides, Pamela, though our fathers were loyal to the English Crown, did you ever know mine or yours to bow to any authority higher than themselves? They were Marcher Earls, they were the law, in Bittenshire and Angleford. None save God was above them.''

Pamela blinked at Roxanne as she gnawed her lower lip anxiously. ''It's all changed, now, Roxy. We're naught but women. We must do as our guardian tells us. And, sweet *Jesu,* our guardian is the greatest king the world has ever known!''

Roxanne did not deign to comment further on Pamela's declarations. Her cousin might submit out of some sense of duty, but not she, Roxanne of Bittenshire. First chance, she'd ride north and then west across the border, into the wonderland that was Cymru—all scree-covered mountains dotted with birch and pine, and valleys with streams and meadows of bluebell, kingcup and anemone. Despite his size, Dafydd, her stallion, could traverse the rocky trails that connected the baronies of Bittenshire and Angleford to Penllyn, where Balin lived.

She would go to Balin, the only man she would ever consider taking to husband.

CHAPTER 3

The evening meal proved tedious, tension straining the hours it took to consume every course. Fortunately for Lucien, he sat at the far end of the table so that he did not feel compelled to initiate conversation that the others would refuse to sustain.

"Mother!" his brothers exclaimed in unison suddenly. Startled but relieved, Lucien turned to see Lucinda of Fortengall breezing into Stonelee's great hall, as welcome as the cold gust of wind that blew in behind her, freshening the stagnant, smoky air. Eagerly, the twins strode across the chamber to greet her, while Lucien rose to follow behind them.

"Peter. Raven. Lucien!" Lady Lucinda's green eyes sparkled when she spied her eldest. "I was surprised when the messenger said you were here at Raven's stronghold. Are Adrienne and my granddaughter well?"

"Yes, Mother. Though Adrienne complains about her unwieldy girth."

"She'll not have that to contend with much longer." Lucinda smiled. "Why did you leave her with the babes due so soon?"

Turning slightly, Lucien gestured to the maidens who remained seated at the high table. "Mother, these are the Ladies Roxanne of Bittenshire and Pamela of Angleford. At King Henry's behest, I've brought them here as my brothers' intended brides."

His words launched a sudden silence during which Lucinda considered the young women with a keen eye.

"I should have brought them to Fortengall Castle," he admitted uneasily, glancing at his stepfather, who had followed Lady Lucinda into the hall and now stood beside her. "But as they are here already, we hoped you could serve as their chaperone."

Lady Lucinda nodded and strode forward, approaching the damsels who had risen to their feet, but remained at the high table. With a welcoming smile, she announced, "I am Lady Lucinda of Fortengall. Now, which of you is which? Let me guess. You're Lady Pamela, and you're Lady Roxanne. Are you ever called Roxy?"

"Sometimes, milady."

"But you are called naught but Pamela. Am I right?"

"Aye, you are." Obviously delighted by the lady's intuitiveness, Pamela flashed her a quick, sincere smile.

"Where are my manners—and my sons'?" Lucinda asked abruptly, turning back to glance at her three eldest sons. "Lucien introduces you to us, but deigns not to explain who we are." She reached out a hand toward her husband, who joined her and grasped her fingers in his own. "My dears, this is the earl of Fortengall, my husband, Lord Ian. He is stepfather to those louts still idling a distance away." Pamela blinked in surprise at Lucinda's unexpected remark, while one corner of Roxanne's shapely mouth curled into an appreciative smirk.

"A pleasure," Lord Ian declared.

The earl was a scarred giant who loomed far taller than either of the Welsh cousins, though they stood on a dais and he on the stone floor. But his manner seemed as congenial as his lady's, and neither damsel felt intimidated.

''My lord,'' Roxanne, and then Pamela, muttered in turn.

''I cannot tell you how excited I am at this news!'' Lady Lucinda continued, still smiling. ''Remind me, Ian, to send word to the king, thanking him for precipitously arranging these unions. I was growing concerned that my eldest twin sons might remain unwed 'til they reached their dotage.'' This last she shared specifically with the young ladies, leaning toward them as though confiding a secret.

''You've other children born as twins?'' Pamela inquired.

''Oh, aye. Ian and I have twin sons together, and another lad, older, who is heir to the earldom. But they're all young yet, not even of fostering age. Now tell me: Where are your homes, and how did you come under the king's protection?''

Concisely, Roxanne explained their circumstances.

Lucinda's eyes narrowed. ''You love the marches of Wales, I can tell. I also sense you care naught for England.''

''Our families are loyal to King Henry!'' Pamela volunteered, her vow uttered on a rush of breath.

''Certainly they are.'' Lucinda took her hand and patted it reassuringly. ''Now, which of you is to wed my son, Peter?''

''I am,'' Roxanne said.

''You?''

''Aye. It seems I'm to wed Lord Peter because your king is inclined to make Lord Percival the Marcher Earl of Angleford.''

''Raven, dear,'' Lucinda corrected her gently, purposely ignoring the mocking glance she noticed Roxanne shooting the lord under discussion. ''All their lives my sons have resented my habit of shortening or otherwise altering their Christian names. Now that one of them has found a designation he feels best suits him, I'm glad to humor him with it. I suggest you do, too.''

''Why?'' Roxanne arched one of her black brows. ''I'm not marrying him. I can simply refer to him as 'your son' or 'your brother' whene'er he must be mentioned.''

Blinking slowly, Lucinda's eyebrows arched. "Somehow, my dear lady, I think that will not do."

Spinning around quickly then, she faced her sons. "Where are your servants, Raven? Someone, come take my cloak! And get your stepfather a mug of mead. Has a room been readied for these ladies? Yes? Then, we shall be going upstairs.

"Come along, girls," she urged, leading them toward the stairs. "I vow your virtue will be safe here at Stonelee." She flashed her sons a wink as she herded the young women past. "But I think, come the morn, Lord Ian and I shall take you to Fortengall Castle. You'll be more comfortable there while you await the day of your nuptials."

The great hall fell quiet. Despite the presence of servants, for all intent, the three brothers and their stepfather remained alone in the cavernous room.

Lord Ian turned slightly, folding his muscled arms across his broad chest. He cocked a skewered, red-gold eyebrow. "Well, my lads. What's this business all about?"

"King Henry's chosen brides for us," Peter explained. "He called for Lucien to ride to London, collect them, and bring them here." His black-eyed gaze drifted toward the stairs, following the path the women had taken. "I can't say I'm displeased. Roxanne of Bittenshire is a comely wench."

"A comely shrew," Raven grumbled. "You're welcome to her."

"Bittenshire and Angleford," Lord Ian mused as the four strolled toward the glowing fire that burned in the hearth near the great hall's outside wall. "Welsh baronies, both."

"Aye," Peter confirmed as the men hoisted carved chairs from the dais and set them before the hearth.

" 'Twill be a great responsibility for you two, assuming the mantle of Marcher Lords. England, by comparison, is a peaceful land these days. But Wales"—the earl shrugged, settling himself into a sturdy chair—"it can be no easy task, keeping harmony among the English settlers and the Celtic natives, even just those who dwell within the barony. But you'll also have to fend off attacks from those who reside in the hills.''

"I'm afraid that responsibility falls solely to Raven," Peter informed his stepfather. He refilled the cup he'd confiscated from the high table with wine from the flagon Raven passed among them. "Bittenshire Keep, according to Lucien, already has a lord to rule and defend it." He explained the situation as it had been told to him. "Nay, I think my lady will have to make herself content at Stoneweather."

Peter and the others looked at Raven, who slouched defiantly in his chair. "I don't know if I care to play the lord baron of Lady Pamela's lands," he admitted. "Truth be told, I'm rather fond of Stonelee. As you said, Lord Ian, England's a peaceful place these days. And my demesne, in tandem with Peter's, leaves its lords and its people contentedly sheltered and very well fed. What, I'm wondering, would make me wish to become a petty sovereign in the rugged wilderness of Wales? I have all I need right here. I've no hankering to don hauberk and sword to fight for the pleasure of it."

Lucien glanced between his two bothers. He'd not forgotten the reason King Henry had given for making him the bearer of ill-favored news.

" 'Tisn't as though this hasn't happened to many a man, Raven," Lord Ian commented. "And when a king urges a wedding, 'tis wise to obey his wishes."

"God's bloody tears, I am not a damnable peasant!" Raven roared. Grasping the arms of his chair, he leaned forward, closer to Lucien. "I resent Henry doing this to me—to us." He cast a quick glance Peter's way. "I should like to pick my own wife, thank you!"

"You never would," Peter said softly. He remained at ease in his own chair, barely turning his dark head to gaze at his twin. "You've been dallying in order to acquire that piece of land which borders your demesne."

"What are you talking about?" Lucien demanded.

"A silly wager. If Raven should remain unwed by the summer solstice of this year, I promised him a piece of land that borders his demesne. That is why my handsome brother, here, would not wed if left to his own devices."

"That, and the likes of Lydia," Lucien added derisively.

Raven scowled at Lucien but denied neither of his brothers' claims. Instead he grumbled, "How do we know?"

"What?"

Raven peered at Lucien suspiciously. "How do Peter and I know King Henry is behind this whole unwelcome business? Because you told us so? Because those wenches told us so? This might all be an elaborate joke!" Smirking arrogantly, he waved both his hands for emphasis.

Lucien's eyes narrowed to slits as he felt his own temper flare. "You obnoxious, ungrateful—" Breaking off his invective, he thrust himself from his chair.

Startled, the others looked after him when he took hurriedly to the stairs.

"You ought not to have made such an outlandish suggestion," Peter admonished his twin. "Our brother wouldn't lie to us."

"He might," Raven insisted stubbornly. Hunkering down in his chair again, he crossed his legs, ankle to knee, and folded his arms over his chest. "As I said, for a jest."

"He wouldn't. *Jesu!* Do you think he'd leave Adrienne, now, when she's near to bearing their second child, just to play a stupid jest? God's teeth, Raven! You are thickheaded and insufferable. The way you've treated Pamela and her cousin is a perfect example!" Standing, Peter gave him a disgusted look.

Mulishly, Raven glared back before jumping up with a snarl and leaning into Peter, nose to nose.

"I did naught to the Angleford lady. If I exchanged harsh words with Roxanne, 'tis because she's a bitch of the highest order! I pray for your sake this whole matter is an elaborate hoax. If not, and you're fool enough to take her to wife on

Henry's capricious order, so be it. But I don't intend to be led blindly to the slaughter!''

The two men's swarthy complexions ruddied more deeply; their eyes blazed like glowing embers.

''Are you saying I'm a fool to obey my king?''

''Aye. It seems I am.''

The two brothers shifted their weight from one foot to another, as though intending to strike the other. But neither raised a hand.

Peter's voice was taut with emotion. ''I cannot believe you're the dangerous dolt you appear to be, brother. Lord Ian is right. To disobey Henry's directive could prove disastrous, especially when one recalls 'twas Henry himself who awarded us the lands where we each now make our homes.

''But you''—with a dark scowl, Peter shook his head contemptuously—''you would defy our sovereign lord, to whom you swore fealty, and risk all—for what? That bevy of women who parade into and out of your bedchamber? Christ!'' He slapped his forehead with his palm. ''Lady Pamela is a sweet, innocent, eager young damsel, full up with trust and dreams. Anyone with eyes can see she'd make a man the most honorable lady wife. But not you, Raven of Stonelee. You're no better than a hound always on the scent of a bitch. You need a new crotch to bury your prick in each and every night. So instead of thinking with your head, you let your cock make your decisions. On the chance you did not know it, brother, a cock cannot think!''

Raven's fisted hands clenched and unclenched; his breathing was fast. ''I warn you, Peter, mind what you say to me.''

''Why? Are you someone I should fear?''

Raven responded by pushing his brother's shoulder hard. Peter stumbled backward but rebounded immediately.

''Enough!'' Lord Ian bellowed, grabbing Peter's arm before he could follow through with an intended punch. ''Sweet Mother Mary, what's got into you two? Are you both mad?''

For several seconds there was only silence. Then: "He started it." The twins spoke as one, as was their habit. When each heard the other, they blinked, startled. When they glanced at their stepfather and saw the expression of incredulity upon his face, they laughed. Soon they were doubled over, holding their bellies, their eyes damp with mirthful tears.

"*Jesu.*" The earl shook his head. "I hear my own young sons muttering that exact remark a dozen times a day. I thought they would outgrow the impulse to point accusing fingers at each other. But, no. Their elder brothers prove me wrong!"

"Well, they shan't be pointing accusing fingers at me any longer." Lucien, returning, made that announcement as he strode into the hall, a roll of parchment in each hand. "Note the royal seals," he ordered as he handed one each to Peter and Raven.

Both men looked at the scrolls, but neither dared insult their brother further by breaking the embossed wax that secured the parchments.

"Forgive me, Lucien," Raven said contritely. "I know you wouldn't concoct such a tale. I need no proof." He waggled the scroll in the air. "I've no defense for my behavior, except to say this whole affair took me unaware. I feel like I've been struck by a battle-ax, and my mood has been dark, I confess."

He looked from Lucien to Peter. "Will you accept my apology as well?"

"Aye." Raven's twin embraced him.

"I must return to Eynsham," Lucien told them. "Adrienne's time is drawing near." His glance darted between the two pairs of jet eyes looking back at him. "Can I trust you? Will you yield to King Henry's wishes and take the ladies to wife? There's no purpose in objecting. His will shall prevail no matter what you do, unless you flee to foreign lands."

"God's tears," Raven mumbled. "If we wed these damsels, we'll be presented with the foreign lands as their dowers."

Lucien took a step nearer to him. "Don't defy his majesty, Raven. Worse, don't defy me."

" 'Twas a jest, Lucien! Nothing more, I vow." He smiled the smile that caused so many maidens' hearts to melt. "I'll wed Lady Pamela and journey to Wales, and I'll brandish my sword to keep the peace. But I shan't pledge to stay there, on my wife's dowerlands. Stonelee's my home."

"That concerns me not. Only that you wed the girl." Lucien looked to Peter. "Have you any complaints?"

"None."

"Good." He turned to the earl. "I trust you and Mother will hold these two to their word, since I doubt Adrienne and I can return to witness the ceremonies."

CHAPTER 4

The earl's castle in the lands of Fortengall lay but a modest ride northwest of Stonelee and Stoneweather when taken, alternately, at a brisk trot and canter; it took some while longer to travel between the estates when riding at an easy pace.

This day's ride was easy. All save Lucien, who'd left Stonelee at dawn to hurry home to Eynsham Keep, rode their horses at a leisurely pace on their journey to Fortengall Castle. Most of them passed their time in quiet thought or easy conversation, as though all were seated at a table instead of mounted in their saddles.

Lord Ian led the procession, amiably pointing out sites of interest. Roxanne paid him no heed. Hailing from a land that had its own chieftains, her father among them, her disdain for the earl's heroic tales was obvious, if one cared to analyze her brooding, belligerent scowl.

Raven could not see Roxanne's face. From a short distance behind her, he furtively watched the girl riding her black stallion and muttered beneath his breath. *Jesu,* but his brother was cursed to find himself betrothed to such a haridelle. As her sire's tenth and last child, she'd surely been meant to be that man's son and heir! She rode like a man, the sharp-tongued witch, assured and arrogant, head bared, shoulders back, spine straight. And, Mother of God, she rode astride as though she had a cock between her legs, not a cleft for delving into!

Raven surreptitiously kneed his destrier and drew up alongside Roxanne, keeping a measurable distance between their mounts' flanks. Though the sight made him clench his teeth, he could not drag his eyes off the female limb clearly visible to him from this angle. Grudgingly, Raven decided the wench had some sense of propriety, for she'd donned men's leggings before raising her skirts to sit square in the saddle. More probably, she did so only to protect her skin from the elements. Still, to spread her thighs across the beast's back, Raven knew the Bittenshire harpy had certainly hitched her tunics onto her lap. Were it not for the fur cloak affording her some remnant of modesty, not only her calves but her thighs would be visible to anyone—any *man*—wishing to ogle them!

Grunting his silent disapproval, Raven turned to gaze straight ahead. His mother, in front of him on the road, glanced over her shoulder and nodded at him before speaking to her husband, who rode beside her. Raven noticed all this, yet all he could see with his mind's eye was Roxanne's amazingly long and tantalizingly curvaceous leg. He began wondering if she wore men's chausses when she rode in the heat of summer, or if she shunned them for comfort's sake and settled her naked bottom into her saddle.

The lord of Stonelee's imagination began running rampant. He could actually see the plump, white flesh of her thighs as she mounted her horse. He could even envision the pink of her woman's flesh and the thatch of ebony curls surrounding it as she lewdly straddled the stallion's back.

"*Christ!*" he ground out, oblivious to his abruptly labored breathing.

"Did you say something to me?" Roxanne demanded tartly, only then acknowledging she'd been aware of his presence.

"Not damnably likely," he shot back, glowering.

"Good."

The wench's behavior outraged Raven on his brother's behalf. She was a woman—no awkward, timorous damsel, but a woman old enough to have been wed a few years and borne a few babes. Her years should have ensured a thorough knowledge of appropriate behavior for one of her class and gender. Yet, she deliberately chose to flaunt herself and defy custom, not to mention make her feelings and opinions known when none cared what she felt or thought.

With a quick jerk of his corded neck, Raven turned in his saddle to look back at Peter and his own intended bride. God's bloody wounds, if he had to wed someone of Henry's choosing, he was damnably relieved to be paired with a shy, retiring maiden the likes of Lady Pamela. Poor Peter. Raven shook his head in pity for his hapless twin. To be saddled with a brazen shrew like Roxanne!

"My lady," Peter addressed Pamela, though they were too far behind Raven, who was consumed by his own dark thoughts, for him to overhear. "Are you . . . comfortable?"

"Oh!" Pamela blinked, startled to discover Roxanne's betrothed beside her and addressing her directly. "Aye."

"Truly?" His expression looked doubtful.

"Well, nay," she confessed after a brief hesitation. " 'Tisn't proper to be so blunt, I suppose, but I must admit my backside's sore. I'd not ridden so much in the whole past year as I've ridden since crossing the border into England."

Peter smiled in commiseration. "I, too, have spent long hours and countless days in the saddle, when I was a mercenary serving other masters. I wore mail and carried sword and shield as well. I assure you, I understand how tender your bottom is."

Pamela blushed rosily. Yet, she looked up at him through

the fans of her lashes and inquired, "You were once a mercenary knight? I hadn't considered that might be so, not when you've a stronghold of your own."

"Raven and I earned our lands," Peter explained, guiding his horse inattentively, with an expert hand on the reins. "Even Lucien, as firstborn, had to reclaim Eynsham, our sire's estate, because it had been lost for years to another. 'Twas King Henry who awarded Raven and me our own fiefs."

"You must have a tale to tell about that. Will you share it with me?"

Instinctively, Peter took a deep breath that righted his shoulders and expanded the width of his broad chest. "Raven and I, as younger sons, and Lucien, landless, earned our coin in tourneys and by selling our sword arms to landed lords. But with Mother's marriage to Lord Ian, we found employment with the king himself—the earl and Henry are old friends, you understand. After a particularly long, hard battle against several baronies that had joined together against the king, we found ourselves the victors. Henry sought to reward us three brothers with one baron's large demesne, which he suggested we divide into three more modest fiefs. Raven and I gladly accepted, but Lucien declined, intent as he was upon regaining his lost heritable lands. Of course, in time, he did indeed regain them."

"You, Lord Lucien, and your twin must have done something especially courageous in that battle against the barons. Otherwise, the king would not have singled you three out for such a great reward. Tell me what transpired, if you will."

Flattered by her interest, Peter launched in to a detailed account. Pamela listened attentively, exclaimed brightly, laughed appreciatively, and interrupted with questions he patiently answered.

Raven caught a few words here and there as his brother regaled *his* intended bride with a tale of their strength and bravery. He would not have minded, except Peter made himself sound like a Viking god with magical powers. And the story went on so long! One would think, he mused irritatedly, it had been a hundred years' war, not a single day's battle.

Again he turned in his saddle, purposely blinking as he swung around so that he would not see the black-haired wench at his right, whose leg remained visible to taunt and infuriate him. When he opened his eyes, he discovered Peter and Pamela riding so close, her skirts brushed his brother's boot. Engrossed in each other, neither noticed when he jerked hard on his reins, halting his steed; they nearly rode into him.

"Raven!" Peter exclaimed, interrupted from his discourse. "I was just telling Lady Pamela about the battle where we rode beside King Henry. The particular one that resulted in our receiving our lands where now sit our keeps of Stoneweather and Stonelee."

"So I gathered." Raven set his mouth in a grim line. "Mayhap it is your bride-to-be you should be telling of your heroic exploits."

Peter glanced at the road ahead. His parents and his betrothed had gained some distance on them, since Raven had forced them to halt.

"You may be right, brother. I shouldn't neglect Lady Roxanne." He addressed Pamela. "If you'll excuse me, milady?"

"Surely." With a smile and a nod, she granted him leave.

"Now you may tell your lady of *your* heroic exploits." Peter grinned at Raven before urging his destrier between Raven's and Pamela's horses, trotting forward to join Roxanne.

Raven brought his mount alongside Pamela's palfrey, and they resumed their journey at an even walk. But the lady looked at the road, not at her betrothed, and she uttered not a word.

Raven could not blame her, as he found himself unable to think of anything to say to this damsel Henry had foisted upon him. 'Twas ironic, he thought humorlessly, because Pamela of Angleford was exactly the sort of female he'd always intended to wed, if and when he married at all. Demure, guileless, obedient, amiable.

"God's tears," he muttered.

"Did you speak, milord?" Pamela inquired.

" 'Twas naught." Another silence fell awkwardly between them. "Tell me of Angleford," he urged, not caring, but glad to have thought of a topic at all.

"There's little to tell. The keep is Norman in design, a fortress built to withstand attacks from the Welsh natives. Not that anyone's attacked Angleford in my lifetime. My sire and Uncle Cedric kept the peace with iron gauntlets."

"I understand it's in the Marches. Where, exactly?"

"Directly to the south lies Bittenshire, Roxy's home. To the north, Angleford borders Penllyn." She flicked an appraising glance toward Raven. "That's the Welsh principality where my mother and Roxy's were born."

"You've kin on both sides. Angleford should be peaceable enough, then, despite its location in the borderlands."

"Aye," Pamela confirmed distractedly. "Milord, what is that?"

Raven turned to see where she pointed. A great stone edifice loomed on the horizon. " 'Tis our destination," he informed her.

"Behold!" Lord Ian shouted abruptly, drawing all eyes to him as he gestured, just as Pamela had done. Addressing the two Welsh maidens riding well behind him, he explained, "Fortengall Castle lies but a short distance ahead!"

The younger riders kicked their horses, drawing nearer to the earl and his lady wife. "It's huge, milord," Pamela volunteered.

"Monstrous," Roxanne mumbled inaudibly.

"Aye, it's a formidable stronghold," Lord Ian agreed. "That's because it has grown with each lord. A grandsire of mine many generations removed chose the site centuries ago. He was a Dane called Joukahainen."

Roxanne rolled her eyes.

" 'Tis larger than even Angleford Keep," Pamela declared.

"Then, Raven shall have to begin building. Won't you?" The earl smiled amiably at his stepson.

"Oh, aye," the younger knight agreed dryly. " 'Tis what I wish to do again, having so recently seen the completion of Stonelee."

"But it is the responsibility of landlords to improve their strongholds," Peter reminded him. His black eyes twinkled when he added, "Besides, once you're wed, you won't be able to while away your time with the leisurely activities you've lately pursued. Design and construction should keep you occupied in a manner that shan't disturb your new bride." He graced Pamela with a wink.

She flashed him an easy smile in return.

Raven glanced from one to the other and scowled. When Roxanne's presence intruded, forcing him to note her smirk, his glower darkened.

"The horses would probably like a run," Lady Lucinda suggested. "Are you ladies willing? The castle's only moments from here if we ride hard."

Without a word, Roxanne responded by separating her horse from the others and breaking into a wild run, leaving the earl's family and her own cousin quickly behind her.

Raven watched her for a moment as Roxanne's cape and hair fluttered in her wake like sail and pennant flying in the wind. His blood boiled. Impulsively spurring his destrier, Rolf, he rode off after her, spewing up clods of damp earth on the road.

"Shall we?" Lord Ian asked those who remained. Immediately, the four set off at a gallop, though they were unable to catch the two who already far outdistanced them.

"Rein in, woman!" Raven shouted to Roxanne as they approached the motte upon which sat the fortress, high above the surrounding countryside. " 'Tis not so easy to gain entrance to Fortengall Castle, nor leave it, either. No one's likely to raise the gate for you!"

Her breathing was hardly labored as she sawed on Dafydd's reins, forcing the beast to halt. "Nay?" A challenge manifested itself in her wicked smile as Roxanne allowed her stallion to prance and paw the earth too near Raven's destrier.

"Nay, you—" Raven snarled.

"Odo! Raise the gate!" Lord Ian's shout interrupted his stepson's rejoinder.

"Aye, milord!" the tower guard responded.

Suddenly, Raven and Roxanne were surrounded by the rest of his family. Glad for the opportunity to be free of her odious presence, he gave her his back and led the procession through the raised gate and into the bailey.

The lady herself fell back, trailing the party as they entered the crenellated walls.

"It's magnificent, isn't it?" Pamela asked her, lagging behind so that she might share a word with her cousin.

"'Tisn't!" Roxanne snapped. "It may be huge, but it's ancient and probably crumbling from within. Fortengall's naught but a big pile of stone laid down in a dreary countryside."

"I don't think this shire is dreary! It's winter, Roxy. Even Wales is nothing but hues of gray and brown all winter. I'd wager that when this land greens up with springtime, it's beautiful."

Roxanne looked at Pamela as though she'd grown a second head. "What ails you?" she demanded. "I'd understand if you were distraught at having to wed that nasty churl Henry has decided should be your lawful husband. But methinks you're under some sort of spell. Why else would you seem taken with things so very English?"

"I *am* English!" Pamela reminded her. "As are you."

"I am Cymry," she countered, "daughter of Princess Rhiannon."

"And daughter of Sir Cedric, whose ancestors hailed from Warwick."

Roxanne's violet eyes widened. "Cedric, Marcher Lord of Bittenshire!"

"Roxy, often times you are very trying." Pamela sighed. "Everyone including King Henry has been kind to us, yet you insist on being bothersome. If you were honest, you'd admit that the twin lords are quite eligible, and no doubt many a fine lady would gladly sacrifice a finger or two to have one of them call her 'wife.' Resign yourself to your fate. It's not so disagreeable, and it could be far worse."

Though her mouth hung open, Roxanne seemed unable to utter a solitary word. As they trailed the others slowly, crossing over the interior bridge into the inner bailey and wading into the pleasant chaos that was life within a barony's walls, her tongue at last began to work.

"Fate didn't hand me this, Pamela," she insisted, furtively glancing toward Raven and Peter, who had already dismounted and now approached them on foot. "The contemptible English king did. But as he is not my king, I shan't—"

"What shan't you do?" Raven questioned.

Roxanne bit her tongue. "Nothing," she mumbled irritably, halting Dafydd beside Pamela's palfrey. She swung her leg over the saddle and lowered herself, with Peter's ready assistance, to the ground below.

"Oh, something, surely," Raven coaxed sweetly, sick to his stomach at the sight of his twin handling the wench so familiarly. He'd have been less alarmed had he discovered Peter caressing a deadly asp.

Roxanne's head snapped to the side. Their eyes met. But before she could speak, a man's voice drew their attention.

"Welcome back, milord, milady."

The four turned toward the keep's main portal. There stood a well-dressed man of middle years greeting the master and mistress.

Taking Peter's proffered arm, Roxanne walked with him while Raven, belatedly remembering his manners, hastily helped Pamela down from her horse. But before she had her feet, he was walking, fast-paced, toward those clustered together on the stone steps. Pamela scampered after him, lest she be left behind.

"My ladies." Lord Ian turned to include both the Welsh maidens as he made his introductions. "This is Frederick, Fortengall Castle's seneschal and one of my oldest friends. If you've a question or a need, don't hesitate to seek him out. He knows every nook and cranny of this old castle. And the servants obey him more quickly, methinks, than they do Fortengall's earl.

"Frederick, may I present Lady Roxanne of Bittenshire and Lady Pamela of Angleford? Roxanne is recently betrothed to Peter, and Pamela to Raven."

"Betrothed! This is good news!" The seneschal smiled and bowed courteously. "The lads will be excited to hear," he added confidentially. "They've been watching your approach from their chamber window."

Following Frederick's lead, everyone entered the great hall. Three young boys scampered down the stone staircase, squealing and squawking, pushing and shoving, like puppies tumbling down a hill. But when they reached the bottom step and beheld strangers accompanying those they knew, the children fell silent.

"Come here," Lucinda urged, hunkering down and opening her arms beseechingly.

The tallest of the three, a fair-haired, blue-eyed specimen missing his front two teeth, squared his shoulders and raised his chin. Striding purposefully toward his mother, he stopped short of entering her embrace.

"Ladies, this is our eldest, Hugh," Lucinda explained. "Hugh, these ladies, Roxanne and Pamela, are soon to wed your brothers, Peter and Raven."

Hugh considered each of the young women cautiously. Then, bowing chivalrously, he stepped forward. Taking Pamela's hand and then Roxanne's, he brushed the damsels' knuckles with his soft, child's lips as though he were a Knight Templar. "A pleathure, miladeeth," he lisped.

Roxanne's eyes went round and her mouth turned down; the moment Hugh released her hand, she rubbed it surreptitiously against her tunic skirt.

Pamela, however, beamed at the gallant little lord. "And who are these fine-looking fellows behind you?" she inquired.

"The carrottopped ruffians are my second set of twins," Lady Lucinda supplied. "James and John."

"Good day, Lord James, Lord John," Pamela greeted them formally as she executed a quick curtsy. " 'Tis a pleasure to find one's self joining a family of such handsome men."

The little twins blinked their green eyes at her. "You be pretty, too."

Breaking into a wide grin at the compliment, she exclaimed, "They spoke as one!"

"So, too, do we," Peter admitted, glancing at Raven.

"Aye, it's a habit all twins have," Lord Ian confirmed.

"Call me Jamie," one of the youngest boys urged, stepping close to Pamela.

"Would you like to see our pet fox?" John asked her. "We found it abandoned when it was a wee babe. He's got a collar and everything, that Master Frederick made of braided leather."

"Aye, we call him Willie."

" 'Cause we used to call him Wiley."

"As he's a fox, and all."

"But it's easier, calling him Willie."

"I'd love to," Pamela assured them, chuckling.

"Later, lads," their father suggested, "after Lady Pamela and her cousin have had time to settle in to their rooms. Mayhap after the midday meal, what do you say?"

"Is that all right with you?" Pamela asked the boys.

"Oh, aye," Jamie and John assured her in unison.

"Run along, now," Lucinda urged them. "You can't be finished with your morning lessons yet."

After some mumbled dissention, the three youngsters scampered back up the stone stairs.

"It seems Lady Pamela has got herself some new admirers," Peter observed. "You've a way with children, do you?"

"She does," Roxanne confirmed before her cousin could reply. "A grimy little army of laborers' mites is forever tagging after Pamela."

"But not you?" Raven asked disdainfully, arching one black eyebrow as he looked at her.

"Nay, not I."

"A pity." His eyes flicked to Peter. " 'Twould have been easier if she'd had some nurturing skills, since you intend to get your brood on her."

"Raven, mind your manners," Lucinda warned before beckoning a servant to lead the ladies upstairs to private chambers.

"I'm certain Peter's offspring will be easy enough to manage. *Yours*," Roxanne added in a soft hiss meant only for Raven's ears, "would be better off drowned, like a litter of kittens in a sack!"

With a flounce, she stormed up the steps, following the Fortengall servant.

Pamela offered both the twin lords an apologetic glance before trailing after her cousin.

"It will never work," Raven declared grimly before his mother, who had caught his eye, could speak. "None of us will ever be happily wed to those Henry's chosen for us."

CHAPTER 5

Roxanne stood on the parapet above Fortengall's inner bailey, leaning on one of the stone notches in the crenellated wall. Aware that she had been there some time, she knew she ought to go down before night descended in earnest. But there was a while left of the daylight, dim with falling snow, and Roxanne was unwilling to waste a moment of her precious privacy.

Any refuge she discovered, she employed, escaping here and there the family that English ruler, Henry, intended to force on her. They had all been confined together at Fortengall Castle for two days now, discussing plans for the abhorrent wedding ceremony designed to link Pamela and Raven, herself and Peter. If Roxanne heard Lady Lucinda make another suggestion regarding that event, which she was determined to avoid, she thought she might slit her own throat! As it was, she felt ready to make a mad dash for freedom. If she reached Cymru, good. If she failed and had to live out her days hiding like a hermit in the forest, that would be all right, too. Anything to be free of these English!

Pamela, however, seemed taken with the lot of them; that she did mystified Roxanne. It was one thing to resign one's self to an unavoidable fate, no matter how miserable that future might prove to be. But to embrace it? To anticipate becoming wife to a knave the likes of Raven of Stonelee? If Pamela had been ordered to wed Peter, Roxanne might have better understood her cousin's acquiescence. He was a good-natured man, and even she could not despise him. But how could Pamela *want* to wed *Raven*?

A sudden insight made Roxanne start. When Pamela married that arrogant knight, they'd return together to Cymru, to Angleford Keep. Perhaps that explained her apparent eagerness to become his bride. If so, it made some sense to Roxanne, because returning home would be Pamela's reward for accepting that rude, insufferable lout as her husband!

But she, Roxanne of Bittenshire, would earn no such reward for marrying Peter. If she obeyed the Angevin's wishes, she'd be naught but an English lord's lady—a lady with no home but Stoneweather, here in this accursed land called England!

Roxanne sighed heavily, her breath a visible, steamy cloud in the crisp, wintry air. Peter was pleasant enough, she admitted to herself reluctantly. He appeared most especially pleasant when compared to his twin. Yet, he was so damnably domestic, Roxanne found it debilitating. So, too, were the rest of the family. Even the earl, who bore scars from countless battles, appeared blindly devoted to his wife and children. The most excitement he had in a day was an argument with Lady Lucinda or a mock battle with his young sons. These English were all too comfortable and complacent in their peaceful land, Roxanne surmised as she gazed out at the horizon, which was fast blending into a seamless canvas of grayish white. It resembled her future, bleak and dreary.

* * *

"Where are the ladies?" Peter inquired of his brother as they passed on the castle stairs.

"Lady Pamela is in the kitchen with Mother. It seems they share a passion for recipes and baking. Pamela is making some sweet concoction that has Mother intrigued."

"And my lady?" Peter pressed patiently.

"You mean that Welsh shrew? She's outdoors, I believe."

"Outdoors? It's snowing and growing dark, besides."

Peter continued down the stairs and Raven turned, retracing his steps as he followed his brother.

"Don't worry, Peter. She shan't succumb to the weather. I doubt she'd succumb to an attack by berserk Nordic warriors!"

"Why must you be so unkind?" Peter demanded when he'd reached the great hall below the gallery.

"It's not that I'm unkind, brother, it's that I see her for what she is. And what she is, is wrong for you."

"Let me decide that. You, however, would do well to show some interest in your own betrothed."

Pulling a face, Raven headed toward the kitchen.

Grabbing his mantle off a peg, Peter walked out into the bailey. "Have you seen Lady Roxanne?" he inquired of the first guard he encountered.

"Aye, Lord Peter. She's 'round the side, up on the wall."

Peter strode in the direction the man had given him and spied Roxanne silhouetted against the pearl-gray sky. With her head bared, she seemed oblivious to the weather. She reminded him of a ship's captain staring out to sea, observing in the vast openness something others would never detect.

Crossing the yard, he climbed the snow-dusted steps set against the curtain wall. "Roxanne," he said.

"Oh!" Startled, she turned to find Peter at her side. "Sweet Mother Mary, I never heard you approach."

"You were deep in thought."

"Nay. 'Tis the wind."

"Aye, that's it. The wind," Peter agreed, though there was

barely a breeze. "Why are you here on the wall? I understand my mother and your cousin are in the kitchen."

Snorting, Roxanne shook her head and looked out again across the dormant fields of Fortengall. "If I concocted something in the kitchen and you ate it, you would most likely die."

"Why? Do you so dread our wedding that you'd poison me if you had the chance?"

She turned her head quickly, her violet eyes meeting his. "I had the chance. But I'm outside on the bailey wall instead of concocting lethal brews in your mother's kitchen."

"What captures your attention?"

"I'm trying to locate the road that leads, eventually, to Bittenshire. I should like to be on it."

"I see. Well, you shall be, soon enough."

"Oh?" Roxanne looked hopeful as she glanced at Peter.

"I make you a pledge, my lady. As soon as it is better traveling weather, I shall take you home for an extended visit."

"Oh."

Peter said gently, "I know you're not keen on this marriage. However, since there's naught we can do but obey our king and join in wedlock, I want you to know I'll do my best to make you content. You'll be my greatest treasure."

Her lashes fluttered as she returned his searching gaze. His promises flustered her, Peter could see. Hoping he'd found a chink in her emotional armor, he seized the moment and reached out to stroke her hair.

"What are you doing?"

"Eh?" His hand stopped, hovering above her crown. "Was I too bold? I only meant to brush the snow from your hair. If you don't shake it off, your locks will be heavy and wet by the time you return to the keep."

Roxanne giggled. It pleased Peter to hear her laughter. Though Raven saw her only as a haridelle, he knew she hid a softer side. He was glad the lady allowed him to glimpse it.

"Why do you laugh?" he asked.

"Because your hair's turning white." She reached up and mussed his snow-powdered locks. When she pulled back her hand, she frowned. "I should have left it full of snow. Then I'd know how you'll look in old age."

"I can't have that." He grinned as he shook his head like a wet hound, sending a little shower of snow flying everywhere. "If you could envision me as a stooped, gray-haired ancient, you might actually dare to defy Henry, refusing to wed me, after all."

With a jerk of her head, Roxanne turned away.

"Still looking for the road that connects Fortengall to Bittenshire?"

"Aye. You're not offended, I hope."

"Not at all. I know the need to feel connected to something or someone dear to you. This may sound peculiar, but I share such a bond with Raven. We were together in our mother's womb, and we've spent most of our lives in close proximity. Yet, when we've been apart, whether separated by many leagues or only the stone walls of a chamber, I know we remain connected. As he can with me, I oft sense what he feels or know what he thinks."

"Sweet Mother of God." Roxanne groaned. "I pity you."

Peter smiled ruefully. "You and he don't get on, do you?"

"Nay." Narrowing her eyes, she peered up at him curiously. "If you two weren't clear reflections of each other, I'd give credence to that old wives' tale, the one that says a woman who gives birth to twins has slept with two men. You and Raven are so different in temperament and spirit, 'twould be easy to believe different men sired you. Only your looks cast that notion into the flames."

"Rest assured my mother was a faithful wife, even to Gundulf, who fathered Lucien, Raven, and me. Not that he inspired loyalty in a wife."

"Oh? Was he a wicked man?"

"More than wicked. But that's another day's tale." Peter

motioned with his head. "You're peering in the wrong direction if you hope to see the road leading north to Wales and the Marches. Take my hand. We'll walk slowly around, and I'll point it out before the light's gone altogether."

Obligingly, Roxanne slipped her hand into Peter's, and they began making their precarious journey along the ledge.

"There." He pointed. " 'Tis the road we traveled to Fortengall as it continues on, due north. It is all but disappearing, between the waning daylight and the falling snow. But it's well-traveled, even in winter. Wardens and reevers from all over the shire must ride to Fortengall to speak with the earl. And people from the villages come to the castle no matter what the time of year. So despite the snow, it will soon be a muddy track again, easily visible.

"I hope you're not planning to be on it anytime soon," he added, looking over his shoulder at Roxanne.

"Nay. Of course not. It is as you said. I need to feel connected to my homeland. The road is like a tie to Cymru."

Peter nodded and then declared, "It's almost dark. Let's go down." Turning full around, he placed his hands securely on Roxanne's waist, nudging her back the way they'd come.

But they had stayed too long already. As she braced herself on the crenellated wall to her right, Roxanne squinted at the ledge beneath her feet. It suddenly proved impossible to discern lines, angles, and shapes. All had become murky and dark, with neither dimensions nor shadings.

"Oh!" Roxanne slipped on a patch of ice, her left foot sliding clear off the wide ledge, her toe pointing like a dancer's in the air above the bailey yard.

His reflexes quick, Peter pulled her closer to him and nearer the wall so that she could plant her foot solidly.

"Are you all right?"

"Aye."

"Be careful. Go slowly."

Roxanne nodded. Like a four-legged beast, the two of them

began again, making slow progress as they groped their way along. Darkness threatened to consume them.

"I—I cannot see the stairs!"

"They're ahead. Only a few more paces. Keep moving."

She took another step and then another. The second of her next two steps brought her soft, leather-soled shoe in contact with another patch of ice. Though she flexed her toes, her foot slipped forward and she lost her balance. Both feet shot abruptly out from under her, and Roxanne fell backward, first hitting Peter full-force in the chest and then going down hard on her rump.

Roxanne cried out, startled and dismayed, until she realized she was sitting securely on the ledge, her legs stretched out before her on the stone-and-mortar catwalk. Leaning on one hand, she turned around to commiserate with Peter. "You must think me a clumsy—"

Her voice failed as shock stole her words away. He was gone. "Peter!"

Panic clutching at her heart, Roxanne sliced the air with her arm. But she connected with nothing, for Peter was neither standing nor sitting behind her. He was clinging to the ledge with his fingers, his legs dangling above the ground far below.

"Roxanne!"

It was all he could manage; there was little more he could say. But she was no timorous maiden. Assessing the dangerous situation quickly, Roxanne promptly rolled to her knees and clutched at his bared wrists, pulling hard.

For a few moments they struggled, Peter's legs swinging beneath the ledge as he tried to gain purchase against the wall with his boots. But he could not, and Roxanne had not the strength required to haul a full-grown man up over a ledge.

"Help me!" she ordered. "I'm going to release one of your hands, now, Peter, and pull with all my strength on the other. Grab my ankle. Pull yourself up—"

Freeing one of his hands so that she could better grab hold

of his other with both her own, she also brought one foot forward and planted it on the edge of the walk.

But Peter did not grab her ankle, knowing full well he could drag her off the ledge with him when he finally fell. And he would fall, that much was a surety.

"Roxanne, release me!" he panted. "I'll get up myself."

"You cannot!"

"I will. I'll—"

She hadn't released him, but suddenly all she gripped in her hand was his leather glove. Peter's fingers had slipped from within, and he had slid away.

"Peter!" she screamed, as a terrifyingly ominous thud drifted to her ears when his body landed. On her knees again, clinging to the lip with her hands, she peered at the yard below. But it was too dark to see him, now. All was dense shadows diffused by whirling snowflakes.

"Help! Help! Lord Peter's fallen from the wall!" she screamed loud enough for those halfway to Bittenshire to hear. And then, despite the fact that she could barely see and that she knew patches of ice lay between her and the stairs, she rushed onward, found the steps, and raced down them to the fallen lord.

CHAPTER 6

"May I taste?"

At the sound of Raven's voice, Pamela whirled about to find herself nearly in his embrace, he stood so close.

"Nay, you may not, milord," she returned, spinning around again, giving him her back as she took a pan from the kitchen hearth. "It must cool."

"It smells delicious, whatever it is."

"It hasn't a name," she admitted as she set the pan aside. " 'Tis something I once concocted on an idle afternoon."

"You'll love it, Raven," Lady Lucinda assured him. "The flaky dough is filled with apples, currants, and honey."

"Aye. Your mother was kind enough to spare me the ingredients, though they be rare this time of year."

"Are you certain I can't taste it?"

"Well . . ." Hesitantly, Pamela consented, cutting a small wedge of her creation and offering it up to her betrothed.

His smile, like the look in his eyes, was blatantly sexual as he plucked the morsel from between her thumb and finger, using only his talented tongue.

Resolutely, Pamela held his gaze. She rarely got his full attention, and now that she had it, she would not blushingly turn aside. During their ride to Fortengall Castle, she hadn't known what to say when Raven sought her out. She found Peter so easy to be with and Raven, well—he was not. Yet, she understood that if she behaved timidly, he'd soon lose interest and go back to ignoring her. Pamela was determined that would not happen.

In truth, the young lady of Angleford wasn't naturally a timid soul, only quiet. And ever since she'd gone to live with her relatives, she'd understood Roxanne needed to be bolder than she. By shouldering her orphaned cousin behind her, Roxanne could then make up for being the last born of the Bittenshire brood.

"What do you think, milord?" Pamela inquired.

"Delightful." Raven licked his lips sensuously. "I think we should name this delicacy."

"What would you call it?" his mother asked.

"Pamela's Delight."

The damsel did not look away, though she found she was disconcerted that Raven of Stonelee was ribald and wicked even under his mother's nose.

"Out, out!" Lady Lucinda ordered abruptly, shooing her son from the kitchen. "Cook is busy with our evening victuals, and we are in her way. She doesn't need you loitering about, taking up good work space with your hulking form."

"Aye, aye!" Raven chuckled, holding up his broad hands as though he feared his mother would swat him. Backing up toward the portal that led to Fortengall's great hall, he kept his black eyes locked on Pamela's. "I insist, though, that my intended feed me my portion of Pamela's Delight when it's served at table, so that I can lick every sweet drop of honey from her fingers."

" 'Twould be unseemly," she pointed out primly, knowing from his quirky grin and twinkling eyes that he played with her.

"Then you may feed me somewhere private."

"Out!" Lady Lucinda commanded sharply. When Raven left, grinning, she explained, "He's unruly. That son of mine needs a woman to prod him into gentility."

Lucinda began rubbing a spot on the scarred worktable as though she were a scullery maid. Abruptly, she put down the rag and sighed. "I can't imagine what Henry was thinking. But then, he's the king. He may do as he will. So the burden of this marriage, the task of making it work, falls upon your shoulders."

"Don't fret over me," Pamela urged. "You may rest assured, my lady, that I'm up to any task set before me."

Lucinda's face warmed with a smile. "Glad I am to hear you say it. And don't let me frighten you, Pamela. I just want everyone to be happy. A bad marriage is a hell on earth. Besides, all my sons are good. I even think Raven's rather special. But he must be brought 'round to the idea of marriage," she added.

"Now, go." She put a hand to Pamela's shoulder, urging her from the kitchen. "We've been in Cook's way too long. Join Raven and the others in the hall. Enjoy some conversation and a cup of mulled wine. You're a guest at Fortengall, after all."

"Will you let me help once I'm your son's wife?"

"Oh, aye!" Lucinda's smile broadened as she waved her hand in the air. "Then I'll work your fingers to the bone."

Laughing, Pamela wiped her hands and scurried through the archway into the great hall, wishing Lady Lucinda were not remaining behind to supervise the meal preparations. She liked the woman who would soon be a mother to her, just as she liked Lord Ian, Peter, and the earl's young sons. She only wished she could feel as easy in Raven's company.

The only way to feel easy in Raven's company, Pamela

decided as her eyes scanned the huge hall and the gallery above, *is to spend as much time with him as possible.* So she was glad that, despite the number of servants setting up plank tables and the many men-at-arms waiting to sit at them, she spied the lord of Stonelee standing alone. Purposefully, she squared her shoulders and raised her chin, intending to go to him.

But then he turned so that instead of his back, she saw his profile. And Pamela saw Raven was not alone. In one arm, he clasped a pretty serving wench to his chest.

"Ah, Bess, my darling girl," he said on a sigh loud enough for Pamela to overhear. "Where have you been?"

"Wilkeshire," replied the maid who was, Pamela noted, well-endowed and blessed with glossy, auburn hair. "My father's aged and doin' poorly, so I stayed with him 'til he was feelin' better. He's on the mend now, thank the saints."

"I'm glad." Raven tweaked her long braid. "Did you just return?"

"Aye. Happy I am to have arrived while daylight remained. What brings you to Fortengall, milord?"

Cautiously, Pamela retreated a few steps, making sure she could still eavesdrop on the couple.

"To see you, my comely wench," Raven declared, bringing his free hand up to brazenly cup one of Bess's ripe breasts. "It's been too long since we shared a bed."

Pamela's mouth gaped open. Quickly, she shut it.

"If you'll recall, milord, for a while I had a husband who assumed that duty."

"But the poor man went to his death, and now you've space on your mattress that goes wanting."

Raven pressed his bearded cheek against Bess's ear. What he whispered to her, Pamela didn't know. But she was not so naive that she couldn't make an educated guess. What she surmised didn't shock her, but she clenched her fists angrily.

Bess threw back her head and clasped her hands behind Raven's neck. Ties meant to hold her tunic securely together over her bosom gaped loosely, exposing shapely white mounds of flesh that Raven stroked familiarly with one thumb.

Pamela, watching, was beyond annoyed by her betrothed's behavior, though she knew she had no right. Such was the way of noblemen, to amuse themselves with women other than their wives. And she was not yet Raven's wife. In truth, they hardly knew each other, having met for the first time only three evenings past. Besides, as Lady Lucinda had so recently advised her, Raven would need some persuading to find contentment in marriage.

It was her responsibility to make him content, first with the constrictions of a lawful, wedded union, then with herself as his lady wife. But now was not the time to begin. If Raven knew she had spied him fondling Bess, he'd resent it. Such resentment would make it far more difficult to win his favor.

Expelling a long sigh, Pamela began sidling toward the archway, intending a discreet exit from the hall. Her eyes still on Raven and the serving wench, her heart skipped a beat when she saw his head come up sharply. He turned in her direction and her heart began pounding, for she feared he had noticed her watching his antics with the maid. But the dark knight's glance passed over her, as though she were a torch or tapestry mounted on the wall. When he set Bess from him, his black eyes appeared vacant.

"Peter."

Pamela heard him clearly mutter his twin's name. But Bess seemed not to have. "What?" the servant asked, frowning at her master's stepson.

"Peter's been hurt!" Raven roared, pushing past her and hurrying to the front portal.

His bellow hushed the chatter and noise as all eyes followed Raven bounding with long strides out of Fortengall's great hall.

"Did I hear Raven say something has happened to Peter?" Pamela turned at the sound of Lucinda's voice. The lady stood beside her, eyes wide with concern as she watched several knights and men-at-arms running from the room.

"Aye." Pamela nodded. "I believe so. He said his brother's name and bolted outside."

"Where is Peter?"

"I cannot say. I haven't seen him."

The heavy, oak-beamed door set into the keep's front wall groaned on its hinges. Shoes slapped against the stones, and voices rose in the yard. Hearing all, Lucinda followed the others at a run. Pamela ran beside her. They had reached the door when they heard a male voice yell, "He's fallen from the wall, milord! Your brother fell from the wall!"

"Torches!" Raven snapped as he strode in the direction the man was pointing. "We need some damnable light!"

Pamela and Lucinda followed him as he charged into the cluster of people crouched beneath the bailey wall, roughly elbowing aside everyone in his way.

"Peter?" He was on his knees immediately, cradling his brother's head in the crook of his arm.

"Don't move him!" Roxanne ordered. "I fear he's broken his leg."

Raven lifted his eyes from Peter's face and glared hard at the girl. "Don't tell me what I should do to aid my brother. What in the name of all things holy have *you* to do with it?"

"I—I was there. Upon the ledge. We realized, suddenly, it had grown quite dark and were making our way to the stairs."

With a dismissive snarl, Raven looked down into Peter's face. "Are you conscious, man? Can you hear me?"

"Yes, I can hear you. You're loud as a raging boar."

Raven chuckled, obviously relieved that his twin was awake and talking. "Is your leg broken, do you think?"

"I'm sure of it."

Lucinda sprinted forward, going down on her knees beside her injured son. "*Mon Petit*, this may hurt you more still, but

I must find the break," she said. Glancing up with a frown, she exclaimed, "I need more light!"

Raven barked an order, and the torch-bearers came near, looming over those kneeling in the snow.

Peter yelped. "God's wounds, Mother! Have you set the damnable thing?"

"Nay. I only just found the break. It's beastly, I'm afraid." She scrambled up, brushing a crust of snow off her bliaut, which was now wet at the knees. Looking about, she spied her husband, who had come to stand near Pamela. Their three young sons clung to the earl's massive legs.

"Ian, *Mon Petit's* leg is broken. 'Tis all I know for certain. We must get him inside."

The earl nodded and barked orders more crisply even than Raven had. Within moments, Peter was being carried into the castle keep. Behind trailed his family, like a royal entourage.

"Sweet *Jesu,* but can you not set me down on a table in the hall? I hate to whine like a babe, but this jostling has my leg feeling as though it's snapping in and out of place with every step these clumsy oafs take!"

"Nay. I'm sorry, *Mon Petit,*" his mother told him. " 'Tis best we get you upstairs to a bedchamber. That way, once I put the bones back in place and you're settled, the worst of the pain will be behind you."

Peter ground his teeth.

"Christ. Give me his head," Raven ordered tersely, relieving a guard of that end of the litter. "I'll lead," he told the man on the other end, "else Peter will be hanging like a dressed deer on the way up the steps!

"Get away," he snapped at Roxanne, who'd been hovering at Peter's side. "You've done enough, have you not?"

Roxanne's head snapped up, and she blinked slowly at Raven. Her lips parted, but she swallowed back whatever she had meant to say and meekly stepped away.

"Is Peter sorely hurt?" young Jamie asked his sire.

"Nay." Lord Ian shook his head and smiled reassuringly, ruffling his redheaded son's hair. "He'll come through it stronger than he met it. But 'twould seem to be a nasty bone break, and they sometimes hurt as much as a sword wound. Trust me, lads," he added, including his other two sons with a glance, "in time you'll all know what both feel like, I'm certain."

"Heaven forbid," Lucinda whispered, crossing herself. Then she hurried after the litter, which was disappearing beyond the keep's gallery.

"My lady!" Pamela called after her, taking the stairs quickly. When she reached her side, she asked, "Where are your supplies? I'll get them for you. I can assist you, too. I know well how to set broken bones and mix a pain-easing potion."

Lucinda glanced at her distractedly. "Have Hugh take you to my rooms. He knows where my herb basket is stored."

As the ungainly procession continued upward and onward, Pamela hurried back down the stairs and enlisted the young heir to Fortengall as her guide.

When she entered the chamber assigned to Peter, Pamela saw that his shoes and chausses had been removed. Lady Lucinda bent over his injured leg, yet the limb Pamela could see was well-formed, hard-muscled, and covered with black, wiry hair. Pamela also saw that Peter's tunic had ridden up high on his thighs. If she dared to peek at the place where his thighs joined, in that shadow beneath the puddling fabric at his groin she would most certainly have seen more than a modest maiden ought to.

With a blink, she glanced demurely away. But just then Lady Lucinda moved aside, and Pamela spied Peter's broken leg. With a grimace, she swallowed back bile burning at the base of her throat. Lord Ian had surmised rightly: Peter's injury was indeed a bad one. A splinter pierced his skin from the inside out, and his whole leg was swelling, flaming crimson at the point of injury.

"Here you be, milady," Pamela announced quickly, purposely setting her mind on the work to be done. She handed Lucinda her huge basket filled with vials and pouches of medicinal herbs. "Hugh and I also found the strips of linen bandages."

"Excellent, Pamela." She took the basket, and as she began sorting through it, she spoke to her husband. "Ian, get me some splints, will you?"

He quit the room without reply.

"Pamela, you and Raven must help me hold Peter down while we pop the bones back into place. 'Twill not be easy. He's a strong man, and he'll fight us."

"I shan't fight you, Mother."

"You will. It's instinct." With a tender smile, she patted Peter's forehead just as she might have were he a young child. "This will help," she informed him, turning sharply and bringing up an open vial and a pygg clay spoon. Filling the bowl with liquid, she popped the spoon into Peter's mouth.

"Christ! If that was supposed to help . . . !"

"Percival?" In her distress, Lucinda addressed her other son not by the name he had taken, but by the name she had christened him. "Would you like some also? You're looking a bit—"

"I'm well, Mother. 'Tis Peter, here, who needs your mending. Please, get on with it."

Raven stood at the head of the bed. Pamela, nearer its foot, noticed that the fit twin looked as much in agony as the injured one.

"Very well." Lucinda moved down the length of the bed until she stood beside the break in Peter's leg bone. "Percival, hold your brother's shoulders down. Pamela, hold his ankle secure against the mattress. This will hurt worse than the fall did."

"I believe it," Peter muttered, nodding at his mother. "The break didn't hurt at all. 'Twas only afterward, when I tried to move."

"I cannot simply slide the two halves of the bone back into place. The split is jagged and must be fitted together."

"Do it!"

Pamela blinked and glanced up at the two identical faces at the head of the bed. It was Raven who'd given the desperate order, not Peter.

Lady Lucinda tried hard to do it. In spite of himself, Peter resisted. His shoulders rose up fiercely against Raven's splayed fingers, and his leg wrenched away from his mother's cunning fingers and Pamela's desperate grip.

Yet, he made no sound. Pamela admired his bravery at bearing up so well in the face of unquestionable agony. Still, they were making no progress. A second attempt and another, yet the leg remained grotesquely misshapen.

" 'Tis brute force you need, sweetling," Lord Ian declared softly. He'd returned to the chamber unnoticed. "You guide the bones, Lucinda, while I pull. They'll go back more easily that way. Lady Pamela?"

At the earl's subtle urging, she relinquished her place at Peter's foot. As he grabbed Peter's ankle in his giant's paws, she scampered along the unoccupied side of the bed and reached across it, grasping the injured man's hands in her own.

"Hold on," she whispered encouragingly. "Squeeze my fingers with your own, milord. 'Twill help you resist thrusting against Lord Raven. Just squeeze and don't worry. I'm much stronger than I look. I shan't break."

Peter gave her a dubious look, but before he could gainsay her, Lord Ian yanked and Lady Lucinda pushed. His eyes snapped shut, and his hands clamped into fists, fairly grinding Pamela's delicate finger bones to dust. He made a small noise, but only Pamela heard him, for the rest heard Raven's agonized groan.

It was done. In hardly more time than the blink of an eye, even the splinter that had been piercing Peter's flesh was realigned.

" 'Tis finished, milord," Pamela advised Peter softly, using her under-tunic sleeve, which was wide as a cathedral bell at the cuff, to wipe the perspiration from his brow. "Your lady mother and I will splint it, and then—"

"Nay." Peter slowly blinked his heavy lids and peered up at the face hovering above him. "My mother knows well how to splint a broken limb. Just stay by me, my lady, if you will."

"Surely I will. Only let me get another drop of potion for you. One that will aid in your sleeping."

Peter blinked his assent, and she scurried around the bed to dive into the herb basket. "Which pouch holds the henbane?"

"That one," Lucinda informed her, intent on her task of securing the wooden splints her husband was holding alongside her son's leg. "The one tied with green string."

Grabbing it, Pamela poured a small measure directly into a costrel of wine. Shaking the large, two-handled cup to mix the herb with the spirits, she brought it to Peter immediately.

Raven, perched on the mattress near his brother's pillows, held Peter's head so that he could more easily drink. He drank heartily, long, thirsty gulps that nearly drained the vessel.

"Do you—do you mind, milord?" Pamela asked Raven.

"Mind about what?"

"If I sit with your brother 'til he sleeps."

"Nay, of course not. Tend him well. I've other matters to which I must attend."

He pushed off the bed and started toward the chamber door. As Pamela followed him with her eyes, she realized for the first time that Bess had shared the room with them all this while. No doubt she had been waiting to be called upon in some capacity. Now that the crisis had passed, she edged toward the door. Pamela suspected Bess had purposely lingered until Raven departed, because she now followed on his heels.

Lady Lucinda edged up the length of the bed and smiled down at her son. "You'll live, Peter."

"That's true enough. No one who hurts as I do could be anywhere near death."

" 'Twill take some long weeks, but your leg will mend solidly. God willing, there'll be no decided limp."

"There can't be. Not—not when I'm wearing splints made by an earl."

Lucinda's eyes widened, her eyebrows went up, and she turned to look at her husband. "Holy Mother, did I send you to do that?" she asked. When Lord Ian nodded his confirmation, she blushed like a damsel. "Servants all around, and I order my husband about like some common lackey!"

"Why should today be different from any other?" he asked good-humoredly, encircling Lucinda's slim waist with his arms. He chuckled, she chuckled—even Peter chuckled, though his laugh sounded dangerously like a moan. "Let's let the lad have some rest, now," Lord Ian suggested. "You, Lucinda, need some sustenance accompanied by a large goblet of wine. Hopefully, Cook has saved us all something to eat."

"Eat! Gracious! Have the children had their supper?"

He nodded again. "And all the castle staff."

"That's good." Lucinda's forehead puckered with a frown. "Ian, I don't feel at all hungry. I should stay—"

"I know you, lady wife," the earl interrupted, "and I shan't have you making yourself ill. 'Twill do no one any good, especially Peter. You'll sup now because I say so, and you'll do it below in the hall.

"Pamela?" Lord Ian turned to her. "You wouldn't mind remaining here with Peter for a time, would you? I know my dear wife will take her ease more readily if you are here to watch him."

"I'd be happy to, milord."

"Ian, nay!" his wife protested.

"Lucinda, aye!" he returned firmly.

"Very well. Pamela, if my son needs anything, if you need anything . . ." The lady allowed herself to be led from the room. Yet she kept talking as she went. ". . . we'll put a page outside the chamber door. I'll have some trenchers brought up to you. And I'll be back to look in on you, Peter.''

"There's no need to hurry, Lady Lucinda," Pamela assured her. "I'll sit with Lord Peter as long as you wish."

The earl shared a look with both Peter and Pamela as he closed the door behind himself and his wife.

When they were gone, Peter looked at Pamela's hand, again holding his, and asked softly, "Did I break your fingers?"

"I think you tried your best. But as I vowed, I'm not so very fragile. See? Every one still works." With a smile, she raised her hand and wiggled her fingers to prove her assertion.

"Your mother's very skilled," she went on. "I've never seen a break as bad as yours. But I'm certain she and your stepfather set it surely."

"I, too. D'you know how I know?" he asked, his tongue swelling thickly and his words growing fuzzy as the medicinals he'd been given began to work their magic. When Pamela shook her head, he smiled drunkenly. "Mother called me Peter."

Pamela frowned. "That is your name."

"Aye. But earlier, I was *Mon Petit*. Her 'little one,' as though I remained of an age with Jamie and John. When Mother's distraught, she's wont to do that, embarrassing as it is."

"I heard her call Raven, 'Percival.' "

"Ha!" Peter barked and then winced at the pain the effort caused him. "He's fortunate she didna' call him 'Percy.' He might've ... ruptured ... something."

His already heavy-lidded eyes closed completely. As Pamela sat beside him on the bed, one of his hands barely encompassed by both of hers, she thought of her betrothed. He hadn't needed to rupture some internal organ to be in pain. He'd been in as much torment as Peter had been. And the pain Raven had felt was as real as his twin's. Pamela knew it.

CHAPTER 7

Roxanne, left behind by the others when they took Peter upstairs, reluctantly retreated to her chamber. She set a little blaze in the fire pit and lighted a few candles. The room, like others everywhere in winter, was gritty with smoke swirling slowly toward the open window. Yet, it was warm and well lit.

She felt horrid. It was all that blasted Henry's fault! Cursing him repeatedly beneath her breath, Roxanne rued the day she'd received the king's missive, commanding her and Pamela to ride to England with the knights he'd sent for them. How dare he? How dare he interfere in lives that should not concern him?

Not that she found Peter of Stoneweather abhorrent. If she hadn't been ordered to wed him, she might have enjoyed his friendship. But she *had* been ordered to wed him, and Roxanne resented that royal command. Besides, she could never love a man who wasn't Cymry, as Balin was Cymry.

That didn't mean she wished Peter harm. Yet, he'd been harmed, and all because he had decided to woo her. Woo her!

As though it were necessary, in light of Henry's order that they wed. As though, too, there were any chance they might actually marry.

"Damn you to hell, you Angevin cockshead!" Roxanne muttered, pacing the hard floor like a caged animal until she gave up and sank down on a stool. When a distant cry reached her ears, she prayed softly, "Sweet Holy Mother, don't let Peter lose his limb. And don't let there be anything worse ailing him. He's done naught to deserve it!"

No more than she and Pamela deserved their fates, though her cousin didn't recognize she was being ill-used by the English king. So it fell to Roxanne to make things right, and she determined to take Pamela with her when she fled. Though they could not take refuge in their fathers' keeps, and only she had Balin to love and keep her, perhaps, she hoped, Balin would also protect Pamela.

Resting her chin in her hands, Roxanne closed her eyes. Her head hurt mightily.

Raven pushed open the door to Roxanne's chamber without a word or a knock. An instant later, she'd sprung to her feet, rounded to face him, and prepared to lash out with a tongue sharply honed by self-serving lies.

But for a brief moment, before the shrew could respond to his unannounced invasion of her sanctuary, Raven witnessed a scene that made his innards twist into a hard knot of outrage.

Roxanne's chamber was cozily prepared for her comfort. The parted bed hangings revealed plumped pillows and an embroidered coverlet, which was turned back invitingly. Precious, scented beeswax tapers sat burning in their dishes, filling the room with the sweet fragrance of roses. A toasty fire crackled and popped in the corner, and before it, idly watching the flames as though she hadn't a care in the world, sat the lethally conniving bitch who'd almost succeeded in murdering his brother!

"What are you doing here?" Roxanne demanded when she'd leaped to her feet and discovered Raven filling up the width of her chamber doorway. "Is it Peter? Is he—"

"He'll live, no thanks to you!" Bellowing angrily, he took two long strides into the room and slammed the door closed.

"Was it . . . only the one leg that was broken?"

"Only? *Only!* Christ, but I wish you could feel what Peter felt. 'Twas torment, I swear. Bad enough should it have happened during battle, or due to some unfortunate mishap. But that *you* should have inflicted such unnecessary pain . . . !"

He left off sputtering, his rage was so intense. Yet, Roxanne did not cower in the face of it. "I inflicted naught!" she shouted back, hands on her hips. "It was an accident!"

"God's wounds, 'twas not! You've no wish to wed him, so you tried to kill him!"

"I did not! How dare you accuse me of such a loathsome deed?" Her expression changed in a flash, one arched eyebrow cocking shrewdly above her violet eye. "Ah, I see the sense of it, now. 'Tis something you, a conniving, deceitful, selfish slug of this putrid English soil would do. Thus, you pin your own evil intrigues to my shadow. I'd best forewarn my cousin, so that she doesn't find herself in unexpected peril!"

"You bitch!" Raven took another step forward and grabbed Roxanne roughly. His fingers pinched her upper arm.

"You bastard!" She wrenched herself free, but it proved a painful process, and by the morning, she'd bear dark bruises from the imprint of his fingers. "Get you gone from my chamber! I did not invite you in."

" 'Tisn't your chamber. You're naught but a guest, and an unwelcome one at that."

"Then you must be naught but a guest yourself," she sneered in return. "I don't recall you being Earl of Fortengall."

Raven paused and inhaled deeply. He saw this conversation

was going nowhere, that he had lost control of it before he'd uttered a word. He had had a purpose in coming here, in facing her alone, without the constraints of polite manners and propriety. He recalled that purpose and pressed on.

"If I had my way," he explained in a suddenly low, menacing voice, "I'd banish you back to whence you came. If necessary, I'd see you dead."

Her eyes, dark as purple pansies, flashed.

"Aye, mistress, that I would, if I felt you were a threat."

"You *do* think me a threat, if you believe I pushed your brother from the wall."

"I think you *were* a threat," Raven corrected. "But you failed in your plan. I found you out, and you'll be a menace no more."

"How dare you!" Roxanne spat again. She brought her hands up to her waist and clenched them into fists, as though intending to fight Raven hand-to-hand.

When she made this move, her chin came up righteously and her bosom thrust forward. Raven noticed this over her threatening stance—the way the light caught her eyes at that angle, the way her breasts plumped above the scooped neckline of her under tunic. As a connoisseur of feminine beauty, Raven was forced to look elsewhere, or he'd have lost himself in contemplation of her full, creamy bosom.

His eyes flicked upward, and he considered her hair. Wild, it was. She hadn't combed it since being out of doors, and the disheveled mass of thick, soft, blue-black curls twining themselves along her shoulders, her chest, and down her back looked enticingly delicious. Raven's fingers twitched. He longed to run them through the ebony vines cascading from her crown to her hips. Instead, he clenched his fists and hid them behind his sleeves as he crossed his arms over his chest.

Backing up a few steps, he leaned negligently against one wall, still glaring hard at the girl. He reminded himself it was less than seemly for a lady of any note to go about with her head unadorned by a chaplet, veil, or headpiece. Worse, for her not even to have plaited her hair into two, thick braids.

Yet, it suited the Bittenshire bitch, Raven thought viciously. It suited an unwed female who dared ride a stallion, and ride it astride, and who had the ripe figure of a goddess.

"I would have you gone," he announced.

"Would you?" she asked. When he nodded, she reminded him, " 'Tis not your concern. It is Peter I'm to wed, not you."

"I consoled myself with that knowledge, my—" He'd nearly said *lady*. Fortunately, the word did not come easily to his tongue, so he caught himself in time and continued, "But I shan't let my reasonable, trusting brother march headlong to his death at your hands, like a lamb led to slaughter. Nay." Raven shook his dark head slowly, his eyes, the irises fully as dark as the pupils, narrowing dangerously. "You'll be dead first."

Roxanne blinked. Except for that brief flutter of her lashes, she betrayed no reaction to his threat. Contrarily, she shook her own dark head and said, "Were I granted the opportunity to slay one of you twins, 'twould not be Peter I'd dispatch."

"You unholy witch!" Springing away from the wall, Raven leaped at Roxanne, grabbed her, and lifted her nearly off her toes. He shook her like a straw doll, hoping her beautiful head would fall from her shoulders. But her head remained fixed, her eyes sparking fire, and then her knee came up hard to his groin.

"Christ!" Raven moaned, releasing her and stumbling back. It was all he could do not to comfort his crotch with his hands as the pain in his privates ricocheted through his innards.

"Dare not touch me again, or you'll be the one who finds himself dead."

Livid, he reached out his long arm and grabbed a fistful of Roxanne's hair, pulling her head back. With his other arm, he pinned her body to his. She stood bowed, the white column of her throat and the swell of her upper breasts exposed. Despite his rage, Raven found himself tempted to touch the damsel even more intimately, mayhap to force himself on her. Ah, that degradation, he thought, would impose some restraint on her otherwise brazen demeanor. Suddenly, he found his lips drawing down toward the base of her throat.

Yet, their skin did not make contact, for again he pulled hard on Roxanne's hair, gaining space between themselves as he regained his reason. He had never forced himself on any maiden, not in all his score and six years. Every female he'd bedded had sought him willingly. He'd no desire to rape any woman, not even to cower a wench who despised him.

"I touch," he growled, "whomever, whenever, I please."

"Oh?" Roxanne breathed hard, straining against the discomfort of her position. "Even your brother's wife?"

"You are not my brother's wife, nor shall you ever be, do you hear?" Raven released her roughly so that Roxanne staggered backward, catching herself on the bed.

"I never asked to be his wife! 'Twould be horrid enough to be forced to take an Englishman to husband, and then let him live with me in Cymru. God's blood—do you think I wish to wed a foreigner and live with him on English soil? 'Twas your king who ordered it so."

She spoke true; Raven knew it. He scowled as he continued to loom threateningly over Roxanne. To defy Henry's decree could prove disastrous. Besides, Peter seemed pleased enough with the Welsh maiden. God's tears, what could he do to protect his unassuming brother?

Raven knew only one thing to do: press on with his meaningless threats. Roxanne of Bittenshire was nothing but a wild creature from the mountains of Wales. It mattered not that her sire was a lord of Norman-English blood who'd held secure for a lifetime a barony his ancestor had carved out of that heathen land. The Marcher Lord's last child was still young and a female in the bargain. She could not match wits with Raven of Stonelee!

"You will not wed Peter," he insisted again, touching the handle of the dagger he kept sheathed in his belt. It pleased Raven to see Roxanne's nervous glance stray to his hand before returning to his face. "I've no care that he may wish it. I shan't let it happen. Instead, I will see that you have a mishap of your own. Only should you fall, wench, it will not be your leg that snaps in two, but your neck!"

With that, Raven spun on his heel, yanked open the chamber door, and slammed it closed behind him. In his wake the candle flames flickered perilously, and even the fire in the pit seemed to tremble.

But not Roxanne. Finally free of his loathsome presence, she still refused to give in to the compulsion to rub her aching arms, throat, and back. She would not even allow the tears burning behind her eyes to be released. Sweet Holy Mother of God, but she hated the English king for putting her in this sorry situation! And if he thought she would meekly bow to his royal wishes, he was wrong. She would not!

Unfortunately, Peter would be offended when she disobeyed Henry's command. Worse, she'd be doing what that swine, Raven of Stonelee, wished her to. But there was no help for it. She had her own destiny, and it had nothing to do with marriage to an English lord and living every day with the threat that it might be her last, at the hands of her husband's brother.

Nay, her destiny lay in Cymru.

Roxanne opened her door and peeked into the hallway. Finally, she saw light seeping from beneath Pamela's door. Swiftly, she padded across the cold stones, slipping into her cousin's chamber unannounced.

"Roxanne!" Pamela looked up from tying the sash on her robe.

"How is Peter?"

"He's sleeping. Not very comfortably, I fear. But between

Lady Lucinda and the earl, his bones are set. Now it's just the discomfort of long weeks of mending that he'll be facing.''

Roxanne sat on the edge of the bed, and Pamela, standing, faced her. ''Why didn't you go to him?'' she asked. ''I'd have thought, as his betrothed, you would show some concern even though you don't care for him overmuch.''

''I don't dislike him,'' Roxanne insisted. ''Between the two brothers, he's by far the better-natured. But you saw how his family hovered over him. Raven behaved as though I'd pushed him from the wall! I didn't think I'd be welcome in Peter's room.''

''He'd have welcomed you.'' She paused before adding, ''Roxy, I don't believe anyone blames you for what happened.''

''They shouldn't! I did nothing! Nothing on purpose.''

Exhaling a long breath, Pamela sat beside her cousin. Folding her small hands in her lap, she said, ''I wonder if we'll delay the nuptials until Peter can stand again.''

''There won't be any nuptials.''

She blinked. ''What do you mean?''

''I shan't be wedding Lord Peter. Nor can I allow you to wed that—that—''

''Lord Raven?''

''Aye. Lord Raven.''

''Of course I'll wed him! Roxy, what are you saying?''

''He came to my room.''

''Raven did? Why?''

''I'll tell you why.'' Roxanne sprang to her feet and began pacing. ''He insists I shall not wed his brother. If I dare try, he's vowed to see me dead.''

''Nay!'' Pamela gasped. ''I should speak with him. He's no doubt overwrought at Peter's injury. Oh, Roxy, you should have seen him—Raven, I mean. He helped set Peter's leg, and I vow he felt all his brother's pain. Not only in spirit, but as though his own leg were broken and being put right.''

''Good.'' Roxanne stopped pacing long enough to give

Pamela a wry look. "Yet I would rather inflict pain on him directly than have him feel an echo of his brother's anguish."

"Roxanne! He's my intended husband. You mustn't speak so."

"Pamela." She dropped to a crouch and took her cousin's hands in her own. "Pamela, you cannot tie yourself to him. Raven of Stonelee threatened me with death if I obeyed King Henry's wishes and wed his brother. How could you wed a man who threatened to murder your own dear cousin?"

"Surely he didn't mean it. He was only upset."

"He meant it! Sweet Mother of God, Pamela—I thought he might try to kill me then and there, in my very own chamber! He's a wicked man and brutal, too."

"You're frightened of him?" she asked dubiously.

"Aye," Roxanne returned softly, slowly nodding her head. "That's it. I fear him to the core of my being. I must get myself gone from here before he arranges a fatal accident. And you must come with me so he doesn't hurt you, either."

Pamela's forehead creased. "He wouldn't ... would he? Lord Peter is so gentle."

"Aye." Pressing her hands to her thighs, Roxanne pushed herself erect again. "Peter is gentle. But his twin is not. Instead, they are reflections of each other. Opposites. Peter is good, but in equal measure, Raven is wicked."

For a long moment, Pamela considered Roxanne's words. But suddenly her chin came up and she stood, too. "You must be wrong, Roxy. Look around you, at Lady Lucinda, Lord Ian, and their sons. Do you recall Lord Lucien? All he could think of was his wife and daughter and the babe that's coming. People like this cannot have an evil one among them. Lord Raven was merely distraught that Lord Peter was so sorely hurt."

"Don't be a fool! Lord Peter himself, this very day, hinted that his and Raven's sire was a wicked man. He wouldn't tell false tales, would he?" When Pamela shook her head, she suggested, "Mayhap, Lord Raven is like his father."

"No, no, no!" Stalking away from Roxanne, Pamela shook her head again. "I cannot believe what you say. Lord Raven may be different from Lord Peter, but he is hardly evil."

"Don't be deceived!" Roxanne reached out and grabbed her cousin's wrists again. "You cannot risk it. If you wed Raven, he will, at best, neglect you; at worst, he may see you harmed."

"Roxy, you can't stop me. I'm honor-bound to wed him, and I shall not defile my father's good name by disobeying King Henry."

"Fool!" Spitting out the word, she tossed Pamela's hands down and spun away from her. "Wed him, then, and die young. But remember I tried to spare you."

She grabbed the latch, but before wrenching the door open, she turned back. "You have the right to remain and sacrifice yourself, Pamela. But I have the right to flee and save myself. I shall go tonight, before darkness wanes. And I expect you to hold your tongue about it."

"I will," Pamela vowed softly. "But Peter—"

"Care for him in my stead. Tell him that I'm sorry. About everything—his fall, the marriage, all of it."

Roxanne finally opened the door, but Pamela stayed her by placing a hand on her shoulder. "Roxy, do you even know how to get to Bittenshire from here?"

"Truth be told, I do." At last, she smiled. "Peter kindly pointed out the road that will take me north to Cymru."

For a moment the cousins looked at each other, each thinking the other strongly misguided. Then Pamela whispered, "God speed!" and they clung to each other in a long, heartfelt hug.

Back in her chamber, as she threw only necessities into a satchel, Roxanne's excitement at avoiding an unwanted marriage, at leaving a despised land, and at escaping a loathsome man was tempered by doubt at leaving Pamela behind. If only, she thought as she hurried, her cousin was marrying Peter, she would not feel so badly. Those two would suit. Unfortunately, she knew there was no chance for them as a couple. Onerous Henry, Angevin King of England, deemed Raven of Stonelee suitable as Pamela's husband and Lord of Angleford. And that was surely what would come to pass.

Sneaking silently down the stairs, Roxanne tiptoed past the sleeping retainers and servants sprawled in the rushes strewn about the great hall. Slipping into the kitchen, she made her way to the postern door and stepped into the night.

Darkness lingered, though it was nearer to dawn than to midnight, and it was cold besides. But torches cast enough light for her to see, even though she clung to the shadows as she made her way to the stables.

"May I help you, m'lady?" the stable man inquired when she peeked into the barn. He sat just inside the entrance, his back propped against a wall, a lantern burning above his head.

"Aye. I need my horse saddled quickly."

"Oh?" Climbing slowly to his feet, he grabbed the lantern from its peg. It cast myriad shafts of weak light through the small holes in its casing. "And which horse would that be?"

"A big, black stallion called Dafydd."

"Aye. That fine beastie I know."

Following him impatiently, Roxanne was concerned about the wickers and whinnies the horses sent up with their hopes for an early oat ration. She didn't think it queer that she'd found the stable man awake rather than snoring on his pallet.

Nor did she deem it unusual that her fine saddle and bridle lay, as though discarded, on the floor near her steed. She felt so pleased to find them easily, she grabbed the bridle and began fitting it to Dafydd's head.

"Hurry," she urged the stable man, slanting her chin toward the saddle. "I must leave quickly."

He was as compliant as any Bittenshire servant to Roxanne's

orders, and shortly she found herself sitting astride Dafydd, leading him out of the stall and into the yard. Moments later, she approached the gate in the outer bailey. She glanced about apprehensively, but she detected no activity at this hour and saw no one who might question her.

Still, as Roxanne had feared, the portcullis remained lowered. Though there had to be other exits in the walls, she had no time to find them. Already the sky was beginning to lighten by soft degrees. So, adopting a bold posture and an authoritative tone, she halted Dafydd near one tower and called up, ''Raise the gate!''

A guard promptly leaned out the window and looked down at Roxanne as she waited in a puddle of torchlight. She felt a tense moment, but to her relief, the man merely nodded, and the iron teeth began slowly to rise from the cavities in the dirt.

The damned chains made a horrendous racket, at least to Roxanne's ears. As soon as the latticework of iron spikes rose higher than her head, she kicked her mount into a canter and ducked beneath them, heading down the motte to the road and north toward Cymru.

Beside the guard in his tower, Raven watched as the Welsh woman galloped away. Unerringly, she chose the right direction despite the diffused light of early dawn and the fact that the road lay buried beneath a carpet of new snow.

She looked a sight, her midnight black tresses flowing behind her as she sat astride her beast like a Viking queen, the muscular stallion churning up snow in his wake as he carried his mistress defiantly away from Fortengall.

Such a vision may have impressed his brother, Peter, but not Raven. He had hardened his heart to Roxanne's wild beauty, and he smiled, pleased, as the brazen bitch took her leave.

''Good riddance.''

''Did you speak, my lord?''

He turned to the armed man with whom he shared the tower window. ''Do you know who that was riding off just now?''

"Ah—I—well, I don't know for certain. But it appeared—"

"Forget who it appeared to be. You don't know. If anyone should ask, most particularly about a lady guest at Fortengall Castle, you never saw her."

"Aye," the guard wisely agreed. Just as the stable man had agreed earlier.

CHAPTER 8

Nearly everyone had gathered in Peter's bedchamber, from his mother, who could not restrain herself from touching his brow, to his youngest brothers, who tore about the room hoping their athletic antics might cheer him. Lord Ian reclined, half seated, on the window ledge, an indulgent expression on his scarred face, while Pamela stood out of the way in a corner opposite the door. From her circumspect position she could not see Peter's face, which was hidden from her view by the hangings draped near the head of the bed. But she had a clear view of Raven, who leaned against the wall near the door.

As she watched, the serving girl, Bess, eased her way past Raven when she entered with a tray. Barely nodding at the lord of Stonelee, she carried the victuals and beer tankard to Peter's bed and set them in his lap. Leaving the invalid with both a cheery word and smile, Bess departed quickly.

Pamela wondered at the woman's behavior. Was it discretion or indifference? She guessed discretion, for Bess had been nearly as guarded the night before when she'd slipped out of this room just as Lord Raven vacated it.

"Good God," Raven groused, drawing Pamela's attention. "How can you stand the racket? Jamie, Hugh, John—come to heel, you young pups. Your brother, Peter, is in misery."

The two younger twins and little Lord Hugh nearly careened into each other as they skidded to a halt and looked up at Raven. Solemnly, Hugh declared, "Mother thaid he wathn't dying."

"Do you think that means he doesn't need some quiet?"

"Let them be," Peter said from his pillowed nest. "I'd rather have too much company than none of it. The latter would be my fate had I broken my leg at Stoneweather."

"You'd not have broken your leg at Stoneweather."

"Mayhap not," Lord Ian put in quickly, coming to his feet and gesturing to his three sons. "But there's no need for this noise. Come along, lads. It's time I led my men on the practice field. Care to accompany me?"

"Aye!" three young voices chirped, and the earl took the children away.

"That's better." Raven approached the foot of the bed and grasped one of the posts. "How did you sleep last night?"

"Better than you, brother, by the looks of it."

Raven shrugged and fingered his unkempt beard. "I suppose my concern for you made me sleepless. I never even took to my bed last eve."

Surprised by his admission, Pamela studied her betrothed's face with a critical eye. He looked haggard. As he'd confessed to spending a sleepless night somewhere other than his own bed, she could easily imagine whose he had shared.

"Nay, no more, Mother!" Peter's protest snagged Pamela's attention, and she spied his arm waving off Lady Lucinda, who approached the bed with a spoon. "No more potions! I just said I slept fairly well. And I should have, considering you dosed me into a stupor!"

"Are you certain?" Lucinda asked skeptically, holding the spoon over the cupped hand she held beneath it. "Rest is what you'll need, Peter, if you're to heal quickly."

"There's naught else I can do but rest, Mother. God knows I'll be confined to this damnable bed for weeks to come."

"Then eat." She set aside the concoction she'd been trying to administer and picked up Peter's eating knife from a table laden with his hastily discarded possessions. Handing it to him, she advised, "You need to keep up your strength."

"That, I shall do," he promised. "But where is the sweet damsel who aided me in eating last eve? And my lady, Roxanne? Why isn't she here?"

Pamela flinched, pricked by guilt. Roxanne was notably absent from among Peter's visitors—she, who above all others should have been present. Her absence was unwelcome confirmation that she'd fled the castle. But how had Roxanne managed it? As she'd lain in her own bed last night, fretting over this very moment, Pamela had decided it would prove impossible for her headstrong cousin to leave without notice, even in the dead of night. But she was obviously wrong. Roxanne had done what she'd set out to do. Already, she was probably halfway home to Wales.

"I think, mayhap, Roxanne is distraught over your injury, Peter," his mother suggested. "When I finished setting your leg last eve and went below, I inquired after her only to learn that she'd retreated to her room. I had a trencher brought to her there, but I haven't seen her yet this morn."

"Mother," Peter said reprovingly, "you didn't seek her out? Have a word with her? Sweet *Jesu*, she probably blames herself for my mishap, as if she were responsible for her slip on the ice. And if she's been all but ignored by the family since I fell, she no doubt feels you blame her, too."

"That's foolishness!" Lucinda protested. But she continued apologetically, "I know I should have seen to her. But I confess, last night she wasn't foremost in my mind. I sat with you for hours while you slept, Peter, until Ian finally dragged me off to bed." She turned and glanced over her shoulder at Pamela. "Isn't that true, dear?"

"It's true—"

"No matter—"

Raven spoke as Pamela did. But as Pamela rushed to Lucinda's side and gained Peter's full attention, Raven left off and she continued, "Your lady mother and I—all of us—were quite concerned for you, milord. It's understandable we didn't think to speak with Roxanne."

"Surely you've seen her since."

"Aye." She nodded, her glance darting briefly toward Raven. "I spoke with Roxy before I retired. Don't fret for her, Lord Peter. She knows she's not responsible for your fall. My cousin"—she blinked and looked at Raven again, though she just as quickly looked away—"my cousin would ne'er accept a burden that wasn't hers to carry."

"Good. She ought not to feel badly about this business. Still . . . I would think she'd have visited me, at least this morn."

Pamela hesitated, feeling Raven's gaze upon her. A third time she glanced his way, this time a moment or two longer than the times before. Conflict swelled within her breast as she debated telling what she knew. But Raven's cold eyes made her decide to hold her tongue for her own sake and Roxanne's.

"Her emotions . . . run high," she explained. "I know Roxanne feels wretched that this"—Pamela gestured to Peter's splinted leg—"happened to you. If she hadn't climbed the wall, you would not have climbed the wall, and certainly you'd not have fallen. In any event, 'tis probably best to leave her for a while. She's been known to do this in the past, to hide herself away when something unpleasant happens."

"She has?" Peter looked dubious.

"Oh, yes." Pamela nodded emphatically. "But she bade me

tell you that she's sorry for everything. And she asked that I tend you in her stead.''

"More foolishness!" Lucinda declared. "I may have been remiss in not comforting Roxanne. She certainly had a fright. But she shouldn't sequester herself in her chamber. I'll go and speak with her immediately and send her to you, Peter.''

As his mother began to pass Raven on her way to the door, he grabbed her wrist and exclaimed, "Nay! Don't. If the wench wishes to be left alone, leave her be.''

"But—"

" 'Tis best, milady," Pamela hurriedly agreed, sharing a look with Raven.

"Why is it best? She's a guest at Fortengall, she's Peter's betrothed. She shouldn't lock herself away as though she were a prisoner in the dungeon. Peter's broken leg aside, there are plans to be made. Plans for your weddings.''

"Mother, let it be," Raven insisted. "Pamela knows her cousin better than we. If she wishes to be alone for a while, what's the harm? 'Tis not as if the nuptials are scheduled for the morrow. And owing to Peter's injury, they may have to be delayed some while longer.''

"God's blood, don't make it sound like I shan't be leaving this chamber again!" Peter complained. He took a long draught from his tankard and licked the foam from his lips. "But you're right. Roxanne is not nearly so brash and indifferent as she'd like us to believe. If she wants privacy and solitude, let her have it. At least until this eve. If she hasn't made an appearance by then, someone should lure her out of her chamber.''

"Milady." A servant rapped on the open chamber door and addressed her mistress. "It is wash day, and—"

"Say no more." Lucinda raised her hand, indicating silence. "I'll be on my way directly." She looked to Peter. "Have you need of anything I may have sent up to you?''

"Nay."

"Then, I'll go now. Eat up," she urged, planting a maternal

kiss on the invalid's brow before indicating the nearly untouched trencher in his lap.

Lucinda bustled out of the room, leaving the twin lords and Pamela behind. Looking between the two of them, she began sidling her way toward the door. "I . . . I should leave you now, also. Lady Lucinda may require some assistance."

"Pamela, you're a guest here at Fortengall, not a servant," Peter reminded her. "However, I would not be adverse to having you wipe my chin free of dribbles and crumbs. I'm not very adept at eating while lying abed."

Pamela smiled weakly, flattered that Peter liked her company but reluctant to offer it. Glancing sidelong at Raven, she suggested, "Perhaps your brother wishes to share a private word with you."

"Nay." Raven's smile did not reach his eyes. "No need for private confidences at the moment. In truth, I should be out on the practice field with Lord Ian. I can't allow myself to go soft if I must protect Angleford Keep from wild Welsh warriors.

"If you'll excuse me." He nodded toward his brother, but his glance held Pamela's overlong before he quit the room.

"Well?" Peter settled his attention on his remaining visitor rather than the food in his lap. "I shan't bite. Why don't you sit beside me? It will make feeding me easier."

"You don't need me to feed you."

"Nay." He grinned conspiratorially and patted the mattress invitingly. "But I do enjoy your company. I only wish I were a less boring companion for you."

"You're not boring," Pamela insisted, darting a glance toward the closed door.

"No? Then why do you look as though you wish to flee?"

Again, she was reminded that Roxanne had fled. Guilt tugged at her conscience for having confided in no one, most especially Peter. "It's not that."

"What, then? Do you already miss Raven's company?"

"Nay!" Her protest was quick and sharply uttered. "That

is, we've not spent much time together, yet. I hardly know him, so I cannot miss him.''

"That's it, then." He nodded as though he'd divined a secret.

"What is?" Pamela approached the bed, picked up Peter's eating knife, and stabbed a piece of cold swan. She held it to his lips, and he bit the morsel off the point.

"You're annoyed my brother isn't wooing you."

"No doubt he's afraid to, considering that when you pursued Roxy, you nearly fell to your death from the bailey wall."

Peter scoffed. "Raven's afraid of naught. Except, mayhap, marriage.''

"Why?" She fed him another piece of meat.

"I don't know." He chewed thoughtfully as she sat, finally, beside him on the bed. "I would guess it's because his life has been good these past few years. The prospect of changing it with a wife and children is worrisome, at least to Raven."

"It doesn't worry you." Pamela picked up an egg and began peeling it.

Peter shrugged and sipped his beer. "I need a chatelaine for Stoneweather, and I need heirs besides. The only way to manage that is to take a wife. I think the king's done me a great service by choosing a woman like Roxanne to be my bride."

"Lord Raven also needs a wife to run his household and give him heirs to Stonelee," Pamela ventured softly as she peppered the peeled egg.

"Aye, he does. And in his head, he knows it. It's his heart that balks at the prospect."

"His heart?" She cocked an eyebrow as she handed the peeled, peppered egg to Peter. "I would think it was some other part of his anatomy that resists being faithful to one woman."

"Little Lady Pamela!" As he took the egg from her fingers, Peter's eyebrows arched in surprise. "I cannot believe I heard such coming from your lips!"

For a moment, she regretted voicing her opinion. But then she noticed the twinkle in his eyes, and she grinned.

Peter chuckled, shaking his head. "Ah, my lady, I don't think my twin yet suspects the trouble he has on his hands."

"Are you saying I'm trouble?"

"Of the most delightful sort."

"You think he'll be delighted?"

"I'm certain of it."

"Well, he shan't be delighted if he doesn't take the time to know me," Pamela said seriously as she dribbled honey from a small pitcher onto a piece of bread.

"He will. He has no choice, now, does he?"

"Sometimes people insist on making choices others won't allow." With a serious frown, she caught Peter's gaze. Roxanne had invaded her thoughts again.

"Sometimes they fight the inevitable," he agreed, accepting the bread Pamela offered and taking a bite. "In the end, though, they do what they must, what is for the best."

Peter's pronouncement consoled her. What did it matter if Roxanne resisted the king's order? What did it matter if Roxanne made it all the way back to Bittenshire? The king's word was law, and Roxanne's sister, Aggie, along with her husband, Thomas, would certainly escort her back to London. Once that was done, Roxanne would find herself swiftly wed to Peter, no matter what her disposition on the matter. Just as she herself would soon wed Raven, despite that his eyes—and other parts of his person—sought out other women.

"If I understand you," she began, sidling up to the head of the bed so that she could share his pillows at her back, "the king's edict is like rust in the gears of Lord Raven's life."

Again, Peter's eyebrows leapt upward. "Aye, Pamela. That's very perceptive."

"Then will you tell me more about this man I'm to wed, so that I may grease the cogs? Methinks he'll be more receptive to marriage if he sees I will enhance his life rather than ruin it."

"You're a clever lady," he said admiringly, his gaze lingering fondly on Pamela's face. "And I'll gladly tell you all you wish to know. But in turn, you must tell me about your cousin. As she anticipates marriage with no more enthusiasm than my brother, I, too, shall have to 'grease the cogs.' "

Pamela nodded, but she felt a prick of anxiety pierce her breast. Poor Lord Peter, she thought, lying abed with his injury and believing his betrothed to be only a short distance away, fretting over his accident. When he learned that she had abandoned him, he would be hurt.

But not for very long, the damsel consoled herself quickly. Roxanne would be forced to return, and when she did, she'd see what a fine husband Peter would make her.

"Very well." Pamela dribbled more honey on another hunk of bread, but this time she took a bite herself and savored the sweetness. "What would you like to know?"

"What is her family like? What was she like as a child?"

Pamela answered that and all of Peter's questions. In turn, he answered her own queries about Raven's past and personality. Between them, they finished the food on the trencher and shared the beer to wash it down. They spent a companionable morning together, as though they were longtime friends. Or better, as though they were each the sister or brother the other had never had.

CHAPTER 9

Pamela felt deflated. She'd been all puffed up after her visit with Peter. While they idled away the morning chatting, there seemed to be no world beyond the space they occupied. They'd had a very pleasant time of it, despite the pain in his broken limb and the secret sitting heavy on her breast.

But now, perched on the bed in the room Roxanne had occupied, an ominous weight fell upon her shoulders. She should never have entered here, she thought ruefully, yet the temptation had been overpowering. Now the confidences she held dear and the disaster they portended filled her mind darkly.

"It's you."

Her head snapped up at the sound of Raven's voice. Pamela found him filling the doorway. Despite the tales Peter had told her of Raven as a boy, she saw him now only as a dark, dangerous warrior.

"You knew 'twould be me," she told him, meeting his level gaze.

"Did I?" He stepped into the room and rested his shoulder

against the stones that framed the doorway. "I understood Lady Roxanne hid herself away in here."

"You know quite well she's gone."

Raven didn't deny it as he looked Pamela over, head to toe and back again. "You knew it, too, yet you said nothing. Why didn't you alert everyone that your cousin has fled?"

"Because I promised Roxy. Besides, 'twill grieve Lord Peter when he hears what she's done. I've no wish to see him hurt sooner than need be."

"How thoughtful of you," Raven said dryly. Stepping farther into the room, he nudged the door closed with the heel of his boot. "But he shan't be hurt. Dismayed, perhaps. His pride a bit bruised. But hurt? Nay. Not more hurt by Roxanne's leaving than he was by her attempt to send him to his death."

"Roxy never meant to kill Lord Peter!" Pamela cried out, shooting to her feet. "He knows it! He told you that his fall was an accident. Why don't you believe your own brother?"

"Because I got the scent of that bitch as soon as she entered my presence. She is deadly."

Pamela gasped, yet she countered evenly, "You are the one who's deadly."

Raven blinked and frowned, surprise evident in his expression. "Me?"

"Aye." She jerked her chin for emphasis. " 'Twas you who threatened to murder Roxanne if she didn't leave your brother before they might wed."

"She told you all, did she?" Reaching her with another long stride, he grabbed Pamela's arm and pulled her close, forcing her to tilt back her head in order to look up at him. "And when do you intend to tell my brother of my part in this?"

"Never."

Raven smiled cheerlessly. "Good. Glad I am to find you know enough not to make charges against your lord husband."

"I wouldn't hold my tongue for your benefit or mine. I'll hold my tongue only to spare Peter."

"My brother has been spared already, my lady. First by fate, which kept him from worse injury when he fell from the bailey wall. And next by me, who sent your hellish cousin riding back to wherever your godforsaken home is."

"Oh? And who but me will spare him from the knowledge that you, his own twin, threatened the woman he would marry if she dared to say her vows? Do you think he would take it lightly if he knew you presumed to interfere? Do you think he'd care not that you pledged harm to the lady he desires to wed? Do you?"

Guilt flickered briefly on Raven's features before he pushed Pamela aside and turned away. "You think me malicious, do you?"

"Nay."

"Speak truly, my lady." He turned to face her again, his expression hardened once more. "Surprisingly, I find you're not afraid to speak your mind when you feel you must. I give you leave to speak it now."

She fidgeted, shifting her weight from one foot to another, and looked down at the toes of her shoes. "Nay, I don't think you are malicious, Lord Raven. I think you are a nobleman, a landed knight, master of your demesne and all the people who labor to serve your needs."

"Somehow I feel you've besmirched my character with that description."

"Nay. 'Tis only that frequently men like you show little regard for others. Your will, your wishes, are all that matter to you."

Raven closed his hands into fists, but his voice remained even. "Men nobly born are born to rule, my lady. Remember it," he cautioned. "While women gently born are born to serve their husbands. Remember that as well."

"I know my place," Pamela assured him primly, purposely keeping her eyes downcast.

"I know you do."

Raven's voice was suddenly gentle. A moment later, she felt his knuckles gently grazing her cheek.

" 'Tis why I was pleased to find King Henry selected you as my bride.''

Pamela closed her eyes completely. She did not believe a word he said. He was too easily distracted by Bess and other women to have a true interest in her. And as he condemned Roxanne so readily, he surely had doubts about herself as well. Yet, Raven of Stonelee could be charming and seductive when he chose to be, and now, suddenly, she felt his mouth on hers.

His kiss was hard, possessive, demanding. But it gave no hint of desire; it was much more a warning. Pamela inhaled a quick breath when he released her, and she stared at him bewilderedly.

Raven's hand fell away from her cheek, and he strode toward the door as she watched his progress. Pausing, he turned back to her before raising the latch.

"You're not to speak of these matters we've just discussed, my dearest. This evening your cousin's disappearance will come to light, but I will deal with Lord Ian and my mother, and most especially Peter. You're not to tell them anything you know or anything you *think* you know. Do you understand?''

"Aye.''

Raven's smile widened, revealing even teeth. He looked almost genial as he graced Pamela with a jaunty wink. "I am indeed pleased you're to be my bride,'' he assured her again before he left.

With a sigh, she plopped down heavily on the edge of the bed. Roxanne had been correct. The twin lords of Stonelee and Stoneweather *were* opposites. But not in the manner her cousin had claimed. Nay. Peter was simply direct and unpretentious, while Raven was a complex man of confusing contradictions. She had her work cut out for her, Pamela knew, if she was ever to understand this dark knight and make him her loyal helpmate.

* * *

"Ian, Roxy's gone."

Though Pamela sat on the floor near the hearth fire playing a rhyming game with the earl's three young sons, Lucinda's words carried clearly across the great hall to her. Looking up, she saw the lady speaking with Lord Ian near the archway.

"What do you mean?" he asked.

"She's gone!" Lucinda repeated anxiously. "As she kept herself hidden all day, and it's nearing the evening meal, I decided to speak with her in private. I went to her room, Ian, but she wasn't there. Only some of her things remain, not she."

"Lucinda, she can't have gone far. We'll find her." Ian paused and looked across the large chamber to Pamela.

"My dear," he said, approaching her quickly with his long, purposeful strides, "it seems your cousin's nowhere to be found. Do you know where she is?"

"Lady Pamela, it's your turn," Jamie declared, ignoring his father's interruption. But Pamela was already on her feet, the game she had been leading the farthest thing from her thoughts.

"I—I haven't seen her all day," she replied truthfully.

"No?" Lucinda, who'd joined them, frowned. "Why not?"

The younger lady grabbed a fistful of her bliaut skirt in each hand and kneaded it nervously. "As I . . . as I told Lord Peter earlier today, Roxy prefers to be left alone when something is upsetting her. She was very upset over Peter's mishap, even though she did nothing purposely to cause it."

"We know she isn't responsible," the earl assured her, smiling encouragingly. "But Lady Lucinda has checked, and Roxanne is not in her room. If your cousin sought privacy, where do you think she'd go?"

Looking up into the earl's kindly face, Pamela felt wretched enough to confess the truth. But she couldn't, for Peter's sake. She glanced at Lucinda, reassuring herself that the lady would understand why she withheld the whole truth. Lucinda would never let one of her sons suffer, not if she could help it.

"I cannot say, milord," Pamela told Ian. "I—I am not familiar with Fortengall. I've no idea where Roxy would go."

Ian turned to his wife. "Have you spoken with Peter? Raven?"

"Nay. I only now found her missing. I spoke with several servants, and all claim they haven't clapped eyes on her the entire day. 'Twould seem no one has seen her since last evening, shortly after Peter was brought upstairs to his chamber."

"I saw her, milady," Pamela put in helpfully, glad to be clinging to a thin thread of truth. "I told you, did I not, that I spoke with her before retiring. She was fine and well then."

"I'm certain Lady Roxanne remains fine and well," Ian declared. "But she should not feel the outcast here among her new relations.

"Frederick!" He hailed his seneschal, who was coming down the staircase, and gestured for the castle keeper to approach. "Have you, mayhap, seen Lady Roxanne today?"

"Nay, milord, I've not." Frederick looked between the two women. "Is something amiss?"

"I doubt it. But the lady's nowhere to be found—at least, not easily found. Would you dispatch some varlets to search the castle and the grounds, and to ask both guards and laborers if anyone has seen the lady about?"

"Certainly, milord."

"Come. We'd best advise Peter that his intended bride has made herself scarce." Lord Ian gestured toward the stairs, urging Lucinda and Pamela to precede him up to Peter's room.

Pamela's chest felt tight as she continued to twist the cloth in her hands, holding up her hems so that she wouldn't trip. Taking the stairs directly behind Lady Lucinda, she asked, "Do you think it is wise? I fear that when he is told Roxy has disappeared, he'll feel that it is somehow his fault. Lord Peter should not be made upset after his recent injury."

"He's a strong man, Pamela," the earl responded before Lucinda might. He trailed the ladies up the staircase. "Besides, 'tis not as if she's fallen down the well or left the bailey's curtain walls. Roxanne will either make her appearance or be found in very short order, I promise."

"Ian's right," Lucinda agreed as she shouldered open the door to Peter's chamber.

"Lord Ian is right about what?" Peter asked curiously when the three of them entered. He looked tired, but his smile seemed genuine.

"We've something to tell you," Lucinda announced, reaching out first to touch her son's brow and then to smooth his coverlet.

"You might tell me where my betrothed is. She's been conspicuously absent since I left her so abruptly last eve." Peter chuckled at his little joke.

Neither his mother nor Pamela joined him in laughter. They shared a quick look before Lucinda explained, "She is why we came to speak to you, Peter. Roxanne is missing."

"What?"

Quickly, Lucinda told him of her discovery.

"I had Frederick send out some lads to look for her. Surely someone's seen her, Peter," Ian put in. "Lady Roxanne can't have gone too far."

"Sweet *Jesu*," he muttered, his brow furled, his lips tight. "Last eve when we were speaking, up on the wall, I thought I had gotten the damsel to trust me a little. You know her, Pamela. That armor she thinks she wears is a fragile illusion. But then I had to take that accursed fall and break my accursed leg—"

He broke off, his glance straying to include his mother and stepfather. "Someone said something to her."

"What?" Lucinda frowned, looking bemused.

"There's at least one among us who hasn't taken kindly to my future wife."

"What are you suggesting, Peter? That—that someone accused her of pushing you off the wall?" Lucinda demanded. "I cannot believe it. I understand she may feel she contributed to your tumble when she slipped on the ice. But no one, no one would have accused her of purposely trying to injure you."

Lucinda turned to Ian to support her contention and spied, at that moment, her other black-eyed, black-haired son stepping into the room. "Raven, have you heard? Lady Roxanne's gone missing."

"Aye?" He seemed not at all disturbed as he continued into the chamber, halting only when he stood directly behind Pamela. "Well, she can't be very far. Besides, didn't my lady, here, explain this very morn that her cousin likes to hide away and lick her wounds when e'er she feels troubled?"

Peter's probing gaze locked on Raven's. "Why would Lady Roxanne feel troubled?"

"You know very well." His eyes fastened on their mirror image. "Obviously she had no great interest in taking you to husband."

"Raven!" Lucinda gasped.

"It's true, Mother," he insisted, glancing sidelong at her. "The damsel made it known to us all that she was unhappy being dragged away from Wales to wed an English lord."

"That may be," Peter conceded. "But I know Roxanne of Bittenshire well enough to be certain she'd no more run away from unpleasantness than you would, Raven. And I don't believe she finds the prospect of marrying me quite as distasteful as you suppose she does."

With a shrug, Raven reached up and put his hands on Pamela's shoulders. She felt the weight of them, like clamps of steel.

"Why she's gone doesn't matter, does it? We must find her and make her feel truly welcome," Lucinda declared. "I'd no idea she so disliked being here among us."

"She didn't," Peter insisted.

"Aye, she did," his twin countered.

"God's tears, Raven!" Peter pushed himself away from his pillows, wincing at the pain the movement caused him.

Pamela longed to assist him and ease his discomfort. But the pressure of Raven's grip prevented her from doing more than inhaling a long, worried breath.

"You know Roxanne's not the sort to cower or hide any more than she's the sort who minces and swoons!" Peter continued, glaring hard at his brother. "You said something to her, didn't you? You blamed her for my fall, my injury. Didn't you?"

"I did not." His reply was calm and clipped, yet he dug his fingers deeper into Pamela's shoulders.

"I know you. I know you better than my own soul. Do not speak falsely to me, brother!"

"Ask her," Raven suggested casually, "when you see her. The wench must still be nearby. After all, she could not get herself out of the bailey without some assistance. And who, here, would assist her? Pamela?"

He spoke her name softly as he lowered his head, his lips brushing her ear. A tremor rippled through her limbs so that she was almost glad of Raven's firm hold. Else, Pamela thought, she might have crumpled.

"Nay." She whispered the word and shook her head, her eyes locked on Peter's. "I did not assist her in any way."

"There."

Raven seemed satisfied and about to press his advantage, except that Frederick suddenly appeared in the chamber doorway.

"Milords, miladies," the seneschal said a trifle breathlessly. "I thought you'd want the news as quickly as possible, so I came myself."

"What is it?" Lord Ian demanded.

"Lady Roxanne's stallion's gone from the stable."

Pamela squeezed her eyes closed lest she make some gesture or some sound that might lead Peter to suspect the truth.

"And the lady?" the earl pressed.

Opening her eyes again, she saw Frederick shake his head. "No sign," he said. "No one has seen her."

"Sweet Mother Mary, she *has* gone!" Lucinda gasped, bringing her fist to her mouth.

"We don't know that, sweetling."

"Of course we know it. If she were riding that huge beast of hers around the castle, I wager someone would have seen her!"

"What did the stable man say?" the earl demanded of Frederick.

"Nothing. He saw naught. Didn't even notice the animal was gone, he insists, until one of the pages took a look for himself and asked where the beast was."

"Find out which page. If I've a lad that bright, fostering at Fortengall, I want to know who he is." Ian paused but a moment before asking, "What of the guards in the tower?"

"Those on the day watch insist no lady left through the main gate. Mayhap she slipped out one of the smaller portals in either of the bailey walls."

"Not likely," Peter snapped. "Both are hidden to the naked eye, except when one knows where to look. Roxanne didn't. Even if she had found a door, she damnably well could not have ridden out of it on that giant steed of hers!"

"Frederick, get me the captain of the guard," the earl ordered tersely. "He'd best bring the night watch with him."

"Aye, milord."

"Lucinda," he continued, reaching out to his wife, "come. We must gather the stewards and speak with the bailiff. I don't know how many visitors we've had to the castle this day. But I suppose we should try and discover whether or not Lady Roxanne might have left with any of them."

Nodding, Lucinda turned to her invalid son. "Forgive me. This is all my doing. I should have spoken with the girl immediately after you were hurt, but I didn't know she was so distraught over the mishap. I confess, though, I didn't expect this behavior from a woman the likes of Lady Roxanne.''

With that last admission, the lady of Fortengall Castle followed her husband down to the gallery.

''Now you have Mother blaming herself,'' Peter growled.

''I have done naught!''

''They're gone now. Mother and Lord Ian. Speak freely, Raven. Confess what you did.'' Peter waited but one slim, impatient moment. ''Damn you! What did you say to Roxanne?''

''He—he did not say anything,'' Pamela blurted, wondering if she imagined it or if her betrothed had really loosened his hold on her.

''How do you know?''

She hadn't imagined it, for Raven's fingers clenched again, gripping more tightly.

''I . . . I told you I spoke with Roxy. Last night, before bed.''

''Aye?''

''What your brother said is true, milord. She was determined not to wed you.''

Peter's expression went suddenly slack. Pamela saw his pain and hated herself for causing it. Even worse was the accusation in his dark eyes. She felt sure he believed she'd betrayed him by keeping silent, by not telling him of Roxanne's determination to avoid the marriage.

Pamela grabbed her skirts in her fists again. She should tell him everything now, tell him how his own brother's threats forced Roxanne to flee for her life. Peter couldn't blame her or Roxy if he confirmed his suspicions about his twin. Once he understood how vile Raven's actions—

As she thought his name in her head, the man behind her released Pamela's right shoulder and began, surreptitiously, to stroke her back.

She could not tell all. Roxanne might have run even without provocation. She was renowned among her family for her impetuous behavior. Besides, her leaving Fortengall—and England—was destined to wreak all manner of havoc. The confusion had already begun, and Pamela could not add to it. Besides, Raven would be her husband soon. She could not earn his regard, let alone his affection, if she turned on him before their vows were even said. And Raven was Peter's twin. She refused to be the blade that severed the invisible ties binding them.

Pamela cleared her throat and let go of the fabric she'd been clutching in her fingers, unaware of how badly she'd wrinkled her bliaut. "Roxanne may have run off for no other reason except that she did not wish to be forced into marriage."

"There." Raven settled his hands possessively on Pamela's waist. "Even her cousin believes as I do, Peter."

Though his twin spoke to him, Peter did not look up at Raven's face. Instead his eyes remained thoughtfully fixed on Pamela's. "So she says."

"You mustn't take Roxy's actions to heart!" she pleaded, desperate to assuage his hurt. " 'Twas not marriage to you that upset her. 'Twas marriage to any English lord! She thinks of herself only as Cymry. She hated the thought of being removed to England, of being torn away forever from her beloved Marches.

"Once," Pamela rushed on, "I even offered her Angleford, knowing she would never get Bittenshire Keep as her own— not with nine elder sisters. I thought if my cousin wed a landless knight, he could rule as Lord of Angleford and she as its lady. I—I would wed a nobleman who already had lands of his own. That way, I thought, at least she'd be in the country she loves so well. And I—I do not care overmuch about where I live my life, so long as . . ."

"What?" Peter's eyes narrowed.

"As long as I have hearth and home and a man who loves me."

Peter settled more deeply into the cushion of pillows behind his head and crossed his arms over his chest. "I suppose someone explained to you that you could not give your dowerlands over to your cousin.''

Nodding, Pamela muttered softly, "Aye. My uncle, Lord Cedric. He said Angleford Keep and its demesne were mine until I wed, and then they would become my lord husband's unless the king himself decreed otherwise.''

"You love Roxanne well, Pamela. Are you sure you didn't aid in her escape?''

"Nay, Peter, nay! I tried to make her understand that all was for the best. But even if you don't know my cousin well, you must realize she's stubborn and willful.''

"Ha!'' Raven barked. "That's a kinder description of the Bittenshire maiden than I would ever make.''

"Brother, remove yourself from my presence,'' Peter ordered tersely. "I would like to be alone.''

"Very well.'' He pulled Pamela along, guiding her toward the door with one arm behind her waist.

Yet she resisted, twisting around to implore, "Forgive me, Peter. I should have warned you. I didn't mean to let Roxy distress you in any way.''

"Hush,'' Raven said gruffly, forcibly leading Pamela out of the room. "Distress is a minor price to pay. My brother already has a broken limb. God knows it could have been worse.''

If Peter heard his brother's hushed comment as the couple exited his chamber, he made no remark. But when Pamela and Raven were beyond his door, Raven halted and held her in place before him. "You did well, my lady.''

The compliment did not please her.

"Believe me, 'tis best this way,'' Raven continued. "My brother would have been as miserable tied in holy wedlock to that—that cousin of yours, as she'd have been if tied to him. You know it, Pamela.''

"You seem to know it. I leave it to you.''

"That's wise.''

"Milord!" A servant bounded up the stairs, halting on the landing. "Lord Ian wishes to see you immediately."

Raven nodded at Pamela. Obediently, she made to accompany him down the stairs.

"Excuse me, milady. Not you. The earl was quite specific, he was. 'Tis only Lord Raven he wishes to see."

Without further word, Raven left Pamela and followed the man down the stairs to the gallery.

She watched him go, unable to reconcile the man Raven seemed to be with the brother Peter had told her about all morning. That one was kind and faithful, strong and selfless. He even had a sense of humor. She hoped that Percival, the brother Peter had spoken of so affectionately, remained at the core of the knight now called Raven. Raven, who boldly threatened Roxanne's life and slyly manipulated her own.

She glanced at Peter's closed door. Pamela also harbored hopes for the man confined to that room. She knew Peter's anger was just, but her silence was honorable, too. It could not come between them! Because, if ever she had hoped for a brother, it was Peter of Stoneweather she'd been longing for.

CHAPTER 10

Raven turned in to one of the galley's rectangular rooms. As all of them did, this chamber had a large window overlooking the great hall, centered directly below. It did not bode well when he entered to discover the heavy draperies pulled closed, blocking the view. Obviously the earl and his own mother, who sat within, had closed the hangings to ensure their privacy.

Instead of suggesting Raven sit, Lord Ian rose from his stool and looked down at him. "Roxanne rode off before this morn's first light, Raven," he said. "At your order."

Raven glanced quickly at his mother, who remained seated, before meeting the earl's eye. "I ordered no such thing."

"You told my man to raise the gate and to forget he'd seen the maid leaving."

Grinding his teeth, Raven rued the watch guard's disloyalty. God's blood, the stable man had kept his word, but not the knight!

"Herbert's my man, Raven, not yours," Ian reminded him, as though he had read his stepson's thoughts. "He may have been willing to hold his tongue if no one asked him of the matter. But under no circumstances would he lie to me when questioned.''

"Why did you do it?" Lucinda demanded.

Raven glanced at her and then quickly away. The look of disappointment in her eyes made him feel like a guilty child.

"I didn't do it. She chose to leave because she's determined not to wed Peter."

"But you aided her!"

"Aye, Mother, I aided her!" Crossing his arms over his chest and widening his stance, at last he deigned to look defiantly at Lucinda. "I aided her to protect Peter!"

"Peter hardly needs protecting. Especially from a young damsel the likes of Lady Roxanne."

"No? Mother, how can you say that? The bitch was so desperate not to wed him, she pushed him off the wall!"

Lucinda gasped. "Oh, Raven. You *did* accuse her, just as your brother suspects you did!"

"I'd no need to accuse her. She's guilty as Eve in the Garden." Disgustedly, he turned away and kicked a stool.

"Sweet Mother Mary," she whispered. "Not only did you know Roxy had run off, you forced her to do it."

Raven neither turned around nor denied his mother's assumptions. It was as good as a confession.

"Why?" she asked softly.

"Because the fool thinks his brother's life is in danger," the earl answered. " 'Twas the wrong thing he did. But I suppose he can't be faulted, since his heart was in the right place."

"That's true." Raven turned to look at his stepfather. "I cannot be faulted because Peter's life is in danger."

"I never thought I'd say this of you, Raven," his mother put in as she rose to stand, "but you're a liar."

His jaw dropped.

"Redeem yourself," she admonished him. "Tell us why you really forced the lady to flee."

He clamped his mouth closed. The muscles in his jaw worked hard as his onyx eyes locked on Lucinda's emerald ones. "I am no liar, Mother. Roxanne of Bittenshire is a shrew. She has a sharp tongue, which she used to express her displeasures, her discomforts, and her generally disagreeable nature. She is forward and bold—Christ! She should have been born a man. You saw the way she rode that horse of hers—that stallion, that destrier, that manly mount! Give the haridelle a sword and shield, and she could ride boldly into battle.

"And yet," he continued, warming to the litany of Roxanne's faults, "she flaunts her femininity like a slatternly whore—baring her legs and spreading her thighs when she sits in the saddle. Even on the ground, she dresses to lure men's eyes—under tunics that reveal the swell of her bosom, her hair unbraided and unadorned. Sweet *Jesu*, Mother! Would you tie your beloved Peter to a slut the likes of that Welsh bitch? If he managed to escape death at her hands, 'twould be all the worse for him. Years, scores of years mayhap, living with that unseemly hag."

Finishing his tirade, Raven stood, glaring, with his hands on his hips. He expected some argument from his mother, but got none. Instead she said softly, "Go after her. You made her leave, you aided her departure. Now, you must retrieve the girl."

"I will not."

"You will." Lord Ian spoke in clipped, forceful syllables. "Despite that you're twins, you and Peter are individuals, Raven. Grown men wise enough to lead your own lives without interference from the other. Not only had you no right to push the lady from our midst, you risk dire consequences by disrupting King Henry's designs. He wishes you brothers to wed the Welsh cousins. Even God shan't be able to help you if you fail to do as Henry commands."

"I would defy the king, my lord, if it meant saving Peter's life."

"His life is not in danger," Lucinda insisted impatiently. "Even if first you thought it, you now must realize the error of your thinking. 'Twas a mishap, Peter's fall. But the bone has been set, and in time it will be whole again. 'Twas a mistake, your allowing Roxanne to run away. Now you must catch her and make things right."

Raven's eyelids drooped ominously as he looked at his mother. His breath came in snatches, his chest visibly expanding and deflating with every short inhalation. His hands at his sides clenched and unclenched. But in the end he did not argue. He might defy the king of England, but he would never, overtly, defy his mother.

"Very well. I shall try to find her. But I cannot promise I'll succeed."

"You'll succeed, Raven," Lord Ian said, more a pronouncement than reassurance. "I have every confidence you will."

With a formal nod to his parents, Raven quit the room. As soon as he had left, Lucinda sank down onto her stool.

"Don't fret, sweetling," her husband consoled her, placing a gentle hand on her shoulder. "Pride alone will ensure Raven finds Roxanne before further harm can be done.

"I am surprised," he went on, "by the muddle Henry has caused with his royal edict. You would think many noble marriages were not arranged, with the way Raven and Roxanne have been behaving. Thank God and Henry those two are not required to wed each other." He frowned at Lucinda. "Why do you suppose Raven dislikes the Bittenshire lady so?"

Slowly, she turned her head and raised her eyes to Ian's. "Is that what you think?"

Roxanne felt like the ancient Cymry heroines, Helie or Arianrod, even like the queen of Cymru who had lived during the English King Arthur's time. The queen who could change herself into other forms and thus deceive her enemies. Roxanne felt strong, invincible. Most of all, she felt free.

It had been like magic, her easy departure from Fortengall Castle. And so it continued to be, for the weather cleared, warmed, and held, making her travel easier.

Not that travel on horseback was ever difficult for Roxanne. She had spent as much time in the saddle as any baron's son, and she rode as well as most trained knights. Of course, she had never ridden wearing armor; her father would not allow it. But her stallion, Dafydd, was strong and loyal, and they rode together joyously, reveling in the brisk breeze that painted roses on her cheeks and in the scent of forest evergreens that brought their heady fragrance to her nose.

Roxanne did not worry about being followed. She knew Pamela would not alert the earl, his lady wife, or Peter. And once they discovered her gone, Raven, the arrogant, self-serving cockshead, would do all he could to delay their going after her. Surely she'd have the better part of two days' lead on any men they sent in search of her. And two days' lead was as good as having no one in pursuit at all. By the time they made Cymru and the mountains, she'd be invisible to them. Better, she'd be under Balin's protection.

Smoke snaked upward into the sky on the horizon. Roxanne knew a village lay ahead. She needed provisions. Fortunately, she had a purse of English coins King Henry had supplied her. From serfs, they'd buy her all she needed and more, allowing her to make little contact with the local gentry as she wended her way northwest to the border.

"Come on, then, Dafydd," she urged her steed, kicking him soundly in his flanks. "We've got days of traveling to get us home again, and I'm none too patient at the prospect."

With an answering nicker, the black horse jerked his large head, as though in agreement, and broke into a fast canter.

* * *

Raven's arse ached. He'd not have admitted it to a soul, but he hadn't been in a saddle this many hours since he'd been knighted by his foster father, Lord Harold of Becknock. Then, he and his brothers had gone off seeking support in their efforts to retake Eynsham Keep, their father's estate, which had been taken by force. He'd been much younger during those hard-riding years, with not even a score of natal days to recount. Now he was long past a score of years, and for many of them he had been a landed lord of leisure. He rode only for sport, or to hone his skills with lance and shield upon the practice field. Or he rode to Stoneham, the village of crofters that supported his demesne. Otherwise, he rode to visit friends and family, or to join Henry and Eleanor's royal court as it traveled about the country.

But Raven of Stonelee did not ride like a soldier anymore. And his two days of riding hard had blistered his buttocks to the point that he winced whenever he kicked his steed into a trot.

Curse the Bittenshire bitch! Why had she come into his life? Henry had not demanded that he wed her, yet they'd met, and the wench caused him untold misery. Really, he ruminated, he should presently have been courting the young lady from Angleford. Though marriage was being forced on him, he deemed Pamela quite suitable. She seemed loyal, obedient, and retiring, and though probably she would not be a good lover, he would never have to fret over her. Pamela would never dare contradict a demand and would always put his comfort over her own. Certainly, she would look the other way when he sought out the sort of females who *were* good lovers.

He, of course, would be an excellent husband to that Welsh damsel. He would not bother her in bed unless they needed to have another heir. He'd make no unreasonable demands. And as long as Stonelee Keep was clean, his table laden with tasty meals, and she neither whined nor nagged at him, he would treat her with respect.

Raven smiled, pleased with his good intentions. Then he frowned at his own discomfort, discomfort caused by Roxanne of Bittenshire. *Jesu,* but he'd like to wring that Welsh harpy's neck when he caught up with her! And he could, Raven realized as his lips curled in a grim smile. Later, he would explain that he'd found her body after she had obviously fallen from that great, devil beast of hers. Everyone knew a female couldn't handle a stallion of that size. 'Twould be easy enough to convince Peter she'd had a fatal mishap while riding alone.

"Nay, nay!" Raven ordered his destrier when Rolf decided to quicken his pace. There was no need to hurry. He had not left Fortengall 'til the morning after his mother and Lord Ian had demanded he do so. As he had no real desire to overtake the wench, he need not endure the agony of a lengthy sitting trot. His steed's even walk was as fast as he need travel. Give the girl plenty of time to cross into Wales and lose herself in the mountains. That way, Peter would be free of the bitch without Raven getting her blood on his hands.

CHAPTER 11

Well into his journey, Raven leaned against a tree trunk and rubbed his hand over his bushy beard. For the thousandth time since he'd first lain eyes on her, he cursed the Bittenshire bitch.

Reaching for a thick branch in the pile of kindling he had collected, he threw it onto his cook fire. It was hours into night; he was cold, and he was hungry. The cold he could chase away by building up the fire, but his hunger was not so easily abated. Already he'd eaten the rabbit he had managed to kill before darkness fell. But the thing had been more skin and bones than meat, and Raven's belly still rumbled.

It was the haridelle's fault not his, despite his having left the castle with only a bit of bread and cheese to sustain him. Raven's meager cache of food had not lasted one day's ride from Fortengall.

It had not been his intent, upon setting out, to ride all the way to Wales. He'd first considered visiting friends in comfort to pass some time before returning to his mother's home, claiming he had been unable to locate the accursed female. But subsequent thought turned him from that plan, knowing such a lie would catch up with him. So, he determined, resignedly, to overtake the wayward wench, assuming he would find her easily once he began tracking her in earnest.

But he had not. And only one monastery along the road had welcomed him with both a pallet and a meal. That forced Raven to sleep outdoors on hard ground, like some lowly foot soldier. Worse, he'd had to find his own food with neither arrows nor spear, because he'd neglected to take the like with him when he'd stormed angrily from Fortengall Castle. He had taken only what he thought he needed, if indeed he happened upon Roxanne—his sword, to cut off the shrew's head, deceptively comely face and all, and his dagger, to cut out her heart, if there was one to be found.

But neither blade proved satisfactory when hunting hare and squirrel. So Raven crafted a slingshot and made camp early while there remained enough light to hunt with the crude weapon. A few nights he had been lucky, if he counted this evening's meager fare.

Snorting in disgust, the knighted lord drew his mantle more closely about his shoulders, burrowing into its warmth as he stretched out on the softening ground, pillowing his head with his saddle. The dampness of the thawing earth seeped through his cloak, his gambeson, and even his chausses. *Jesu,* he thought sourly as he tried, in vain, to ignore the dank cold of his clothing. He hated the Welsh witch, with her blue-black tresses, her blue-violet eyes, her blue-veined, alabaster skin. Fortunately, contemplating her innumerable character flaws lulled Raven's mind into weary sleep.

Twigs snapping underfoot awakened him with a start. Instinctively, he was on his knees, ready to spring to his feet, his hand gripping the hilt of his sword. Blinking, he accustomed his eyes to the darkness and scanned the area surrounding the indistinct camp, looking for unnatural movement among the trees.

They sprang at him all at once, two afoot, one leaping down from above. The nearest man, lunging toward him, brandishing a sturdy log, swung his primitive club in an arc toward Raven's head. It grazed his brow, but Raven was too quick for it to do further damage. Rolling forward and away, he left the villain to lose his balance when he made contact with little else but air.

On his feet with sword unsheathed, something whizzed past his ear. Whirling around, Raven discovered he had just missed being plugged with an arrow. Outraged, he advanced on the shooter. But before he had gained more than a stride or two, a shout diverted his attention.

The last of the outlaws brandished an ancient sword. Ignoring the archer, Raven concentrated on the swordsman. They looked near the same age, but Raven suspected this one was more skilled at stealing eggs than he was at combat. Still, the man seemed strong and agile, and his rusty sword was as dangerous as any knight's.

They thrusted, they parried. Raven deflected an awkward blow, and the outlaw stumbled, going down on one knee. Yet, before Raven could press his advantage, the cur sprang up again, swinging wildly. Their deadly dance continued.

Broadswords being heavy, it was not long before both Raven and his foe were breathing hard. The erstwhile thief, however, panted heavily and sweated into his eyes. When he paused to use his sleeve to wipe the moisture from his brow, Raven leaped forward, cutting the man from left shoulder to right hip.

The wound was long but shallow, yet the outlaw's frayed tunic split wide and the skin beneath was striped red with oozing blood. He blinked at Raven in disbelief; then, dropping his battered sword, he sank to his knees.

The lord of Stonelee had little time to catch his breath. Another arrow sailed past, this time brushing his shoulder.

Silently thanking all the saints that this archer proved such a dismal shot, he whirled about to face the inept bowman. "You're a dead man!" he shouted, spying his ungainly foe fumbling for another arrow in his quiver. Giving him no time to free it, Raven sheathed his sword and stalked forward, balled his fingers into a fist, and slugged the outlaw in the jaw. The fellow went sprawling.

Straddling his hips, Raven peered down into the hapless villain's face. He was a boy, Raven saw, hardly old enough to take a knife to his whiskers. And he was clearly unconscious, his eyes closed, his breathing easy. With a snarl, Raven leaned over and grabbed the bow from the boy's limp hand.

"Aaaggghhh!"

Dropping the weapon, Raven expelled a noisy breath as a man's full weight fell upon his bent back. He managed to right himself, but still the miscreant clung to him, his feet hooked about Raven's thighs and his hands clasped beneath Raven's chin.

"Get . . . off!" Raven demanded, punctuating his order with a quick twist and an elbow jab to the fellow's ribs.

The man's feet dropped to the ground, but he tightened his grip around Raven's neck. Grunting, Raven bit his hand hard.

The flesh tasted like sweat, dirt, and grease; Raven grimaced and spat. But he'd at least freed himself of the clinging madman. And while the ruffian wailed and sucked his wounded hand, Raven picked up a stubby branch as thick around as his own wrist, and clubbed the man soundly on the side of the head.

He fell like a stone, as the others had, his eyes crossing before they fluttered closed.

Panting, Raven looked around at the sprawled bodies littering his campsite. Two were still in their own worlds, but the worst injured among them remained awake. To him, Raven spoke, promising, "I'll not kill you thieving bastards. Even you shan't die of your wound, if you clean it properly. But I vow, if you

e'er cross the path of Lord Raven of Stonelee again, my kindness will not be repeated!''

Stomping off toward the fire, Raven touched his fingers to
his temple. They came away smeared with blood.

"Curse you, Roxanne of Bittenshire," he muttered angrily
beneath his breath. Collecting his few belongings and the
archer's quiver and bow, he strode over to Rolf and swung his
saddle up onto the stallion's back. "Because of you, I've gone
hungry and sleepless, and now my head aches damnably." He
pulled the girth tight, nearly squeezing the air from the animal's
lungs. He wished he were strangling Roxanne. "I could have
been killed!" he complained indignantly, mumbling to himself
but seeing his quarry so clearly, it seemed as though she stood
beside his destrier. "Killed! Taken from this earth before my
time." He slipped the bridle onto the horse's head and pulled
himself into the saddle.

"There'll be no more tarrying, woman," he informed the
image still floating, conveniently, directly before his eyes.
"And when I catch up with you, methinks I'll do the world a
favor by taking you from it!"

Roxanne spied a village and debated. She still had a good
while of afternoon light left for traveling. She had no need to
stop so soon. Yet, having been on the road—when there was
a road—for several days, the supplies she'd obtained earlier
were almost depleted. And she was tired of sleeping wrapped
in her mantle like some wild Scot wrapped in his plaid. Even
she sometimes shivered, huddling near the small fires she made
to provide a little warmth and light as she stole some rest during
each day's darkness. Now, a pallet on a dirt floor in some
humble crofter's hut would seem a luxury.

Roxanne trotted her steed briskly down the main road and
halted in the middle of the small hamlet. Villagers swarmed
toward her like moths captivated by her light.

"There's naught to be looking at," she informed the curious crowd from her lofty perch on Dafydd's back. "I am Lady Roxanne, on my way to my father's keep, and I find myself in need of food and accommodations."

"I am called Elmo, m'lady," a middle-aged man introduced himself, doffing his cap. He spoke French as Roxanne had, but he spoke the nobles' language poorly. "Where is your escort?"

"Dead."

Elmo turned to the other villagers, prattling in Old Saxon, the tongue of English peasants. When they gasped and groaned in a combination of surprise and sympathy, Roxanne elaborated with a tale that came easily to mind.

"My brother and I were traveling the king's roads, minding our own business, when we encountered a stranger. A big man he was, even for a knight. Dark as the devil's own—black hair and beard, and eyes blacker than midnight.

"He frightened me," she continued when Elmo repeated her words in his crude tongue for the benefit of her audience. "And my dear brother did not like the looks of him, either. Yet, after exchanging a few words, we parted and went our own ways."

Roxanne found herself enjoying being the center of attention. Peasants with rapt faces hung on her every word, as Elmo translated them.

Warming to her story, she went on. "My brother hadn't noticed, but the black knight watched me with a lustful eye. Even after he'd disappeared from sight I shivered, remembering how he'd leered at me, as though I were naked."

When her narrative was interpreted, she watched the women shiver, clutching their shawls tighter over their bosoms, and the men frown angrily, as if their own wives and daughters had been accosted by this evil knight.

"Still, I believed we were safe, as the knight rode off in the opposite direction. But when my brother and I stopped for the night, he came out of the trees and attacked!"

This brought gasps of outrage from everyone in the crowd.

Roxanne refrained from smiling, and instead nodded her head vigorously, emphasizing the truth of the translator's words.

"Still on his mighty steed, he dispatched my brother with his bloody sword, sending my beloved—ah, Felix—home to God. Then he leaped from his saddle and—and—"

As Elmo conveyed her story in the Saxon tongue, Roxanne paused and sniffed, wiping her eyes with her tunic sleeve. She was surprised to find the fabric moistened. Then, realizing she had brought herself to tears, she covered her face with her hands lest the peasants see she giggled rather than wept.

They watched her shoulders shake. Finally Elmo ventured, "M'lady, you need tell us no more. We understand. But how—how'd you get yourself away from such a strong, wicked knight?"

Willing her expression serene, she raised her head.

"He's mighty and villainous, evil to the core. But he's stupid."

When mouths dropped open all around her, Roxanne knew the meaning of her speech had been conveyed accurately. In her heart, she smiled as Raven's image loomed before her. And it was Raven's image, not his twin's. She recognized the differences between them, even though few others would be able to.

"I tricked him. When he thought I was securely restrained so that he might . . . might . . . might have his way with me"—she paused for effect, inhaling a shuddering breath—"I hit him on the head with a rock as big as a mellon. Then I . . . I stole his horse and rode fast away."

For a moment, everyone standing in the rutted path studied Roxanne with silent fascination. Some peered at Dafydd, believing him to be a knight's destrier.

Then Elmo explained, "M'lady, our lord's manor is but a short distance to the west. He would supply you better food and greater warmth than any here could."

Roxanne had no desire to make the acquaintance of another

English noble. All she wanted was a pallet somewhat softer than the hard ground, and a hearty meal, no matter how humble.

"I'm tired, my good man," she informed him. "If only you knew what I'd been through, looking over my shoulder to see if that evil knight is in hot pursuit riding blindly through the forest and along unfamiliar roads. I fear I'll drop if I have to go another few paces. Please," she begged heart-wrenchingly, leaning down to give the peasant a closer look at her fluttering lashes. "Could you kind people allow me a floor to sleep upon and, mayhap, a crust of bread to nourish me?"

He assured her that he would, that the whole village would, even before he'd spoken to the others and gained their consent. Reaching up, he assisted Roxanne from her saddle as though he were a noble squire, not an elderly serf.

"This horse needs oats and water," she announced. "I'll pay anyone willing to supply the feed."

Before Elmo could translate her offer, a sturdy youth of perhaps ten and five years strode forward and reached for Dafydd's reins. "I'll tend him for you, m'lady."

She blinked at him in surprise, and he shrugged, explaining, "Elmo's not the only one familiar with the Norman tongue. Those of us who work at his lordship's manor must know and speak it."

"Oh." She pinched a penny from the purse at her waist and flipped it to him. When he caught the small coin, she promised, "There'll be another one for you if you brush him down now and saddle him by dawn on the morrow."

"Very good, m'lady." Tugging first on his forelock, he then tugged on Dafydd's reins, about to lead the horse away.

"Boy!"

"Aye?" He paused and turned to her.

"I need a bow and arrows. I'll pay for them with good coin." She watched his expression turn skeptical and added haughtily, "I can shoot an arrow as straight as any man."

"I've no doubt that's true, m'lady. But the people of Twittenham will protect you from the Black Knight, just as we would all our women.''

An impatient sigh escaped her lips in a hiss; Roxanne wished she could roll her eyes without insulting this chivalrous lad. No black knight, most especially Raven of Stonelee, would be pursuing her. She didn't need the villagers' protection. She only wanted the weapons to shoot game and feed herself. She'd no wish to be at the mercy of English peasants again, or worse, at the mercy of English noblemen.

''You're very kind,'' she said sweetly. ''But I must continue my journey, and I'll be riding alone when I do. I'd feel better if I had some means of protecting myself.''

''You're wise, my lady. I'll locate the best in the village and bring it to you.''

With that assurance, he took Dafydd off.

''If you'd like to stay with me and my wife,'' Elmo offered, ''we've a bit of extra room in our hut. All our children are gone, grown up or dead.''

''Thank you. You, too, are very kind.''

As the peasant led her to his home, Roxanne noticed the crowd had dispersed. Most of the male children and some of the girls followed the boy who'd taken Dafydd. Yet, many adults, the majority women, had gathered together in animated groups.

''What's happening?'' she asked Elmo.

He grinned, revealing broken and missing teeth. ''We're goin' to have a party,'' he confided in a jovial whisper, ''to celebrate your visit, m'lady. We're roastin' a pig and makin' some pudding. 'Twill be a long time before we eat this eve. But when we do, your belly'll be full, that I vow.''

Again, Roxanne sighed. Sometimes she wondered if she'd ever cross the border into Cymru. But then she resigned herself to the night's festivities and even enjoyed a slight anticipation. Although the company and comforts the villagers offered were humble, they were far more appealing than the prospect of huddling alone again under a tree, her belly rumbling and her body shivering.

"He's comin', Kip!" a young Twittenham resident announced, tugging on his elder brother's sleeve. The older boy was the youth who'd earned a couple of pennies tending to the gracious lady's horse.

"Who's coming?" he asked distractedly, tying together another sheaf of faggots for the family's fire.

"The Black Knight!"

"What!"

"It's true, Kip. At least three of us saw him ridin' out from the woods. He's just as the lady described him, big and dressed in black. An' he's got a wound on his head, from where she hit him with a rock!"

Kip dropped his bundle of branches and began running toward the town. As his brother kept pace beside him, he asked, "How long 'til he gets here, d' you think?"

"Not long. Kip, the lady left yesterday morn. Why are you lookin' so worried?"

The older lad slowed and stopped as they reached the first dwelling on the edge of the hamlet. "If he killed Lady Roxanne's brother, a knight like himself, and then tried to have his way with her, think what he might do to the people of Twittenham!"

The younger boy's eyes widened with understanding when Kip opened his mouth, shouting an alarm that brought people out of their cottages and off of their crofts.

"What is it?" Elmo demanded, being the first to reach the brothers standing in the road.

"Mick saw the Black Knight riding this way."

"God's blood, that means he'll be here soon." Elmo turned as the other villagers converged on him and the pair of boys. He explained what he knew and ordered curtly, "Women, into

your houses with your babes. Light no candles, douse your
fires, and secure your doors. Men, come with me. Quickly,
now. We've no time to dally.''

The village looked deserted. That was the first thing Raven
noted as he squinted in the half light of dusk at the crude
dwellings lining the bumpy, rutted road. He wondered if disease
had wiped out the population and, fearing such had happened
recently, reined Rolf in. He'd no desire to die of some plague
while in pursuit of Peter's worthless betrothed. But then, he'd
no intention of wasting still more time circumventing the village. The road, rough as it was, at least provided a direct course
to the River Wye and Wales, his destination.

Raven sniffed. He smelled no death, only the lingering scents
of wood smoke, grease, and pig shit. Cautiously, he spurred
his destrier into a canter and entered the town, riding fast.

He hit the ground hard. When the warhorse's forelegs buck-
led beneath him and he went down, Raven vaulted out of the
saddle, somersaulting into the air before making contact with
the earth.

Dazed, his neck and shoulders ripped with pain, Raven
gasped. Something had tripped Rolf, he realized that much.
Something worse than a bump or a hole in the road. But before
he could sit up and divine the obstacle that had felled his steed,
a hail of stones flew over his head.

''What, by God's bloody wounds—''

A barrage of pebbles and rocks, thrown by hand and shot
with slings, pelted Rolf's hindquarters. With a whinny and a
snort, the stallion bolted away at full gallop.

Disbelieving, Raven rolled over and leaned on his hands and
knees. Turning his head, he tried to see who would commit
such a crime. But before any one of the villains came into his
view, a cracking blow against his back sent him sprawling on

his belly in the dirt. Other blows, wielded with tree trunks, he was sure, rendered him unconscious.

Raven woke to daylight. Blinking blindly up at the cloudy, gray sky, he felt too confused at first to know why he hurt so badly. Then it came back to him, and he forced himself into an upright position despite his pain.

He sat in a field, short, brown grass pricking his palms when he braced himself with his hands. Looking around, Raven felt dismayed and relieved—dismayed because he'd no notion at all where he was, yet relieved because he saw Rolf standing nearby, nibbling the dry, stunted grass.

Whomever had attacked him had taken Raven some distance after rendering him unconscious. Probably, they'd lain him over Rolf's back to do it. So even if he knew the village where they had assaulted him, Raven realized he'd not easily find it again.

Nor would he try. Time was critical, and for all Raven knew, he might now be farther from the marches than he'd been yestereve. And surely the borderlands was the place where the one behind his assault had run for refuge.

Coming slowly to his feet, Raven searched his person. A few rents in his traveling tunic, but no fresh blood. His gold-handled dagger remained sheathed in his belt and his broadsword in its scabbard at his side. At least the madmen who'd assaulted him had not been reckless enough to steal his weapons and risk his righteous vengeance.

So he still had the means to cut off her head and cut out her heart. With a humorless smile, Raven imagined doing just that to the beautiful, malicious Roxanne.

CHAPTER 12

"I'll take that."

"What?" Bess frowned as she turned to Lady Pamela, who'd entered the hallway behind her.

"The trencher, the flagon, which you've brought up for Lord Peter. I'll take them."

"But, milady . . ."

Pamela did not wait for the servant to protest, nor did she bother to explain. Instead she grabbed the heavy tray and pushed past Bess into Peter's bedchamber. She didn't knock, but shouldered open the door, blowing inside like a gust of wind before kicking the door closed behind her.

She was nearly as startled by her actions as the bang of the door when it shut. Flustered, she stood where she was, her back to the timbered portal. When she finally settled her gaze on Peter, she found him smiling at her curiously.

"You're not Bess," he said.

"Certainly not."

"I expected her to bring me my meal."

"I . . . was on my way up the stairs. I relieved her of the duty."

"Why?"

Why, indeed? With quiet efficiency, Pamela came forward and set the tray on Peter's lap. She did not know why she'd done what she had. She did know she didn't like Bess. She suspected that if the servant could be so free with Raven, she was probably equally as free with Raven's twin. As Roxanne was nowhere about to protect her betrothed from that loose-moraled maid, Pamela felt obliged to protect Peter on her cousin's behalf.

"No particular reason," Pamela finally answered. "Would you like me to take your food back downstairs and send Bess up with it again?"

"Nay." Peter chuckled and shook his head. "But I wish you'd listen to what my family keeps telling you, Pamela. You're not a servant here at Fortengall."

"Yes, but I like to keep busy. Your mother seems to think needlework is the most strenuous activity I, as her guest, am allowed. When my mother lived, there was always much to do at Angleford. I miss those days, she and I together."

"I'm sure you do." Peter's gaze was somber. "I know it's not much of a challenge, but you could help feed me my supper."

Pamela took her knife from her girdle and began trimming a candlewick on the table beside his bed. "I wish that *you* would listen to what *I* keep saying: you don't need me to feed you."

"You're right." He leaned forward, craning his neck around the hangings clustered at the head of the bed, in order to better see the damsel. "But I so enjoy it when you do!"

Sheathing her dainty knife, Pamela turned to him, hands on her hips. "Have you always been such a lazy lout, or is this new to you?"

"Lazy!" Peter feigned outrage at her remark. "Remember you're speaking to the lord of Stoneweather!"

"Och!" She waved her hand in the air. "I think I'm speaking to young *Mon Petit*," she countered, "as your mother, Lady Lucinda, might say."

"You're cruel." With a sigh and a pained expression, Peter collapsed against the pillows behind his back. "Poor Raven hasn't a clue what a hard-hearted wench you are."

"My heart is not hard," Pamela countered, pretending to be affronted by his lament. "And I'll feed you like you're still a babe, if that's a comfort to you."

"It is." He flashed Pamela a grin as she perched beside him on the mattress and raised a spoon to his lips. "Besides," he continued around a mouthful of stew, "to be truthful, I have had a headache for days, and this morn I awoke sore all over. I still feel battered and bruised."

She dropped the spoon back into the bowl, spattering gravy on the tray, all humor gone from her expression. "You don't feel warm," she announced, frowning pensively as she placed her hand lightly on Peter's brow. "Is there anything else amiss? Problems with your stomach, your bowels . . . ?"

"God's teeth! What a thing to ask me!" he complained. "Never, in all my years, has a maiden asked me about my bowels!"

Briefly, Pamela felt contrite. It had been an intimate query, after all. Yet, Peter would soon be her brother-by-marriage, and already she counted him as her friend. Moreover, he was disabled, an invalid who could easily succumb to all manner of contagion while his broken bones knitted.

"We are not at a party, my lord, nor a picnic, nor a feast," she pointed out as she slipped off the bed. "You've been seriously injured, and I'm helping to care for you. If there's anything wrong with you other than your broken limb, may-hap—"

Peter's arm snaked out, brushing the tied-back bed hangings

like an asp darting out of the grass. Grabbing her wrist and holding Pamela imprisoned, he ordered sternly, ''No. You are not going to tell my mother. She hovers over me enough as it is. Good God, you'd think I was one of her younger twin sons, not her eldest! Besides, there's naught wrong with me, except for this damnable leg. The other, well, I probably slept rather stiffly last night. After all, I can hardly turn or stretch with my leg as it is.''

''You're sure?''

''Quite.''

With a nod, Pamela sat again. But she did not pick up the spoon. Peter grabbed it, dug into the bowl of broth, venison, and vegetables, and wolfed down the food, proving himself hardy. ''What did you do with yourself today?'' he inquired.

''Lady Lucinda and I discussed the wedding plans. She made a list of all yours and Lord Raven's friends and neighbors, as well as those nobles Lord Ian must invite out of courtesy.''

''What of your friends and Roxanne's? What of your kin?''

''My only family is Roxanne's, and though there's enough of them when you add up the husbands and children, I doubt any can reach Fortengall Castle in time for the ceremony. Mayhap we'll have some sort of feast when I return with Raven to Angleford.''

''Mayhap some of Roxanne's sisters will accompany her back to Fortengall.''

Pamela blinked at Peter. ''Do you think she'll make it all the way home to Bittenshire before Raven catches up with her?''

''They've been gone quite a few days already, Pamela.'' He shrugged. ''And your cousin had a solid lead on my brother. I'd not be surprised if she arrives home before Raven overtakes her.''

''And then he'll have to convince her to return.'' She lowered her lashes, looking down at her hands.

"Do you think that will prove so difficult?"

"Nay! Not because of you," Pamela hastened to assure him. "If she balks at returning to England, 'twill only be because of how well she loves Wales."

Peter took a gulp from his tankard and set it aside. "How well does she love it?"

"Too well," Pamela admitted, watching him intently, concerned her honesty might upset him. " 'Tis as though she is part of the land, the craggy mountains, the valleys of heather. She was beside herself when Henry's knights arrived at Bittenshire with the royal missive, informing us we were to come to him in London. We knew what it meant: English husbands. And to Roxy, that was unthinkable."

Peter remained quiet.

"She'll reconcile herself, Peter, I know she will," Pamela continued quickly. "Once she takes the time to know you, she'll be happy. Surely, she'll come to love you, and it shan't matter that you'll live together here in England. Besides, you will take her back to Wales for long visits, won't you?"

He nodded, his eyes searching Pamela's face. "You don't feel as your cousin does. Why not?"

Shrugging her shoulders, she glanced away. "Roxy loves the land. I love"—Pamela turned quickly back to him—"people."

"Good fortune for Raven."

"Why? With me, he gets a piece of Wales he doesn't want."

"As you feel certain Roxanne shall come to care for me, I believe Raven will, in time, be glad to rule as Marcher Lord of Angleford."

"Do you think so?"

He smiled and nodded encouragingly. "I know so. And I know my twin better than you know your cousin."

Their eyes held a long moment; then, as one, their gazes drifted to the tray on Peter's thighs. A big, fat tart remained untouched upon it.

"Would you like to share?" Peter asked.

"I shouldn't. I haven't supped yet, and I wouldn't want to spoil the meal I'm sure your mother's having kept warm for me."

"Is there some law, by Church or country, forbidding us to begin a meal with sweets?"

"Nay, I think not."

"Then, share it with me."

"But it's yours."

"Now it's yours as well."

Peter picked up the pastry, lathered with clotted cream, and stuffed it into Pamela's mouth. Unable to do less, she bit off half of it, getting cream on her nose and juice on her chin.

"You may feed me like a babe, but you eat like one!" he laughed, taking a modest bite from the remainder of the tart.

"Oh? Is that so, milord?" Pamela grabbed the last bit of tart from his hand and smashed it against his lips.

Peter hadn't had time to open his mouth as the pastry catapulted toward it. Blackberries, cream, and crust clung to his cheeks and dribbled into his beard.

"You wench!" he roared, laughing more heartily as he reached over Pamela and grabbed a damp rag from the washbowl on his bedside table. When he'd dragged it over his face, removing the debris from her assault, he pitched it back into the basin.

"That's not very chivalrous," she complained with counterfeit indignation.

"Because you've a spot of cream on your nose, I should have given you the rag?" He removed the dab of white froth with the tip of his finger and stuck it in his mouth, licking it clean. "I think not. The only thing you're going to get is this!"

With one hand, Peter set aside his tray on the far edge of his bed. With the other, he grabbed Pamela's waist and hauled her onto his lap. There he held her, tickling her ribs while she thrashed, giggled, and begged for mercy.

"You wretch!" she shrieked, laughing helplessly. "Unhand me! I might cause your leg further injury!"

"It's already broken; what worse could you do? Nay, I'm not releasing you 'til I've determined you've had enough," Peter declared, continuing to tickle her sides until she kicked convulsively.

It was then that Pamela's tunic skirts slithered high on her legs, revealing naked limbs from thigh to shoe. Along the inside of her calf ran an ugly scratch from ankle to knee.

"God's wounds, what happened to you?" Peter demanded, ceasing immediately his playful torture.

" 'Twas nothing." Modestly, Pamela tugged her skirts down, though she remained seated in his lap. "I was outdoors with your brothers. The young ones, that is. We were playing a game. They hid from me, the Wicked Witch of Woolsey Woods, and I cackled and hunted them down. I—I don't recall, but somehow I got myself caught in a patch of brambles. I scratched myself on a thorn trying to get free."

"Did you have Mother look at it?"

"Don't be silly. It's naught but a scratch."

"Did you tend it yourself?"

"Nay!" Pamela shook her head impatiently. "I told you, it's nothing."

"That's not always true," Peter argued. "It depends on the sort of brier you tangled with. Some are poisonous."

"Do you think I'm going to die from this paltry wound?"

"Nay, I do not, because I'm going to look at it again to make certain there's no putrafaction."

"Putrafaction! I cannot believe what I'm hearing!" Her shock no longer feigned, Pamela tried to scramble away.

But Peter clamped his arms tighter about her waist. "If you can speak to me of bowels, Little Lady Pamela, I can speak to you of putrafaction. Now, be still. I want a better look."

Mortified, Pamela did as he bid her, enduring the indignity of him raising her skirts and exposing her naked calf. Embarrassed, she closed her eyes tightly. At least, she consoled herself caustically, Peter's examination would be as brief as her short limb!

"There's nothing unusual about the cut, is there?" she demanded through clenched teeth. She could feel Peter's fingers skimming the inside of her calf just beneath the scratch, and she felt a queer tingle in her belly. "I know it's red, but it only happened a few short hours ago," she prattled, wishing he'd be done with his scrutiny, wondering why she continued to endure it.

"Peter. Pamela. What are you two about?"

Opening her eyes at the sound of that censuring female voice, Pamela saw Lady Lucinda standing in the doorway.

"Nothing." In a flurry of skirts and limbs, she scrambled off Peter's lap and the bed, finding the floor with her feet. When she stood, her tunics tumbled back into place.

"Nothing?" Lucinda's eyes left her and fixed on Peter.

"Pamela had a tussle with a thorn today, Mother, and the thorn won. She insisted the injury was slight, but I insisted on examining it to make certain that was so."

"Is it?"

"Aye. Already it's scabbing and beginning to heal."

"I told you," Pamela muttered, giving Peter a sidelong glance.

"That's good." Lucinda stepped farther into the room. "I came up because you never joined us for the evening meal, Pamela."

"I'm sorry. When I brought Lord Peter his tray—"

"I thought I had servants to do that."

"You do!" Mortified, Pamela skirted the lady and backed up to the door. "I happened into Bess on the stairs and offered to carry it up, since I was already on my way—"

"I see." Lucinda turned, examining the table at Peter's bedside. "What's this?"

Both he and Pamela glanced at the rag his mother had plucked from the washbowl. It was smeared with berries and cream.

"I had a mishap while eating my tart," he explained.

"Oh?"

"We behaved childishly," Pamela admitted, her face flushing warmly. "I meant only to keep Peter—Lord Peter— company. But as you're here now, milady, I'll go to my chamber."

"Don't you want your supper? Cook has a trencher for you. All you need do is ask one of the servants, and she'll bring you your meal in the hall."

"Nay." Stepping back through the doorway, Pamela shook her head. "I'm not hungry. I think—I think I'll go straight to bed. I am tired."

"I see. Well, sleep easy, Pamela, 'til the morn."

"I shall, milady. Good evening." She nodded her head respectfully toward Lucinda and cast a quick glance at Peter. "My lord." With that, she scurried from the room and down the steps, her face flaming with embarrassment and her heart hammering with relief.

"Lady Pamela's been spending a great deal of time with you, hasn't she, Peter?" Lucinda asked her son when they were alone.

"Roxanne asked her to tend me in her stead. She's only doing as her cousin, my betrothed, wishes her to."

"I doubt very much that Roxanne asked Pamela to sit on your lap while you fondled her leg."

"Mother!" He eyed her sternly. "I know it may have appeared that we were engaged in some sort of bawdiness. But she did scratch herself badly, and I did demand to see it for her sake! After all, she's been helping you nurse me since my fall. It seemed only reasonable that I take an interest in her injury."

"Yes, dearling."

"Mother!" he said again, impatiently. " 'Tis bad enough

you treat me like a child because I'm bed-bound with this broken leg. Don't treat me like some wayward youngster whose bad behavior has earned him a possible thrashing!''

"I'm not, Peter. I've only been agreeing with you."

Their gazes met and held before Lucinda finally looked away. Rounding Peter's bed, she retrieved his meal tray. "Would you like another tart?" she asked as she headed to the door.

Peter merely grumbled in reply, and Lucinda closed the chamber door behind her. Instead of taking the tray to the scullery or calling for a servant to take it from her, she hesitated on the landing.

Pamela of Angleford was an innocent, if ever a maid could be. That much Lucinda knew of the girl, having spent so much of the past sennight in her company. And her son, Peter, didn't lie. But that did not mean more trouble wasn't brewing.

"Sweet Holy Mother of *Jesu*," she muttered. What had Henry done, deciding Raven should wed Pamela and Peter, Roxanne? Everything had gone upside down since Lucien arrived with the news and the ladies. Peter was injured and lying abed; Roxanne rode recklessly toward Wales; Pamela, left alone by Raven, spent too many hours in Peter's company; and Raven! Lucinda threw back her head and shook it wearily as she gazed above. Raven was feeling so much, all of it painful to him.

With a sigh, Lucinda lowered her head and turned, beginning her slow descent down the stairs. There was nothing she could do but keep her misgivings to herself. In the end, life would run its course as it was destined to.

"Lucinda." The earl, standing with his seneschal in the great hall, spied her from the corner of his eye as she approached. Turning to her, he asked, "Did you find Pamela?"

"I did. She was . . . entertaining Peter."

" 'Tis good they get along so well, considering their intended spouses have left them as they have. If the young lady gets on so easily with Peter, surely she and Raven will be compatible, too. Don't you agree, sweetling?''

"Oh, aye." She nodded, sharing a sidelong glance with her old friend, Frederick. "Because, of course, as twins, Peter and Raven are so very much alike."

CHAPTER 13

Raven stood in Bittenshire's great hall. He had traveled hard to make up for lost time, and journeying into Wales was hard in any case. Despite the pleasing valleys and the lowlands that bracketed the rivers, most of this country was mountainous. Still on the cusp between winter and spring, the landscape was as dreary as the footing was precarious. Rolf, Raven's destrier, struggled along the narrow, rocky trails that were not suitable to his wide, long-legged gait. He managed to get his rider where they were headed only out of sheer stubbornness and the noble dedication that had been bred into him.

Following the River Wye to Offa's Dyke, which he crossed before heading into the Cambrian Mountains, Raven became lost more times than he'd ever dare admit. The natives he encountered all spoke some vile tongue that was as unintelligible as a newborn's babbling. None of them even understood French. That much Raven had determined whenever he repeated his request for directions in a slow, booming voice, as though Wales' population was, to a one, both dimwitted and deaf.

Obtaining no useful response, he'd had to rely on his internal sense of reckoning, which required the sun to mark his course, north by northwest.

That had been nearly impossible. This wild land, it seemed, rarely saw sunlight. What it saw were pewter skies and rain, from mist to drizzle to blinding, stinging downpours. Depending on the sun or the stars to determine one's way was nearly futile. Thank *Jesu*, the young lord thought, for his own keen instincts.

He would also thank the lord and lady of this keep, if ever they returned to greet him, for relieving him of the smell of damp wool that had engulfed him since the day he'd crossed the border into Wales. Arriving during a pounding rain when neither the earl nor his wife was available, the stronghold's chief steward had seen Raven provided with a hot bath, a hearty meal, and a comfortable bed. Availing himself of all three, he now felt much more his usual self. Waiting to meet Roxanne's sister and the lady's husband tried his patience. After thanking them for their hospitality, he would demand to know where they had put the wench, so that he could drag her out and skin her alive.

"Lord Raven?"

A large, fair-haired man approached. "Lord Thomas?"

"Aye." He smiled. "Earl of Bittenshire, I am, thanks to my wife and King Henry." Thomas gestured to a stool near the hearth fire. "And you are the man Henry's decided should wed Roxanne."

"Ah—" Raven was about to correct the earl's mistaken assumption when a female voice called out a greeting. Having lowered himself nearly onto the stool, he quickly reversed his descent and stood to meet the lady approaching from the hall's entrance. Thomas of Bittenshire jumped up as well.

"Aggie. Please meet Roxy's betrothed."

"My lord." She extended her hand. "My name is Agatha, but do call me Aggie. Everyone does."

Raven brushed her knuckles with a polite kiss as she glanced around and inquired, "Where is my sister?"

"Isn't she here?" he demanded.

"Roxy at Bittenshire? Nay, of course not." Aggie glanced at her husband and back again to Raven. "Isn't she with you?"

Raven knew not what to make of this unexpected news. He'd presumed Roxanne had returned home to this keep. Where else would she go?

Impatiently, he gestured to the stools clustered before the fire. "Please. Let us sit so that I may explain. The story's a bit complicated."

The lady settled herself beside her husband, and Raven sat, too. "I am Raven, Lord of Stonelee. King Henry's commanded me to wed your cousin, Pamela. 'Tis my brother, Peter of Stoneweather, who is supposed to wed Roxanne."

"Why are you here?" the lady inquired.

He answered with another question. "Have you heard nothing from Henry or Roxanne?"

"We did receive a message from the king," Thomas explained, "informing us he'd decided on suitable husbands for the maids."

"But though he included your names, 'twas unclear just whom my sister and cousin were to marry," Aggie put in. "Nor did His Majesty say when the nuptials are to take place."

Raven exhaled loudly through his teeth. "It was left to us, the when and where of our marriages," he informed the pair. "After Roxanne and Pamela arrived in England, we gathered together at my stepfather's keep, Fortengall Castle. My mother has been quite helpful in planning the ceremony, after which Pamela and I intend to ride to Angleford. I expect it shall take me a little while to see that it runs efficiently even while we're not in residence."

"You don't sound as though you intend to settle there," Thomas observed.

"I have other lands in England," Raven reminded the earl

bruskly. Hunkering forward, resting his arms on his knees, he asked again, "You're certain you've had no word from Roxanne?"

The earl and his wife shook their heads. "Why did you think we would?" Aggie asked.

"Because she's here. In Wales."

Aggie's eyes went round; her mouth dropped open. "Nay! Why would Roxy be in Wales when you—that is, your brother—"

"Peter had . . . an accident. He broke his leg and is confined to bed until it mends. I'm sorry to say," he informed them grimly, "your sister took his confinement as an opportunity to return to her homeland."

"She wouldn't!" Lady Agatha gasped.

"She would," Lord Thomas countered, turning to his wife. "That wench is too headstrong—"

"Is there something wrong with your brother?" she interrupted, ignoring him as she addressed Raven. "Some . . . disfigurement?"

"Nay! Not unless his recent injury leaves him with a limp. Otherwise, he looks exactly as I do. We're twins."

Aggie closed her mouth and peered at her hands, which she had folded in her lap.

"It's Balin," Thomas declared.

"What?" Raven asked.

"Balin of Penllyn," he elaborated. "Roxanne fancies herself in love with him."

Raven tensed. Had he been a jilted bridegroom, he could have felt no more insulted.

"Who is Balin? Where is Penllyn?"

"Balin is a cousin of ours, son of our mothers' brother," Aggie explained. "Penllyn is an ancient principality that none of the Marcher Lords has ever conquered. In truth, none has made an attempt in the past thirty years, not since my mother, Rhiannon, married Cedric, and her sister, Ceridwen, married

Arthur of Angleford. They hailed from Penllyn, and they were princesses. When they wed Marcher Lords, all the English earls ruling the borderlands left Penllyn undisturbed. We live side by side as friendly neighbors.''

"Balin is now Prince of Penllyn," Raven surmised. When Aggie nodded, confirming his deduction, he inquired, "Is the principality nearby?"

" 'Tis not too distant. Bittenshire borders Angleford, and Angleford borders Penllyn. I'll lead you there on the morrow," Thomas offered.

"No." Raven's tone was sharp. He had found his way to Bittenshire; he could find his way to Penllyn. Besides, he did not want any witnesses when he finally got his hands on that treacherous shrew. 'Twas one thing, he thought murderously, for her to run in fear of him back to the bosom of her family. 'Twas another altogether for her to run to the arms of a Welsh prince!

"No?" The earl cocked one golden eyebrow curiously.

"No. She's a proud woman, Roxanne is. She will be humiliated when I catch up with her and take her back to Fortengall to wed Peter. I think it wise that we keep her humiliation as private as possible, else she'll have naught to lose and may run away again. 'Tis best if she doesn't realize her family knows of her foolhardy actions and the price she pays for them.''

Lady Agatha's dark eyes sought Raven's. "You know my sister very well, don't you, milord?"

Too well, he thought. Yet, he only shrugged.

"We all know her well," Thomas barked, rising from his stool, "with the exception of our king, who should know her better! *Jesu,* but I fear he's made an unsound decision, forcing her to wed and live in England. Aggie, you know how she feels about Wales. And as she has no hope of having Bittenshire as her own, you'd think Henry would have been clever enough to wed her to a son of a Marcher Earl.''

Sighing, the fair-haired lord shook his head. "As you no

doubt suspect, Lord Raven, Roxy is spoiled, wild, and totally impossible. She wishes to stay in Wales, thus she'll do all in her power to remain. She'll defy King Henry no matter the problems she causes for others, and she shan't show any remorse.

"I've often thought that by the time she came into this world, my wife's parents were both too tired of childrearing to pay her any heed. They let her have her way, and she ran about the countryside like some orphaned waif. Never given a sense of duty, she now dares to shame us by running away from the man the king himself chose to be her husband. And Henry! *Jesu,* what must he think?"

Thomas settled his questioning gaze on Raven, who explained, "Henry doesn't know. When we discovered her missing, and Pamela suggested she had run off rather than wed an Englishman, I came after her in Peter's stead. His injury prevented him from coming himself, or, of course, he would have."

"Of course."

"But I'll get her back, I vow, and none shall be the wiser."

"That's kind of you, Lord Raven," Thomas said, thanking him. "What of Pamela?"

"Pamela is perfect," Aggie assured her husband before Raven could reply. "She has a keen mind, is soft-spoken and agreeable. Certainly she is any nobleman's ideal lady wife. Isn't that so?"

Raven nodded, a bland expression on his face disguising his surprise at Lady Agatha's sharp tone. And then he realized the great hall was filling up with people as servants began readying it for the evening meal.

"Lord Raven," Thomas said, "two of Aggie's sisters are visiting here, along with their husbands and children. Though you shall be wedding Pamela, not Roxanne, we are kin to both damsels. Allow me, please, to introduce you."

Thomas headed off across the room, determined to gather

his in-laws together. Meanwhile, Lady Agatha rose from her stool.

"Roxanne is not spoiled," she confided to Raven in a low voice. "Far from it. My youngest sister was, in truth, neglected. Not purposefully, of course, but simply because she was born last among many. Until Pamela came to live at Bittenshire Keep, Roxy was oft left to her own devices. She used her freedom to run about the countryside forging friendships among the villagers and hill people. They, you see, made time for her when her own kin did not. If Roxanne has become willful and independent, milord, 'tis because she's always felt it necessary to depend upon herself. Yet her mettle will make her a strong, loyal helpmate to the man she marries."

"You should convey this to my brother, once he weds her."

"Nay." Aggie's dark eyes held Raven's. She did not even blink. "Lord Peter will learn about her in time. But you need to know Roxy now."

"Why?"

"You are here, he is not. You will track her 'til you find her. When you do, Lord Raven . . ."

"Aye?"

Aggie shrugged and finally glanced away. "What you see may displease you."

Raven twitched. Everything about the wench had displeased him so far. "What do you suppose I shall see?"

"A woman who attempted to make her own choices." The lady, a fairer, plumper version of Roxanne, looked Raven directly in the eye again. "She hasn't yet learned that women rarely have that privilege. So I beg you, milord, not to judge her harshly. Be patient. Tolerant. And don't betray her to your brother."

She is the one who has betrayed my brother, he fumed. But he held his tongue.

Then Thomas was striding toward them, two lords and two ladies accompanying him. Raven recognized the women as

Roxanne's sisters, for they all shared a certain look, though none was nearly as comely as the youngest of their clan. No woman, he found himself thinking before he blotted the notion from his mind, could ever be as beautiful as the violet-eyed Roxanne.

Roxanne sat on her stallion, looking up at Bittenshire Keep. Her heart felt huge within the confines of her ribs, swelled up with sorrow and longing. How she wished she could break the cover of trees, which hid her from the sentries' view. How she wished she could ride up to the walls, announce herself, and see the bridge lowered over the moat as the portcullis was raised for her to enter. How she wished she could run into Aggie's arms, welcomed both by her sister and Thomas.

But such wishes could not be made real. Roxanne knew she should not even be so near to home, for at any time a band of English knights, in Stoneweather's or Fortengall's employ, might appear. If they spied her, their mission would be easy enough—half a dozen burly, armed soldiers could quickly overpower her and forcibly return her to Peter. Worse, to Raven who, never far from his twin, would never be far from her, either. Close enough to make his move and dispatch her to eternity.

A shiver ran up Roxanne's spine. Until that moment, she had not really feared Raven of Stonelee. It had been an act, a role she had played because it suited her. His threats had been the perfect explanation to offer Pamela for her furtive departure from Fortengall. Now, though, she felt uneasy as she recalled Raven's dire warnings. They had been real, not pretense.

It was almost dark; torches burned within Bittenshire's bailey, and dim patches of yellow light flickered weakly through the narrow arrow slits of the sturdy keep. Cautiously, Roxanne glanced over her shoulder, imagining that several mounted knights led by Lord Raven of Stonelee had materialized behind her.

But she was alone. Aloud, she said, "If I need protecting, Balin shall provide it for me."

Gently kicking Dafydd, she urged him to turn. Roxanne had another full day's ride before reaching Penllyn, but she would seek shelter tonight from Hywella, her dear friend. Some thought the old woman a witch because she lived alone in a secluded bough hut far from villages and her countrymen in the hills. But Roxanne knew the truth. Hywella had lost her husband and all her children to one cause or another, and now she shunned company, preferring a solitary life. Yet, she would welcome Roxanne because she always did. And tonight Roxanne needed someone who would smile at the sight of her.

CHAPTER 14

Roxanne walked back to the hut Hywella called home. She had gone out upon waking to relieve herself and now she strolled leisurely, relishing the sights and smells of Cymru.

Hugging her friend's shawl about her shoulders to ward off the damp chill the departing night had left behind, Roxanne heard a bird chirp its morning call. Glancing up, she noted not only the small, drab wren, but that the branch on which it sat appeared weighted with bright green balls. The leaves were budding, she realized; springtime was coming to Cymru.

It gladdened Roxanne's heart to be here to see it. She thought every season had its merits, but spring and summer in Cymru were the better of the four. A little quiver brought gooseflesh to her arms as she realized how close she had come to missing it—not only springtime in her homeland, but her homeland itself. She could not bear to be exiled from this place. She loved every clod of dirt in this country, every mountain, valley, and fen. She was certain she would shrivel up and die, were she denied the majestic view of the mountains that appeared from a distance verdant green, lush purple, and at their peaks, cool blue. As well she would expire if she never saw a valley blooming pink and blue with heather.

"Back, are you?" Hywella observed when Roxanne approached.

"Aye." She smiled, glad to hear the language spoken that was music to her ears, glad to be able to speak it again herself.

"Porridge is hot. Best fill your belly, girl, if you're going to be riding all day." The wrinkled old woman, with her plait of silver-streaked black hair, nodded toward the iron pot hanging over a cook fire just outside her crude abode. She reached over with a hand speckled brown with age and handed Roxanne a bowl.

Roxanne filled it and another, and brought them inside the hut so that they both could eat. While they sat on their rough stools, their backs bowed as they spooned up their breakfast from the bowls balanced between their knees, Hywella said, "He's looking for you."

"Who is?" Roxanne demanded tightly. One of Lord Ian's knights? One of the English king's?

"The man you're to wed. He's looking for you. I saw it in a dream."

She sighed, relieved. Hywella had seen no one with her rheumy eyes. She remained safe, far ahead of any English knights sent after her. But why had Hywella made such a remark? Eerie pronouncements were the reason so many believed her old friend a witch. Yet, Roxanne had always believed the woman only said such things to unsettle those who came to see her, for Hywella desired no company and wished to frighten them off. The warnings and predictions she peddled were pure fantasy.

Why, then, did Hywella speak such foolishness now? She had voiced her pleasure when Roxanne arrived yesterday, and as she would be leaving soon, she had not overstayed her welcome.

"Why do you say this to me?" she asked.

Hywella shrugged. "Because it's true. I dreamt it."

Roxanne let her spoon slide down into the thick, congealing mess in her bowl. She met the woman's milky gaze and felt the porridge she'd already consumed settling into a hard ball at the bottom of her belly. "Who? Who is looking for me?"

"I told you, Roxy. The man you're bound to marry."

Dread, a sudden cold, damp gust, made her shiver. The pleasure and contentment Roxanne had been enjoying in Cymru was supplanted by the foreboding chill. "Peter of Stoneweather?"

"Nay. I think not. No such name came to me." Hywella shook her head.

"Of course," Roxanne agreed. Whether or not the old woman had truly dreamed of someone looking for her, it couldn't have been Lord Peter who Hywella saw in her sleep. He lay abed at Fortengall Castle, his mangled leg held together with splints and bandages. "It could only be—!"

Hywella's unruly black eyebrows arched when Roxanne exclaimed. But the girl bit her tongue.

"I needn't tell you his name," she said a moment later as a rush of pleasant anticipation made Roxanne smile. The emotion was so strong, it sucked under the wave of trepidation she'd felt earlier. Teasingly, she added, "You saw his face while you dreamed. He's young and strong, virile and handsome, is he not?"

Hywella nodded seriously.

"I'd best hurry to him then, if he looks for me. I have no wish to disappoint him."

Roxanne stood, setting her bowl of cold porridge aside. The old woman also rose, clutching the younger woman's arm with her bony fingers.

"Be cautious, Roxy," she warned. "It is not what you think. He does not know you're to be his wife."

"I'm aware he doesn't know. Not yet." Roxanne beamed

happily. "But when he learns the way is clear for us to wed, he'll be as delighted as I am!"

It took her only a few moments to saddle Dafydd, say her farewells, and head out, up into the mountains. Mayhap, Roxanne mused as she rode away from the little bough hut, Hywella was indeed a witch. Everything she'd said made sense, though she knew nothing of the recent events in Roxanne's life. Clearly she'd advised her that the man she would marry was looking for her, though he did not know they were to wed.

It could only be Balin of Penllyn, Roxanne thought giddily. She had made her way back to Cymru and was making her way back to him. But Balin had no way of knowing she'd escaped King Henry and the marriage that English monarch had arranged.

Yet, still he loved and longed for her; he waited and watched, too. It was easy for Roxanne to imagine Balin standing on his mountaintop, gazing at the horizon, hoping she would come.

Her heart swelled with love as she embraced the image of her handsome prince, and she rode faster.

Raven felt awkward riding the scruffy, sturdy little cob instead of his tall, powerful destrier. Thomas of Bittenshire had assured him the smaller horse would be more nimble and surefooted when traversing the mountainous terrain, so Raven had agreed to take him. But he had insisted on bringing Rolf with him also, and now the massive warhorse followed the stocky little beast Raven rode, as though he were a pack animal.

Having set out before first light, Raven believed he would reach the land called Penllyn before night fell again. As he rode along, keeping a wary eye on the burgeoning gray clouds overhead, he wondered what he would find when he reached Prince Balin's abode. Roxanne was certainly there with him. Would the Welshman try to hide her? Or would he be reasonable and allow her to return to England for marriage to Peter?

Jesu! the voice in Raven's mind muttered. Anger and frustration kept him irritable. His plan had been to get Roxanne away from Fortengall so that Peter would have no opportunity to marry her. His keenest desire had been to protect his brother so that the bitch couldn't send him from this earthly world the first chance she got. Yet, now he was concerned some petty, heathen prince might try to prevent him from seeing King Henry's wishes carried out.

"Madness," he muttered to the nameless animal beneath him. " 'Tis naught but madness, and has been since Lucien appeared at my door with those two Welsh females in tow."

A beam of sunlight, narrow at its source, wide where it washed the ground, suddenly broke through the threatening clouds that abruptly, delightfully, parted. Raven raised his head to let the warmth embrace him. It had been a long, dreary winter he'd passed in England, a long, damp journey he'd endured in Wales. This sunshine brightened his spirits as much as the landscape, which seemed a stunning, radiant green at its edges.

"Spring is nearly here," he told himself as he shrugged off his cloak and lay it across his lap. He gazed at the rolling land surrounding him, admitting to himself that Wales wasn't so hard and ugly after all. Not with sunlight glinting off every blade and stone, not with the oaks and ash preparing to unfurl their budding leaves.

His stomach rumbled, and spying a clearing with some short, hardy grass tufting in clumps beneath the trees, he halted. Swinging his leg off the cob, Raven tethered the beast and its far mightier relation so that the horses might eat. Then he grabbed some bread and meat from the pouch Bittenshire's cook had packed for him, and, sitting down with his back against a tree trunk, began a late, leisurely, midday meal.

Realizing that he'd nearly dozed off as he surveyed the land beneath half-closed lids, Raven suddenly sat up straight. Eyes opened wide, he leaned away from his backrest and peered at the trail. "God's blood!" he swore, blinking to ensure he saw what he thought he saw. " 'Tis the bitch! I got myself ahead of her, though she set off a full day before me!" He pushed himself to his feet, still crouching, and slapped one muscled thigh. "Saints be praised, the poison-tongued shrew is going to ride straight into my arms!"

Roxanne glanced over her shoulder still again. She knew that ahead, not a few more hours' ride, stood Penllyn Hall where Balin watched and waited. But behind her could be anyone, most likely men Peter or Lord Ian of Fortengall had sent to bring her back to England.

There was no one behind her, though. Not even a lamb or a weasel. So Roxanne righted herself in her saddle again and kept her eyes forward. Not that she saw much of what lay before her. She knew the route to Balin's home so well, she could have found it blind or in the dark of a moonless night. Dafydd knew it nearly as well. Thus, Roxanne allowed herself to sink into her private musings, most of which had to do with the feel of Balin's arms about her, the taste of his lips pressed to her mouth.

She shrieked. Even as the scream escaped her, she wondered how she managed it, with her heart stuck in her throat. Indeed, it seemed to be cutting off all her air.

No, it was not her heart lodged in her throat that made breathing all but impossible. It was the outlaw who had leaped from a tree limb and landed on Dafydd's rump. He'd grabbed her hard around the middle, and when the stallion reared, sending them both tumbling off his shining black backside, the man rolled, pinning her beneath him. Not only were his arms squeezing the life from Roxanne, so, too, the weight of his body pressed her into the ground.

"Cease your struggling, woman, if you wish to see another day!" Raven ordered. "Oooooph!"

He'd been sprawled across her, his legs splayed on either side of her well-rounded hips while he attempted to subdue her. But Roxanne had managed to bring up one knee, hitting his stones hard. Raven felt as though she'd brought a hammer down upon his manhood. Not only did he exhale a moan of pain, but he released his hold, rolling off the wench while grabbing his cods tenderly with both his hands.

Roxanne did not jump up and attempt escape. She lay on the rock-strewn trail, gasping for breath and trying to regain her wits. Suddenly, the pieces of her shattered reality settled into place, and she recognized the face that had loomed over hers—Raven of Stonelee's. Even if she hadn't known Peter stayed confined at his mother's keep, she would never have mistaken the good twin for the evil twin. The dark one, the cruel one, the hateful one—the one who had vowed to see her dead—was the one lying but a scant distance away from her.

Roxanne pushed herself up, ignoring the stinging pain of stones pressing into her palms. She looked up the length of trail visible to her and spied her stallion waiting docilely. In the next instant, she scrambled to her feet, intent on reclaiming her mount.

"Aaaagghhh!"

Her cry was unintelligible, a combination of startled fright and pain. Raven had seen her, from the corner of his eye, about to bolt. He had reached up, grabbed Roxanne's unbound hair, and yanked her back down beside him again.

"Let . . . me . . . go, you filthy swine!" she ground out as he positioned himself above her, straddling her hips again.

This time, however, he put his weight on his calves as he knelt and wrapped a hank of her hair around his fist, as though it were a silken rope. He jerked the coil that pulled tautly from her scalp, making Roxanne wince.

"Not damnably likely!" he snarled down into her flushed face. "Not after all I've been through trying to track you down. You'll be coming back with me!"

"I shall not!" She tried twisting away, but the grip he had on her hair caused her more pain, she suspected, than her knee to his groin had caused him. It was effective; she lay still beneath him for a moment that was punctuated by their hard, jagged breathing. The moment did not last long, however. Almost immediately, Roxanne tried to repeat the effective move that had brought Raven low a moment earlier.

"Bitch!" He sat back on his rear when he felt her leg move, and pinned her thighs to the ground. "Twice you've wounded me thus. I shan't give you the opportunity to make it thrice!"

"You deserved it." With blue-violet eyes, she glared at him hatefully. "If I kicked you in the cods every day for the rest of your life, I doubt you'd be hurt as often as you deserve!"

Raven clenched his free hand, controlling the urge to strike her. He never hit women because as a child he'd watched his father, Gundulf of Eynsham, strike everyone from the serving women to their daughters to his own mother, Lucinda, who was oft beaten near to death. But, curse the saints, Roxanne of Bittenshire certainly invited beatings or at least a cuff to the jaw!

She seemed to read his mind. "Go ahead," she taunted. "Hit me! 'Tis what you're dying to do! 'Twill make you feel more the man if you bruise and break a helpless woman—will it not, *Percival?*"

His obsidian eyes narrowed to slits as he shook his head ever so slightly. "The name my mother gave me does not offend me, milady. 'Tis only that the name others gave me suits me better still. But call me by my Christian name, if you care to."

He spoke so calmly, with such sincerity, Roxanne wanted to scratch out his eyes. She tried to, bringing up her hands to rake his face with her nails.

Before she could get close enough to claw him, Raven released the knot of hair he'd been gripping so tightly. Using both his hands to catch her wrists, he pushed back her arms and braced them against the ground above her head.

"It will be as long a journey back to Fortengall Castle as it was from there to here. I'd advise you to bring in your claws if you'd like to travel comfortably on the back of your own mount. If you do not, I shall keep you bound and gagged on the fore of my destrier the entire ride back into England."

"Back . . . into England?" Roxanne's bosom rose and fell as she ground out the words and gasped for breath. "Why in the name of all things holy would you wish to take me back to England? 'Twas you who urged me to leave there. 'Twas you who warned me not to wed Peter. Why—?"

She did not finish her query, yet Raven understood her question. Unfortunately, he had no reasonable answer.

"Get up," he growled, leaning back on his haunches, gaining his feet, and pulling Roxanne up with him.

"Nay!" Purposely, she let her knees bend weakly, crumpling back to the ground like dead weight. She nearly pulled Raven down with her, but he managed to stay on his feet.

"Up!" he ordered heatedly. This time, when he yanked her up, he pulled her close. Releasing her hands, he wrapped his arms about her waist, securing his hold.

She was garbed only in bliaut and under tunic; no mantle swathed her curvaceous form. He, too, was cloakless. Raven wore neither gambeson nor mail but only his tunic, and it was not so thick that he couldn't feel Roxanne's breasts tickling his chest with every deep breath she took. He saw, through the fabric layered over her bosom, that her nipples had hardened. They made little points in her bliaut. Despite his passionate dislike for the damsel, he discovered himself swelling in his braies.

Roxanne was glad he did not demand conversation of her, not even a retort of any kind. Her throat had gone dry when his arms encircled her waist. Never had she felt a man like Raven of Stonelee pressed the length of her. Not that she had any experience, except for Balin. But he did not feel like this. And how was *this?* she wondered as she glared at her captor's rugged face. *This* was a perfect fit, as though their bodies were halves of a whole. She was tall; he was taller. His lips might have caressed her forehead if he but leaned forward. His chest met her chest, making her breasts tingle. And below their waists, she felt the bulge of his lust burgeoning against the apex of her thighs. There would be no need, if both were so inclined, to jiggle and angle and squirm themselves into position. 'Twas as if they'd been made for each other.

Roxanne found that thought so reprehensible, she belatedly resumed her struggle against Raven. Bringing her hands to his chest, she pushed against him. Though she didn't manage anything close to freedom, she succeeded, at least, in putting space between her sensitive breasts and the hard muscle of his chest.

"Why?" she hissed, demanding an answer to her desperate query.

"I've been overruled."

CHAPTER 15

Raven had taken his saddle from the cob and returned it to his destrier's back. With a stinging slap to the smaller horse's rump, he sent the little beast back to Bittenshire on its own. Tying Roxanne's stallion securely to a tree branch, he lifted the wench into her own saddle. She could hardly mount on her own, as he'd bound her hands tightly in front of her waist.

Roxanne felt lighter than Raven expected. Despite her amply rounded bosom and distractingly curvaceous bottom, he found her waist rather small. Mayhap her slim waist caused her other attributes to appear more abundant. But he wouldn't know unless he saw her nude.

Roxanne's expression was mutinous as she watched Raven secure her bound wrists to the saddle. But she made no move against him nor even muttered an angry word, until his hand brushed her calf. She was, as usual, clad in men's leggings beneath her skirts, so no skin was exposed to the knight's eyes. And perhaps his touch had been inadvertent. But the lady wasn't inclined to give him the benefit of her doubt.

"Dare not touch me again!" she warned, eyes flashing.

Raven blinked, startled from the faraway place his thoughts had wandered. Looking up at his captive, he informed her, "I fear I must. I cannot trust you to follow me back to Fortengall of your own accord. Thus, I shall keep you bound. I doubt even you, expert horsewoman that you are, can mount and dismount with your hands tied and your wrists lashed to the saddle." Dismissing her along with her complaints, Raven strode to Dafydd's head and untied the reins.

"My legs are not bound!" she pointed out, her cry harsh.

"They will be, if you don't hold your tongue," he snapped without so much as a backward glance. He climbed onto Rolf's back and wrapped a lead rope attached to Roxanne's saddle around his fist. "I'll truss you up like a feast-day goose. Imagine how I'll be forced to touch you then."

Roxanne imagined it well, as Raven led her back the way they'd come, toward Bittenshire, Offa's Dyke, and England. Her wayward thoughts infuriated her. She hated this Englishman, this Norman-blooded knight who served King Henry. He'd been rude and nasty since the first; he'd been cruel and threatening, too. Now he was purposely ruining her life, even though he believed returning her to Fortengall Castle, to Peter of Stoneweather, would ruin his brother's life as well.

Nothing made sense to Roxanne. Why had Raven of Stonelee, the knight who urged her to flee to Cymru, come to retrieve her? And why ... why had she felt a rivulet of fire course down her nether limb when he touched her there? Certainly, the touch had been unintentional, for she knew Raven detested her as much as she did him. Yet, that made matters worse, for Roxanne now harbored a secret, shameful desire—the desire for Raven to touch her in just such a manner again.

Ahead of her on the narrow trail, Raven kept his eyes fast on the hard, uneven stone-strewn path before him. He'd learned firsthand that sturdy, sure-footed cobs negotiated this terrain far better than mighty destriers. But as he'd chosen to ride Rolf just as Roxanne did her destrier, he kept a short rein on his beast and his gaze never left the ground.

He thanked the saints for the distraction. If he allowed himself to think of anything but the precariousness of their journey, he worried what notions might fill his head. Raven suspected his mind would be cluttered with visions of the woman riding behind him, her ebony tresses gleaming blue-black in the sunlight, her bosom bouncing with every step her stallion took, her slim, well-shaped legs clenching the beast's flanks, taut as they might be if wrapped around his own waist. . . .

So determined was the lord of Stonelee to concentrate only on the ground beneath him, he wasn't aware when the patches of gray clouds above swirled and expanded, joining together, overlapping until there remained neither blue sky nor shafts of sunlight to penetrate their veneer. Only when the first drops of rain splattered against his face did he realize the weather had turned again.

In no time at all, the spotty, fat, cold droplets shrank as their numbers increased. One raindrop could not be differentiated from another as a seeming river poured down upon them. Grim, yet resigned to the unceasingly miserable weather, Raven twisted around to check on his prisoner.

It was hard to see Roxanne despite her proximity because of the driving downpour. Squinting, Raven opened his mouth, intending to inquire after her well-being. But suddenly Rolf lurched and went down hard on his forelegs.

Alarmed, Raven swung forward but found himself helpless as the beast slid and rolled to his side. Rolf was down now, completely, his hind legs stiff as his forelegs pawed the air. Yet, as they were on a slope, the horse continued to slide.

Hitting his shoulder hard, Raven grimaced as his leg bore the destrier's weight, caught between the beast and the slick, muddy trail. Instinctively, he let go the reins and drew his leg up, free of the animal.

He also released the rope tied to Roxanne's mount as he

rolled clear of his own helpless horse. But as he scrambled up, Raven saw it was too late. Rolf's fall and his own, while clasping the lead rope, had brought the other beast down, too, and Roxanne with him. The second stallion skidded into the first, pushing Raven's steed even farther down the incline.

Abruptly, both horses stopped their unnatural, uncontrollable, descent down the trail. Rolf quickly regained his footing, planting himself squarely in the mud, his stance wide to support himself. Roxanne's stallion also attempted to heave himself upright, off his side and off his rider, to regain his balance and his own footing.

Even as Raven stumbled over to Roxanne, his boots making sucking sounds in the muck, he felt a stab of dread pierce his heart. He knew that, had she been free, Roxanne would have curled into a ball and rolled away so that she wasn't crushed by her steed or kicked by his flailing hooves. But, being bound, she remained pinned beneath her horse. And she was silent, neither crying in pain nor shouting at him for having allowed this to happen. She lay still as a stone.

''Roxanne!'' Crying her name, Raven pulled his knife from his belt and cut the leather tie that kept her wrists against the fore of her saddle. Grabbing her beneath her arms, he hauled her out from under the beast who, freed of his ungainly burden, managed to stand on his own. ''Roxanne!''

Her blue-violet eyes were open, staring at him peculiarly. She didn't blink, and Raven feared she might be dead. He became suddenly, totally frantic at that possibility. It didn't occur to him that his reaction was as queer as her stare, nor that he should have been thinking, *Glory be, the bitch is dead; Peter is free of her forever! I cannot be blamed for her fatal mishap while she rode a horse too strong for her to handle. 'Twas her desire to return to Wales, with its treacherous mountain passages and brutal, blinding rains. Her fate was all her own doing. . . .*

These were not Raven's thoughts. In fact, he had no coherent thoughts at all as his heart pounded in panic.

"Roxanne?" He dragged her to the edge of the path, cradling her in his lap. "God's wounds, Roxanne, do you hear me?"

Rain pummeled down into her unseeing eyes for another moment. Then her lashes fluttered, and she wheezed, gasping, before finally inhaling a full, ragged breath of air.

The damsel had had the wind knocked out of her, Raven realized, relief swelling blissfully within his breast, soothing away the painful knot of anxiety.

Roxanne's eyes focused. The searing ache in her lungs, as she'd tried to inhale but could not, had momentarily blinded her to all but the need to breathe. Now that she could gasp deep gulps of air, she saw clearly the man holding her. His hair lay matted against his skull; water dripped off the tip of his nose and glistened in his beard. He looked fierce and thoroughly disreputable, yet at that moment Roxanne deemed him the most handsome man she'd ever seen. More pleasing to look upon than Balin, more desirable than Peter.

"You varlet! You knave! You cockshead!" Planting her elbow in Raven's ribs, she rolled off him onto her knees. Using her hands to push herself up, she managed to find her feet again. "You're as ignorant of this land as your stupid English horse!" she announced, hands on her hips. "Yet, you would try to lead me through these mountains? Are you mad? You nearly killed me!"

No longer having a burden, even a fairly pleasant one, nestled in his lap, Raven leaned back on his elbows and looked up at the shrieking shrew. The waves and soft curls of her hair had gone straight with the weight of water clinging to every strand; it lay flat and cleaved to her ears, her shoulders, her bosom. The wool bliaut and under tunic she wore were just as heavy with rainwater, and smeared and spattered with mud. Yet . . .

Raven surprised himself as he ignored her tirade to focus, instead, on her appearance. Or, perhaps, he was not so surprised.

Since the age of ten and two, he had been noticing women's attributes. Roxanne's hair, wet and streaming, allowed him to see the full shape of her face. He realized immediately that her glorious head of night-black curls, which usually flowed wild and free, was superfluous. If she routinely hid her mane beneath a wimple, the wench could not be more comely. And her figure—*Jesu!* The fabric covering her was far from transparent, yet it clung, exposing her feminine form. The way she stood facing him with her hands on her hips, her breasts were thrust forward, her hardened nipples preceding the soft mounds themselves, making his fingers itch to caress them. And the raindrops trickling down Roxanne's throat, converging like a stream running into the crevice of her exposed cleavage, well . . . It made Raven want to lick up every drop with his tongue. As well, the torrential rain pounded her gowns against her body, pushing the cloth into the juncture of her thighs. It appeared as though her loins had been purposely outlined, on the odd chance that Raven did not know precisely where they were. As if guided by a marker, his glance drew down to her most tantalizing attribute, that spot a man might invade and lose himself within.

He despised himself for it. At worst, this harpy was responsible for Peter's near demise, a devil woman who should be relieved of her life. At best, she was destined to be Peter's lady wife, his own sister-by-marriage. He'd no business coveting her body.

She was still haranguing him when Raven shoved himself up and stood to face her. Abruptly she fell silent, her luminous eyes locking on his. But he said nothing to her. He made no excuses or apologies. He did not even point out that she was, for the time being, his captive, and therefore he was bound to lead them out of Wales, not she.

Wordlessly, he gave her his back and strode to the two waiting horses, where he checked their legs for soundness. Satisfied, he led both Rolf and Dafydd over to Roxanne. There, he handed her her own stallion's reins. "Walk," he ordered, leading his destrier down the muddy slope before her.

Raven heard Roxanne muttering curses and complaints, but he paid her no heed. He remembered seeing an abandoned shepherd's hut. As it was late in the day already, and he was thoroughly miserable in wet clothing once again, Raven determined to take shelter there for the night.

Roxanne ceased her muttering long before they reached the shelter. She was furious, more for letting him catch her than for her current, sorry state. Yet, she was glad for the little hut, once she saw it, though she'd have confessed her relief to no one, least of all the lord of Stonelee.

Chivalrously, he unsaddled Roxanne's horse as well as his own. He'd been half tempted to let her struggle with the task, especially when she simply dropped her stallion's reins and walked on into the little bough house. But Raven could not bring himself to be that heartless, even if the wench deserved it, for her wrists remained bound together.

Thus, he entered after her, carrying both saddles and bridles. When he unceremoniously dropped his load onto the dirt floor, he looked up and around. " 'Tis dry, at least."

"You mean it's not leaking too severely," Roxanne countered.

Raven heard the unmistakable sound of water dripping through the roof. "So there's a bit of rain coming in. Only in that corner."

"And that one."

Turning, he saw she was correct. "We'll just have to make do with the center of the room, then." He looked back at Roxanne. She was sodden and shivering, though she stood stoically. "I'll get a fire going. 'Twill help dry us out."

"Ha! What will you use for kindling, milord? Sopping leaves

and soggy twigs? And what for the steady, warm blaze that shall last us through the night—a nice, damp log?''

Raven's eyes narrowed dangerously, but Roxanne felt a twinge of triumph. How easy it was, after all, to set down the arrogant English knave! Yet, she wished they could have a fire, even a small one near the open portal. Because, if her chattering teeth were any indication, she would soon freeze to death.

"Did you take my belongings off Dafydd?" she inquired.

"Dafydd?"

"My horse. His name's Dafydd. I rolled my cloak with food and clothes, and tied it to his rump. Did you bring the bundle with you?"

"If it was tied, it's still on your saddle. See for yourself." Raven toed the two saddles laying at his feet.

His was atop hers. Kneeling, Roxanne pulled Raven's saddle aside and began working at the leather strings that secured her bundle to her saddle.

Sighing in annoyance, she looked up at her captor. "Would you mind undoing my bonds? 'Twould make it easier."

"Why should I make things easier for you?"

"Why not?" she snapped irritably. "Where in the name of all things holy am I going to run this night? It is nearing evening, if you didn't notice. The weather is accursed, and there's no moon. I should just like to get my things untied here, and—"

"And what?" He took a step closer to Roxanne. "Get out of those cold, wet clothes?"

Gritting her teeth to keep them from chattering and to restrain herself from saying something that might earn her a stinging blow, Roxanne glared up at Raven. "Aye."

A corner of his mouth quirked in a smile. "I would not be displeased to see you shed of those wet, muddy gowns. Thus, I'll do all in my power to assist you." He squatted beside her and worked loose the cord that bound her wrists. "I'm capable of more assistance than this, if you should require it."

They were eye to eye, but Raven held Roxanne's gaze for no more than a few moments before his glance meandered downward.

As though he'd dared to touch her with his hands, Roxanne leaped up and away. " 'Twill be full dark soon. I can wait. Night here, under a starless sky, is black indeed. Be assured you shan't be seeing anything you're not entitled to."

"Go ahead, then. Catch a chill—and your death from it. 'Twould be a blessing all around, as I see it. But I shan't stand here freezing for another half hour. I intend to change my garments while I can still see to do it."

With a nonchalant shrug, Roxanne backed still farther away and left him to it. She hoped he was wrong, that it would not take fully half an hour more before the night was black as pitch and she could finally relieve herself of the hideously heavy, icy garments clinging to her body. And as she looked through the doorway, she was pleased to know he was wrong. The rectangle of gray light brightening the inside of the hut to a dismal, dim degree was fast disintegrating.

"Oh!" The startled grunt escaped Roxanne's lips without her intent. But the beast, the craven lord of Stonelee, had planted himself firmly in front of the narrow doorway. He had tugged off his boots and now proceeded to shed his clothes. The pale light behind him glowed faintly on his skin as he exposed it.

Roxanne definitely saw skin and sculpted muscles and matted thatches of hair. Raven had casually undone his belt, setting his knife and his sword aside, safely out of her reach, and pulled his knee-length tunic off over his head. Bared to the waist, he was too compelling a vision for her to look away. Rainwater dripping into a muddy puddle could not compete with Raven of Stonelee stripping. So she stared, curiously fascinated by his seminude, masculine form.

Raven was formed well. His shoulders were broad, his chest cleaved into two, muscular halves. A light fur, as black as the hair on his head, covered him from neck to navel, though the downy pelt tapered into a narrow line as it disappeared into his chausses.

He loosened the ties that kept his leggings anchored, but this time Roxanne managed to smother her gasp. Shock should have caused her to cover her maiden's eyes. But she wasn't easily shocked, so her eyes remained open, and she watched in fascination as Raven tugged his chausses down his legs, taking his undergarment with them.

Kicking the damp, offending articles aside, he paused for a moment. If he glanced her way, Roxanne would not have known; the light behind him put his face in shadow. Besides, she was not looking at his face. She stared instead at the place on his body to which the dark trail of springy hair led. Where it led was to an astoundingly large, male appendage.

His root hung limply, but it was large. Roxanne knew this, for she'd seen more than a few naked men in her parents' keep, though all quite by accident. Raven, she determined, was not what one would call beautiful, like some angel who flitted about God's throne. But he was certainly pleasing to the eye, from his bearded face to his broad shoulders, from his flat belly to his muscled thighs. And Roxanne found his prick fascinating. Any woman would. Were it hardened and lengthened and nudging between a damsel's thighs . . . !

Her inhaled breath was so noisy and sharp, Raven looked up and leaned forward, peering at her. "Are you well, wench?"

"I'm no wench. I am a lady."

"That is a matter for debate." Raven crouched, searching through his satchel. He muttered a muffled curse.

"Is something amiss?"

"Aye. My only other pair of leggings are my best. I can't risk ruining them while riding through this miserable country."

"Cymru is not miserable!"

"Again, 'tis a matter for debate."

Raven rose and shook out his damp chausses. Then he walked away and pushed the garment's hip band between two of the

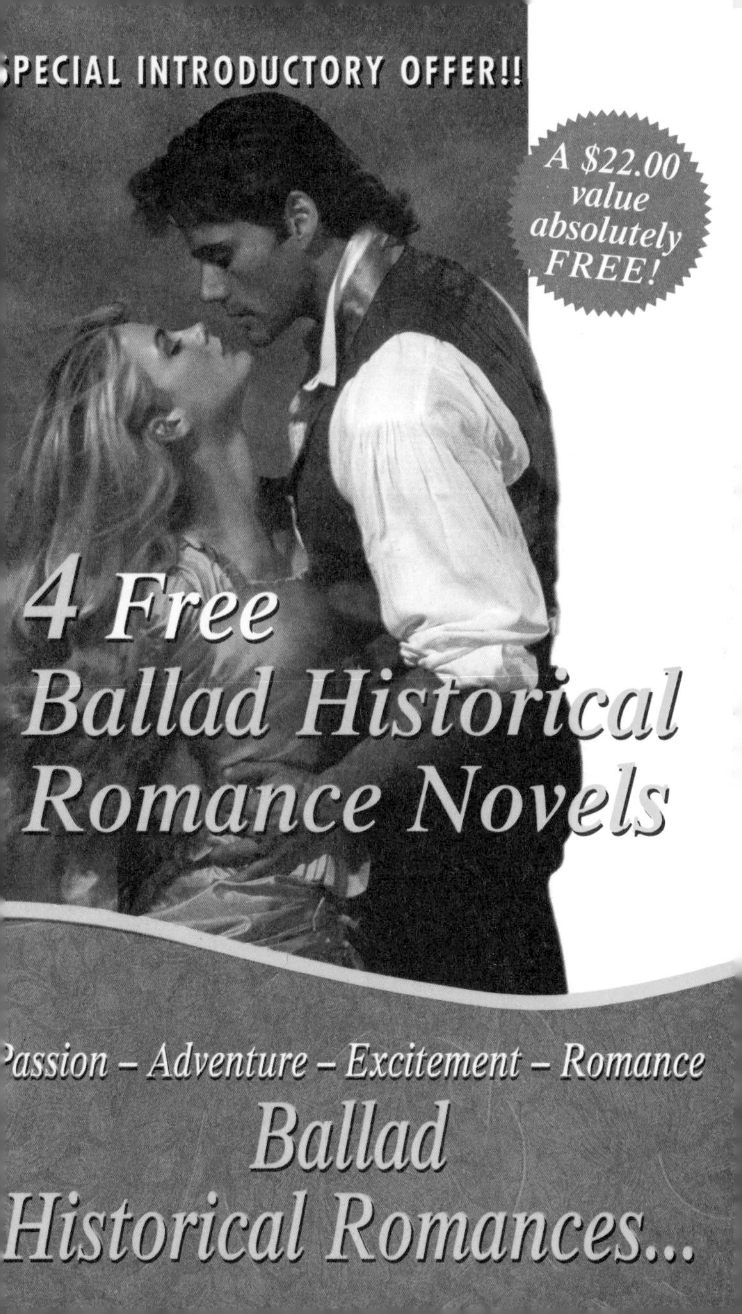
SPECIAL INTRODUCTORY OFFER!!
A $22.00 value absolutely FREE!
4 Free Ballad Historical Romance Novels
Passion – Adventure – Excitement – Romance
Ballad Historical Romances...

INTRODUCING *BALLAD*,
A BRAND NEW LINE OF HISTORICAL ROMANCES

As a lover of historical romance, you'll adore Ballad Romances. Written by today's most popular romance authors, every book in the Ballad line is not only an individual story, but part of a two to six book series as well. You can look forward to four new titles a month – each taking place at a different time and place in history.

But don't take our word for how wonderful these stories are! Accept our introductory shipment of 4 Ballad Romance novels – a $22.00 value – ABSOLUTELY FREE – and see for yourself!

Once you've experienced your first four Ballad Romances, we're sure you'll want to continue receiving these wonderful historical romance novels each month – without ever having to leave your home – using our convenient and inexpensive home subscription service. Here's what you get for joining:

- 4 BRAND NEW Ballad Romances delivered to your door each month

- 25% off the cover price of $5.50 with your home subscription

- a FREE monthly newsletter filled with author interviews, book previews, special offers, and more!

- No risks or obligations…you're free to cancel whenever you wish… no questions asked.

To start your membership, simply complete and return the card provided. You'll receive your Introductory Shipment of 4 FREE Ballad Romances. Then, each month, as long as your account is in good standing, you will receive the 4 newest Ballad Romances. Each shipment will be yours to examine for 10 days. If you decide to keep the books, you'll pay the preferred home subscriber's price of $16.50 – a savings of 25% off the cover price! (Plus $1.50 shipping and handling.) If you want us to stop sending books, just say the word… it's that simple.

If the certificate is missing below, write to:

Ballad Romances, c/o Zebra Home Subscription Service, Inc.,
P.O. Box 5214, Clifton, New Jersey 07015-5214

OR call TOLL FREE 1-888-345-BOOK (2665)

Visit our website at www.kensingtonbooks.com

FREE BOOK CERTIFICATE

Yes! Please send me 4 Ballad Romances ABSOLUTELY FREE! After my introductory shipment, I will receive 4 new Ballad Romances each month to preview FREE for 10 days (as long as my account is in good standing). If I decide to keep the books, I will pay the money-saving preferred publisher's price of $16.50 plus $1.50 shipping and handling. That's 25% off the cover price. I may return the shipment within 10 days and owe nothing, and I may cancel my subscription at any time.

The 4 FREE books will be mine to keep in any case.

DN110A

Name _____

Address _____

City _____ State _____ Zip _____

Telephone ( ) _____

Signature _____

(If under 18, parent or guardian must sign.)

Orders subject to acceptance by Zebra Home Subscription Service. Terms and Prices subject to change.
Offer valid only in the U.S.

Get 4 Ballad
Historical Romance Novels
FREE!

A $22 value — FREE! No obligation to buy anything — ever.

boughs that helped form one wall of the hut, effectively hanging the leggings to dry.

He seemed nonchalant, as though he were quite alone instead of in the company of a gently reared young woman. Roxanne marveled at his ease, though she knew it was born of arrogance. She marveled, too, at what she could see of his backside. It was not easily visible; the daylight, gray as it had been, was nearly gone. She had to lean and angle her own body forward, and squint to get a better view.

It was worth it. As Raven raised his hands to work the garment between the two, close-fitting tree limbs, the muscles in his back flexed visibly. So, too, did the muscles of his upper arms. Even his buttocks flexed a bit, and Roxanne, unable to deny her admiration of his tight, round rump, thought she could make out two dimples, one on each side, not far below his waist.

"Looking for something?"

Abruptly, Roxanne straightened her posture. Her cheeks flamed, but she knew he couldn't see her face. Nor could she see his, though she surmised he had spun around to confront her.

"Ow! God's blood!"

Raven had returned to the pile of possessions he'd dumped on the floor. Apparently, he had stubbed his toe on one of the saddles. In the darkness, Roxanne grinned.

She sensed more than saw his movements and assumed he had donned a dry tunic. She also had the distinct impression he had sat down. Now she heard him chewing.

"What are you doing there?"

"Eating." He swallowed. "Aren't you going to get out of those wet clothes and have a bite from your own stores?"

He did not even offer to share what he had, he was so accursedly rude! And strutting around like a cock in a hen house had been worse than rude, Roxanne reflected. He had flaunted himself, as though she had no sensibilities. Now, he would let her go hungry while he filled his own belly.

Exhaling loudly through her nose so that the insolent lord of Stonelee would well know her displeasure, Roxanne stomped toward her own bundle of belongings. Unfortunately, Raven sat right beside them, and she tripped over his leg.

He caught her before she fell. His hands gripped her ribs, and she felt the weight of her breasts settling against the back of his wrists. Frantically, Roxanne sought the floor with her fingers, straining to balance herself without Raven's assistance. Her fingers met not with cold dirt but with a firm, manly bulge draped in soft wool. If she had been purposely reaching for his cock, she could not have found it more surely.

"I didn't know you cared," Raven whispered seductively.

"Damn your soul to the depths of hell, I do not!" Roxanne brought her hand up as though it were scalded. She then promptly fell backward onto her rump. "You are—are—"

"What?"

Staring hard at the indistinct image she knew to be Raven, Roxanne thought of a dozen things he was. Unfortunately, every descriptive word that happened to come to mind was flattering. At least, he would think them flattering!

"Vile! Despicable! The belly of a slug! Need I go on?"

"Only if you're going to take off those wet gowns."

"I am. But as I vowed, you shan't be seeing anything you oughtn't."

Taking her things to one of the dry corners in the hut, Roxanne undid her girdle and angrily yanked off her bliaut, her under tunic, and her thin linen shift. She would have dearly loved to dry her skin with her fur cape, but it was more wet than dry. So she pawed blindly through her things, which had fallen out when she unrolled the mantle, and determinedly tugged on replacement garments for all three she'd removed. Only then did she peel off the pair of men's chausses she always wore when riding astride. Yet she didn't replace them.

She had no others. She could not find her foodstuffs, either. They had been in a separate pouch, though rolled into her cape. Roxanne assumed the bag had been lost when Dafydd went down on the hillside. Now she had nothing to eat, but she would gladly have wasted away before asking Raven for a morsel.

There was nothing to do but sleep. Huffing and puffing, and making great noise as she went about it, Roxanne spread out her cape and then lay down on it. Some of it was dry, for it had been rolled and not all of it exposed to the rain. But it proved difficult trying to align her body with a warm, dry patch. Besides, she had nothing at all with which to cover herself, and as night settled in, the air had grown chill.

Roxanne lay in what she now considered her half of the hut, curled on her side, shivering. Though her stomach grumbled, her thoughts were not on food. Her thoughts were all on the man occupying the other half of this leaky shelter. The cruel, suspicious man who thought she had tried to kill his brother and then had pledged to kill her if she did not flee. The man who accosted her by leaping down from a tree. The man who nearly got her killed by tying her up and setting her on a horse that slid down a muddy trail. The man who stripped naked and strutted before her as though she were a common slut, not a lady born. The Englishman who despised Cymru. The man who . . .

. . . had an air about him. Something altogether different from his usual pompousness and angry disdain. Roxanne had no word for it, but whatever it was, she found it compelling. Raven had some secret, sensual allure, a force that tried to draw her near. It seemed as if, subtly, he attempted to bewitch her, to bring her close enough that she would, he might—what?

Again Roxanne shivered. Raven of Stonelee was dark, not only in coloring. He had a dark nature. Yet, something of that darkness was not evil. It was seductive.

"Here."

She started when she heard his voice. Raven had come up behind her and now knelt beside her. When she rolled halfway toward him to peer at him suspiciously, he thrust something into her hand.

"What—what is it?"

"A fig. I've more. And bread and cheese, too. I have a wine skin as well, if you're parched."

"Nay. I'm not thirsty." She propped herself on one elbow and considered the offering he'd placed in her hand.

"Aren't you going to eat?" Raven asked.

"I'm not very hungry."

The moment she spoke, Roxanne's stomach growled again, loud enough for them both to hear.

Raven laughed. "You're hungry. Eat. I vow, 'tis a dried fig you have clutched in your hand, not some fat vermin I stepped on with my boot. Nor is it poisoned. Go on."

Suspiciously, Roxanne brought the fruit to her lips and guardedly tasted it with her tongue. Satisfied that he told the truth, she popped it whole into her mouth and ate it quickly.

Raven handed her another palmful of figs. When she'd consumed them, he gave her some bread and cheese.

"Are you sure you want no wine?"

Roxanne blinked, staring hard at the faceless figure sitting so near her in the dark. She'd been right about starless nights in Cymru. When darkness fell, it cloaked everything. Eyes opened or closed, a body could see no more or less.

In that darkness, with Raven's deep voice speaking gently, Roxanne nearly lost her old dislike and new fear of the man. But not completely. Not enough to risk consuming potent spirits.

"Nay. I'm fine. But my thanks for the food."

"Move over."

"What!" Her question was a single syllable screech.

"You were hungry. You're still cold. I could hear your teeth chattering on the other side of the hut. Move over and we'll share your mantle beneath us. We can share mine as a cover."

"No!"

"God's blood, woman!" Raven's tone had lost its gentleness. He sounded annoyed, angry. "I've no desire for you and wouldn't have, even if the king weren't intent on you wedding my brother. For *Jesu's* sake, move over and let us warm each other!"

Roxanne debated only a moment before giving in and scooting to the far side of her fur mantle. Because it was not far enough and provided little space between them, she immediately gave Raven her back. He draped his wool cloak over them as he stretched out beside her.

He didn't find her desirable. That was all she could think of, now. She found him desirable despite his foul temperament, though she'd not admit it under threat of death. But she, who was surely loved by one and all who knew her, was not good enough for him! The cur. The varlet. The damnable cockshead!

Raven's breathing had become the slow, easy breathing of a restful slumber long before Roxanne herself succumbed to sleep. Later, when she woke, she discovered him still asleep.

She discovered something else, as her heart caught in her throat. During their sleep, she and the despised English knight had turned to each other. Now Raven's arm lay heavily across her ribs and waist; her own hand rested trustingly upon his shoulder. But worse and more appalling, their tunics had rucked up, exposing both their nether regions, if not to an intruder, at least to each other beneath Raven's cape. His substantial manhood lay snuggled against the juncture of her thighs, as though it attempted to nestle in the thatch of her dark maiden hair.

Aghast, Roxanne refrained from crying out. Instead, inquisitively, she wriggled her hips just a little. To her amazement, she discerned the Englishman's root was no longer limp. Not hard, exactly, but growing hard for certain.

Immediately, Roxanne went still. In the moonlight slanting through the open doorway, she saw that Raven of Stonelee looked far less fearsome in his sleep. He was handsome, despite that his ebony locks had grown longer and his beard fuller, making him appear wilder than he had upon their first meeting. Again, without his meaning to, he seemed to have the power to draw her to him. She was tempted to move her hand from his shoulder and secretively caress his face.

Moonlight! Belatedly, Roxanne noted what she had overlooked when first she'd opened her eyes. The moon had come out. Pausing to listen, she noticed there was no longer that tedious dripping in both corners of the hut. Nor did light stream down from the heavens, but the rain ceased. The night was good for riding now, riding on to Penllyn.

Stealthily, Roxanne slid from beneath the covers and groped for her shoes. The only things she dared take with her from the hut were Dafydd's bridle and saddle. Even then, she held her breath as she tiptoed outside and readied her mount for riding. Yet, by the time she led Dafydd through the brush and back to the trail, she saw no sign that Raven had awakened.

She was free. Roxanne intended not to lose her freedom again. Not to Raven of Stonelee, certainly, who had threatened her with death, and worse, found her not at all appealing!

CHAPTER 16

Pamela climbed Fortengall Castle's staircase, anxious to tell Peter the news. Lady Lucinda had just confided to her that at the end of this very week, she saw no harm if her son began to move around a bit. But when she reached his chamber, she noticed the door stood ajar and heard, from within, familiar voices. One belonged to Peter himself, and the other to a woman with whom Pamela was all too familiar. The lord and the servant chatted companionably; they laughed, too.

Anger swelled within her bosom. Bess was up to her tricks again! If Roxanne were here, Pamela knew her cousin would grab the brazen wench by her braid and throw her out of Peter's sickroom. Well, she thought righteously, it was up to her to throw Bess out, since Roxy wasn't at Fortengall to do it herself!

She pushed the door open all the way—its hinges groaned as loudly as the chains that raised the castle gate—and planted herself on the threshold. Before her, the pair on the bed froze in an outrageous tableau that only fueled Pamela's ire.

Bess half stood, half knelt beside Peter on his bed; she had only one foot on the floor. Her skirts were hiked up, exposing a naked knee that pressed into the mattress. As she leaned over the invalid, her plentiful bosom fairly brushed Peter's cheek as she held a costrel at his groin.

Peter's flat belly and well-muscled legs were fully exposed, his tunic drawn up above his hips. The sight of his bared limbs alone might have given Pamela pause, but what else she saw made her gasp. He was handling his own prick, which he had pointed down the throat of the two-handled cup Bess held.

"Pamela!" Peter exclaimed, ceasing abruptly the emptying of his bladder. Yet, Bess neither set aside the costrel nor backed away to stand on both her feet. She remained hovering over Peter as she stared at the unexpected intruder.

"What are you doing?" Pamela demanded of Bess, striding toward her.

"Helping my lord to piss."

"His arms are not broken." She grabbed the vessel from Bess's grasp and slammed it down on the trunk at the foot of the bed. "He could hold the cup himself."

"But—"

"But naught!" She leveled a chilling gaze at the servant. "If Lord Peter needed to relieve himself and his page, William, was nowhere about to aid him, you should have given him the cup and closed the bed hangings to allow the man his privacy. Have you no notion of propriety? Have you no shame?"

Bess finally slid off the bed and began sidling toward the doorway. "I meant no harm, milady. I didn't think it was wrong. 'Tis not as if I've never seen a man's cock before. Especially Lord Pe—"

"Enough!" he warned.

Bess glanced at him. "But, my lord, I—"

"Get out," Pamela ordered, pivoting on the balls of her feet and stalking slowly toward the doorway, forcing Bess to stumble backward.

"Pamela."

Ignoring Peter's entreaty, she kept pace with the servant until both had crossed the threshold. Then she grabbed Bess's sleeve and hustled her down the steps. Only when they'd reached the gallery did she let go, and only then to nudge the woman into a small, unoccupied chamber.

"I shan't have it," Pamela declared stiffly.

Bess's forehead furrowed. "What . . . ?"

"Your—your familiarities with Lord Peter. They're unacceptable, and I shan't have it."

"He can't get up, and he needed t' piss! What else should I have done?"

"I told you what you should have done! Is that your difficulty, Bess? You can't hear? Or do you not understand the words spoken to you?" Her voice had gone up a level in pitch and in volume.

"Lady Pamela, I don't understand your concern," Bess admitted. "I've done naught. Besides, I've known Lord Peter an' his brothers since we were all quite young. They're like brothers t' me, the both of them!"

"Don't lie to me! You'd never sleep with your own brother, yet I know you share my intended husband's bed! I saw you the night you returned to Fortengall Castle. You were in Lord Raven's arms. He kissed and—and fondled you!"

Bess had the good grace to blush. But before she could stammer out either a denial or an excuse, Pamela rushed on. She leaned close to the servant so that there was no need to raise her voice above a whisper.

"Lord Raven is away at this time, but beware, Bess. I'll not tolerate your sleeping with him when he returns. Not even before the marriage ceremony. If such were your plans, you'd best abandon them. As for Lord Peter, he is my cousin's betrothed. You may think he's free and willing because he's yet to say his vows and his bride-to-be is nowhere near, but think again. *I* am here, and I shall protect Roxanne's interests."

Inhaling a deep breath that appeared to increase the size of her breasts, Bess returned Pamela's steady gaze. "Milady, there's no need. I've not been with Lord Peter in many years. Not since before I wed. An' not since my husband died, either."

Pamela took half a step back and considered Bess appraisingly.

"What you said about Lord Raven an' me," she went on, " 'tis true. We were bein' a bit familiar with each other after I returned from carin' for my father. But it went no further, I vow. That night Peter took his fall, an' I ne'er saw the lord of Stonelee again. Besides, soon afterward I learned he's pledged to take you as his wife. I'd ne'er share my bed with him, knowin' he was soon to wed. Certainly, not after. Nor would I spread my legs for Peter.

"Lady Pamela," Bess pleaded, "you needn't threaten me! Sweet *Jesu*, Lady Lucinda would flay me alive if I did such with either of her sons, now that they're goin' t' take wives! Besides, I love the lady dearly, and would ne'er do ought which might displease her."

Pamela continued to study the servant for another long moment. Slanting her chin toward the door, she ordered at last, "Go. Should Lord Peter need assistance of a private nature, call on someone else to aid him. If his page or no other is near, call me. I'm obliged to tend him in my cousin's stead."

"Very well, milady." Bess bobbed her head respectfully and hurried out of the gallery chamber. Scurrying down the remaining steps leading to the great hall, she did not bump into Lady Lucinda, who stood on the stairs several steps above the gallery.

The earl's wife hadn't meant to listen to the young women's conversation. And Pamela was right to upbraid Bess, if she had cause to believe the maidservant made free with either Raven or Peter. Those three had been close as peas in a pod since first they met long years ago. And the games they played were not children's games. If their amusements continued, Pamela was correct that the time had come for them to cease.

Lucinda could not help wondering, though, why Pamela of Angleford was so concerned over Peter's behavior. She sensed the damsel's fury was not all on her cousin's behalf.

Heaving a heavy sigh, she retreated soundlessly up the stairs before Pamela emerged from the gallery room and encountered her. At the top of the steps, she entered the highest chamber in the keep.

Standing before the seat in the wide solar window, Lucinda gazed outside, beyond the bailey walls to the demesne that surrounded the castle. She wished she could confide her concerns to Ian, but he was gone away with her youngest sons, Hugh and the little twins, to visit his friend, Neville of Kurth.

"God's tears," she mumbled tiredly, turning and settling onto the cushions, the open window at her back. Raven was in Wales pursuing Peter's intended bride, whom he claimed to despise though Lucinda knew it wasn't so. Peter was lying abed with Raven's betrothed as his steady companion, while Pamela took the burden of Peter's care upon her shoulders as though it were her duty, when it was not. The threads of the king's hastily woven tapestry seemed to be unraveling.

In his room, Peter watched his door, which remained open, and wondered who would be the next to enter. Since Pamela had gone, taking Bess with her, he'd pulled down his tunic and tossed a rug over his lap. Modestly. Pamela's abrupt appearance, her catching him bared before Bess, had shamed him, even though all he'd been doing was pissing. Still, he felt as though the little lady of Angleford had caught him swiving the wench!

It was foolishness, Peter chided himself. Pissing was a natural act. And how, by God, was he going to perform this perfectly natural act, which should have been as easy as exhaling breath, with his broken leg bound and totally useless? Of course he needed assistance. He was no better off, at the moment, than a babe in swaddling! And why shouldn't Bess assist him? Christ, but they'd seen all of each other many times before. And then he *had* been plowing the wench! Now, he thought nothing of drawing out his cock in front of Bess for the purpose of relieving himself. God's teeth, it would have been nothing to either of them if she'd held it in her hand! 'Twasn't as though he could do anything *pleasurable* with it in his present state!

Peter's teeth clamped together, and he breathed hard through his nose. Who better to tend him than a trusted servant, an old, dear friend? What would Little Lady Pamela have him do otherwise? Would she be willing to set her virginal eyes on his naked loins in order that he find some relief? Would she dare wash his body, his chest, his legs, his buttocks? Would she hold not only a cup, but his prick, while he pissed? Would she?

He did not need to raise the covers to see what was happening to that very same appendage he'd been contemplating. Peter could feel it thickening against his thigh. The more he tried not to imagine Pamela wrapping her fingers around his sex, the clearer the vision became and the harder his manhood.

"God's bloody tears!" he ground out in frustration, bringing up his good leg and bending it at the knee. Cautiously, he tried to turn slightly on his side so that one thigh pressed down on the other. He hoped to squeeze the life out of his errant cock, but it had a will to thrive that surprised him.

Why did he think of Pamela? The Angleford lady wasn't his intended bride. She belonged to Raven! Little Lady Pamela would only be his sister-by-marriage; already, she seemed like the sister he'd never had. She sat with him when he was grumpy, played games with him when he was bored. They chatted away the long hours, sharing stories of their childhoods, their dreams, their beliefs. She asked him about Raven, his brother's character and habits; he asked her about Roxanne.

Pamela was good company. Despite her being painfully

young and solemnly mild-mannered, she could give as good as she got, at least with him. When Peter exhibited the petulance he believed was his right, under the present circumstances, she would have none of it. She forced him to be civil, if not entertaining, else she departed the chamber with a flounce, declaring she would return with his supper or to play a game of Nine Men's Morris only when he was prepared to be gracious again.

Truth was, Peter realized with a pang, he missed Little Lady Pamela when she deserted him. Other companionship did not quite do. His page, William, wasn't clever enough to play a good game of draughts; his young half brothers were so rambunctious he really feared one of them might crash onto his leg and break the bones again. And his mother! He would gladly die for her, but Lucinda of Fortengall could be a smothering tyrant when one of her own fell ill or injured. Often he wished he were recuperating at Stoneweather Keep. Then he realized Lucinda would have traveled there to tend him, if that was where he'd fallen.

But Pamela of Angleford . . . had the perfect touch. She indulged him when he needed it and scolded him when he needed that, too. She was clever and witty, and she had the most delightful giggle—something he'd first learned the evening he'd hauled her onto his lap and tickled her. She was pleasing to look at in the bargain. All in all, Little Lady Pamela made the perfect—

Sister. Peter filled in the blank, completing his thought the moment she came into view. He had not heard her footsteps on the stairs, but suddenly she stood in the doorway.

"My lord."

"There's no need to be so formal," he returned. "We will soon enough be kin, and"—he arched one eyebrow, continuing with a note of chagrin—"you've seen most all of me there is to see. I think that puts us on equal footing."

"Very well. Peter. May I come in?"

"What? You've given up bursting unannounced into people's private bedchambers?"

Peter bit his tongue. He'd meant to tease, not accuse. Yet, he could not take back the words as he'd voiced them.

Eyes downcast, Pamela said contritely, "You're right. I had no business coming into your room as I did. 'Tis why I've come again, to ask your forgiveness."

"I shan't grant it."

Her eyes flew open, and she hesitated on the threshold instead of entering the room.

"You've done naught that requires forgiveness," Peter explained quickly, concerned she might run off.

Pamela's fine, arched eyebrows came together in a frown. "But I did, my—ah, Peter. I burst into your room and reprimanded your servant. Even though Bess behaved badly, 'twasn't my place to chastise her."

He smothered a smile behind his hand. Ah, this wench could be deceiving. Appearing for all the world like the most innocent angel, when she believed she was in the right, she took a stand—even under the guise of issuing an apology.

"I shouldn't have had Bess assist me with that particular task. I should have sent for William, or demanded some privacy, at the very least. It must have looked—"

Peter left off when he saw Pamela's color heighten. "Please," he urged, "come sit by me. There's a stool nearby."

Hanging back a brief moment, Pamela closed the door and walked slowly into the room. Peter felt inordinately glad she was staying. Yet, it disheartened him to see her ignore the stool in favor of remaining on her feet some distance from the bed.

"Whatever it appeared," Pamela continued, " 'twas no business of mine. If Roxy wants to be sure no loose serving maid attempts to seduce you, she ought to be here to intervene."

"Seduce me?"

"Mayhap 'seduce' is too strong a word," she conceded. "Nonetheless, you are my cousin's business, not mine."

"Aye, that's true," he agreed. "But Roxanne is gone, as is Raven. And I thought we were friends?"

"Of course we're friends!" She seemed eager to confirm it. "I know you better than I know your brother, and I'm to marry him. Perhaps, though, that is why I reacted so strongly when I saw Bess touching you—touching your—" Unable to finish the sentence, she fell silent, eyelashes fluttering.

"Any lady would have been distressed to see us engaged as we were. I suppose I'm lucky 'twas you who came upon us first and not my lady mother!"

Pamela smiled. "I suppose you were. She'd think you a wastrel, after finding you the other night with me in your lap and my skirts nearly up to my—"

Again she let her remark go unfinished, another flood of crimson coloring her cheeks.

"Still"—determinedly she took a deep breath and continued—"though we are friends and each betrothed to a close relation, if I took it in my head to tryst with one of Fortengall's knights—say, perhaps, Sir Herbert—I would not expect you to censure me or call out that knight to defend my honor."

"You wouldn't?" Peter's eyebrows arched in surprise.

"Nay, I would not. Truth be told, I'd never do it. But if I did, 'twould be my business. Mayhap your brother's as well. But not yours."

Peter frowned thoughtfully as he considered Pamela with a scowl. A lady carrying on with a man always concerned someone else—her sire, her guardian, her husband. How could Pamela believe otherwise?

He deliberated pointing out this fact. But his counsel was sidetracked by images of Pamela cavorting with Herbert. Why Herbert? Did she consider that fair-haired, blue-eyed knight such a handsome fellow she actually *fancied* him?

Peter cleared his throat. Dropping his gaze to his immobile leg, which remained propped on a pillow in the exact position it had been in since the hour it was set and splinted, he said solemnly, "In defense of Bess, we've known each other quite a long time. She has, on prior occasions, seen me without my braies. 'Tis why it never occurred to us it might be deemed unseemly for her to aid me as she did. I'm glad," he added, "you pointed out the error of our thinking."

"You're not angry?"

"With you? Certainly not."

"Well"—Pamela smiled tightly as she rocked on her heels—"I suppose I'd best be going and let you rest." She turned away, but before taking a step she exclaimed, "Oh!"

"What is it?"

She turned back to Peter. "I forgot to tell you why I came up earlier. I've news. In two days' time your mother says you'll be able to get out of bed with the aid of crutches. No going below to the great hall, of course. But you will be able to visit the jakes on your own."

"Ah." He twiddled his fingers against his chest. "I'm pleased to hear it, and annoyed that I'm so pleased to have a pretty damsel bring me such news."

"Think on it this way," she suggested, her smile softening. "Bess will no longer be able to tempt you by offering her assistance with a cup. Spared such enticement, you'll more easily remain true to your betrothed."

Peter made no reply, not even when Pamela departed with a nod. But he was thinking hard.

Roxanne of Bittenshire is off, God knows where, most likely with my brother by this time. As she left me, I shouldn't think she'd require any explanations for my behavior. I doubt the wench cares a fig what I do, or with whom. And Little Lady Pamela doesn't care, she told me so herself!

Yet, he did not quite believe Pamela's professed disdain. It pleased him well the Angleford damsel cared what mischief he might be up to, and with whom.

But something did bother Peter. Interrupted by Pamela's

earlier intrusion, his bladder had never been completely emptied. Now it let him know the need was urgent.

"William!" he shouted, straining forward, away from his backrest of pillows. He hoped against hope the irresponsible young fellow was at his post in the hallway beyond. Pamela had closed the door behind her. He could not see. "William, I need you—now!"

The page did not respond to his call, and Peter fell back again. His pillows seemed to have rearranged themselves, and they were no longer comfortable. As well, his leg throbbed.

Glaring at the bedside table, he spied the bottle of potion and the spoon that his mother used to dose him when his broken bones pained. Pushing himself forward again, he reached out, straining to grasp the clay bottle. But his fingertips only grazed the vial—it might have been on the other side of the chamber, for all the good it was doing him.

"William! Curse you, boy, I want you in here now!"

Where was he? In the kitchens eating? In the stables playing? Or in the garderobe doing what he himself should be doing, standing on his own two feet, holding his own accursed prick in his hand, pissing like a man?

"William!" he bellowed, and at last the chamber door flew open, the towheaded lad rushing in breathlessly.

"Milord?" he asked, looking warily at Peter.

"I need a pot to piss in, and I need that damnable bottle on the table, and I need—"

He broke off, realizing that what he needed he had no right to ask for: Little Lady Pamela.

CHAPTER 17

"How fare Neville and Beatrice?" Peter inquired of his stepfather. He referred to the lord and lady of Kurth, whom Ian had recently returned from visiting.

"Good. However, their daughter's children seemed to be falling ill with some affliction, so Beatrice advised me to take my leave and return the lads to Fortengall. 'Twas why I cut my visit short."

"No doubt Mother is glad you've returned early. She's never quite at ease when you're away."

"Aye." Ian leaned forward on the stool he sat upon, bowing his large frame over his long legs. "Lucinda has always presumed that if I'm away from Fortengall, I'm putting myself in some sort of danger. She refuses to recognize that I've not been a mercenary knight since before she and I wed. Nor does she take into consideration that England has become a peaceful land in the years since King Henry replaced King Stephen on the throne."

The huge man let out a long sigh. "Nay, she suspects that

when I leave these bailey walls, 'tis with the purpose of engaging my sword with some villain or other, and purely for the excitement.'' Ian shot Peter a rueful smile. ''The woman does not see me for the old man I am. She thinks I still enjoy the thrill of combat, as if there were any thrill in that I once enjoyed.''

''She loves you as she's loved no other, and she worries about you. Be glad, my lord, my mother sees you only as handsome and virile, even if you think otherwise. No doubt she'll view you that way 'til the day you die.''

Ian nodded in agreement, and a silence fell between them.

Clearing his throat, Ian asked tentatively, ''Is there any young damsel who thinks you handsome and virile? Any wench who might love you enough to believe it even when you're aged and bent?''

Peter chuckled. ''I doubt it, Lord Ian. Even if such a woman exists, she's not confided in me.''

''What of Lady Pamela?''

''Lady Pamela?'' He furrowed his brow and looked at his stepfather askance.

''Aye. Since Raven left the castle to pursue her cousin, you've spent a great deal of time with the maid from Angleford. What do you think of her?''

''I think . . .'' Peter paused, lowering his gaze as he carefully considered his response. ''I think she is very nice.''

''That's all?''

''Aye.'' His eyes met the earl's. ''As well, of course, she's comely. And very pleasant company. I think she'll make Raven an excellent wife.''

''Do you!'' Ian boomed, smiling congenially. ''I think so, too. I told your mother, since you and Pamela seem to be getting on so well, she and Raven will manage nicely together also.''

''Mother's concerned?''

"Nay, not concerned. At least, no more than she always is about her children."

"Why?"

"Why," Ian repeated with a frown. "Peter, I believe Lucinda has noticed the considerable time you and Pamela spend together. She's been wondering if, mayhap, 'tis not a good thing for either of you. After all, you're pledged to Roxanne, and Pamela to Raven."

"Not good for us?" He cocked an eyebrow. "How is her entertaining me while I lie in this damned bed day after tiresome day not good for us? It's good for me, I'll tell you that!"

"Don't upset yourself, lad," the earl urged hastily.

But Peter was upset. He found he disliked discussing Pamela, and the fact that Lord Ian asked him about her was peculiar in the extreme. Certainly his mother had sent the earl on this mission because catching him with the damsel in his lap had aroused her suspicions.

And it had all been so innocent! He'd seen the ugly scratch on the tender flesh of her leg and had examined the wound. Why did his mother have to fret about such a trivial matter?

"How do you feel about Roxanne?"

Peter blinked. "How should I feel?"

"I don't know," Ian admitted with a shrug, hunching over his thighs and threading his fingers together. " 'Twould be understandable if you're angry with the wench for running off."

"Were it true that she fled simply because she could not bear to have me as her husband, I suppose I might be. But I've no doubt my brother, Raven, had more than a little to do with her going. I won't blame her for what was surely his doing."

"And Raven? Do you blame him?"

Exhaling loudly, Peter wished he were back on his feet and his twin back at Fortengall so that he might battle his brother with fists. He needed some brutal, physical outlet for his frustration, and Raven, curse the fool's harsh tongue, needed some sense knocked into his seemingly empty head.

"Aye. At least, I hold him accountable. 'Tis bad enough I'm abed with my injury. But because of him, my intended bride is missing, and he's gone, too, in search of her! Still," he added thoughtfully, "I know Raven's actions, whatever they've been, were born of brotherly concern. I cannot blame him either, for his misguided deeds."

"That's good." Lord Ian nodded and abruptly leaped to his feet. "Your mother and I would hate to see a rift grow between you two. We understand the king's edict abruptly altered both your lives. But it's not as though he demanded you wed some unseemly hags with paltry dowers. Henry seems to have done his best by all of you. I'll wager that in a year's time, you'll look back on all this with wry humor."

Peter smirked. "Do you?"

"Aye." Ian was already making his way to the door. "I'm sure you'll be as happy with Roxanne as you feel Raven shall be with Pamela."

He grabbed the latch and pulled open the door. "I'll leave you now to rest. Or should I send William in to you?"

"You mean the young wretch is there, outside the door?"

The earl peeked around the corner. When he turned back to Peter, he was smiling. "Aye, the lad's where he should be. Do you have need of him?"

"Nay. I'd prefer to be alone, milord."

He lied. He'd have preferred to be alone with Pamela. Like a ray of sunshine, she brightened his otherwise dreary days. How could he lie about, waiting idly, helplessly, for Raven to return with Roxanne, for all of them to sort things out and marry, if he did not have Little Lady Pamela, her stories and songs, her games and her giggles?

He couldn't, Peter decided. And he wouldn't.

* * *

"Ian, what did Peter say?"

Lucinda had been standing in their bedchamber doorway, waiting for her husband's approach. As soon as he appeared, she clutched his sleeve and posed her question.

"Very little. But enough to please you, sweetling." Patting her shoulder, the earl urged Lucinda into the room.

"What? What did you ask him? How did he answer?" she demanded as Ian heaved himself into his heavy, carved chair, which groaned under the assault.

"Peter thinks highly of Pamela and believes she'll make Raven a good wife. He is annoyed by his brother's actions but holds no grudge. As for Roxanne, he holds her blameless for abandoning him, knowing as we do that Raven in some way instigated her leaving."

Ian tugged off his shoes and kicked them aside. Leaning back in his chair, he stretched his legs and wiggled his toes.

Lucinda's gaze strayed from his face to his feet and back again. "That's it? You were gone all that while and that's all that was said?"

"Sweetling, what else is there?" He frowned up at her.

"You dallied in Peter's chamber for some time. There must be more!"

"We spoke of other things. My visit to Kurth Keep. You."

"Me?" Her hand flew to her heart.

"Your love for me, if you must know." Ian grinned, reached up, and took his wife's hand, pulling her down onto his lap.

When he began fondling her breast, she slapped his fingers away. "Ian, please! This matter is of great concern to me."

"There is no matter for you to be concerned about, Lucinda. True, the king's pronouncement and the two Welsh maidens abruptly transformed your sons' lives. But for the better, methinks. Peter thinks so, too, or so he led me to believe. Why can't you accept it?"

He kissed her temple. Though Lucinda did not resist, she did not respond to his attentions, either.

"But Roxanne running away, and Raven going after her . . ."

"How could Peter go after her, with his broken leg? Besides, they'll be returning any day. Surely Raven's caught up with the lady by now. Once they are back, all shall wed according to Henry's plan."

"You don't think it's unwise, Pamela spending so much time with Peter?" Lucinda turned her face to Ian's.

He kissed her on the nose. "Nay, not at all. Peter enjoys her company. The poor man would probably be quite bored if Pamela didn't entertain him."

"But, Ian, I caught her on Peter's lap! Her skirts were up—"

"Didn't you tell me she has a bad scratch on her leg, and Peter said he was examining it? How else could he look at the wound if he did not raise her skirts a bit?"

Lucinda exhaled loudly and shook her head. "You don't understand."

"*You* don't understand," he corrected sternly. "Sweetling, Peter and Pamela are friends. Better they should be allies than adversaries, like Raven and Roxanne, eh? Now, let it go."

"Very well."

"Dearest." Ian's eyes narrowed as he considered his wife's frowning countenance. "You ask for my advice, and then you plot to counter it. Why did you have me speak with Peter if you don't wish to accept what he said?"

"I'm not plotting," she argued, lowering her eyes guiltily and ducking her head beneath her husband's chin to rest her cheek on his shoulder. "If you insist, I'll accept Peter and Pamela's relationship as that of simple friendship. But you mentioned Raven and Roxanne—they've both been gone many days. I ne'er expected 'twould take so long for them to return."

"She's clever, that girl is, and determined, too. Probably, she made Raven work hard to find her. But he has found her by now, most certainly," Ian assured Lucinda as he stroked her cheek with his thumb.

Her breath blew warm and moist through the earl's tunic, onto his skin. "That's most likely true," Lucinda agreed softly. "But we've no idea how they've gotten on since Raven overtook Roxanne. There could be trouble on that score."

"There is no trouble. At worst, Raven has the maid trussed up like a prisoner of battle as he carries her back to Fortengall Castle. She may well be furious with him. But in the end, that will be to everyone's advantage."

"How?"

"She'll be so pleased to be free of Raven, she'll thankfully take Peter to husband without further complaint."

"I pray you're right and that nothing else happens to further delay the nuptials."

"Naught will happen," Ian insisted. "I am the earl here, and I command it to be so."

Pamela sat on a stool in her chamber, clad only in a shift and bed robe, running her fingers through the waves her braids had crimped into her long, light-brown tresses. Her scalp prickled, so she dropped her head forward, scratching her head with the sort of delight many an old, fat lord felt when he scratched his plump belly.

She smiled languidly as she sat upright again, stretching her arms overhead and flinging her hair over her shoulders so that it settled in silken coils against her back. She had recently left Lord Ian's table, pleasantly full from a good meal and pleasantly tired from a day of activity. Not since her mother passed away had Pamela been called upon to handle so many of a chatelaine's duties. She'd enjoyed the toil, but even so, she wondered what had prompted Lady Lucinda to ask for her assistance instead of refusing it. Perhaps it was due to the lady's preoccupation with her three youngest children. While dining with Lord Ian and his seneschal, Pamela had learned the earl's wife was fussing over the boys, who did not seem their usual, spirited selves after returning home with their father.

She missed Peter. Except for a brief visit that morning, before Lady Lucinda caught up with her and suggested a dozen matters she might assist with, Pamela had not spent any time with her bedridden friend. She had lingered after the evening meal in prolonged conversation with the earl and Master Frederick and had not made time to tell Peter a story, or sing him a song, or even to bring him his supper tray. He must be, she thought, quite bored and feeling singularly neglected.

Feeling guilty, Pamela impulsively picked up a candle and opened her chamber door. The corridor appeared empty and eerily quiet. Were it not for the burning torches in their braces on the wall, and the lingering scents of cooked meats still wafting up the stairs, the castle seemed almost deserted. Confident she would not be noticed skulking about in her nightclothes, Pamela tiptoed up the cold stone steps to Peter's room.

He heard her coming. It galled him to admit it, but he had been listening for her all day long. Her footsteps were nearly silent, but he caught the sound of her bare feet padding across the stones even before her melodic voice called from beyond the door, "Peter? Are you awake still?"

He considered staying quiet, feigning sleep, to punish her for ignoring him. But he couldn't resist the opportunity to see her. "Aye," he answered. And then the door opened, the hinges creaked like old bones, and Pamela peeked inside his room, holding her candle aloft.

"Am I disturbing you?"

Aye. "Nay."

She came forward, and as Peter peered at her through a narrow opening in the bed curtains, he sucked in his breath. Pamela looked like a Yuletide angel with her glistening hair streaming in loose waves to her waist, and the long, bell-shaped sleeves of her saffron robe covering all of her hands but her nails. The tie cinching her waist emphasized its small circumference; as well, it held the light fabric of her robe close to her body, accentuating her pert bosom.

He snapped his eyes shut as he muffled a groan.

"Peter? You're not ill, are you?"

"Nay, I'm accursedly well. In truth, there's naught I'd like better at this moment than to saddle my destrier and head out for a long ride!"

"You sound strange," she informed him before she halted abruptly, having encountered William's body sprawled upon a pallet on the floor.

Peter rolled his head against the pillow and spied her looking down at the sleeping page. "Ignore him. He won't wake, I assure you."

"But our voices—"

"If the squeaking hinges didn't disturb him, I doubt our voices could penetrate the lad's clogged ears. If I blew a hunting horn at his head, I suspect 'twould fail to wake young William!"

Pamela stepped over the boy and set her candle down on the table. "You're angry with me, aren't you?"

"No." At the moment, Peter's feelings toward the lady of Angleford were many. None involved anger.

"You are angry, and you've every right," she insisted, parting the curtains farther and slipping between them to sidle onto the bed beside Peter. "Ever since Roxy and Raven left the castle, and you've been forced to lie abed with your injury, I've kept you company as best I could. But today I didn't. I'm sorry."

"Why didn't you?"

"I was very busy." She smiled happily. "Peter, your mother begged my aid! So often I've implored her to let me help with some small task, and always she's declined my offers. But today she sought me out, as though I were truly her daughter.''

"Did she?''

Pamela nodded. "Lady Lucinda had me running from one end of the keep to the other, from the solar to the scullery and back again.''

"And this evening?''

"Oh." She bowed her head contritely. "Lord Ian asked that I stay with him and Master Frederick at the high table, even when supper was done.'' Pamela's head came up again. "I think because, with Roxanne gone and your mother occupied elsewhere, the earl wished a bit of feminine companionship.''

Peter sniffed the air and caught the sweet fumes of mulled wine on Pamela's breath. "My mother is meddling, and Lord Ian's abetting her,'' he complained.

"Meddling? What makes you suspect that?''

"As I explained to you once before, Pamela, the castle keep will run just fine without you lending a hand. Besides, my mother should have been seated at the high table with her husband. Why wasn't she?''

"I fear your young brothers may not be feeling well. She was tending them.''

"Oh?'' Peter felt a little ashamed. If Hugh, James, and John were ill, then, mayhap, Pamela's absence had not all been contrived.

She nodded, gracing him with an apologetic smile, and Peter quickly forgot about everything save this damsel. With the hangings draped about the bed, it seemed as though they were in a tent. Alone in a tent, on a dark night, with only a sliver of silver moon to dispel the gloom.

His eyes scanned her face, her throat, her—in the thin candle-light from beyond the curtains, he saw that the edge of Pamela's robe had parted to reveal a hint of bosom above her flimsy, linen shift. He felt a rush, hot and tingling, surge through his nether regions.

Pamela is my sister! he reminded himself, closing his eyes against her innocent beauty. *My sister-by-marriage. Almost. And already, my friend. That's all. That's all she will ever—*

"Peter, are you certain there's nothing wrong besides your leg?"

He heard Pamela's words, but more, he felt her warm breath against his cheek.

Snapping open his eyes again, he found himself staring into hers. The amber orbs seemed to draw into them all the light there was, so that they glowed luminescently. Peter had a sudden urge to kiss the lady's eyes.

"I assure you, I'm well enough," he insisted gruffly. "On the morrow, when I have my crutches, I'll run up and down the castle steps."

"I doubt that. But you will be able to get around a bit, that's for certain." Tenderly, she smoothed the covers over Peter's chest and splinted limb. "I think it's best you get some sleep now. 'Twasn't my intention to disturb you at this hour. I only wished to explain my absence and say good night."

She grabbed the curtain, parting it, about to slip away. But Peter grabbed her other hand. "Sing to me," he begged.

"I cannot!" Pamela shook her head and frowned. "My caterwauling would surely wake William."

"You have a pretty voice. It soothes me. Please sing to me until I sleep. If you're really so worried you'll wake that useless page, then lie beside me and sing softly in my ear."

She hesitated a long moment. Then, with a nod, she agreed. "Very well," she said, snuggling down beside him, taking care not to bump his injured leg as she settled herself in the crook of his arm.

She sang a song in Welsh. Peter didn't understand a word, but he would have listened to Lady Pamela singing the whole night through, had he been able.

He was not able, though it wasn't he who fell asleep. Pamela drifted off, and for a long while, Peter lay there contemplating every gentle contour of her pixie face.

When the lord himself fell asleep, the lady still slumbered beside him.

CHAPTER 18

Prince Balin's home was neither castle nor keep but a hall, the sort King Henry presently restricted his nobles to building. A long, low structure of timber and stone, outbuildings and huts surrounded it. In another place, the structure would have been encircled by high walls for defense. But Penllyn Hall required no such barriers to keep enemies at bay, for it sat high on the side of a mountain. None could reach it without being spied from the watchtowers. And those at the hall had the advantage over invaders, for Welsh archers were the greatest in all the world. They had the finest longbows, the strongest arms, the truest aim, and their arrows flew better in downward flight than angled toward the sky.

Roxanne knew she would be expected. Not because Hywella had told her so, but because she knew she would be seen by her cousin's men long before she reached the road, the last leg of her journey. Yet, despite her rush to get there, Roxanne paused alongside the stream she had used as her guide to Penllyn Hall. Perched on her stallion's back, she looked out at the view, at the morning sun creeping higher behind the mountains to the east. The buttery yellow light deepened the fragile shades of color coming back to the land, and it set to sparkling the water coursing down the stream.

This place, the heart of Penllyn, was nearly the most beautiful place in the world. Perhaps it was the most beautiful, and only her emotions allowed Bittenshire to vie with it. But Roxanne knew she could happily live out her days here, as Balin's wife, as his children's mother.

That thought spurred her to hurry forward again. When she saw the pennants with their red dragons, Cymru's oldest emblem, waving in the breeze above the towers, her heart fluttered as lightly as the silk fabric did in the wind.

Obeying his rider's command, Dafydd rushed headlong into the stream, splashing water onto Roxanne's bared legs, her skirts, and her bodice. But she smiled happily as they took to the rough road that snaked the final span to the Cymry prince's home.

"Lady Roxanne, is that you?" the first mounted guard she encountered called out in their native tongue.

" 'Tis I, Gawain, returned from that accursed land called England!" She beamed, flashing her teeth, as he turned around to join her, keeping their horses apace.

"Balin said you'd be coming. He rode out on some business, but we were advised it wouldn't take him long. He asked that I give you his greetings."

Roxanne's heart leaped. Mayhap Hywella truly was a witch!

"How long has he known I was bound for Penllyn Hall?"

Gawain shrugged. "Since the watch first spied you and notified him. He went out to look for himself, while his horse was being saddled, and he said to me, 'Gawain, I'll be damned, but it looks as though that is my cousin, Roxy, headed up the mountain.' As I told you, he'd have stayed to welcome you himself, but some pressing matter demanded his attention."

Roxanne felt a twinge of disappointment. Quickly, she

shrugged off the one emotion that was not ebullient. "I'm so glad to be home!"

"Home?"

"Cymru, Gawain, Cymru! All this land is my home, not just Bittenshire."

As soon as she neared the hall's front entrance, Roxanne leaped off Dafydd's back and tossed her reins to a servant. "Is Melwyd at home?" she inquired. When Gawain nodded, she rushed inside and called out to her cousin, Balin's sister.

"Roxy, it is you!" Melwyd greeted her with a kiss on each cheek and took her hands in her own. "I thought I'd heard speculation that you'd been spied riding toward Penllyn Hall. I believed the watch's eyes deceived him. Why aren't you in England? Isn't that where you're supposed to be?"

Roxanne looked at Melwyd, whose dark blue eyes and pale blond hair were so much like Balin's. "I fled. I escaped."

"What?" The princess, who was no older than their cousin, Pamela of Angleford, gasped in surprise. "Why? What happened?"

"I'll tell you all, but will you feed me first?"

Melwyd ordered food and drink brought to her cousin, and the two ladies sat down at a plank table. While she ate, Roxanne gave Melwyd a brief accounting of that which had transpired since King Henry ordered her and Pamela to London.

"I cannot believe it." Melwyd shook her fair head slowly. "I understand why the English king felt obliged to find husbands for you and Pamela. The lords of Bittenshire and Angleford have always been Norman, beholden to the English monarch. The reigning sovereign must see to the welfare of their orphaned children, especially unwed daughters. But why would he foist English lords on you two? Surely there are eligible sons of other Marcher Lords, sons of mixed blood, sons whose heritable lands lie in Cymru."

"Because the Angevin bastard rules most of the Christian world!" Roxanne exclaimed. "He hopes to rule all the isle before he dies, and if he does, Cymru will be swallowed up by England. He has no sense of our separateness, that we are not all descended of Saxon or Norman blood, but mostly sons and daughters of Celts with our own tongue and our own ways. Melwyd, I've no doubt he handed Pamela and me to those brothers—they are, in fact, twins—simply because it was the easiest way to get us off his hands. He doesn't know us; he does not care how miserable we would be, tied to English lords living on English soil."

"Twins?" Melwyd's eyebrows arched upward before she suggested hurriedly, "Have some more wine. Calm yourself. You're safe now, Roxy.

"But what of Pamela? Why did she not return with you?"

Roxanne swallowed a large draught of apple wine and tilted back her head to look up at the rafters. "She's resigned to her fate. Besides, if she weds Raven of Stonelee, they must return to Angleford so that the knave can rule there as its lord. Whereas I'd be forced to live out my days at Lord Peter's keep, a place in the south of England he calls Stoneweather."

Melwyd eyed Roxanne curiously. "You said 'if' Pamela weds Raven of Stonelee. Why would she not, if she is so resigned?"

"Because Raven is the one who followed me back to Cymru! The beast left her to come after me. Now, who knows what will happen?"

"But I thought . . . Roxy, I'm confused. I presumed the lord Henry ordered you to marry followed you to Cymru."

"Nay." She shook her head impatiently. "Peter of Stone-weather had a fall and broke his leg. Raven accused me of pushing his brother off the bailey wall. I'd no choice but to leave Fortengall Castle, their parents' stronghold, after such an accusation. So I slipped away in the dark of night and rode toward home. But Pamela's betrothed came after me."

"Why?" Melwyd's eyes widened with curiosity.

"I don't know why!" Roxanne snapped. "He just did. It

makes no sense to me, either, but he was not inclined to explain to me the reasons behind his pursuit.''

"Raven of Stonelee, the lord who is to wed Pamela, is the man you spent last night with in an abandoned bough hut?''

"Yes.''

"Roxy!'' The younger woman gasped.

"Don't act so shocked. It's not as if it were my idea. I— we—had no choice. The weather was foul, it was nearly night. We were lucky to find shelter at all.''

"But . . . alone with a man, a man not your husband nor even a relation!'' Melwyd leaned closer to her cousin and asked in a whisper, "Is he old? Is he ugly?''

Roxanne said nothing, but her mind raced. Raven, old? Raven, ugly? He was as far from either as Balin was. Yet he was as far from Balin as God from the devil.

"Well? Is this Lord Raven too old to satisfy a woman, least of all a young wife? Is he so dreadful to look upon, he might frighten a woman into bearing a dead babe? What?''

Roxanne did not answer. At that moment, the prince himself strode into the hall.

He scanned the dim interior of the dwelling until he spied Roxanne sitting at the table with his sister. Quickly, he made his way through the myriad of servants and relations also in the hall, and stood before her.

"Balin!'' Roxanne sprang up, threw herself at him, and hugged him hard. For a moment he stood stiffly, arms akimbo, until, at last, he wrapped his own arms gently about her.

"Balin, I am so glad to see you! I am so glad to be here! I feared I'd ne'er see Cymru again, let alone you.''

"I thought Henry had married you off.'' Balin stepped back, resting his hands on Roxanne's shoulders.

"She refused to wed an English lord,'' Melwyd piped up, rising and joining the couple. "She ran away.''

"What?''

Roxanne looked into Balin's handsome face. His expression was hard.

"Aye, it's true. But the brother of the man Henry declared I should wed urged me to go. He threatened me if I dared to wed his twin. And though he himself is supposed to marry Pamela, the bastard followed me back to Cymru!"

"Why would he do that, if he wanted you gone?"

"She doesn't know," Melwyd eagerly supplied. "But she spent—"

Melwyd did not finish the sentence because Roxanne kicked her ankle sharply.

"Lord Peter, who I am supposed to wed, had an accident. He cannot travel. I suppose he sent his brother, Raven, after me. Certainly Raven would not have followed me for any other reason. He hates me as much as I hate him!"

Roxanne intended to put as much enthusiasm into the last of her speech as she could. To her own ears, however, she sounded less than emphatic.

Balin did not appear to notice the uncertainty in her voice. Releasing Roxanne, he rubbed his brow with his fingers and thumb and looked down at the floor.

"What is it?" she asked anxiously. "Balin, I thought you'd be pleased I'd returned unwed."

"Where's Pamela?" he asked sharply.

She blinked. "Pamela remains in England at a place called Fortengall Castle. The parents of the two brothers Henry desires us to wed reside there."

"Ian of Fortengall is your betrothed's sire?"

"He is not my betrothed. You—" Roxanne broke off, silenced by the unfamiliarly hard glint in Balin's eye. "The earl is stepfather to Lords Peter and Raven, aye."

"By all the merciful gods." His expression grew darker as he strode away and then back to Roxanne and Melwyd.

"Why? What is it?" Roxanne clutched Balin's sleeve.

"Nothing."

"You lie!"

The prince arched one warning eyebrow.

"Then—then you are not telling me all," she insisted softly, searching his face for a hint of pleasure at her being there.

But he continued to scowl. "Why is Pamela still with her betrothed and his family, and not here at Penllyn with you?"

"She didn't want to come," Melwyd informed her brother. "Roxy says she has quite accepted her fate, even though the men—did you hear Roxy mention they are twins? Even though they are both old and horrid to look upon."

"Melwyd!" Roxanne snapped, glaring at her cousin.

"They cannot be so old," Balin informed his sister, "if they are the sons of the earl of Fortengall's lady wife. I'd judge them to be in their prime." His eyes darted from Melwyd to Roxanne. "If Pamela remains and weds the lord Henry has given her to, then they'll both be returning to Angleford Keep, shan't they? How long, Roxy, before you expect them to arrive at Arthur's keep?"

"You've not been listening to me, either of you!" Frustrated, she looked back and forth between brother and sister, prince and princess. "Henry decreed I should wed Peter of Stoneweather. He is now at Fortengall Castle confined to bed with a badly broken leg. Pamela is betrothed to Raven of Stonelee, but he's not in England, planning his marriage to our cousin. The scoundrel's hot on my trail, with the intention of taking me back to England to wed his brother!"

The scowl faded from Balin's face and he blinked, as though seeing Roxanne for the first time. "That's good. Their wedding will be delayed at least until he—Lord Raven, is it? At least until he returns. And one man alone . . . Roxy, how far behind you is he?"

"Not far enough."

"A day's ride? Two?"

"Two, I would think. He's lost in Cymru, and his mount is a huge warhorse unsuitable for riding in the mountains."

Balin chuckled. "This, from a lady who rides her own huge stallion?"

"But Dafydd was born and bred here. He's as Cymry as you or I and familiar with the land. Besides, he's not near as huge as Raven's destrier."

"Let us hope his horse breaks a leg, falls, and crushes the wicked lord beneath him," Melwyd suggested merrily. "Then you two can wed, and—"

"Sister, shut your mouth!" Balin ordered, and the young girl complied immediately. He stared hard at her for a moment, as though trying to convey a silent message. When he looked at Roxanne, his glance was wary.

"I would speak with you in greater detail about your adventure," he told her. "But I fear I've much to do this day. I should return by the evening meal. We'll talk then."

Balin pressed a dry kiss to Roxanne's forehead. It was far less than she'd expected, but she hid her disappointment.

When he stepped back, he perused her garb with a critical eye. "It appears your journey was a hard one. The stream is still rather cold for bathing, but I suppose Melwyd can see some water is heated for you to have a wash."

"I'm Cymry," Roxanne declared, attempting to deny the Norman blood, the English blood, that flowed through her veins. "The stream will serve me as well as it serves you."

"That's my Roxy." Balin winked, and her heart did a little flip-flop. He loved her still.

Raven reached Penllyn Hall midafternoon. He was livid, more at himself than Roxanne, for having let her slip away. But, despite their crude accommodations, it had been cozy snuggling up with the wench. He had slept the sleep of the dead until the lack of her warm body beside his brought him awake with a shiver.

He could not know how long she'd been gone; barely first

light when he woke, he'd set out hurriedly. But he did not overtake her.

It mattered not, though, because Raven knew where she was headed. And Thomas of Bittenshire had drawn him a map with landmarks to guide him. He had also advised Raven to approach the prince of Penllyn's abode on foot, not on horseback, and via a circuitous route. That route had brought Raven near Balin's stronghold by approaching from higher up the mountain, behind and above the hall. When he spied the place, unprotected by walls or moat, he understood why the Welsh chieftain did not need such fortifications. A single man, afoot, could—slowly, arduously—make his way almost to the top of this mountain and down again. But an army could not. An army could only march straight up to Penllyn's front door, and the guards, armed with their wicked longbows, would keep the warriors from getting too close.

The sun, which to Raven's surprise had remained shining the entire day, was damnably hot by this afternoon hour. Combined with his strenuous climbing and hiking, and the weight of his quilted gambeson and hauberk, he was sweaty and itching. When he detected the certain sounds of a nearby stream gurgling down the hillside, he made his way to it.

Raven spied no one in the vicinity, laundering or fetching drinking water. Cautiously, he stripped off his shirts and covered his sword with them, leaving all on the bank. Then, his dagger clamped between his teeth, he walked into the stream.

The icy water shriveled his manhood when it lapped Raven's crotch, yet he happily doused his head, his arms, and his naked chest. He felt so refreshed, he nearly forgot the untenable circumstances that had brought him to this accursed land.

Giggling. Voices. Female laughter and chatter.

Raven's ears pricked up like a wolf's, and he looked downstream to the source of the sounds. He could not see the Welsh women who conversed in that confounded language he would never understand. But he knew they were nearby. Cautiously,

Raven retreated from the stream, cursing the splashing noises his strides through the water made. Immediately he dressed, strapping his sword belt to his waist.

The breeze must have carried the women's voices from afar, because it was some distance downstream that Raven finally spied them. He saw two, one a young damsel sitting on the shore. She had shining yellow hair and was garbed more finely than any Welsh peasant would be. Raven knew her to be a lady and suspected she might be kin to the prince of Penllyn.

But the other wench captured his rapt attention. In water that reached only her knees, stood Roxanne of Bittenshire. She was nude. Finally, Raven had the opportunity to determine if her small waist made her seem so deliciously curvaceous or if she were more endowed than most maidens of her years.

Crouching in the underbrush, he watched as Roxanne pranced, kicking water toward the girl on the bank. She bent over to scoop up handfuls, which she spilled over her breasts, and knelt so that the water lapped at her belly and ribs. Then, jumping up and springing high, she laughed as she waved her hands overhead, which caused her breasts to jiggle and bounce.

Raven's balls hurt. His cock hardened so, he imagined it might poke a hole through his braies. If he kept watching Roxanne, he expected he would shoot his seed right into the bush he hovered behind. But *Jesu,* what man wouldn't?

He continued to watch as Roxanne stretched on her back, floating in the shallow stream to rinse herself clean. He watched as she stood and ran, spewing a glistening wave in her wake when she scampered to the shore. And he listened as she chatted with her friend in that curious tongue. He did not detest the language so much when he heard Roxanne speak it. Somehow it suited her. In fact, this wild, mountainous country and the frolic in a crisp, cold stream under an unseasonably warm, mellow sun, suited her. Roxanne was as wild, robust, and vigorous as the land she obviously loved so well.

But he would take her from it. He had to. Not for Peter's sake. Not even for King Henry's. For his own.

"It was good you waited to bathe," Melwyd told Roxanne as she handed her cousin a drying towel. "The days are warming up nicely now, but it takes some time. If you'd come down here this morn, you'd have frozen your nipples off."

Roxanne threw back her head and laughed.

"What's so amusing?"

"I can imagine it, my nipples hard as small, round icicles hanging from a door lintel. I could just reach down and snap them off, tossing them away." As she spoke, Roxanne pulled one nipple taut, as though she were trying to break it off her breast.

She had no idea the effect she had on the voyeur in the bushes.

"You are glad to be back in Cymru," Melwyd observed. "I've never before seen you quite so light-hearted."

"I escaped the devil's clutches," Roxanne replied, seeing Raven's face in her mind. She pulled on her shift and reached for her under tunic. "You'd be feeling merry if you'd escaped a monster, too."

"Glad I am I shan't have to worry about it." Melwyd toyed with a twig for a moment before looking up at Roxanne. "Balin's given his blessing to my wedding Owain."

"Owain!" Roxanne stopped in the middle of lacing her bliaut side seam. "That's wonderful news."

She grinned. "He's meeting me here soon."

"Melwyd!" She scowled at her cousin as she knotted her ties and reached for her girdle. "Why didn't you warn me? I've been cavorting like a mermaid in the sea. He might have seen me naked!"

"He only has eyes for me."

"Oh!" Feigning wrath, Roxanne shook her wet head and

shot her damp towel at Melwyd. "Well, I'd best hie myself off to the hall then, to let you have some privacy." She yanked on her shoes. "Does Balin know you two meet?"

"No. And you'd best not tell him. He thinks we only see each other while chaperoned."

"I trust this wedding is coming soon, before a babe does."

"We don't—I never—it's not like that, Roxy!"

"Mayhap not yet, but it could be, if you keep meeting secretly," the older girl advised. Even as she warned Melwyd, Roxanne thought of Raven pressed against her in their makeshift bed. "Will you be long?" she asked.

"I'll be back before supper."

"I'll see you then." Picking up the towel once again, Roxanne left the bank and walked toward Penllyn Hall.

Raven did not follow Roxanne. He knew she would go to Prince Balin's abode, and he considered the opportunity the other wench afforded him by lingering alone at the stream. The situation was precarious, full of potential, fraught with danger, so he did not form a plan. But he had the kernel of an idea in his mind, so he lingered.

He felt his nebulous hopes dashed when a young man joined the girl. Not really anxious to watch them swiving, Raven was relieved when their amorous indulgences went no further than fondling and kissing with their tongues. This couple also chatted in Welsh, so he could not determine their identities. But Raven felt certain the damsel was highborn. If he had any luck, she'd be a close relation of Balin's. Someone the Welsh prince would not sacrifice for Roxanne, not even if he loved the damsel from Bittenshire.

CHAPTER 19

Roxanne expected to feel a flush of warmth when Balin joined her at the high table. She did not, and she knew a niggling concern over Melwyd's absence. The princess hadn't returned since Roxanne left her at the stream.

"Where's my sister?" Balin inquired.

"Which one?"

He gave Roxanne a look. True enough, the hall was crowded with Balin's younger siblings. But they both knew the particular one to whom he referred. "Melwyd, of course," he said.

In the space of a heartbeat, Roxanne decided not to tell him the truth. She cherished the rare moments she and Balin were alone together; Melwyd and Owain had a right to enjoy their own precious moments.

"I believe she said she had a headache," Roxanne fibbed. "Probably, she is lying down. Should I check?"

Balin's eyes scanned the curtained chambers along the far wall. "Nay. It is noisy enough in this place during the meal hour. If her head hurts, taking to her bed will do little enough to ease the pain."

Platters and bowls were passed down the length of the master's table, at which Roxanne and Balin sat. Everyone ate with gusto, and there was much conversation. Much, among others. Little, between the two.

"Where did you go today?" Roxanne finally asked Balin as they lingered over the last of their meal.

"Roxy." He sighed, and his startling blue eyes met her softer, violet-tinged ones. "Roxy, I will speak with you of what took me off this day. But first I must know your intentions."

"My intentions?"

Balin nodded. "Regarding King Henry's decree. He declared his wish that you wed that English lord—"

"Peter of Stoneweather."

"Yes. Yet you fled him. And now his brother is after you, intending to take you back."

"So?" She felt an anxious knot twisting in her chest.

"If you do not return before Henry learns what you've done, it will go hard on your family."

Roxanne had never thought of that, not once. All she'd thought of was herself, and how she could not wed an Englishman and live on English soil. Never had it occurred to her that Henry would deal harshly with her sisters and their families when she failed to obey his edict.

"They—they can disown me. It was hardly my family's doing that I fled from my bridegroom. Besides . . ."

"Besides what?"

"It was Peter's brother who ordered me gone! He accused me, falsely, of trying to kill Peter and threatened to murder me if I dared go through with the marriage. Could the foolish knave who rules England actually blame my sisters for me fleeing under such circumstances? Could he even blame me?"

Balin nodded thoughtfully, pushing aside the remains of his meal.

"Still. Assuming you could explain to him your motives for running away, and assuming he accepted them as valid, Henry would still feel obliged to arrange another match for you."

"To another English lord?" Roxanne screeched in horror. "I won't! I refuse! Besides, you and I—"

Balin stood abruptly and grabbed her wrist, pulling her up with him. "Come outside," he demanded. "With me."

She had fantasized about such an invitation since she'd ridden away from Fortengall Castle. But now that he presented the opportunity, Roxanne found it wanting.

Still, she went with Balin as they picked their way through the crowded hall until they reached the main portal. Outside, she matched his long strides until they'd gone well beyond the nearest outbuildings and the glow of the torches burning in the yard. If the night were not starry, Roxanne couldn't have seen Balin's face, even though he stood directly before her. Fortunately, the moon shone down, lighting his handsome features.

"Roxy," he began softly, "you know I loved you when I was a lad. I always wished to make you a princess just as Rhiannon, your mother, was born a princess."

Roxanne's heartbeat quickened. Music from a harp in the hall drifted out to them, and she felt the plaintive melody wrap itself around them. Suddenly, the evening seemed romantic.

"I still love you, Balin."

"I know." His smile was quick, and then it was gone. He took both her hands and held them against his chest. "But my father's gone, like my mother before him, so I rule Penllyn now. And things have changed."

His words shattered her illusion of romance. "Changed?" Roxanne repeated, her voice cracking. "How have they changed?"

"My concerns are greater than they used to be when I was merely the chosen heir. I can no longer put my own desires first. I must put my people's needs first."

Her heart thudded. "Do you believe, as your wife, I wouldn't put the people of Penllyn first? *Jesu*, Balin! Pamela keeps insisting I've English blood in my veins. But I don't. I'm a child of Cymru!''

"Don't do this." He shook his head, tightening his lips into a thin line, and glanced distractedly at the sky above.

It pained Roxanne that Balin avoided looking directly at her. "Don't do what?" Her voice was thin. "Don't love you?"

Slipping her hands from beneath Balin's, she slid them up to his shoulders and then around his neck. He looked down at her when she did this, and Roxanne immediately took advantage of the opportunity by raising herself on tiptoe. She kissed him hard and passionately, probing his lips with her tongue.

For a moment, Balin did not respond. He stood rigidly straight in her embrace. But her ardor drew a moan from deep in his throat, and the prince at last grasped her to him.

Despite his belated enthusiasm, something seemed sorely amiss. Roxanne had always felt delighted, excited, when they had kissed before. Now kissing him seemed only a challenge, and the reward—his returning her purposeful ardor—less than satisfying.

"I must think." Balin suddenly released her and strode away, giving Roxanne his back. "I will admit, Roxy, that it is not so easy being a ruler as I had once believed."

Following him, she urged, "Talk to me, please. Tell me what's wrong. You said you'd tell me where you went today. Where did you go, Balin?"

"To meet with the leaders of my army."

"What?" She ran around him so that she could look Balin in the eyes. "What army?"

"A force of warriors from Penllyn."

"Warriors? You mean shepherds and farmers who pick up horns and weapons to rush down out of the hills and attack the Marcher Lords? Those sort of warriors?"

"Yes. Precisely."

Roxanne took a step backward. Her mind filled with a flurry

of thoughts punctuated by memories of random comments Balin had made since her return.

"Penllyn has been a peaceful principality for many years, Balin," she said. "Since my mother wed Cedric, and Pamela's mother wed Arthur, none of the English lords ruling the borderlands have dared attack Penllyn. None would now. Whom do you fear, Balin?"

"I fear no one."

Her heart felt as though it were clutched in an ever-tightening fist. "Who, then, do you plan to attack?"

His eyes held Roxanne's, and for the space of several moments he did not reply. But she knew his answer before he spoke it, for only one barony of any consequence bordered the land of Penllyn.

"Angleford," he said.

"Angleford!" A simmering rage boiled over when Balin confirmed Roxanne's darkest suspicion. Flying at him, she pummeled her fists against his chest. "You dare to steal Pamela's birthright from her?"

"The first lord of Angleford stole that land from the prince of Penllyn!" he ground out, grabbing her wrists. "Now's the perfect time to retrieve it. The keep is a strong one, and once I secure it, it shall serve this Prince of Penllyn well!"

"You—you—" She pushed herself away from him. "You are doing this for your own glory, Balin! You'll risk the peace and your people's lives all for your own eminence!"

"Nay, it is for my people's sake I do this!"

"What of Pamela, our cousin? My parents kept her lands in trust so that she would have them upon her marriage. Angleford is hers, Balin, hers! Yet, you stand there, callously informing me you intend to take it from her!"

"She will not care, Roxanne," he insisted, taking a step that brought him near to her again. "You know Pamela better than I, and even I know she'll be content wherever her husband wishes to keep her. She's not like you; she doesn't love the land. Besides, were she to wed and reign as chatelaine of Angleford Keep, the stronghold would not be hers. It would belong to her husband, that same English lord you claim to loathe!''

Roxanne's breath came in jagged gasps, and her head swam. She knew Balin spoke true. Yet, it was wrong to take Angleford from Pamela, wrong to exile her to England.

''When?'' Roxanne demanded. ''When do you plan to storm the keep? Before she returns to Cymry with her knighted husband?''

''Yes. Of course. By all the gods, Roxy, I don't intend to put Pamela in danger. It is why I was glad to know her wedding will be delayed until this English lord, Raven of Stonelee, returns again to his homeland. She won't arrive at Angleford Keep with her new husband until it's lost to them both.''

''How kind of you!'' Roxanne snarled.

''It is the most kindness I can afford to spend on anyone, especially Pamela of Angleford.''

''Pamela of Stonelee, don't you mean? It's where she'll be required to live, in that accursed England!'' She stared hard at Balin, wondering if he was so pleasant to look upon after all. ''Still, you can't think Raven shan't attack you even if you wrest Angleford from the knights employed to guard it. He will, or he'll die trying!''

''You hold him in high regard, do you?''

''Yes. No! I don't know.'' She shook her head in confusion. ''I do know he's a hard man, and he won't take lightly this stealing of his wife's estate.''

''Let him take it hard, then. I care not. But now is the time for me to make my conquest, while there's no lord in residence to lead a defense, and your sister's husband, Thomas, grapples with the newness of being the earl of Bittenshire. Later, I shall defend Angleford as I do all of Penllyn.''

''But Raven of Stonelee is in Cymru even now! He cannot be more than a day's ride from here!''

Blue eyes bore into violet ones, issuing a challenge. "I know. You've told me. That is why I need you, Roxy."

"Need me?" She lowered her voice and frowned suspiciously. "For what?"

"To put the cur back on your scent before he reaches Penllyn Hall. To let him catch you and take you back to his brother."

"What!"

"It is a perfect plan—at least as perfect a plan as I can devise, considering your untimely arrival here has nearly brought my enemy to the door. If you are both on the road back to England, Pamela's betrothed shall not hear of what's transpired at Angleford until it is too late."

Like sediment in a cup of wine, the swirling confusion of Roxanne's thoughts began to settle. She saw everything clearly now. "What of me?" she asked in a harsh whisper. "You would send me back to wed an English lord?"

Balin answered with the slightest nod. Yet, that nearly indiscernible gesture ignited Roxanne's fury once again. He did not love her! He would not wed her! And worse, he'd sacrifice her to an English noble! "You toad! You—you—!"

Unable to think of anything vile enough to call Balin, she whirled around, intending to run again, this time from the man she had loved so well and so long. But he reached out, caught her shoulder, and pulled hard.

Both her under tunic and bliaut tore. As he spun her back into his embrace, the garments' sleeves slid down one arm, exposing the limb nearly to her elbow and immodestly baring almost all of one breast. The prince caught Roxanne against his chest and held her firmly. With one hand pressed to her back, he cupped her bottom with the other and plundered her mouth.

"If you love me, Roxy, you'll do this for me," he growled, releasing her lips just long enough to speak before grinding them against his own again, so viciously she felt his teeth.

* * *

Raven made his way toward the hall with the Welsh wench held tight to his chest, facing straight ahead. She would not dare move away, for the edge of his dagger lay against her neck.

He had surprised the damsel's escort and slugged him soundly before taking her captive. Now that full darkness had descended, he was bringing her to the prince with the intention of trading her, whoever she was, for Roxanne of Bittenshire.

Spying the object of his mission and a fair-headed young man, Raven stopped. The couple stood well beyond the outbuildings, locked in a passionate embrace. When Raven saw the Bittenshire bitch and the man he presumed to be Prince Balin, he halted so abruptly, the maid in his arms nearly pitched forward. He tightened his hold about her ribs to keep her upright, and if she hadn't made desperate, choking sounds so that he loosened his grip, Raven might have suffocated the girl quite unintentionally.

Yet, his attention stayed on the man and the woman who remained oblivious to his presence. Never had Raven felt quite as he did at that moment, spying Roxanne wrapped in the Welshman's embrace, her gowns already beginning their slow, sensual descent to the ground. He felt a red-hot hatred blossoming in his heart, though he didn't know who inspired it, Roxanne or Balin. He did know he couldn't allow their tryst to continue. If he saw the man strip Roxanne down to her resplendent, ivory skin, he believed he might kill them both.

"Unhand her!" Raven shouted.

Balin and Roxanne turned and stared; as they did so, they parted slightly. She tried to extricate herself from his grasp, but he held fast to one hand. Her free arm, Raven noticed, was bared; so too was most of one breast.

"Raven!" she gasped. He couldn't tell whether she was shocked, outraged, or merely surprised.

Without responding to her cry, Raven nodded toward Roxanne and informed the Welsh prince, ''She's coming with me.''

''Is she?'' Balin replied in French, Raven's tongue.

''She is. Or this wench will take her place.''

''Balin, please!'' Melwyd cried in Welsh. ''He's English. He must be Pamela's betrothed, come for Roxanne! If he doesn't get her, he'll surely slay me!''

''He'll not slay you,'' her brother promised.

''Raven would not kill Melwyd!'' Roxanne exclaimed. ''You've no need to—''

Abruptly, she broke off. She had believed for so long that Balin would protect her, the fact that he would not nearly slipped her mind. Yet, as the prince transformed himself from beloved hero to scorned enemy, she found Raven her only immediate ally.

''Stop speaking that gibberish,'' Raven ordered, thrusting Melwyd forward so that the four now stood in a close circle. The knife at her throat glinted ominously, reflecting the moonlight.

''Raven, don't,'' Roxanne urged, in French again.

''Nay, don't,'' Balin repeated in that same tongue. ''Roxanne will go with you. She knows she must.''

She knew. But the shock and hurt of Balin's betrayal still stung as she turned to look at him.

Raven saw the look, and the rage in his chest burned hotter. This was the man she loved—a man who handed her off easily to one of King Henry's men, a knight who might slay her as effortlessly as he threatened to slay the wench he now held captive. How, Raven wondered, could Roxanne be such a fool?

''Let my sister go,'' Balin ordered evenly, his eyes locking on Raven's. ''I said Roxy will return with you to England, and so she shall. Willingly. Isn't that so, cousin?''

Balin glanced at Roxanne, a meaningful smile raising the corners of his mouth. Roxanne's lips curled in a sneer as she finally wrenched her arm free from his grasping fingers.

"Aye, I'll go. Willingly, to be sure!" Pulling up her torn sleeves to cover herself decently, she stumbled toward Raven.

"Let Melwyd go," she begged gently. "She's done naught. And Balin spoke true. I'll go with you."

"Why should I believe you?" He moved the blade of his dagger more directly in front of Melwyd's throat. She whimpered, and tears streamed down her cheeks.

"Because I give you my word, and my word means as much to me as the Cymru soil upon which I stand."

Raven's eyes held Roxanne's. For a timeless moment he peered hard at her, trying to read more than her mind—trying to see her soul. Finally, he swung his dagger away from Melwyd's throat and pushed the girl away. Balin caught her and held her.

"Rest easy, Lord Raven of Stonelee," the prince said jovially. "I respect King Henry's wishes. I'll send no one after you, I vow."

"I fear I must take you at your word. But if your word is false, I'll cut Roxanne's heart out. That, I vow."

"Ask her." Balin angled his chin toward Roxanne. "You seem to put some store in my cousin's pledges. She knows the truth. Roxy, tell him."

Swallowing hard, Roxanne looked up at Raven. "He won't send his men after us. He has his own reasons not to."

On foot, without his destrier, Raven had no choice but to accept promises from the lying Welsh who surrounded him. Resigned to the risk, Raven turned around silently. Without looking at Roxanne, he reached out, grabbed her hand in his, and pulled her along.

Brazenly, the pair left the prince's lands by way of the hard, dirt-packed road. Raven listened for footfalls or hoofbeats behind them, and he kept his free hand on the hilt of his sword. It occurred to him he should not have sheathed his dagger; if the Welsh attacked, he could use the knife to take the Bittenshire bitch's life in those brief moments before the warriors took his. As it was, with the fingers on his sword hand twitching, it appeared his last desperate act would be to defend her. Why, in the name of all things holy, would he ever consider protecting this haridelle?

Yet, he did not free his dagger, and they continued to walk through the silent night. When they had gone far enough, Raven pulled Roxanne off the path into the trees.

She kept pace with him, and her familiarity with the land relieved her of having to watch her footing. Which was good, because Roxanne's mind reeled.

She knew how things had appeared to Raven—Balin's embrace, her own dishabille. If the situation had developed as she'd believed it would, Raven's assumptions would have been absolutely correct. But nothing had gone as she'd hoped, and Raven could not begin to understand what had truly transpired. He could not know that she would have gone with him of her own volition, even if he'd not held Melwyd as a hostage.

Yet, as they trudged through the starlit woods, Roxanne resented Raven's judging her. Peter might have that right had he been here, had he seen her and Balin together. But not Raven. Besides, he had demanded she leave Fortengall Castle and abandon his twin. Had he expected her to enter a convent? *I think not!* she fumed indignantly.

So Roxanne did not speak as they walked. She knew she would have to, before Raven attempted to take her back to England. For Pamela's sake, she had to explain all about Balin's deceit, appealing to Raven's honor—if he had any—to protect Angleford Keep from the Cymry prince. Of course he would do it, not for Pamela, but for himself. No knight would willingly lose such a stronghold to a foe. Raven of Stonelee certainly wouldn't.

But she delayed making her appeal. Determinedly, Roxanne held her tongue, vowing not to speak until Raven first spoke to her. Then she'd confide in him, not a moment before.

* * *

Hours passed before the couple reached the place Raven had left his destrier to graze. Relieved to see him, Raven ran forward, stroked Rolf's mane, and then knelt to untie the animal's bindings he'd used to hobble the stallion's legs.

"Roxanne," he called out over his shoulder, "come here quickly. We've a way to travel still this night." He checked his saddle's girth. "Roxanne?"

A wave of anxiety surged within his breast when the wench neither replied nor appeared. If she had run off from him again, he would kill her when he caught her and be done with it.

"I—I—"

Hearing her voice, Raven located the wench—crumpled in a shivering heap on the bank of the stream. In the fragile, silver light he saw her sitting, knees drawn up, head bowed, her arms drawn tight around her legs.

"Are you ill?" he demanded gruffly as he approached, bringing Rolf with him.

"Nay." Roxanne shook her head. "Only—only tired, is all. I—I had little sleep last eve."

"I'd imagine not," he commented sourly. "Yet, there's no need for you to walk farther. Rolf is strong enough to carry both of us. Now, get up. I've no time for dawdling. Peter probably expected us back at Fortengall days ago, and we're still in this damnable land, nowhere near the border even."

Roxanne reached up and took Raven's proffered hand, needing his strength to regain her own footing. But the hand she gave him was not the one he'd been holding fast to all these hours. This one was cold as ice.

"God's teeth! You're freezing!" His exclamation sounded more an accusation than an observation.

"If you'll recall, I left Penllyn Hall rather abruptly. Besides, I left my cloak with you."

Raven began untying the bundle on Rolf's rump. "Mayhap you'd not be so accursedly cold if your bliaut covered you decently. Take some advice, woman. If you're going to shed your clothes for a man, untie them first. Ripping them in a craven frenzy is fair destructive."

He could not quite interpret the expression on her face when he turned to Roxanne with her fur mantle in hand. But Raven suspected the look was malicious.

He wrapped the cloak about her quaking shoulders. All these hours, she had been holding together the rents in her tunics with one hand. Now she let go, and the torn half of her gowns sagged, baring her arm and her breast.

Raven's gaze traveled down to the pebbled nipple, erect in the chilly night air, and he felt his prick twitch. Slowly, he raised his right hand, nearly giving in to the impulse to warm Roxanne by placing his palm over her bosom. Instead, he raised his eyes and found Roxanne peering at his face, not his errant fingers. Brusquely, he grabbed the edges of her cape and pulled them together, covering her from neck to knee.

Taking the reins, he mounted the horse. When he was seated, he slipped one foot out of its stirrup and reached for Roxanne. She took his hand and put her own foot in the vacant stirrup, hoisting her skirts. This bared her unclad leg to Raven's view, and again his manhood stirred.

"Sweet Holy Mother Mary," he muttered, hesitating before drawing her up behind him. "You rode to Penllyn Hall wearing naught beneath your skirts?"

"Women never wear anything beneath their skirts, as I'm sure you're quite aware."

"Aye." He grit his teeth. "But women never ride stallions, certainly not astride!"

"My leggings were wet when I left you."

"Then you shouldn't have left me."

He gave her a look full of meaning and then hauled her up, jerking Roxanne into his lap instead of behind the saddle on

Rolf's rump. She was cold, Raven told himself, and she needed the warmth of his body, his arms, to take away the chill.

Roxanne didn't protest. She seemed content enough as they rode along; snuggling against him, she dozed. And then woke with a start. It was still dark, so it took a few moments to orient herself. When she realized they'd returned to the shepherd's hut, she asked, "Are we stopping here?"

"Aye." Raven helped her slide off Rolf's back and then swung himself down to the ground as well. Immediately, he began relieving the destrier of his saddle. "We can have a brief sleep before we set off again."

"Set off?"

"Aye. To England." He dumped the saddle on the ground.

"Raven, we cannot."

"God's bloody wounds, woman!" He straightened so swiftly, grabbed Roxanne's shoulders so abruptly, she stumbled and nearly fell. "You've caused me naught but grief since first I laid eyes on you! Henry did not even declare I should wed you, yet I'm the one who's borne the brunt of your shrewish schemes and deadly actions! I warn you, wench, give me no more cause to wish you dead, or I'll make my wishes real!"

"Balin is going to attack Angleford."

"What?" Raven thought he'd misheard her.

"Balin intends to attack Angleford," she repeated. "Now, before you return with Pamela as her husband and as Marcher Earl. Now, while there's no lord in residence to lead that keep's knights in a winning defense."

He looked hard at Roxanne, searching her face. "But I'm in Wales, near Pamela's estate. Does this Welsh prince think I shan't ride there immediately and prepare to defeat him?"

"He expects I'll accompany you to England, and that you'll be well away from here when he makes his raid. Balin believes you shan't hear of his plans until they have already been played out and Angleford restored to the boundaries of Penllyn."

Raven crooked a finger beneath Roxanne's chin, tilting her

face up to his. "Why does he think you'll keep silent, when you're privy to his secrets? Angleford is your cousin's dowerland, after all. Your loyalty must be to her."

"It is. That is why I'm telling you, so that you'll remain here to defend Pamela's home."

He stood very, very close to Roxanne now, and he leaned down just a bit so that their faces were closer still, their breath warming each other's cheeks. "But why doesn't Balin know this? Does he think you more loyal to him than Pamela, because he is a prince?"

"Nay." Her voice was soft, her gaze unwavering. " 'Tis because he foolishly believes I'm still in love with him."

CHAPTER 20

Pamela woke with a start. She felt bemused, befuddled, unsure of where she was and why. It came to her then that she resided at Fortengall Castle, not Angleford or Bittenshire Keeps. But something still seemed amiss.

A soft snore made her flinch. Jerking toward the edge of the bed, eyes wide with alarm, she cautiously turned her head. Belatedly she realized she lay in Peter's bed, not her own.

"Sweet Mother Mary," she whispered beneath her breath, pushing herself upright, careful not to disturb the man slumbering beside her. Swinging one leg over the edge of the mattress, she sought the floor with her toes and groped her way between the bed hangings.

It was much lighter than it had been when she'd come to visit Peter late last night, despite the fact that the candles had all guttered out in their dishes. Pamela made out slivers of sky around the edges of hide anchored across the narrow window. Like a black pearl, the darkness seemed infused with an iridescent light as dawn pushed the night aside.

Tightening the sash at her waist, Pamela leaned down and peered at the page still sprawled on his pallet. "Thank you, Lord," she muttered prayerfully, finding William still fast asleep. Then, sprinting over the boy, she lunged for the door and lurched into the hallway.

Voices. Footsteps. Doors opening and closing. Was it so late, Pamela wondered frantically, that the servants were already up and about? Could Lady Lucinda, always an early riser, be up and about as well?

Footsteps on the stairs, descending from above. Panicked, Pamela hurried into the corner garderobe.

In truth, she needed to relieve herself. But she was so anxious, she did not think she could. So she stood in the privy, trying to ignore the malodorous air, and listened for voices in the corridor, on the stairs.

"How many in the village?" Pamela heard Lucinda ask as the lady reached the landing beyond Pamela's refuge.

"A score of children," Master Frederick replied. "But at least six adults, too."

"And in Tysdale?"

"Even more, according to the man I sent there."

"Tysdale is near to Kurth. I'm certain that's where the boys contracted it. Ian said Neville's grandchildren seemed ill while he, Hugh, and the little twins were visiting."

"Are you going to check on Peter?" Pamela heard Frederick ask, and presumed they stood outside his chamber door.

"Aye," Lucinda confirmed. "He's ne'er had the crimson rash, nor has Raven or Lucien. How they escaped it in childhood, I don't know. But both Lucien and Raven were gone from Fortengall before the illness showed itself here, so my concern is for Peter."

There is sickness! Pamela realized, quickly forgetting her earlier concern that someone might catch her in Peter's room. More important now was the scourge that had invaded this peaceful shire. Lady Lucinda would need all the help she could enlist, and Pamela intended to offer her assistance.

Emerging from the garderobe, she approached the lady of the keep. "Pamela!" Lucinda exclaimed. "Why are you up so early? Are you unwell?"

"Nay, milady, don't fret. I'm fine. But I heard you and Master Frederick speaking. I gather many have fallen ill."

Lucinda shook her head as the seneschal, nodding to both the ladies, left them and hurried down the stairs.

"That damnable crimson rash has reared its ugly head. The little twins and Hugh are down with it, burning with fever, their skin covered with red spots."

"I'm sorry. But children are often afflicted. Most recover."

"Aye." Lucinda nodded as she reached for the latch on Peter's door. "If they were well-fed and healthy before succumbing to the illness. I myself suffered with it when I was a small child. Ian did also, or so he assures me."

"But not your eldest three?"

"Nay." She looked grim. "And as you may know, when grown men and women fall prey to it, 'tis much worse than it is for the youngsters. Sometimes adults fail to recover." With a frown, she asked Pamela, "Have you had the crimson rash?"

"Nay."

Lucinda closed her eyes. "After all that's gone amiss since you and Roxanne came to us, I pray God you don't fall ill."

"I shan't, milady," she vowed. "I'm quite healthy."

"Makes no matter. No one knows how this pestilence is spread."

"Is the well befouled?" Pamela asked. "Have the stores been checked for vermin?"

"The water in the well is sweet, and I have servants inspecting the foodstuffs. However, having lived long enough to see outbreaks of this disease time and again, I suspect we do not poison ourselves with food and drink. The crimson rash always comes this time of year if it comes at all. I believe simply being near those who are ill is enough to make another succumb.''

"Yet, all do not," Pamela reminded her helpfully.

"Nay, all do not. And those who suffer and survive never fall prey a second time. But that does you and Peter no good."

Lucinda opened her son's door and dropped her voice to a whisper. "I hope I do not find him feverish. With his bones still mending, he isn't as strong as he should be. If he sickens with the crimson rash now, it could take him to his grave!"

"Peter is not sick, milady," Pamela hastened to assure her. "He slept like a babe all last—"

Breaking off as she realized her blunder, she closed her mouth abruptly. Instead of venturing a small lie that might explain away her knowledge of Peter's health and sleeping habits, she opted for silence.

She followed Lucinda into the bedchamber as the lady strode forward and wrenched open the curtains enclosing Peter's bed. She flinched when the bed's occupant came into view. Though he remained asleep, one arm flung carelessly across his brow, the covers had obviously been thrown back and now lay double over his chest. Beside him, the linen-covered mattress and pillow retained the imprint of both a head and a body. It looked like an empty nest, except obviously no bird had nestled there.

Pamela sucked in a breath, bracing herself for the lady's inevitable accusations. But, to her surprise and relief, Lucinda seemed not to notice the telltale evidence. Already she was shaking her son awake.

"Wha . . . ?" Peter slowly shook off sleep, until he spied his mother looming over him. When his eyes were wide and alert, his glance darted toward Pamela before returning to Lucinda. "What is it, Mother?" he asked dourly. "Is there a problem?"

"I believe so."

"Mother." Peter pushed himself into a sitting position, again glanced over Lucinda's shoulder at Pamela, and declared, "I'm a grown man."

"That you are." She straightened her stance and crossed her arms over her chest. "Yet, that fact is unimportant at the moment. Right now, I need speak with you on a matter of dire consequence."

"And what is that?"

Succinctly, Lucinda told Peter of the outbreak of crimson rash there, in the castle, and in nearby towns.

"This is terrible," he muttered softly. "I wish there were something I could do to help. I know you'll make yourself ill, trying to nurse everyone. But with this accursed leg—!"

"Peter, how do you feel?" Lucinda asked impatiently.

"Me?" He frowned. "I'm quite well, except for my injury."

"No fever?" She touched his brow. "No rash?" She examined his arms.

"Nay, none. Mother, the crimson rash is a children's affliction, is it not? Since I never fell ill with it as a lad, I doubt I shall fall ill with it as a man!"

"You cannot be sure. The disease does not discriminate. And unlike most children, many of the adults who are stricken don't survive."

"What are you saying?" Again he glanced at the damsel standing behind his mother. "Pamela, you're not ill . . . ?"

"Nay."

"But she never had the sickness as a child, either," Lucinda put in.

"My . . . lady?" a sleepy voice said, drawing everyone's attention to William. He sat among the tangle of his blankets, rubbing his eyes.

"William!" Lucinda exclaimed, turning her back on Peter to crouch beside the page. Raising his tunic, she examined the boy's skinny chest. "Have you ever had the crimson rash?"

"What?" He blinked, not fully awake yet and confused.

"A sickness called the crimson rash. Have you ever had it?"

"Oh, aye!" he exclaimed cheerfully. "We all were down with it one year, my sisters and I. 'Twas springtime, if I recall, and I hated being abed, scratching myself night and day, when I should have been out of doors riding my pony."

"Thank *Jesu*." The lady grabbed the page by the scruff of his neck and hauled him up. "Many at the castle have come down with the illness, William, so I'll need those who are well to do the chores they cannot. Go to the kitchen, now, break your fast, and await me in the great hall. I'll come down later to tell you what I need you to do."

"I don't wish to get that cursed rash again, milady!"

"You won't, I promise. Now, go!"

Obediently, the page scooted from the chamber. When he disappeared out the door, Pamela volunteered eagerly, "I can help tend the sick. Especially the children."

"You'll not be tending any of the sick," Lucinda countered with a shake of her head. "As neither of you have had the rash before, both you and Peter must remain sequestered. I'll not risk your succumbing to this pestilence and worse"—she made the sign of the cross—"dying of it."

Pamela shared a look with Peter before turning back to Lucinda. "What would you have us do?"

"I fear there's nothing for it, but that you must remain in your bedchamber and Peter in his."

"You're mad!" he complained irritably. "Mother, today is the day I'm to get my crutches. Nothing, not even a plague, shall keep me confined to this bed!"

" 'Tis not as if you intended to joust or dance," she reminded him tartly. "Still, I'll find someone to assist you so that you're able to get up and about for a short while."

"Who?" Peter demanded.

"Who?" Lucinda rubbed her forehead distractedly. "I cannot say. Best it be a man with some strength. And best it be a servant who's already had the illness."

"Best it be me," Pamela announced.

Lucinda's head snapped to the side, and she stared hard at her young guest. "You?"

"Aye." She nodded her head for emphasis. "Lady Lucinda, you'll need every hand available to you, as more and more fall ill. Why waste the services of an able-bodied serf when you can use me?"

"Nay. Absolutely not."

"Please hear me out, milady! You intend to keep me isolated so that I do not encounter those who are ill with this malady. You intend to keep Peter isolated as well. Best you keep us isolated together, so that I may tend him. 'Tis the most reasonable course of action."

" 'Tis not! You are a guest here, not a serving maid."

"I like to be helpful, milady. I truly enjoyed assisting you yesterday."

"I shouldn't have imposed on you."

" 'Twas no imposition."

"Pamela speaks truly, Mother," Peter put in. "Last eve she told me how pleased she was to have work to do."

"But . . . tending you, Peter, is far different from selecting plump stewing hens, or mixing tisanes."

"Yet, I would not be bored," Pamela explained, "as I would be, confined to my chamber with no company."

"The same holds true for me, Mother," Peter agreed. "I can't tell you how wearisome it is being so much alone here."

Lucinda shook her head stubbornly. "I cannot allow it."

"You will." Peter was uncompromising as he addressed his mother. "Lady Pamela and I get on very well, and besides, she's quite skilled at ministering to the ill and injured. Since you will not let her assist in caring for the sick, I shall let her care for the injured—me."

"Peter." She spoke softly. "Pamela is Raven's betrothed. If he learns you two remained together for the length of time it takes this illness to run its course, he might think—"

"My brother is on the road, alone with my future wife. I do not lie here suspecting him—them—of anything untoward."

"Lady Lucinda," Pamela ventured, seeking to put her mind at ease, "though orphaned young, I was reared to be good and God-fearing. I'd ne'er do anything to shame Lord Raven, myself, or either of my parents, God rest their souls. Yet, I tell you true, my lady, if my mother knew I'd not done all I could to assist you now, she would be ashamed of me."

The older woman considered the younger with a long, appraising glance before her eyes flicked to Peter. "You're so keen on getting to your feet again. Pamela's but a wisp of a girl, hardly strong enough to pull you up and set you on your crutches. If she's your only nursemaid, you may be confined to that bed another sennight or more."

His eyes sought Pamela's before he replied, "The lady of Angleford has a strength to match your own, Mother. I've no doubt she will give me all the care and assistance I require."

Setting her mouth in a grim line, Lucinda finally nodded her assent. "Pamela, there's an unoccupied chamber next to this one. 'Tis a good deal smaller than the room you've been using. But if you settle into it, 'twill make caring for Peter easier."

"Very good, my lady." She smiled, pleased with her victory. "I'll gather my things immediately."

"I will go below to the great hall. Ian and I must make an accounting of those who are down with the rash. 'Tis full light now, and more will have awakened with fever than went to sleep with it."

"Mother, my crutches!" Peter reminded Lucinda as she followed Pamela from the chamber.

"I'll get them," Pamela volunteered before Lucinda could reply. "And some food for you, also. Don't fret, Lady Lucinda. I'll not go near any sickrooms, but I'll see to Peter's needs."

When Lucinda nodded and quit the room, Pamela scampered

back in. Retrieving the costrel Peter used to relieve himself, she tossed him the empty cup and yanked the hangings closed about his bed. "There!" she called to him triumphantly. "I am indeed a capable assistant!"

He anticipated her return. During Pamela's absence, Peter managed to reach the ewer on the bedside table. He used the water to wash his face, dampen his beard, and comb his hair back with his moistened fingers. Smoothing his covers modestly over his legs and hips, he ran his tongue over the front of his teeth while he watched the door.

"Here you are, my lord," Pamela said when she reappeared, properly dressed and carrying a tray. Depositing the meal tray on Peter's lap, she promptly rushed out of the room again. The next time she entered, she toted a pair of crude crutches.

"Not very knightly, are they?" she observed with a smile, propping them against the wall just inside the door. "Have you everything you need for a while? Are you comfortable?"

"Aye." His eyes met hers. "You're not planning to run off again, are you?"

"I thought I'd finish moving my things into the room next door."

"Delay a bit," Peter urged. "I think we need to talk."

"Very well." Closing the door, she approached the bed but grabbed a stool instead of sitting beside him on the mattress.

"How did you happen to be with my mother so early this morn?" Peter asked.

"I was in the hallway when I heard her coming down the steps. I hid in the jakes."

"A pleasant place to cower!" He chuckled. Then, his expression serious, he admitted, "I expected the worst when I awoke to find her looming over me. But I take it you weren't discovered sleeping in my bed."

"Nay. I woke just before dawn. William still slept soundly. I thought all the household would still be abed. But they weren't, because of the sickness.

"Peter," Pamela continued, leaning forward and looking into his eyes, "you shouldn't have let me sleep here. Why didn't you wake me?"

"There seemed no need. You looked so peaceful. And soon enough, I myself slumbered."

"It wasn't right, my being with you that way."

"What way?"

"You know! Beside you in your bed! Can you imagine what your lady mother would have thought if she'd come in and found us? 'Tis only by the grace of God I awoke a short time before she came to look in on you."

"That may be," he agreed. "But we were spared discovery. Let's not dwell on it."

"Aye, let's not." She reached out, lifted a hunk of warm, fresh-baked bread from the tray, and handed it to Peter. "You must eat. You'll need your strength today, if you intend to work with your crutches."

Instead of plucking the bread from her fingers, he grabbed her hand and brought it toward his mouth, forcing her to stand and lean toward him. As he bit from the loaf, his black eyes held hers. "Are you up to aiding me?" he asked.

Pamela pulled her hand free. "Certainly. I am not very big in stature, but as you said, I'm strong."

Nodding in agreement, Peter looked pointedly at the bread she still clutched in her fingers. When Pamela offered it to him again, he took it. Yet, he used one hand to capture her wrist as he plucked the morsel from her grasp, and he lingered a moment before releasing her. "Gentle and strong. A perfect nursemaid."

She pulled back her hand and lowered her lashes. "I hope so. I must reassure your mother of my worthiness."

"Worthiness?"

"To join her family. She disapproved highly when she discovered me on your lap. And today she voiced her concern over Raven's reaction to my tending you alone."

"Raven?" Peter's liquid eyes froze; they glinted like black ice under a winter moon. "Is he forever first in your thoughts?"

Pamela matched Peter's scowl with one of her own. "Aye, of course. He's to be my husband, after all."

"Ah, yes. Your husband. Though he's off in the wilds of Wales with my intended bride!" He leaned back against his pillows and looked toward the ceiling.

"He had no choice," she insisted defensively. "My cousin was gone, yet you could not go after her, not with your leg so badly broken. It was hardly Raven's doing."

"Wasn't it?" He slanted his gaze toward Pamela.

Flustered, she glanced down at her shoes and plucked at the skirt of her bliaut, twisting the wool with her fingers. "I—I don't know. I only hope they soon return to the castle."

"I don't."

Pamela's head came up; she eyed Peter curiously.

"We've the beginning of a calamity here in this shire, with the crimson rash spreading. Such pestilence always worsens before it improves. I know not if Roxanne suffered the illness as a child, but my brother surely hasn't. I wouldn't want him to return while this scourge rages. No matter how angry he may make me, I wouldn't wish him sick, let alone dead."

The damsel stepped forward and put her small hand into Peter's much larger one. "Don't worry for him," she urged gently. "I'm certain that if Roxy and Raven approach Fortengall anytime soon, they'll learn of the situation and not venture forth until it's safe. As for you, I'll keep you safe. We'll both stay well away from those who are indisposed. And I'll see to your needs until you are able to see to them yourself. Eventually, I'm sure, all will come to pass precisely as King Henry planned."

Peter lowered his gaze to contemplate the delicate hand

touching his. Despite how small it was, it seemed the perfect companion to his callused palm and long fingers. "Are you?" he asked, shockingly aware that he now hoped otherwise.

Pamela nodded slowly, and when he looked up to meet her gaze, he found the little lady staring at him curiously.

CHAPTER 21

"Halt and declare yourself!"

Raven, with Roxanne behind him, reined in his mount at the edge of Angleford's moat and called out, "I am Lord Raven of Stonelee, soon to be your master by King Henry's royal decree!"

The tower guard leaned out the window and shaded his eyes from the morning sun. "We have had no word on this matter, my lord!"

Rolf began prancing, shaking his head. Snarling in annoyance, Raven used both reins to control him, though he knew his own impatience had conveyed itself to his steed.

"Have you not had word that Henry sent an escort for the ladies Pamela and Roxanne at Bittenshire? That he had them brought to England for the purpose of marriage? I am the knight Henry's chosen to wed Lady Pamela; therefore, Angleford's to be my stronghold!"

The knight above dropped his hand so that the riders could no longer see it. When it reappeared, it grasped a mighty longbow which, though it seated no arrow, proved very effective as a wordless warning. "Have you brought some proof with you, sir? All may be as you say, but I dare not let you into the bailey without proof."

"Holy Mother of *Jesu!*" Raven muttered angrily, as much to Roxanne as himself. "The fool will soon be under full attack, yet, he quibbles with me, his lord and master!"

"Be glad he is cautious. Were he reckless enough to allow you inside without argument, you'd have his head."

Roxanne had spoken softly near Raven's ear. Now she leaned away and to one side, making herself more visible to the guard. "Llewellyn, is it you? 'Tis I, Lady Roxanne of Bittenshire! Let us in, I pray you!"

"Lady Roxanne?"

"Aye, 'tis the notable, honorable, and most beloved Lady Roxanne, daughter of the late earl, Cedric of Bittenshire!" Raven growled. "Now, lower the drawbridge and raise the damned gate!"

"Aye, milord. Milady." Llewellyn nodded and disappeared. Soon, the heavy wooden drawbridge came down on squeaking hinges even as the portcullis rose on equally creaky chains.

Peevishly, Raven spurred Rolf's flanks, and they galloped across the bridge, the destrier's hooves thundering over the boards. Inside the bailey walls, Roxanne slid off the horse and Raven followed, tossing the reins to the nearest servant. "Rub him down and feed him well," he ordered tersely.

Roxanne led the way up the steps into the keep. As he followed, Raven surveyed the barony. Angleford's walls enclosed a veritable village. And inside the keep itself, Raven discovered a great hall carpeted with rushes, at the fore of which sat a raised dais and a high table. It all looked exceedingly familiar to him, all very Norman.

"Lady Roxanne." A serving wench bobbed respectfully before the young woman, though her glance kept straying to the black-bearded knight beside her.

"Annie, where is Master Felix?"

"I'm certain the seneschal is on his way, milady. But I'll go search him out, just to be certain."

Annie scurried off, and Raven grabbed Roxanne's elbow. "Annie? Felix? Why haven't these people any of those accursed names I can't pronounce? And that servant speaks French!"

"Because this is the Marches, and in the Marches the lords are English of long-standing Norman tradition. Fully half or more of those who labor here come from English stock. But never fear, Lord Raven," she addressed him mockingly, "you'll hear those names you think so foreign and that tongue you cannot understand. A great many Cymry also live and work at Angleford."

Crossing his arms over his chest, Raven peered down at Roxanne. She was all bite and spittle, now that she was in familiar surroundings. But last night, in the bough hut, she'd been as fragile as Roxanne could ever be. Exhausted and shivering, she had compliantly cuddled against him.

"Bittenshire is much the same as Angleford, isn't it? Not that I had the leisure to note the servants' names. But I recall when they addressed me, they did speak the king's French."

"What? You were there?" She sounded shocked.

"I was. I assumed that's where you headed when you left Fortengall Castle. As you were not in residence, however, I spent a little time with Lord Thomas and your sister. 'Twas the new earl who told me where you'd likely be and how to get there."

Roxanne clamped shut her open mouth and glared at Raven. Her jaw worked, and he thought she would say something, most likely unkind. But she did not, either because she wasn't as rash as she oftentimes seemed to be, or because, at that moment, Master Felix made his appearance. He was a sandy-haired man of middle years, whose sturdy legs supported a barrel-chested body and a head that seemed supported only by his shoulders.

"My lord—Raven, is it? Raven of . . . ?"

"Stonelee. And Angleford. At least, I shall be Lord of Angleford when I wed this damsel's cousin, Lady Pamela."

The castle keeper nodded his head bemusedly as his eyes strayed to the woman beside the lord. "Lady Roxy! Why are you here? I mean to say, shouldn't Lady Pamela have returned to Angleford with her betrothed?"

"She's still in England at a place called Fortengall. There she awaits the return of this"—she glanced sidelong at Raven—"this lord who will be her husband."

Though the seneschal had no need to know, Roxanne launched into a gaping-holed explanation of how she, instead of Pamela, came to be with Raven in the borderlands. As Raven waited impatiently for her to finish her tale, he considered Felix's attire. Unlike Fortengall Castle's seneschal, Frederick, who garbed himself in finely stitched tunics made of the softest, most vibrant-hued cloth, this official dressed in rough raiment of drab colors, shades of brown and green. Were he in the forest, he'd have blended well with the trees. And, despite the nature of his household duties, he was armed much as Raven was, with sword and dagger both. This seneschal was a warrior.

Raven realized, suddenly, that Roxanne and Felix had slipped into Welsh, and that he could no longer understand what they said. "Enough!" he ordered, his eyes snapping as he glared at her, wondering what she'd said in that tongue beyond his ken.

Turning to Felix, he demanded, "Has the lady disclosed what brought us here to Angleford Keep?"

"Nay."

" 'Tis of grave concern." Raven glanced at the high table. "Have a meal brought to us, with a flagon or two of wine. Call for the captain of the guard to join us. I would speak with you both, for there are plans to be made. Urgent plans."

Servants brought the victuals quickly, while Felix disappeared to seek out the captain.

"Sir Edwin, milord," Felix said when he and two others

joined Raven and Roxanne on the dais. He indicated the knight to his right. "Edwin is the captain of the guard. Gruffydd, here, is his next in command." With another nod, he motioned to the mail-clad man on his left.

Raven noticed immediately that both knights, though no older than himself, were scarred near as badly as his stepfather, Lord Ian. The metal links sewed securely to their leather hauberks to form sturdy mail were as battered and bent as the fingers on their hands. These two had not acquired the injuries that left such scars simply by hunting stag in the forest.

"Raven of Stonelee." Introducing himself, he gestured for Edwin, Gruffydd, and Felix to sit down opposite.

"The lord of Stonelee is betrothed to Lady Pamela," the seneschal explained. "Some matters required Lady Roxanne's return to Wales, and as her own betrothed, who is Lord Raven's brother, is temporarily indisposed due to injury, 'twas Lord Raven himself who accompanied her."

As Raven absorbed this version of their wild ride through Wales, the captain of the guard nodded at Roxanne.

"Milady," he muttered respectfully, taking her hand and brushing his lips across her knuckles. "Forgive me for seating myself without first acknowledging your presence."

The captain's behavior was correct enough, Raven decided, except for the familiarity of the smile he flashed Roxanne.

"You need no forgiveness, Edwin." She smiled at him.

And Raven bristled. He felt the short hairs on the back of his neck rise. He wanted to snatch Roxanne's hand from the knight's inappropriately lingering grasp. Instead he barked, "Leave us now, my lady. We've men's business to discuss."

Her mouth fell open, and she turned to him with wide eyes. Raven could see her tongue, and he knew that on the tip of it clung a torrent of epithets she was dying to throw at him.

But his dark warning, sent silently with a flash in his eyes, wasn't lost on the damsel. As he watched, she hesitated. Then she snapped closed her mouth, pushed herself out of her chair, and stormed to the keep's stairs, disappearing up them.

Raven returned his attention to the men seated at the table. "Balin," he said.

"Prince Balin? Of Penllyn?" Felix inquired.

"Aye." With a nod, Raven took a sip of his wine. "He means to attack this keep."

"Attack Angleford!" Edwin cried in disbelief. "Why would the Welsh prince do such a thing, milord? Who told you this?"

"The lady who just went upstairs. 'Twas with him she had some urgent business." He swallowed back the distaste that declaration left in his mouth, knowing as he did the exact nature of her "business" with the young, virile, handsome prince.

"And he told her? He told her he intended to attack Lady Pamela's stronghold?" Felix demanded.

"He did."

"But weren't . . ." He frowned, shaking his head. ". . . weren't you with her? Did you not escort Lady Roxanne to Wales? Why would he confide in her with you there beside her? Doesn't Balin know you'll rule as Lord of Angleford once you wed Lady Pamela?"

Raven set his jaw and looked down at his fingers, still clasped about the stem of his pewter wine goblet. He certainly could not share the precise details of what had occurred in Penllyn, or why. These men were strangers to him. Besides, he had to lead them in a defense of this barony and its people. Risking his men's scorn was not an option.

"Prince Balin did not know I accompanied Lady Roxanne back to Wales and into Penllyn. She had need of her privacy, so I granted it to her. He has no notion I'm here in Wales. And his plan, as I understand it, is to wrest Angleford away from you who are charged with holding it before I arrive with Lady Pamela."

"Why?" Sir Gruffydd asked.

"Because the valley in which this keep sits was once part

of Penllyn, was it not? Balin wishes to win it back, thereby broadening his borders.''

All three of the Angleford knights muttered to themselves and each other. Finally Felix said to Raven, ''Penllyn has always been at peace with its neighbors. And Balin is blood kin to Pamela, since his own sire was brother to Princess Ceridwen, the lady's mother. How can he think to steal her birthright?''

''In Balin's defense, he feels the first lord of Angleford stole it from some now-dead Prince of Penllyn. As reigning prince, he deems it his right to take it back. As for his cousin, Pamela, he intends to keep her from harm by making his move while she is still in England, wedding me.'' Raven smirked and shook his head. ''Unfortunately for him, he has no idea I am in residence already, able and willing to thwart him.''

'' 'Tis an irony,'' Edwin noted. ''We always expected serious attacks from other Marcher Lords, not a peaceable neighbor.''

''Well, the unfathomable is now reality.'' Raven leaned forward, putting his head nearer the others'. ''I would wager he'll be here within days and that he intends to lay siege.''

Both Edwin's and Gruffydd's eyebrows shot up. Instead of either commenting, they turned as one to Angleford's seneschal.

''My lord,'' Felix said softly after clearing his throat, ''the natives do not lay siege.''

''Nay? 'Twould seem the wisest course of action. Angleford, like Bittenshire, lies in a deep valley. Should Penllyn's men surround us, they could hold their ground for months, starving us out. They'd never have to fire off a single arrow.''

''They like to shoot arrows,'' Sir Gruffydd explained. ''We Welshmen are the best longbow archers in the world.''

The knight did not flinch under Raven's blatantly suspicious glare. ''My lord Raven,'' he went on, ''do not doubt my loyalty to Angelford. Aye, my name is as Welsh as the prince of Penllyn's. But my mother was English, daughter of an armorer brought to this demesne to ply his craft. Most all who live and labor for the Marcher Earls of the borderlands are of mixed blood, Welsh, English, and Norman, as are most of the Marcher Earls themselves. Thus, our only loyalty is to our lord, not an assortment of blooded kin.''

''Gruffydd's correct,'' Felix agreed. ''You'll find no traitors at Angleford, and Penllyn's warriors will rush down out of the hills, too many to count, blowing their horns and screaming their cries.''

''So?'' Raven scoffed, leaning back in the lord's chair and crossing his arms over his chest. ''Tribes of untrained soldiers charge from the hills, making a great deal of ear-splitting noise—what matter? We'll keep the gate down and the draw-bridge up. No harm shall come to any within Angleford's walls.''

The captain of the guard, his man, and Felix exchanged looks. ''They'll attack the village, milord. You did not come upon it, riding in as you did. It lies some distance due west in a line directly behind the keep. Of course, Angleford's guard should have to defend it.''

Raven looked at him as though he were dimwitted. ''Knowing, as we do, an attack is imminent, I shall simply bring the villagers to the keep, holding them safe within its walls.''

''That's reasonable, but the bailey cannot hold so many for very long. Besides, the village is no tiny hamlet. 'Tis a town filled with tradespeople and craftsmen. They have property and possessions, merchandise, which none shall willingly abandon.''

''They'd rather die?''

''Aye,'' Edwin answered, ''many would. Wouldn't you rather die than flee your home and leave it to be plundered and destroyed?''

Raven didn't respond; there was no need. Leaning forward again, he stroked his whiskered chin with his fingers.

He knew he should ask the captain's advice. The knight was, after all, the head of the guard charged with defending

Angleford Keep. Edwin was familiar with this place and with this land. By the look of him, he was also passing familiar with a good fight.

But Raven was not of a mind to ask advice. He was the lord here—if not officially, then in spirit. Though he only truly loved one place, Stonelee, this place would soon enough be his. He'd be damned to hell before he'd give it up, especially to Balin of Penllyn, Roxanne's—!

"Send word," he ordered Felix. "Alert one and all, from those who toil at the keep to the villagers beyond the walls. I want everyone inside the bailey by nightfall on the morrow."

Felix nodded.

"Sir Edwin, I would meet with the guard. All the knights and men-at-arms. They must know who leads them now."

"Very good, milord."

The men stood, and Raven strode between the captain and Sir Gruffydd, heading out of the hall, the keep, and into the yard.

Roxanne watched him go. She had stormed up to Pamela's chamber, slammed the door, and promptly tiptoed back down the stairs to peek around the wall at the men remaining in the great hall. She had overheard all that they said, and she was furious!

"To think I am forced to put my trust in that cockshead!" she complained later, soaking in the bath Annie prepared for her while muttering that a body oughtn't bathe *too* frequently, or she might get a congestion that could lead to her death. "All he intends to do is hide behind the bailey walls, hoping Balin and his men will tire and scatter. As if Cymry would ever turn tail before either victory or death!"

Roxanne's fury did not wane as the day progressed. In truth, her anger grew hotter as she idled away her time, not with strategic planning of Angleford's defense, but with searching through the late Lady Ceridwen's clothes to find something suitable to wear. Yet, while she was involved in such feminine endeavors, her thoughts were not on colors and ornamentation. She kept reliving those minutes when Balin confessed his true feelings. They were so opposite those she'd expected of him. Despite his mention of love, he did not love her, he demanded love *of* her—and blind obedience to his demands.

While Roxanne sat on a stool in Pamela's childhood bedchamber and Annie dressed her hair, she felt tears welling in her eyes. Frequently, she had to dash the damp streaks from her cheeks with the backs of her hands.

She had never felt so betrayed by anyone as she did by Balin. And now she was stuck with Raven. Raven! Just the thought of him brought his image vividly to mind. Even his scent seemed to fill her nostrils. When the recollection of his smell, of musk, leather, and a hint of wool, nearly made Roxanne dizzy, she mustered her complaints against the English scoundrel, to counteract his spell. One by one she counted them out, from his cruel accusations at Fortengall Castle to his cowardly, weak-kneed plans to defend Angleford Keep.

"There you go, m'lady," Annie chirped as she secured a sheer veil atop Roxanne's head with a jewel-encrusted circlet. "My, but you look as much a princess as Lady Ceridwen. Or your own mother, Lady Rhiannon."

Having scampered around the stool to better see Roxanne, the servant rubbed the smudges from a polished piece of tin with a fistful of apron. Annie handed the shiny metal to the young lady, urging her to look at her own reflection. "Am I right?"

Roxanne peered into the crude mirror, able to see only one eye, her nose, and part of her mouth at a time. Even those features blurred. But she knew the dusky blue bliaut and matching veil suited her, and that the blue and red stones in the circlet would wink and sparkle in the torchlight. She mused that Raven of Stonelee might find her comely if he saw her thus. Especially having seen her only mud-spattered and rain-drenched during their miserable ride together.

What, by all the saints, am I thinking? She sent the mirror skittering onto a clothes trunk, as though it were a pebble she'd skipped across a pond. It clattered noisily when it landed, but she ignored it, turning away from Annie, lost in her own thoughts. *Raven belongs to my cousin. I pity Pamela for her bad luck! Peter is by far the better man when it comes to those two brothers, and he is mine. Not Raven, never Raven . . .*

Roxanne strode to the window and looked out. She saw nothing of the bailey below. The harsh, cruel, hard-hearted, cutting-tongued Lord of Stonelee—and Angleford—was the only image before her eyes.

I hate him. I would not be here with him if it weren't for Pamela. I must remember Pamela! And I must not be thinking of making myself desirable to her betrothed. I don't want him. I would not have him if he begged me to be his!

Whirling around, leaning on the window ledge behind her, Roxanne faced Annie. "These were Aunt Ceridwen's clothes; now they are Pamela's. I shouldn't be wearing them."

"Don't be foolish," the servant chided. "They're too big for Lady Pamela, and besides, she's a generous soul. She'd want you to make use of them. You need to be properly garbed when you preside over supper in the great hall."

"I don't feel up to presiding over supper," Roxanne declared, sitting again on the little stool. " 'Tisn't as though we're entertaining guests. The new Marcher Earl can preside. I shall remain here in this chamber. Annie, bring me up a trencher, will you?"

The woman shook her head. "Milady, you can't mean what you say. 'Tis only right that you act in Lady Pamela's stead."

"I will do what I please!" Roxanne hissed, annoyed by the servant's arguing. "Now leave me be, 'til you bring me a tray."

"But . . . I . . . very well, milady," Annie finally managed, though she appeared mystified by Roxanne's mood. Nodding obediently, she backed through the portal and closed the door behind her.

Raven was annoyed in the extreme. From his place at the center of the high table, with the empty chair beside him, he perused the hall still again, knowing full well Roxanne was not among the throngs come to sup this evening.

"Where is Lady Roxanne?" he demanded of a scullion setting a platter of roast pork on the table.

"I haven't seen her, milord," the youth replied.

"God's teeth!" He snapped before leaping up and pushing back his chair. Angrily, he stomped toward the stairs and climbed them, two at a time.

The wench's goal in life was to annoy or anger him at every opportunity. She was too bold and far too daring for a female. She spoke her mind instead of holding her tongue, and she deliberately set out to accomplish her own ends, never once considering the ramifications of her brash actions. Yet, could she be a hag? A homely crone a man could easily dismiss? Nay, she could not. She had to be bewitchingly beautiful, so that a man wanted her even when he knew he should not.

Raven put his hand on the latch of Pamela's bedchamber door—he knew Roxanne used her cousin's room. It occurred to him that he would enter here a thousand times in the future, only to find the fragile, obedient lady who would then be his wife. Yet, he didn't anticipate it. What he anticipated was seeing Roxanne, wild, infuriating haridelle that she was.

He threw open the door. She was sitting on a stool, her head bent in thoughtful contemplation. But she promptly flew up, a swirl of sparkling azure, raising her arms in a gesture of surprise that made the wide sleeves of her under tunic meld with the skirts of her bliaut. Roxanne seemed like a winged fairy materializing before him.

Raven felt a tightness in his chest and a surging in his loins. He wanted this woman. Worse, he loved her.

"How dare you!" she shouted, her indigo eyes glaring at him unflinchingly. "You may have thought I'd no right to privacy at your stepfather's keep. But let me assure you, I've a right to it here at Angleford!"

"Why?" Raven kicked closed the door behind him and stomped across the room, grabbing Roxanne by her upper arms.

"Because it is my cousin's keep! I—I've spent much time here, growing up. It—it is almost a second home to me!"

"Is it?" Raven's eyes narrowed as they bored into Roxanne's. "I thought Penllyn Hall was a second home to you."

She flushed guiltily, and it piqued his ire. "Fortengall belongs to my mother and her husband," he told her. "Angleford is mine. You've no rights here, Roxy, not even to privacy."

She blinked up at him, her expression startled. He realized, just as she surely had, that he had, for the first time and quite easily, called her, "Roxy."

Roxanne felt indignant and insisted righteously, " 'Tis not yours yet! You have not taken your vows with Pamela!"

Raven jerked hard on her arms, pulling Roxanne closer. "Who I wed has naught to do with this. 'Tis a matter of honor."

Their eyes locked for a long moment. Then Raven's gaze traveled upward. Her sweet-smelling hair shone, even in the gentle candlelight and despite the veil adorning her ebony locks. The flimsy fabric flowed in soft blue folds down either side of her face to her shoulders, and as he followed its lines, he noticed it sparkled with flecks of silver. Allowing his glance to leap up again, he also noticed that the stones in her circlet glowed warmly. Yet all the glitter seemed to be reflected a hundredfold in Roxanne's violet-blue eyes.

"Un—unhand me, you cur!" she demanded, wishing to sound forceful, knowing she sounded as weak as a mewling kitten.

"I'll unhand you if and when I choose." He cocked an

arrogant brow. "Remember, I am lord here. If not forever, at least for this night. My will prevails, not yours."

What did Raven will? What did he desire? Roxanne wondered hopelessly, hopefully, as her lashes fluttered.

The knight expected to be graced with that mutinous expression the lady wore so often and so well. But instead, he saw uncertainty in the damsel's face. Instead of hard, her gaze appeared soft, soft as her lips, which she wetted with the tip of her moist tongue.

Raven might have rued the stirring he felt at his groin, except he suddenly realized that Roxanne knew—knew that she felt about him as he did about her. Though she was obviously pained to know her unruly heart had gone astray, that knowledge warmed him in regions not generally discussed in mixed company.

Jesu, he thought, fighting the desire to fondle her breasts. How he would love to take his time exploring all her womanly attributes. Yet, he dared not. If he loosened his hold, she might wrench herself free. Raven had no mind to let her go. Not now. Not ever.

The lord of Stonelee licked his own lips and felt the lady tremble as she watched him do it. Cautiously, he released her shoulders and slid his hands down her arms to her elbows.

Roxanne lost her balance slightly, swaying as though entranced while she stared at Raven's tongue. Despite the fact that she knew she should be thinking anything but, Roxanne imagined his tongue tickling her own body—her ear, her throat, her belly. . . .

He saw that his move had upset her balance slightly. Yet instead of tugging away or stepping back, Roxanne leaned into Raven. Taking it as a silent invitation, intentional or not, he clasped her more firmly to him, his splayed fingers against her ribs.

"I shan't let you fall," he whispered near her ear, his lips grazing her lobe.

"Oh!" Her response was breathless, hardly a true word. Yet, it was all Roxanne could manage; she felt stricken.

"I shan't let any harm come to you, ever." He ran his lips along her jaw even as his hands began deftly undoing the lacings at the sides of her bliaut.

She knew full well what he was about. She did not resist, except to say—without the haughtiness she would have liked to have managed, "I—I recall you vowed to harm me by your own hand."

"Did I?" Raven kissed Roxanne's chin, fluttered a kiss over her lips, and then retreated to safer territory, her cheek, her ear. "I believe there was a condition that, wisely, you did not meet. Is that not . . . true?"

"Oh!" A startled gasp, prompted not by his question but his kisses.

"I've no quarrel with you, Roxy." He tugged the outer garment off her shoulders and let it puddle around her ankles. "In truth, since you advised me of the danger to Angleford Keep, I must consider you . . . my . . . ally."

As he spoke, Raven stealthily slipped his arms under hers, keeping Roxanne's sagging body upright, while quickly plucking the laces free that ran down the back of her under tunic. "Aren't you?" he whispered, his lips blazing a trail down her throat, his tongue wetting a path over the swell of her breasts. "My ally?"

"Ohhh."

Her insides had dissolved to a consistency of pudding. No, porridge—warm and runny, barely cohesive. The sensation seemed to be spreading outward; Roxanne's knees had gone watery. She could barely stand of her own volition.

Her second garment pooled on top of the first. Roxanne remained clad only in a shift of sheer linen, fine hose, and soft, kid slippers, while the circlet and veil adorned her head. She looked like a Celtic goddess, and Raven wished he could step back and take the time required to memorize every detail of her scanty garb and voluptuous figure. But he dared not. He'd gone rock hard, and he needed this woman in the most intimate, desperate, primitive manner a man ever needed a woman. The damsel could not be allowed to think, lest she flee him. So in order to keep her senses reeling, he needed to keep her close.

Lowering his face to hers, Raven kissed Roxanne deeply. Still plundering her mouth with his tongue, he reached up and removed her head ornaments, flinging them with certain aim onto a nearby table. Next he slipped an arm behind her knees and lifted her, carrying Roxanne to the bed as if she were a child. There, he sat her down.

She was relieved he'd taken her to bed, not only because she knew what would surely happen, now, between them on this soft, wide mattress, but because Raven had relieved her of having to stand firm—on her feet, on her principles.

"I am your servant, my lady," Raven vowed sincerely, kneeling before Roxanne to slip off her borrowed shoes. He realized, as he raised one well-shaped foot to his lips in order to press kisses on the inside of her arch, that he had never called Roxanne a lady before. He wondered if she realized it, too.

Yet, he did not spend too much time pondering, for as he lifted her foot to caress it against his cheek, her shift slid up her thigh. The wayward garment afforded him a peek at her thatch of ebony maiden hair and the soft, moist petals of her woman's flesh tucked within. It nearly undid him.

Raven strove for control and maintained it. Still on his knees, he reached out, gently but purposefully tugging Roxanne's shift off over her head. To his delight, his relief, she raised her arms without protest, mutely assisting him.

Roxanne wanted this. She wanted to be relieved of her virginity, and she wanted only this man to take it from her. How could this be? Only yesterday, she'd have insisted it would never happen in her lifetime. But Raven of Stonelee had proved himself the man she wished to gift with her innocence—that sweet sacrifice a maiden could bestow but once.

She gave herself up to his seduction, and Raven knew, in that instant, she was his. She was also nude, except for her stockings, which he had not enough patience to remove. Besides, he felt enamored of the look of her, naked except for her clad legs. It was, for once, a reversal of her frequent mode of dress. So eagerly and more quickly than he'd ever recalled managing before, Raven shrugged off his own tunics and shoes. Wearing only braies and chausses, he climbed upon the bed and straddled Roxanne. Lifting her slightly, he settled her across the center of the mattress and lay down gently atop her.

"I—we—"

"Hush, sweetling," he ordered, his deep voice as entrancing as his words. "I shan't hurt you. I vow I shan't hurt you."

"Ohhh."

Smiling at her acquiescence, Raven's kissing, stroking, and fondling became more heated, more intense, more demanding. The lady's response did not really surprise him. She was a lusty lass, and he adored that quality in a woman. Most especially, he adored that quality in this woman. Now, he determined to prove to her no man could be his equal. Roxanne of Bittenshire had to desire him above all other lovers, most especially that accursed Welsh prince, Balin.

Raven escalated his assault on her senses. It took all his will not to succumb to the titillation of her response.

"Please, please!" Roxanne begged as he palmed her hot, slick sex. She felt such an intense craving, she not only begged aloud, her body thrummed with its physical need.

"Aye? What is it you wish, sweetling?" he asked, raising his lips from the erect, pink nipple he'd been suckling.

"I—" She panted and stared at him with glazed eyes. Confusion and uncertainty made her stammer, "I—I don't know. I do know, and yet—I do not. Methinks—"

"Here. This is what you seek," Raven interrupted, as he

took one of Roxanne's hands and pressed it to his straining, swollen manhood.

The muddle in her mind sorted itself. A flash of intuition, bolstered by instinct, cleared her head abruptly. Roxanne's thick lashes fluttered, her eyes focused on Raven's face, and she began undoing the ties that held up his leggings. She discovered her fingers as adept as his had been when he'd loosened her bliaut strings.

Again, Raven nearly lost control when this time, Roxanne raked his hips and buttocks with her nails as she slid his remaining garments down his thighs. Panting, he rolled off her and quickly stripped away his chausses and braies, flinging them aside. Immediately he climbed back above her, settling between her thighs, poised to enter her, ready to ride her.

"Here," she breathed, repeating what he'd said and done moments earlier. Yet, Roxanne did not gently cup his freed manhood. She encompassed his sex with her fingers, stroking it with innate skill.

"Good God, woman! You cannot expect me to—"

"But I do. I . . . expect . . . this!"

With a triumphant little smile, Roxanne spread her thighs farther and drew the head of Raven's rampant staff to the cleft secreted between her legs. When she tugged at him a bit, he reclaimed the power he had ceded to her and began to thrust himself inside without her guiding hand.

"Oh!"

He smiled down at her face at the sound of her exclamation, with which he had now become intimately familiar. Bracing himself with his hands, he plunged his blade into her sheath.

The initial probe had caused a rush of sweet sensation to sweep up Roxanne's hips, belly, even her breasts. Then her half closed eyelids snapped open at her virgin's pain. But she was not nearly so surprised by the breaching of her maidenhead as Raven, who had never expected to find the barrier he had so clumsily broken.

"Dear God! Roxy, forgive me," he pleaded, knowing he had been brutal when he should have been exceedingly gentle. "I believed you and Balin—God's tears, I'd have warned you, had I known."

"I knew," she informed him, remaining as still as he. "I just forgot for a bit."

"It shan't hurt anymore, I vow. That one painful moment should be the worst you'll e'er endure."

"I know that, too." Roxanne wriggled her hips, testing the feel of him. Her discomfort, sharp and jolting, had fled as abruptly as it appeared. Raven felt wonderful inside of her. His manhood filled her up, sealed her whole. So now, rather than grimacing in pain, she smiled provocatively. " 'Tis what I wanted."

"Nay," he insisted softly, craftily, as he pulled his weapon nearly all the way out of her sheath while raining kisses on her face again. " 'Tis . . . *this*"—he pushed himself into her once more—"that you wanted."

It was indeed what Roxanne of Bittenshire wanted—what Raven of Stonelee wanted, too. And together they had it, as neither might ever have imagined in their wildest dreams.

Later, cuddled under the covers in the bed, the hangings drawn closed to ensure their privacy, Roxanne dared to ask something in the afterglow of their lovemaking she'd not otherwise have ventured. "If I am your ally, Raven, what are you to me?"

"Your lover, sweetling. Always. Your lover."

Annie knocked. When she had no response, concern made her curious. The servant stepped into the lady's room, carrying Roxanne's trencher, at just the moment Raven spoke. Though she couldn't see him through the bed hangings, his voice was unmistakable. And though she could not see Roxanne, either, the woman knew full well to whom the new Marcher Earl of Angleford spoke.

Thus, before the night had passed, everyone at the keep had been apprised of the news that Lady Pamela's betrothed, Raven, Lord of Angleford, had bedded Roxanne of Bittenshire.

CHAPTER 22

Pamela sat near Peter's window. He had been sleeping since she'd entered, and she had considered retreating to her own chamber. But she knew, though he never admitted it, that he felt distressed when she was away from him.

Pamela felt distressed when she was away from him, also, and distressed when she was near! For something about Peter of Stoneweather had recently changed, and it wasn't only that he now got along on crutches.

Bedridden, he'd been a different man. Unlike his twin, he had made Pamela feel safe—so safe, she'd not even considered his gender. At most, he was a surrogate brother to her, and sisters did not think of their brothers as virile and attractive men.

But Peter of Stoneweather was a virile man. He had been when they had first met, but somehow, she'd forgotten it while he remained indisposed. Yet, since the first moment he had hauled himself up on his crutches, he had exuded an aura of masculinity that fairly intoxicated her senses. No longer always on his back, dependent on her ministrations, he towered over her when standing, and the muscles in his arms flexed with potent strength. It made no matter that she assisted him in his efforts to walk. Peter's male presence incited in Pamela a sense of frail vulnerability. Even when he returned to bed, she could not forget how easily he might overpower her—because, in some secret corner of her heart, Pamela wished the lord of Stoneweather would indeed overpower her, forcing her to do what she dared not.

Sighing, Pamela glanced at the pile of cloth laying atop a trunk. It was a beautiful bolt of fabric, the color of amethyst, which Lady Lucinda and Lord Ian had gifted her with to make a wedding tunic. Already it had been cut to her size. Now she should be sewing the seams. But Pamela had no desire to stitch, most especially a bridal bliaut for her wedding to Raven.

"Any spots?"

"What?" She jerked at the sound of Peter's voice and turned to him, surprised to see he'd awakened.

"Any signs of the crimson rash?"

"Nay! Why? Have you broken out?" she asked anxiously, already on her feet and rushing to his side. She even reached out to lift his arm and examine it, but stopped herself abruptly before touching him.

"Nay." He shook his head. "I only asked because you had such a pensive frown on your face."

"I was lost in thought."

"Were you? What were you thinking about?"

"Ah . . ." Pamela glanced at the trunk, at the cloth. "My wedding bliaut and—and my wedding."

"To Raven."

"Aye. Who else?"

"Who else, indeed. Well, get on with it, why don't you? There's little enough for you to do, confined almost like a prisoner in this chamber with me. How many games of draughts and Nine Men's Morris can be played in a day? Do your sewing now, so that you're ready for my brother when he returns.''

"No.'' She shook her head firmly. "You're my first responsibility.''

"I'm not your damnable responsibility!'' he shouted peevishly. "I've had those accursed crutches many days now. I can use them well enough. Feel free to return to your own chamber, milady, if you'd like!''

"I wouldn't like!'' she insisted, wondering how their easy compatibility had transformed into such a taut, tenuous relationship. "What say you we have another go at using your crutches? I'll stay right beside you, should you need me.''

"Nay. I—'' Peter shook his head sharply, yet his expression suddenly softened. "Very well,'' he agreed.

She felt glad his ever-altering mood had taken an abrupt swing for the better. In the early days, when he'd been testy, she'd left him to wallow. Now she felt his bouts with melancholy were somehow her doing, and she made every effort to cajole Peter into a better humor.

Pamela grabbed the wooden implements from their resting place at the head of Peter's bed and reached out a hand to him.

"Thank you.'' He smiled congenially as he accepted her assistance, and swung his good leg over the edge of the mattress.

Pamela flinched as a hot spark seared her palm at the feel of Peter's warm flesh against her own. Yet, the sensation wasn't unusual, and it proved the reason she avoided touching him whenever possible.

But she couldn't avoid him now. Purposefully, she held his hand tight as he stood on his uninjured leg. Then, with her free hand, she slid one crutch under his arm. Only when Peter seemed steady with that prop did she release his hand to offer him the second crutch. "Do you want to sit in the chair by the window?''

"Nay. I want to get out of here. Let's be daring,'' he suggested with a cocky smile. "What say we try for your room?''

Pamela shrugged. It was no farther to her chamber than to the garderobe. "I suppose we could," she conceded. "But why would you want to? My quarters are small."

"But they are not *these* quarters," he explained, "which is why I wish to visit there. Anything, to get out of this room and not be idling in the stinking jakes!"

"Very well. You lead, and I'll walk directly behind you, my hands on your waist."

"I expected that you would."

He winked before moving away from the bed so that she could step behind him. Never had he winked at her before, and the effect was shocking. Pamela nearly giggled. But she could not indulge in such frivolity, as Peter was already making his way across the bedchamber, forcing her to keep up with him.

"You're doing well," she said encouragingly.

"I told you I'd mastered the art." They emerged in the corridor. "What if I try to walk using only one crutch?"

"Peter, no!" Running around him, Pamela looked up into his face. "You couldn't possibly manage with only one."

"I could, if you gave me a shoulder to lean on."

She wanted to decline, but Peter's contentment was her only ambition these days. She nodded.

Grinning, he set one crutch against the wall and held out his arm, beckoning Pamela to his side. When she put her small frame next to his, he hugged her close.

The pressure of his fingers gripping her shoulder did not unnerve her; oddly, she felt secure in the awkward embrace. Slipping one arm about his waist, she impulsively reached up and placed a hand encouragingly over his.

Cautiously, they took a few steps forward. "Are you all right?" Pamela asked, raising her face to his. To her surprise, he responded by leaning down and kissing her nose.

"Quite all right, thank you."

Peter had kissed her! It was an innocent peck, a brotherly buss. But, by God, it had been a kiss!

Pamela felt gay and wildly giddy. But she willed herself to contain her unruly emotions, drew a deep breath, and cautioned, "Be careful." Scampering forward, she opened the door to her chamber before returning to Peter's side to assist him again.

"Help me to the window," he urged, leaning heavily against Pamela. "I believe it has a more interesting view than the one my own looks out upon."

"Different, mayhap, but hardly interesting. However, if you lean out and look to the east, you can see some of the meadow."

"Gazing at a meadow. What a delight!" He chuckled as they reached the window, and Pamela disengaged herself to drag a chair nearer to it.

"Nay." Gripping the stone sill with one hand, Peter set his second crutch aside. "I think I shall stand for a bit."

"It won't be too tiring?"

"I'm injured, Pamela, not wasting away from disease. I'm as strong as Raven, I'll have you know."

"I know," she assured him hastily.

He leaned against the wall beneath the window, gripping the sill with both hands. When he put his head through the opening, the breeze ruffled his shiny black hair.

"Sweet *Jesu,* but this is pleasant." He glanced back at Pamela. "Come. Join me."

Obediently, she did. Though any window this high up in the keep was of a decent size, it was not so large that there could be any space between them. Pamela was excruciatingly aware of his ribs, hip, and thigh pressed snugly to her own body. She cursed herself for noticing such. He was Roxanne's betrothed, and she should not be having wayward feelings about him. The problem with wayward feelings was, one could not control them.

"It smells like springtime, doesn't it?" Peter asked, again gazing at the bailey below.

"Only because the wind's shifted. Earlier today, the stink of the middens wafted through the yard."

He chuckled. "Is there no poetry in your soul, Little Lady Pamela? I thought all young women had romantic natures."

"When appropriate, my lord, I sometimes indulge in whimsy," she assured him, her spine stiff.

"Ah." He looked at her appraisingly. "Then, you don't feel it's proper to wax poetic or indulge in romantic notions when in my presence?"

"Nay. 'Tis not. Once we're wed to—oh!"

Unexpectedly, Peter lost his balance and lurched toward her. Instinctively, Pamela reached for him. In turn, he wrapped his arms tightly about her waist.

Awkwardly, careful of his injured leg, she managed to drag him to the chair. When he was seated, she admonished, "Sweet Mother of God, Peter! You've just barely regained the use of your good leg after weeks abed. You cannot stand without assistance and not expect to fall!"

"You're right," he agreed contritely.

"Mayhap we should get you back to your bed."

"Nay. I would sit here and enjoy the view awhile."

She sighed but agreed indulgently. "Very well."

"Sit with me."

"There's not another chair."

"No matter." Peter grabbed Pamela's hand and tugged her down into his lap. Startled and dismayed, she tried frantically to spring off. But Peter's bad leg had not affected his arms. With them he kept her pinned, seated on his hard-muscled thighs.

"This is not at all proper," she said primly. "If your mother happened by—"

"She won't. She's tending Hugh and the little twins, and all the others at the castle who've succumbed to the crimson rash. Besides, how could I enjoy this pleasant view if I knew you were denied it or forced to stand? Indulge me, sweetling. Sit with me and look up at the sky. Ah! I can, indeed, see a bit of the meadow where Lord Ian always holds Fortengall Fair!"

He called her *sweetling!* Such was an endearment lovers used. Hearing it caused her pulse to quicken.

"Pamela?" Peter touched a hand to her chin, forcing her to face him. "Is something amiss?"

"Nay. I, uh . . . nay," she repeated lamely.

"Look," he urged gently, pointing to the bailey wall on the opposite side of the yard. "Do you see there, on the parapet? The first bird of spring, I'd wager."

"Yes." She nodded distractedly, unable to see the bird, not even looking for it. "The yard is rather quiet, though, don't you agree? There's much less bustle and noise than normal."

" 'Tis because there's much more sickness than normal. What did Mother say last time she came to the door? Children have fallen ill left and right, and more than a few grown men are laid low with the scourge."

"Aye. At least your younger brothers are bearing up well." Pamela sighed distractedly, knowing she should jump from Peter's lap. Failing that, she determined to sit perfectly still. "If it is mostly the little ones who are sick, you'd think there'd be more laborers about."

"Nay." He gave her waist a reassuring squeeze. She swayed toward his chest but immediately righted herself again. "Parents are home tending their stricken children."

She nodded, agreeing with his assessment, thinking only that the time had come to end his visit to her chamber. Suddenly, Pamela became aware of something niggling at her like a bedeviling insect bite. Yet, she had no small blemish on her skin; rather, a hard, firm bulge in Peter's braies nudged audaciously at the cleft in her buttocks!

Turning wide-eyed to the man who held her, she expected some confirmation of her unspoken accusation, or at least an apology. But Peter smiled benignly. So Pamela resumed a more subtle attempt to slide out of his lap, which, to her mortification, only worsened the situation by inflaming Peter's lust. Rigid in his embrace, she declared sternly, "You must release me, my lord. It cannot be good for you, my weight upon your injured leg."

"Nonsense," he argued easily. "My leg is broken below the knee. Aye, if you perched on it there, I don't doubt you would break it again. But where your bottom's resting, I assure you it feels quite good."

Flushing crimson, she dared not face him. Didn't he know? Apparently not. He couldn't know and remain so nonchalant.

"Little Lady Pamela, are you vexed?" he asked softly, touching her cheek with his fingertips to force her face to his.

"Nay," she lied. "I'm not vexed."

"You appear vexed," he insisted. "Let me reassure you."

He drew her closer still, and Pamela watched, captivated, as his lips came so near hers they all but touched.

"I must insist . . ."

"On this?" he whispered, his warm breath tickling her nose.

Peter eliminated any space between them as he fluttered his lips unthreateningly over Pamela's own. Like a sorcerer, he drew her to him, bound her to him, without so much as a cord or a command. Unable to resist, she closed her eyes and gave herself up to Peter's gentle kissing, which resembled a butterfly flitting over the petals of an unfurling flower.

The knight's kiss remained gentle for some moments, but not forever. His tongue, hard and strong, insinuated itself between Pamela's soft lips. Surprised, she gasped, opening her mouth wider and inadvertently allowing him easier access.

When she issued this instinctive invitation, Peter accepted. Grasping the back of Pamela's head with his hand, he held her in place and leisurely explored the recesses of that warm, moist cavity behind her parted lips. Submitting to his onslaught, she sagged against him, palms against his chest.

Her conscience screamed *wickedness!* but the throbbing of her sex and the pounding of her heart silenced the warning. Thus, it was with regret that Pamela felt Peter's tongue retreat. Not ready to relinquish this instrument of titillating pleasure, she selfishly nipped at the moist tip before it escaped completely. As it lingered at the entrance of her mouth, Pamela clasped the invader with her lips, holding snug the velvety, pink muscle with which she was being assaulted so sensuously.

Again, Peter's tongue drove deep; again, it retreated. Pamela thought, distantly, that she might be swooning. Yet, she was keenly aware of her own ragged breathing and her nipples, aching painfully when her bosom rose and fell, as the wool of her bliaut scraped the silk of Peter's robe.

He drew her down against him so that her back rested in the crook of his arm. Pamela raised her unfocused gaze to the soft, ebony pools of his eyes, and discovered them nearly hidden behind his heavy, black-lashed lids. Passion slackened the features of his handsome face, baiting her own churning feelings and beckoning them to the fore. Suddenly Pamela knew she would not lose consciousness. Never would she miss a moment of this tender, erotic onslaught.

Instinct kept her from passivity. Unaware of what she did or why, she locked her fingers behind Peter's neck, securing him to her by mimicking his embrace. Then Pamela began to suck as a baby suckles a breast. The silky walls of her mouth contracted around him, her gentle tongue massaging the underside of his own rigid tongue.

Peter's hands moved. She felt one kneading her bosom, assuaging the discomfort. Pamela arched into him, needful of more of his expert fondling. She thought how splendid it would be if his fingers could find their way into her tunics to caress her bare and heated flesh.

But then she felt again the swelling at his groin as it prodded her bottom. She knew that if Peter in fact rid her of her clothes, somehow that male appendage would make its way into her secret cleft, despite that he remained crippled and she still a virgin. No matter how dearly her body craved it, such could not be permitted, and Pamela's conscience shrieked that message so woefully that she reluctantly reacted.

Flailing her arms, Pamela managed to loosen Peter's hold. With a cry, she jumped from his lap. Before he could detain her again, with a touch or a word, she fled the tiny chamber.

"Pamela!" Peter shouted, glaring at the door. "Pamela!"

He reached for his crutch and propped himself up. But no sooner had he made a clumsy attempt to walk than it went skittering out from beneath his arm.

"God's bloody wounds!" he swore, unable to retrieve the implement, unable to walk at all without it.

Pamela stumbled into the hallway and leaned against the wall, breathing raggedly. She'd been sinful—and worse, she'd sinned with her cousin's betrothed, her own intended husband's brother! She had to find the castle priest; she had to confess!

"Pamela?"

Inhaling a breath, she strained for composure as her eyes beheld Lady Lucinda approaching on the stairs. The earl's wife looked pale, her green eyes smudged with dark shadows. But Pamela didn't notice her appearance because the unexpected encounter heightened her panic.

"Is something wrong? Neither you nor Peter are ill, are you?"

Pamela shook her head as she tried to find her voice. "N-nay. We're both well. Except for Peter's leg, that is."

"Then, what is wrong? Surely something is."

"I"—she clutched her bliaut where it lay across her bosom and looked helplessly at the lady—"I . . . simply . . . had to get away."

"Away? From Peter?" Lucinda frowned. "Did he do something to upset you?"

"No. Not apurpose. But"—Pamela sighed raggedly—"'tis difficult, milady, being confined so long with only one person for company and companionship. I need—"

"What do you need?" Lucinda asked gently.

She looked right and left, her head snapping from side to side as though she sought an escape route. Then she cried plaintively, "Air!" And before the lady could dissuade her, Pamela ran haphazardly down the stairs, disregarding all the precautions she'd previously taken to avoid those who'd been exposed to the crimson rash. Flying past the guards, she wrenched open the keep's front portal and tore across the bailey.

Lucinda did not follow her. Retrieving the crutch she found abandoned in the hallway, she called her son's name. She found him not in the bedchamber he always used when visiting Fortengall, but in the smaller room where Pamela now slept. Discovering him helpless, clutching the back of a chair, she hurried forward to assist him.

"What's happened between you and Pamela, that she would leave you stranded this way? Did you have an argument?"

"Aye," he confirmed glumly, refusing to meet his mother's eyes. "'Twas nothing serious. Only . . ."

"Only what, Peter?"

He shrugged. "In close confines for too long, the most friendly of people can become . . . vexed with each other."

"Vexed, is it?" she repeated, and Peter noticed that though his mother seemed distracted, she did not seem disturbed. "Well, I'm sorry if your friendship's been strained. But hopefully, you shan't have to continue in isolation much longer. Hugh, John, and Jamie are doing much better, and there have been no new victims of the crimson rash today. If such continues, you will be able to come down to the hall. By then, Raven and Roxanne should have returned."

"I'm pleased," Peter said with little enthusiasm.

"Do you want to return to your own chamber now?"

"Nay. I'll sit here awhile longer."

"Then I shall return later to help you."

"You need rest, Mother. I beg you, get off your feet. And don't worry after me. Pamela will return to assist me."

"Will she? Methinks the damsel intends to be gone awhile. Nursing you has apparently tried her sorely."

"'Twas nothing, not even a squabble. She'll return soon."

"Mayhap you're right," Lucinda agreed as she crossed her arms over her chest. "Pamela of Angleford is a dutiful girl, and I am grateful for her assistance. But she's young, Peter, so do not abuse her good nature, I beg you. Raven has already done enough of that."

His obsidian eyes glittered. "I would ne'er exploit the lady of Angleford Keep," he declared, "and I take exception to you implying I might. As for my brother, he'll have some accounting of his own to do, once he returns to this castle keep!"

Nodding tiredly, Lucinda retreated without further comment. When she was gone, Peter sank into his solitary thoughts— and smiled secretively.

Pamela ran, but not because she was either insulted or frightened. Nay, she ran because she realizes she desires me as much as I do her! There is no denying it, now. Our attraction is too great to ignore or overcome.

Peter knew full well more trouble would come of this, that it would rise up like an ugly monster from a murky sea and threaten to destroy his and Pamela's timorous, fledgling love. But he intended to face the beast and best it, whether it wore Raven's face or King Henry's.

Idly, he stared out the window. When he spied Pamela in the pale, brown meadow beyond the curtain walls, his heart seized with longing. He knew, even if she did not, that the Little Lady of Angleford was destined to be his.

CHAPTER 23

"Lucinda!" Lord Ian grabbed his wife's arm and spun her around, directing her toward the high table in the great hall. "You will sit down, and you will eat!"

"Ian!" she protested wearily.

But it was no use. The great scarred giant of a man was no match for a slim, exhausted woman. He fairly whisked her off her feet as he pulled her along behind him; she quickly found herself in her chair looking down at a trencher of steaming food.

"Eat," he directed again, looming above her on the dais as though prepared to thwart an attempted escape.

With a nod, Lucinda plucked her eating knife from the sheath on her girdle. Only then did the earl sit down beside her.

"You shouldn't be so loud," she chastised him, glancing about the hall at the bodies asleep on their pallets. "You'll wake the servants."

" 'Tis a rare servant who could not catch a midday nap while supposedly about his duties. One and all will sleep through my spoken words." Despite his argument, Ian also looked around the quiet hall. "The fact that so many have gone to bed, though, proves you're pushing yourself far too hard. You steal but a few hours' sleep every night, and I fear you miss more meals than you take. You're going to be ill yourself if you keep this up much longer."

"I can't fall ill, Ian. You know it. I suffered the crimson rash ages ago, as a child."

"I do not speak of this malady, sweetling. I speak of you working yourself into your grave. I shan't have it," he warned, setting his jaw and glaring at her emphatically.

Lucinda swallowed a morsel of meat. Since her eating knife now hung suspended in her limp hand, Ian took it from her, speared a turnip cube, and popped the vegetable into her mouth.

"It has been fully ten days since the boys came down with fevers and rash. They have left their beds already, and others who took sick are on their feet as well. Lucinda, the scourge is waning. In another sennight, few will remain abed."

"But there are many more right now."

"All with family and friends to tend them."

She nodded, accepting another bite of food her husband fed her. Yet, her expression remained sad.

"What is it?" Ian inquired gently.

"I'm thinking of the ten and two we lost. Old Kip and Mary's baby, among them."

"Aye." Ian nodded. "But Kip was past seventy, and the infant barely out of the womb. The number who died altogether is small, Lucinda."

"Mayhap, if I'd done more—"

"Lucinda, cease!" Her husband grabbed her shoulders, forcing her to turn in her chair and face him. "You did all you could."

She seemed to disagree, but when, finally, she nodded her ascent, the earl added, "I would think you'd be relieved,

Lucinda, that this sickness is passing. Mightn't you now be able to free Pamela from her duties as Peter's nursemaid?''

"Oh, aye! Ian, I'm glad you reminded me. I've seen so little of them, I'd nearly forgotten their circumstances.''

"Forgotten? God's teeth, Lucinda, I thought you were concerned about their growing friendship even before this illness struck. Yet, you've forgotten their circumstances?'' He peered at her suspiciously. "My lady, you must be far more fatigued than even I supposed, if such is the case.''

"I'm not,'' Lucinda insisted before taking a sip of her home-brewed beer. "But several days ago, I encountered Pamela intent on scurrying from the keep. She was quite overwrought.''

"Overwrought?''

"Aye. Apparently Peter's company had worn thin, and the damsel sorely needed a respite from his constant presence.''

"Sweet *Jesu.* They're not now as contentious as Raven and Roxanne are, do you think?''

Lucinda's eyes widened with an expression Ian could not interpret. Abruptly, she pushed back her chair and stood. "I must go to Pamela,'' she announced, "and explain that the danger is past. She may return to her own chamber, and William can return to his post in Peter's room. I—''

She swayed dizzily, and Ian caught her, scooping her into his arms. "It can wait 'til morning. Now, you are going straight to bed where you shall sleep until you're fully rested.''

"Ian!''

"Don't argue with me, woman. 'Twill make no difference if you speak with Peter and Pamela now or on the morn. But I fear for your health if you do not get yourself to bed without delay.''

Lord Ian was wrong.

Peter sat in his chair, crutches handily nearby, thinking hard what to do. Pamela was in the neighboring chamber, avoiding him. She had been avoiding him since the afternoon he'd nearly seduced her. Always about when needed, she never denied him assistance when he required it. But she seemed able to stay just beyond his reach, using a stool where previously she might have perched on his bed, and often retreating to her solitary quarters where before she would have lingered to keep him company.

Seduction now seemed nearly impossible. Any day, Peter knew, his mother would announce the crimson rash was on the wane. Pamela could return to her old room while he himself went downstairs among the company in the great hall. And Roxanne would surely return with Raven at any moment—his blundering brother was not so poor a knight that he couldn't track and overtake a damsel traveling unescorted.

Time was running out, Peter realized grimly. And Pamela now kept him at a distance. But he would be damned if he'd dally any longer, allowing the forces of fate to interfere in his destiny.

Sounds on the stairs distracted him; he heard his mother and the earl heading to their own bedchamber. Their departure from the great hall signaled the end of the day. The rest of those in the castle would find their beds soon.

Without hesitation, Peter stood, securing the crutches beneath his arms. He was better at this than Pamela knew. Tonight she would discover he was better at other things than she ever dared imagine.

Skillfully, he approached the door and maneuvered it open. Next, he made his way along the corridor to Pamela's chamber.

She was undressing. It wasn't so late in the evening yet that she could not have challenged Peter to a board game of one kind or another. But she had not dared. Spending daylight hours with the lord of Stoneweather proved taxing; spending evening hours with him was nearly debilitating, frayed and frazzled as her nerves had recently become.

Pamela had never been so frightened in her life as she was the day Peter restrained her, petted her, and kissed her. Being with a man and enjoying those feelings did not horrify her. Lady Ceridwen had prepared her daughter to experience those emotions precipitating the physical act of sex. Secretly, Pamela had anticipated them with some eagerness. But she expected to learn from her own husband, not her betrothed's brother!

She shivered though she felt no chill. In truth, her skin felt aflame! With a damp cloth, she swabbed her body down.

The lady's door stood ajar. How naive she was, Peter mused, smiling to himself. If Pamela had any idea of the sort of thoughts that consumed him, if she had any inkling of what he was capable of, she would have closed her door tightly and barred the portal against him. But in this tiny room, she believed herself safe. How foolish of her, yet how lucky for him.

Stepping close, he peered into the open space between the door and its frame. His pulse leaped at the vision he spied.

Pamela's back was to him as she faced the table where her washbowl sat. Languidly, she raised one arm high, running a damp cloth from her wrist to her shoulder. Next, she lifted her other hand above her head and then, Peter presumed, she scrubbed her breasts. "Sweet Mother Mary," he muttered silently. He would love to be the one bathing her breasts. But he'd not use water and a rag; he would use his moist tongue.

Pamela flipped her unbound hair, honey-brown and streaked with paler strands that glittered golden in the flickering, yellow candlelight, over her shoulders. The mane settled heavily, a shawl whose fringe skimmed her waist but left her bottom exposed. Rinsing out her cloth, Pamela then bent forward to wash her shapely calves.

That action parted her wealth of hair. It streamed down either side of her face, revealing again her alabaster back, the delicate knobs of her spine. Peter's loins seized as he contemplated slipping up behind her, catching her pert breasts in his hands, and pressing that slim back to his chest. Imprisoned against him thusly, he knew her bottom would rub his thighs. . . .

Jesu! What a derriere she had, he realized as his manhood hardened. Peter's member was not contained in any way, for he wore only a bed robe. Now it threatened to part the edges of fabric, anchored together only with a loose cord tied at his hips. If he shifted his weight slightly, he knew his masculine appendage would surely show its head—already it aimed at the enticing cleft between Pamela's feminine, fleshy globes.

He groaned. She heard him. Pamela spun about in surprise, crossing her arms over her chest to cover her breasts with splayed fingers. But her stance provided minimal modesty, and the darkish curls in the V of her thighs so beguiled Peter, he came forward without hesitation.

When he stood inside the small chamber, he did what the lady should have done: He closed the door tightly and barred it.

"Peter! You—" She lunged for her own robe, which lay at the foot of her bed. But before she could pull it on, the knight stopped her, not with a restraining arm but with a word.

"Sweetling, nay. Leave it off. I would look at you."

She froze in the act of picking up the garment. With the robe clutched in one hand, she gazed at Peter, wide-eyed.

"You're beautiful, Pamela. More beautiful than I imagined. That seems impossible, but it is true."

He came toward her, swinging his legs through his braced crutches. When he stood directly before her, he tossed one crutch aside and used that arm to embrace her.

She stiffened. "Peter, no! 'Tis wrong. We shouldn't—!"

"We must." He brought his mouth down hard upon hers, stealing her breath, routing her will. When he released her lips and drew a deep breath, he added hoarsely, " 'Tis what I want, what you want, what must be."

They kissed again, and Pamela succumbed, sagging against

him. His sex emerged at last from the folds of his silken robe and snuggled against her flat belly.

"The bed," he whispered against her ear, and Pamela helped him to it, clinging to his side. When he was seated, he dragged himself to the middle of the mattress, shrugged off the robe to fully display his potent desire, and reached up, beckoning her.

For a moment the girl faltered, her eyes on his face. He was such a dark man, from his blue-black hair, waving in soft wisps against his neck, to his eyes, nearly as black, yet, warm and liquid, to his beard, just as sooty as every hair that sprang from his flesh. . . . Pamela's gaze traveled lower and lingered.

It was as though she'd touched him. Peter's hard appendage quivered like an arrow that had just pierced a board. In a whisper, he beseeched her to do in fact what she'd done only by implication.

His tone was urgent, and Pamela did not hesitate. Leaning toward him, she crawled up onto the bed, one knee at a time. Then she slithered up beside him, stretching out alongside his hard, hot body. Peter dwarfed Pamela with her head near his shoulders and her toes not even reaching the ankle of his uninjured limb. Yet, she did not seem intimidated. Reaching out boldly, she grasped his shaft with her fingers. She could no more encompass it with her small hand than she could cover Peter's body with her own. So she stroked the muscle's length, from head to scrotum.

"*Jesu!*" he moaned, throwing back his head so that the knob in his throat protruded. "Sweetling, how I've longed for you to do precisely that!"

While Pamela continued her gentle, tentative caresses, Peter twisted his upper torso to fondle a breast with his hand. When she gasped and closed her eyes, he leaned down and lathed the nipple his fingers neglected with his searching tongue.

"Peter!" She arched her back and turned her face toward his. As he kissed her there, on lips and nose and eyes, she released his cock and began, blindly, to explore his body with the palm of her hand and the tips of her fingers.

He lay back with a groan and succumbed to her examination. Purposely, he distracted himself with nonsensical thoughts as he endured the exquisite torture of her exploration. More than once he thought he would lose control, as Pamela traced the indentation marking the two, muscled halves of his chest, as she tongued his wide, pebbly nipples, and as she raked her nails through the springy hair that flowed like a river from his chest to his groin. Yet, he managed to refrain from spilling his seed, though his sex felt heavy and ached for release.

Pamela saw the knob in Peter's neck slide up and down the column of his throat. She heard the sounds he made. But he didn't speak until he covered her hand with his own, and she stilled her movements.

"Cease," he demanded, his voice little better than a frog's croaking. "Climb astride me so that I may give you the sort of pleasure you've given me."

The damsel demonstrated no false modesty and did not protest out of either guilt or shame. Instead, she drew herself up to her knees and climbed over Peter's belly. When he touched her woman's flesh, and she jumped at the shock of his gentle handling, she didn't throw herself off in terror or surprise. Instead she closed her eyes, threw back her head, and braced her hands on his thighs.

"Pamela."

At the sound of her name on his lips, her eyes opened a crack. Meeting his gaze, she leaned toward him, a wary expression on her features as her hair tumbled down, tickling his shoulders. "Aye?"

"Pamela, I believe I want you more than Adam desired Eve. But I cannot take you this way."

She stared hard at him a moment. "Very well," she conceded without argument, turning aside and sliding her thigh across his belly as she promptly began taking her leave.

Peter grabbed her wrist before Pamela's bottom and its moist, musky heat was only a taunting memory. She looked at him in confusion, and he saw her eyes glaze with shining tears.

"Do not say you love me," she warned, her voice high. "You are correct, Peter. We cannot love each other. Not like this. 'Tis wrong and can never be."

"I do love you. And we shall have each other."

"Nay!" she cried sharply, her tears falling freely now. "A madness overtook me, that I was so willing to give myself to you. Roxanne, your brother . . ."

"Speak not of them now," Peter growled, yanking on Pamela's arm, forcing her to fall forward, above him, and to brace her hands beside his head. "This moment is ours. It has naught to do with either your cousin or my twin."

"How can you say that?" she demanded hoarsely. A tear from her eye plopped on Peter's cheek. "You're to wed Roxy and I, Lord Raven."

"Never!"

"But, the king!"

"The king be damned." He reached up and locked his fingers behind her back. She fell against him, her breasts cushioned in the springy hair matted on his chest, his hard staff nestled in the flesh of her soft belly. "You'll be *my* bride, Little Lady Pamela of Angleford. I'll not allow you to wed any man save me."

In disbelief, she opened her mouth in a little *O*. Peter, unable to resist, raised his head and pressed his lips to hers. Pamela at first failed to respond, but then she gave in to the enticement of his kiss. Relinquishing the bedclothes she had clutched in her fingers, she tangled them instead in Peter's glossy hair.

" 'Twill never happen," she argued breathlessly when she came up for air. "No one, from the king, to your mother, to our own intended spouses, shall allow us to wed each other, Peter. You know it, so do not torture me!"

"Torture you?" He smiled. "Sweetling, 'tis you who are

torturing me. And if I cannot join my body to yours in a very short while, I shall embarrass myself in front of you."

"But—but you said we couldn't. I—I don't understand!"

"I would wed you now, Pamela, before any can thwart the nuptials. If we are already man and wife before they learn of our love, none can undo our wedded union."

She made a *moue* with her mouth and shook her head slowly. "Even if we dared, how could we? There is no way we could bring secret witnesses and a priest to this chamber without someone knowing. You suggest impossibilities, Peter."

"Nothing is impossible if you truly want it, sweetling." He reached up and stroked her jaw with his knuckle. "Do you? Do you want to be my wife?"

"Oh, aye! I do. But . . ."

"No more arguments. And no witnesses or priest, because we require neither to speak our vows. 'Tis the law, and has been for long years: two people may wed alone by consent, providing their vows are said in earnest and there are no impediments to their union. You know there are no impediments, Pamela, or Henry would not have commanded you cousins to marry we brothers."

"Aye," she agreed softly. "But King Henry wants you to wed Roxy and I, your brother. He'll be furious if we disobey him."

"For you, I shall defy him and risk his royal fury."

"But I'd not have you dead! Oh, Peter." Pamela fell against him and hugged his neck. He could feel her tears wetting his shoulder. "I would rather love you secretly and know you are alive and well, and husband to Roxanne, than have you as my own a short while, only to see you slain at Henry's order!"

"I'll not meet such a fate, dearest." He smiled as he lifted her shoulders so that he could better see her face. "If we must, we'll flee to some hidden corner of the world where even the great king cannot find us. You'd come with me, aye?"

"Oh, aye! Where I live out my days, I care not, as long as I'm with the man I love, the one who holds me dear."

"I hold you dear." He let one of his hands slide up and down the curve of Pamela's bottom. "And I shall hold you forever. Beginning this night."

Peter rolled Pamela off him, keeping her cuddled at his side. As he propped himself on one elbow, he considered her naked charms. Her eyes were dark gold and glistening, her hair delectably disheveled, and her cheeks bloomed rosily, the color having blossomed with her awakening passions. He thought how most every man in the land would love to behold such a nubile, naked bride as they made their wedding vows.

"I," he began somberly, "Peter, Lord of Stoneweather, take thee, Lady Pamela of Angleford, as my wedded wife. I shall be faithful to you all of my days, and I shall spend those days ensuring that you and our children shall be always safe, sheltered, and well-fed. Never shall I love another."

It was enough, and he was impatient. Pausing, Peter looked to Pamela, waiting for her to speak her troth.

Her lashes fluttered. He smiled encouragingly.

"I, Lady Pamela of Angleford, take thee, Lord Peter of Stoneweather, as my one, true husband. I come to you a virgin and vow never to know another man as long as we both shall live. All my children will be yours, have no doubt. And I shall care for you and them 'til I die." She paused and took a deep breath that made her breasts quiver. "I love you, Peter."

"No more than I love you."

He glanced down at his hands and removed a gold signet ring set with onyx, as dark and gleaming as his eyes. Taking Pamela's hand in his own, he then slipped it on her middle finger.

Pamela gazed at the ring and at her hand in Peter's. When she looked up, she appeared suddenly shy as she asked, "Are we truly man and wife?"

"As truly as if we'd been wed in a great cathedral with a bishop saying mass and royalty witnessing our troth."

She grinned, and the tears trickling anew from her eyes were joyful tears.

"Come here, wife. I must make this marriage binding, now."

Peter drew her over him again. His sex had lost its rigidity during their vow-taking. But the instant Pamela's smooth belly fell flat against it, his root went hard as any warrior's wooden staff.

Pamela hugged him, wrapping her arms behind his neck. She squirmed before straddling his hips and drawing herself farther up his length. This brought her breasts directly before Peter's face, and he suckled them greedily, pleased to note that the cleft secreted between her thighs had pressed against him and was slick with need, a need he shared.

"Lift up," he urged, using his hands to guide her hips. Pamela raised herself, watching silently as her husband nestled the head of his penis into the folds of her sex. "This first time, you will probably know some pain, dearling. But slide yourself down upon me slowly, until you have all of me inside."

Obediently, Pamela complied, lowering herself over the blushing knob at the end of his staff. Cautiously, she sidled lower, taking him into her. "Oh!" she gasped, startled, at the first sting of pain.

" 'Tis a virgin's curse," Peter explained. "But I vow that after this, I shan't hurt you again. From this moment on, I vow never to hurt you at all, for any reason under the sun."

As he spoke, he reached forward and rubbed his thumb over the nub swelling between those folds of pink, feminine flesh. Pamela closed her eyes, and her head lolled back. Immediately she began to undulate in response to his skillful stroking.

As she moved, her sheath clenched his invading member. With each twist and turn, it also closed down upon that masculine appendage, drawing more and more of it closer to her womb.

"Ahhh!" Her cry mingled pleasure and pain. Her head came up, her eyes opened.

Peter smiled as his languid gaze met hers. He continued to stroke her, and Pamela's breathing quickened. As well she began to move her hips in a primitive dance as old as time.

She had all of him.

Reaching out with one strong arm, he pulled his bride down against his chest. His hand remained between them, pleasuring the core of her sex.

Pamela continued to writhe, intuitively pleasuring him. Suddenly she peered into Peter's eyes with an expression of astonishment. At that same moment, she stiffened and shuddered with the unexpected release of her first, tumultuous climax.

To see his wife thus, an innocent cresting the waves of pleasure he'd aroused in her, sent Peter flying over the precipice of his own fervent desire. Smothering a moan in Pamela's smooth, round shoulder, his warm seed poured out of him and into her.

"We are one," he whispered when he got back his breath. "We are man and wife, and no one shall separate us. Ever."

CHAPTER 24

Roxanne woke amid the rumpled bed clothes, sat up, and stretched her arms overhead. She felt wonderful, yet, for those first few moments of wakefulness, she could not understand the source of her euphoria. Then it came to her, as the subtle soreness between her legs brought back images of the night just spent and the knight with whom she'd spent it. Frowning, Roxanne gazed at the empty space beside her.

"Are you awake?" Raven inquired, drawing back the bed hangings to look at Roxanne. He was dressed. She was not, but she made no attempt at all to cover her naked breasts.

"Aye." She nodded casually, hoping she appeared composed. She didn't know how lovers behaved with one another come the morning after. But she would not let her inexperience show.

"Are you hungry?" he inquired, and again she nodded.

"I would think so. We had no supper last eve, though I did spy a tray of food on the table when I rose this morning. Was it there when I . . . ?'' He left off, raising his eyebrows in mute question.

"Nay. Annie surely brought it up after we had—"

Roxanne didn't finish her thought, either. Yet, both Raven and she leaped to the same conclusion.

"Don't concern yourself, Roxy. The woman's naught but a servant, after all."

True, the Angleford servant was of no consequence. Yet, the woman surely knew what had transpired here last evening, and that knowledge vexed Roxanne. "Raven."

He sat down beside her, and before she could continue he kissed her soundly. As his tongue explored her lips, he possessively fondled her breast with his fingers.

"I admit I'm famished, too," he said when he released Roxanne and came again to his feet. "I'm going downstairs to break my fast. There's much to do this day before Balin arrives to attack the keep with his warriors."

"Raven—"

"Later, Roxy. Later."

With that, he stepped outside the wall of curtains shrouding the bed. She heard his footsteps as he departed the room and the sound of the door creaking closed behind him.

A sudden fury consumed her. Balin had sent her away after only the rudest of kisses. Now Raven dismissed her after ravishing her body, breaching her maidenhead. How dare he!

She threw back the covers and leaped off the bed. Roxanne of Bittenshire was no slut to be used and discarded like a village whore! If Raven didn't realize this on his own, she would make him understand the consequences of his reckless behavior.

Dressing herself in the gowns Raven had removed the night before, Roxanne used her fingers for a comb and was still tugging on her shoes when she began her descent down the stairs. The first people she spied in the great hall were two, twittering serving wenches. They smiled slyly at her until she glared back and ordered them to work. But Roxanne knew that they knew—they all knew—about her and Raven.

He was at the high table, not seated and eating but standing before the dais, speaking with Master Felix.

Lifting her skirts, Roxanne walked quickly across the length of the large room, intending to call out to him. But when she neared Felix, she halted midstep and remained silent.

"Nearly everyone knows, my lord," the seneschal was telling Raven. "The servants in the keep, the barony's guards, knights and archers alike. It is . . . unfortunate."

"It is . . . none of their business!" Raven snapped, imitating Felix. "Why should I care what those employed at Angleford think of me, their lord? I rule here. They're of no importance."

"That is hardly true in this instance, Lord Raven. You are not yet wed to Lady Pamela, and therefore have no real claim to Angleford. But because Prince Balin rides this way intending trouble, you need everyone's loyalty, most particularly the guards'. Men do not readily risk death for a lord to whom they owe no fealty. Certainly not one they do not respect."

Raven stiffened. Roxanne saw it in his stance.

"I've done naught to lose their respect. As you say, Felix, I'm not committed to this barony, yet, I am willing to risk my life to defend it. What more might they expect of me?"

Felix shrugged and looked down at his feet. "I suppose they expect you to honor their lady, Pamela of Angleford."

Roxanne cringed and watched Raven through narrowed eyes as he laughed disdainfully. Lounging against the plank table, he waved a hand negligently through the air, demanding, "Are the people of Angleford so naive they don't know noblemen take mistresses? Did Lord Arthur sleep with none save his lady wife?"

Roxanne glanced down at her bosom. The pain she felt was so sharp, she instinctively looked for a wound. But no crimson blood blossomed on her bliaut; the cut was invisible.

Felix flushed, but he widened his own stance as though to

hold his ground. "The people of Wales know the ways between men and women as well as the English do, my lord. I cannot say whether or not Arthur dallied with wenches other than Lady Ceridwen. If he did, he was *discreet*."

"Lady Roxanne and I were discreet," he insisted, standing tall again. "No servant had any business entering her chamber without permission. And having done so, the woman had no right to carry tales. If I were, in fact, the reigning lord of this demesne, I'd have her dismissed or worse. As seneschal here, you might consider taking just such action against the servant."

"You may be right, Lord Raven," Felix agreed calmly. "But that is not the real issue here. 'Tis not as if you took your ease with a serving wench. You, ah . . ." He cleared his throat. "You spent the night with Lady Roxanne, your betrothed's blood cousin. Some, who are particularly fond of Lady Pamela, no doubt feel you betrayed her."

Raven snorted. "And who might these 'some' be? You, Felix? Well, brace yourself. If you think on it a moment, you'll realize it's worse than that. Not only did I sleep with Pamela's cousin, I slept with my own brother's prospective bride. They're one in the same, Roxanne is."

Having not moved a muscle, having hardly breathed, Roxanne felt a new flush of anger surge through her veins. Raven was far worse than Balin. At least her cousin, the prince, had simply rejected her. But the Englishman had seduced her for his own selfish reasons and had the gall to boast of his abuse!

Her hands made fists, but though she'd been publicly scorned, she dared not act on it. She remained Cymry, and Cymry retained their dignity even when humiliated, so that later they might exact revenge.

"That is hardly an argument in favor of your cause," Felix told Raven.

"I need not argue with anyone, not in this barony!" he shouted back. "I came here to warn you all, to give my aid and leadership in defending this keep. I need not have come.

I've a fine estate of my own in a land that suits me far better than this wet, wild place called Wales. I care not a whit about Pamela's dowerlands. Were she to lose them to Prince Balin, I'd ne'er be forced to trek through the mountains under rainy skies to return here again.

"Nay, I need not have come. But I did. And I shall stay until this conflict with the Welsh prince is ended. But don't dare reprimand me, sir. Whether I swive a scullery maid, my brother's wife, or Queen Eleanor herself, 'tis none of your accursed business!"

Roxanne felt as though she'd been chiseled of stone. Her bones seemed heavy, her feet secured to the floor. It flashed through her mind how she would kill Raven, Lord of Stonelee. She had to slay him now, not only because he'd used her ill, but because he could never become Marcher Earl of Angleford in fact. Certainly she craved her revenge, but more critical, she felt honor bound, after her fall from grace, to spare Pamela the fate of becoming that black devil's bride.

"My lords, they've attacked the village! Cymry have stormed down from the hills. Prince Balin of Penllyn leads them!"

Every head in the hall turned to the man who'd run into the keep, shouting his news. Roxanne turned, for the messenger entered the hall behind her. But she didn't turn as quickly as Raven, and their eyes met for the briefest moment.

Raven was dressed for battle, in hauberk and mail. He had no helmet, but he pulled up his leather hood and put his hand on his sword hilt as he headed for the front portal, shouting orders as he went. None questioned his authority, inside the keep or outside in the bailey where he mounted Rolf, who was already saddled. Even Felix, who remained on the stoop, his sword at the ready to defend those within the walls, nodded obediently in response to his instructions.

As Raven rode beneath the raised portcullis with Sir Edwin at his side and a contingent of armed men following on foot, he saw Roxanne's face with his mind's eye. She had heard every word he'd said to Felix, and she didn't know that most were lies. He knew, though, that he'd broken the pledge he had made to her only last night, his vow never to hurt her. He had hurt her as only a man can hurt a woman, and that had not been his intent.

The thunder of hooves and booted feet on the wooden drawbridge was deafening. Edwin pointed, showing Raven the way to the village even as he rode ahead to take the lead. But the lord of Stonelee hardly noticed the noise or the course he was to take, because his thoughts remained with the lady of Bittenshire who remained at Angleford Keep.

I would have explained, had I time. But there was no time, and Roxy should know it. "Later," I told her, and later 'twill be that we speak of yesternight and the morrow. But not until Angleford and its people are safe from Balin's onslaught.

Having convinced himself, for the moment, Raven's senses suddenly filled with his surroundings as he and the captain rode hard along the rutted dirt track leading from the keep to the town. Like fish swimming upstream, they charged through the lines of villagers who had already begun their retreat from town to keep. The colors of their clothes and their bundles, the shapes of their carts and beasts of burden, whizzed past Raven. He could smell Rolf's sweat and the scent of pines; he felt the damp wind pushing against his face and heard the clank and jingle of swords and armor. His pulse quickened as his blood flowed fast through his veins, a rush of reserved strength surging into his limbs at the anticipation of impending battle.

Raven was almost swallowed up by the moment—the danger, the pace, the exhilaration. Yet, suddenly he envisioned Roxanne's face. Her eyes looked as brittle and cool as cut amethysts.

He hadn't ordered her to remain within the keep's walls, he

realized. He had not assigned a guard to protect her. He'd left without a word, any word.

Raven knew he had made a grave mistake.

Within the bailey walls, the rush of activity quickly burgeoned into pandemonium. The remaining knights and archers calmly took up their positions near the gate and on the parapets. But the stronghold couldn't be secured because of the town's people, including clinging children and crying babies, who kept arriving in breathless, straggling clusters. Sir Gruffydd, who had been given command of the keep's forces, ordered the bridge to remain down and the portcullis raised high so Angleford's people might continue scurrying into the sanctuary of the bailey.

In the first moments after Raven and his forces departed, Roxanne had given up plotting her bloodthirsty revenge. Retreating to Pamela's chamber, she'd torn off the fine garments that had once been Lady Ceridwen's and donned the coarser tunics she'd worn on her journey from England. Beneath them, she tugged on her own pair of men's leggings, which Raven had returned to her with the bundle of her belongings. Over them she pulled a gambeson, the thick, quilted woolen shirt knights often wore as armor. She belted all the layers at her waist, making sure her dagger was in place. Then, at her side, she anchored a short, light-weight sword. Roxanne was not very skilled with that weapon, but she still had her longbow and a quiver of arrows, purchased in the English village. She was a fine archer, trained since childhood to shoot straight and far. Hopefully, she would not have to defend herself in close quarters with a blade. At a distance, with bow and arrow, she'd prove a worthy opponent.

When Roxanne returned to the great hall, her hair tied back from her face with only a practical bit of leather cord, she was armed as well as any knight. But she spent her time ushering the frail, the female, and the children into the keep and other buildings within the bailey walls.

She was in the yard when she heard the shouts. Looking up at the men on the walls, she saw them pulling back their bow strings and the arrows flying forth. The projectiles whistled through the air, but Roxanne could hardly hear their sound over the racket at the gate.

Both men and women screamed, and she spied the bloodied bodies—villagers all—just inside the gateway. As she approached at a run, her skirts hitched high, men's shouts and curses mingled with the clank of metal on metal. The battle had reached Angleford's bailey-bound knights just at their door as Balin's men breached the bridge and stormed the portal by trampling the villagers still hurrying toward safety.

"Bring it up! Draw up the bridge!" Sir Gruffydd shouted. Roxanne heard his voice above the others'. She also heard the squeal of chains as the portcullis dropped, unhampered. It sounded like the earth cracked open when its iron teeth slammed into the ground.

But it was too late. Though the prince's forces could no longer enter Angleford's bailey without first scaling the walls, too many warriors had already gained entry. Like madmen, they shrieked and screamed, more naked than clothed as they swung their clubs and aimed their arrows.

Roxanne heard the arrows whistling, and she saw not all came from Penllyn's bowmen. Many of Angleford's men-at-arms who stood on the wall had turned around to face the inner bailey. They were shooting at the invaders who had penetrated the sanctuary of Angleford's yard.

It took her only an instant to realize she was vulnerable to both sides in this battle, so Roxanne dashed to the wall, hovering in its shadow. Fingering an arrow in the quiver at her back, she pulled it out and notched it in her bow. Biceps flexing, she drew back on the string, aiming it at a Celt whose back faced her. She sent it flying. A moment later, he went flying forward 'til he sprawled in the dirt. The wooden shaft protruding from between his shoulder blades still quivered.

Roxanne repeated her efforts several times over, though she did not always wound or kill. She didn't think of herself as a slayer, a murderer of her countrymen. It was all she could do to concentrate on what needed to be done, for clods of damp dirt and debris flew everywhere, stinging her eyes; people, serfs, and soldiers alike fought, brawled, ran, and crumpled; and a cacophony of sound besieged her ears, from children's bawling to men's cursing to cries of fright and grief. Also, there were horses—Roxanne couldn't fathom where all the beasts had come from. Peasants in any land owned almost none, and the Cymry who lived in the hills owned fewer still because the terrain was not easily traveled on horseback. Yet now there were horses within this valley keep's walls, little cobs and ponies that whinnied and snorted in their fright and excitement.

She saw the tall steed from the tail of her eye, and the sight of him made her breath catch in her throat. In disbelief, she watched the black stallion prance in her direction while his rider swung his sword in wide arcs, hacking at any unmounted foe in his path. It was Dafydd, her own beloved stallion, whom she'd left behind at Penllyn Hall. Now he carried Balin on his back, the Prince of Penllyn.

The Welsh chieftain spied Roxanne at nearly the same moment she did him. He pulled hard on Dafydd's reins and halted before her. She'd never seen such a look in her cousin's eyes before.

"Traitor," he snarled, glaring at her contemptuously. "You were to take the English bastard back across the border with you. He should not have been here when I attacked! But you told him, didn't you, Roxy? And now you fight *me!* To keep me, a prince of Cymru, from retaking this piece of land from the Marches and reclaiming it as Penllyn territory once again!"

Dafydd had danced a few paces forward; now Balin kneed

the beast, urging it so near to Roxanne, she'd have stepped back if the stone wall were not directly behind her.

"You bitch," he continued, shaking his head in disgust. "I believed you loved your homeland, that you loved me—"

"You?" Roxanne took a step forward. "I risked the fury of the English king to come to you and be your bride. But your only intent was to use me. You expected me to sacrifice my life, my happiness, to aid you in achieving your own ends. If I'm a traitor, Balin, it is because you first betrayed me!"

The prince's eyebrows shot up in surprise. Then a nasty smirk ruined his handsomeness. "In truth, I'd considered it a sacrifice to give you up, Roxy. Now, at least, I know I've lost nothing in losing you. You're unwilling to make sacrifices for the true people of Cymru, and you've not enough pride to keep from playing the lover scorned. Glad I am to see what you really are. Glad I am to know the error of my thinking."

She blinked. Dust didn't sting her eyes; blinding confusion muddied her vision. Was he right? Was she selfish, an ignoble traitor who'd brought about this mayhem simply to spite a man who had more concern for the people he ruled than love for her?

Nay. Her insight burned as bright as a flash fire. Straightening her shoulders, Roxanne shook her head defiantly and said, "The true error in your thinking, Balin, was to believe you'd a right to our cousin's land. Pamela was born to a Cymry princess, same as you. And just as Penllyn rightfully came to you, Angleford must come to her."

"You delude yourself, woman," Balin scoffed, turning Dafydd away from her. "And I haven't time to continue this conversation. The battle's far from done. I would see it finished, I the victor."

Cranking chains and squeaky hinges distracted both of them. Looking toward the gate in the bailey wall, Roxanne saw the portcullis inching its way upward. The next moment she heard the thud as the drawbridge came down on the far side of the moat.

Hooves pounded the bridge's timbers. Before Balin could direct his mount more than a few strides forward, two horses galloped under the iron spikes and into the yard. On one rode Sir Edwin, captain of the guard. On the other sat Raven, lord of this keep. Behind them, a swarm of Angleford's armed knights followed. The warriors fanned out, blood lust in their eyes, war cries on their lips. Horns sounded, swords clashed, arrows sang.

Yet Raven and Balin faced each other as though they were the only two knights in the lists, squaring off for competition. But they did not challenge each other for a lady's colors; they were combatants who knew losing could well mean their own deaths.

Someone knocked Roxanne down. She scrambled up, leaving the relative safety of the wall to better see Raven and Balin do battle. They charged each other, wielding their swords while she, unconsciously, unsheathed her own short sword.

She was a little amazed at how well Dafydd behaved while Balin deflected Raven's sword and thrust his own. The stallion, though smaller than Raven's warhorse and never trained for battle, behaved as though he were bigger and well used to the noise and chaos of warfare. But suddenly, Raven drew blood and Balin lost his balance, tumbling off his mount. An instant later, the English lord was off his own destrier, meeting his enemy on even ground.

Impulsively, Roxanne called for her horse by whistling the note that usually brought him to her. Though he'd skittered far afield when freed of his burden, his ears pricked up and he pranced to her. Whispering calming words, she scrambled up onto his back, still brandishing her sword as her eyes remained trained on Raven and Balin.

The two parried and thrust, stumbled and danced. Bodies and debris lay strewn in the dirt around them, yet neither dared look where he stepped. Still, neither one fell hard enough, long enough, to be skewered by the other. Roxanne found herself thinking how ironic it was, what sweet, divine justice it was, that these two selfish, arrogant, coldhearted knaves should be determined to dispatch each other to hell.

Then one of Balin's men grabbed her leg and tried to pull Roxanne from Dafydd's back. Startled, she hesitated wielding her sword. In that instant, the warrior inadvertently pricked the horse's haunch with his pike, sending the stallion rearing. Roxanne held on with all her strength, and when Dafydd's hooves slammed back to earth, she was filled with such outrage she swung wildly at the Cymry fighter, scoring his chest left to right. With a yelp of agonized pain, he stumbled away from her, dropping his weapon to clutch at his bloody wound with both hands.

The man and the incident immediately forgotten, the damsel looked about wildly, trying to find the two men she'd loved unwisely and unwell. They had maneuvered themselves away from her, deeper into the center of the bailey. Though she could hear their voices and the sounds of their swords clanking against each other, she could not see them through the multitude.

Roxanne rode forward, deftly urging her mount over, around, and through the tangle of inert bodies and rushing people who blocked the path between herself and Raven and Balin.

Raven was wounded. He had fallen over an upended keg, thus giving the Cymry prince the advantage. Before, when Balin had fallen off his mount, Raven had granted him the opportunity to find his footing before continuing their fight. But now, the Welshman afforded no such leniency to the Englishman. He tried to run Raven through, but Raven's own strength and skill with a sword prevented him from doing more than piercing his shoulder. Blood seeping through his leather shirt where the metal rings had been sliced away, Raven held his weapon high, like a shield, and moved it quickly, this way and that, to block all Balin's moves.

Roxanne's racing heart skidded to a halt so that she no longer felt its frantic beating. It seemed to her the dirt, the noise, the blood, the fray that surrounded her disappeared behind some magical curtain. All that remained, all she remained aware of, was Raven, Balin, and herself. And she felt terrified for Raven in a way she would never have imagined.

The magical curtain tore abruptly, as others moved into her view. Three Penllyn men, carrying clubs, approached Raven's back. He was unaware of them as he crouched in the dirt, fending off Balin while trying to gain purchase with his feet. He was doomed to fall before the prince, if someone did not assist him.

With her short sword sheathed, Roxanne clutched her last arrow in her fingers, notching it in her bow. "Raven, behind you!" she warned shrilly before releasing the shaft of her own weapon. Her arrow whooshed through the air, and its point made a thudding sound as it impacted with Balin's right shoulder. She could have sent it straight into his heart. But at the last possible moment, she altered her aim enough to spare him death.

The prince cried out and fell, dropping his sword as he clutched his shoulder. But Roxanne spared him neither notice nor pity. She watched Raven. He'd turned at her warning and now faced the trio of half-naked warriors. His back was safe again, as though his twin had been there to guard it. Only it was Roxanne of Bittenshire who watched his back, giving him leave to smite the others who would kill him.

Raven slew them all. When he turned tiredly, his right side sagging with the weight of the broadsword clutched in his hand, his left side stained with blood, he looked up at her. "I thank you, my lady. I owe you my life."

As soon as he spoke, the curtains in her mind, which had sheltered her from the rest of the melee in the yard, parted wide. But the sounds of battle had waned to near insignificance, and Felix was running toward them.

"Lord Raven!" he shouted breathlessly, panting as he halted

before Angleford's self-proclaimed lord. "We've won! The Welsh beyond the bailey walls have retreated, and those within are defeated, whether or not they choose to admit it."

" 'Tis my understanding the natives frequently retreat when met with firm resistance, only to descend again, determined to win the next foray."

"Aye, milord, that's their way when there's someone to command them. But I see you've felled their leader," Felix noted, jerking his chin toward the prone prince of Penllyn. "They shan't be returning, I'll warrant."

Raven glanced disdainfully over his wounded shoulder at the injured man. "As he's a prince, you'd best see he's cared for in some comfort. Charge a servant or two to bring him inside the keep. Have them tend his wound properly." Turning, his eyes again flicked up to Roxanne, who remained seated above him on her horse. To her, he added, "Unless you'd like the privilege."

The lady betrayed no reaction to his remark, except that her glance moved briefly over Raven's bloodied arm. "The only wound I plan on tending is on my stallion's rump." With that, she reined her horse around, walking the beast slowly toward the stables.

CHAPTER 25

Roxanne, to Annie's utter mortification, had bathed once again. The warm water had felt soothing. But now that she lay, exhausted, in Pamela's bed, she felt as though she'd been run down by an ox cart. It had been a long while since she'd used a bow so frequently, and the short sword she'd brandished had been heavy in her hand.

As she lay on her back, looking up at the canopy, she tried to keep her mind blank. Roxanne had presumed her fatigue would aid her efforts. But obviously her wits had not been dulled by either fright or fight. Her thoughts spun at full speed, an array of images holding sleep at bay.

She loved Raven. It was impossible, yet true. She'd known it the moment she realized he might be killed by Balin's men. When, with her aid, he'd dispatched the club-wielding Cymry warriors, she had been giddy with relief.

But then the cur had had to ask if she wished to tend Balin. After all she'd done, she had not expected such a snide, contemptuous remark. But then, numbed by the intensity of her love for the man, she'd conveniently forgotten Raven's disdainful remarks earlier that same day.

Roxanne's lids were heavy, but they would not close completely. Unthwarted, tears rolled down her cheeks in fat, wet droplets that veered down her jaw and dampened the tendrils of hair curling over her shoulders.

Raven impatiently endured being stitched up by a crusty old crone whose needle was as dull as an old man's teeth. Then, discovering a man's bed robe in the lord's chamber, he donned it and headed to Roxanne's chamber.

He didn't knock, but presumptively pushed open the door and stepped inside. Abruptly, he stopped beside the bed. The hangings were pulled back, giving him a clear view of Roxanne lying there—a clear view of her tearstained cheeks.

Raven's heart spasmed. She'd looked like a Viking queen earlier today, brandishing both sword and bow, her voluptuous figure disguised by the heavy wool gambeson. She'd behaved like a Danish warrior woman, slicing at her enemies with that short sword and sending arrows surely into the flesh of others, including the man she'd once loved, Prince Balin. But now she appeared delicate and wan, a soft, young girl who needed comfort and protection—*his* comfort and protection.

Believing her asleep, Raven gently lowered himself onto the bed beside her. For a time he studied Roxanne, her presence invading him like sinewy tendrils that insinuated themselves beneath his skin. "Roxy."

She opened her violet-blue eyes and looked straight at him. She hadn't been asleep. She had known he was there. Yet, she'd avoided acknowledging his presence as long as she'd been able.

"Are you hurt?"

"Oh, aye. I hurt." Roxanne did not elaborate, but her gaze didn't falter. Her look induced Raven to grimace guiltily.

"And you?" she asked, her glance straying to the bandage exposed where his bed robe gaped open. "Did someone tend your cut?"

"Aye."

"Is Balin—"

"I would speak—"

They both broke off before Raven asked, "You wish to know what's become of . . . your lover?"

"He's not my lover, as you well know!" The lady pushed herself up off her pillows. Her face was but a handbreadth from Raven's now, her cheeks pink with anger. "You know I had no lovers at all before—"

"—me." Grabbing her wrists, Raven pushed Roxanne down again. "Can't you bring yourself to say it? Are you so ashamed of taking me to your bed last eve?"

"Aye! You used me ill. But I didn't take you!" She blinked but continued glaring at him. "You burst into my chamber just as you always do, and—and you seduced me!"

"Methinks 'twas the other way 'round." Raven chuckled as she squirmed, trying in vain to free herself from his grasp. "Wasn't it?"

"Nay, 'twas not, you hard-hearted bastard!" Roxanne struggled against him some more, but Raven kept her wrists pinned to the pillows behind her head.

"Well, whoever enticed whom, the entire keep knows we are lovers. So you'd best admit it to yourself, my lady."

"I . . . will . . . not! If you take your ease with a milkmaid, does that make you two lovers? Only fornicators! That's all I am, a fornicator who betrayed my cousin, Pamela, and my intended, Peter. Just as you betrayed them!"

With a growl, Raven pressed himself closer to Roxanne. Their lips nearly touched. "We are lovers!" he hissed angrily. " 'Tis bad enough all those we're hurting. But you dare not demean what we shared in this bed last night. 'Twas not mindless rutting between us, Roxy, and you know it!"

"Do I?" Her eyes glistened. "I heard you talking with the seneschal. I know that I mean no more to you than you do to me. Certainly, you—you don't love me."

For a long moment, Raven remained hovering above her, his breath and Roxanne's mixing. She was defiant, but there was a wary look in her eyes, as though she feared he would rear back and strike her. It pained him that she had overheard and believed what he'd said to Felix. It sickened him worse that she thought he would use his brute strength to harm her.

Abruptly, he closed the negligible distance between them, bringing his mouth down hard upon hers. Roxanne endured his kiss without resistance or response. His weight, his hands, kept her beneath him.

But then his kisses changed. Slanting his mouth over hers, he began sucking her upper lip. As Raven's mouth coaxed a reaction from Roxanne's, he released her wrists and slid his hands behind her head, holding her to him tenderly.

With her hands freed, she might have pummeled Raven's shoulders. Instead she reached up and gingerly locked her fingers behind his neck, careful of his wounded shoulder.

"I love you, sweetling," he confessed. "I suspect I've loved you some while. I certainly loved you last eve." He cocked his head to the side. "And you? Do you love me?"

She hesitated. "I'd not have—you know. Last eve, in this bed. With any man. Not if I weren't in love." She looked down at her covers instead of up into Raven's face. "If I had no love for you, I'd have let Balin kill you this day in the bailey."

He smiled ruefully. "I'd wager, that if he'd had the opportunity earlier today, you'd have aided him with my demise."

Roxanne sucked in a deep breath, her eyes snapping open wide. "God's teeth, I would have! Mayhap I should have, after all you said to Felix. But I couldn't, when I discovered you'd fallen and Balin had the advantage over you."

Her damp, clotted lashes fluttered. "What shall we do?"

she whispered. "I can't wed your brother and remain your mistress."

"You're not my mistress, nor shall you ever be." His voice was stern as he sat erect again. "Roxanne of Bittenshire, you are my beloved, and soon enough you'll be my lady wife."

"But—but Pamela! And Peter! And, heavenly God, the churl you call your king!"

Raven looked away from Roxanne, folding his hands together as he rested his elbows on his thighs. "Pamela is a sweet, biddable young maiden, and if I could help it, I'd not hurt her for the world. But she's better off not being wed to a man who loves another, and I think she's wise enough to know it. As for Peter . . . unlike me, he's slow to anger. But when his temper flares, none would willingly witness it. No doubt, I shall have to endure his fury's heat, for furious he'll be. Yet, for most all our lives we've been two halves of a whole. There's too much between us, Roxanne, for my brother to despise me forever."

"And—and Henry?"

"Jesu." Raven dropped his head back and looked toward the canopy above. "The king has a temper worse than my own. It's his red hair that's the cause of it, no doubt. But we've been friends for long years. There must be a way 'round his decree." He turned to face Roxanne, whose brow furrowed with lines of worry. "What can it matter to him if you wed me instead of Peter?"

"The matter is that 'twas not his decision. A king's word is law. If we marry, we'll disobey him. Disobeying a king's command is punishable by death."

"We're not going to die, either one of us. At least, not by Henry's order." Raven took Roxanne's hand in his. "If need be, we'll hie off to some far corner of the earth where even the mighty English monarch cannot find us.

"Don't fret," he urged, leaning down to plant a gentle kiss on his beloved's brow. "You'll be my wife, and I'll care for you all your days, if you'll have me."

"I'll have you," she whispered in response, reaching up to grab a fistful of his ebony locks in her fingers, so that their next kiss could not be broken 'til she allowed it.

Raven was not as sure of their future as he tried to sound. But the lady's declaration and response to his offer inflated his heart with a kind of gladness that even their passionate loving had not inspired. He had broken his other vow to Roxanne, the one not to hurt her. But this vow he would keep. He felt bound to because, not only did he love her, she loved him.

"Peter! Pamela! I've news that will please—"

Lucinda of Fortengall stood in the open doorway of her son's room. She was alone.

Her heart seized in panic. Tearing up the corridor, she tried the latch on the door of Pamela's room. It moved freely enough, but the door would not swing inward on its hinges. The portal was barred.

"Peter! Pamela!"

"A moment, please," her son replied, and again Lucinda's heart lurched. She didn't have to peer into the tiny chamber to know what had happened between the occupants. Her worst fears had come to pass.

The bar was lifted, the portal opened. Peter, in his bed robe and leaning on crutches, stood to the side of the doorway. Pamela lay in bed, her wide eyes anxious as she peeked timidly over the edge of the covers.

Lucinda did not move.

"Mother, come in," Peter urged hospitably as he hobbled back to the bed and sat down beside Pamela. "Is there some news you wished to convey?"

"Aye. But it seems of no consequence, now."

"Is it Raven? Is he here, or have you had word from him?"

Her glance flicked between the young, nearly naked, lord and lady. "Nay. I came to tell you the crimson rash is on the wane. I felt it was safe for''—her eyes narrowed on Pamela as she said pointedly—''Raven's betrothed to return to her own chamber. I had the impression she was anxious to do so. But now—''

''Mother,'' Peter interrupted. ''There is something you need know. The woman sharing this bed with me is no longer Pamela of Angleford, but Pamela of Stoneweather, my lady wife.''

''Your wife? Peter, what say you? How could you and Pamela be wed? You've been secluded for more than a sennight. Father Simon has not visited. He's been riding 'round to Fortengall's villages assisting those who are ailing. When—?''

''Last eve, milady,'' Pamela explained, clinging to her husband for support. ''We made our vows to each other last eve. I'd not have . . . given myself . . . to Peter, were I not his bride.''

For a long moment, Lucinda stared at the couple. Then her shoulders sagged. ''I intended to tell you both last night that Pamela could safely leave this chamber, and henceforth the servants could assist you, Peter. But Ian insisted the morn was soon enough. If only . . .''

''Mother''—his tone was firm—''whether or not Pamela was free to leave me, she and I would have married. Nothing you might have said could have dissuaded us.''

''But your brother!''

''I know.'' Slowly he nodded. ''I shall have to make peace with him somehow. I'm sure I can. He's my twin, after all.''

''That may be.'' The lady sighed. ''But what of Henry? Will he accept your marriage? Even if he does, I dare not imagine the consequences you may suffer for what you've done.''

''He'll accept our marriage, Mother, because it's true and binding despite the lack of witnesses. Whatever the king's response, we shall weather it.''

''Ah,'' Lucinda muttered thoughtfully, noting how her son held his young bride's hand. ''To be young, fearless, and in love.'' She shook her head and turned away. ''I'd best tell Ian.''

She closed the door behind her, and Peter returned to his bride. He found Pamela looking pale and distraught.

"Peter, what have we done?" she asked frightenedly. "Last eve, in the dark, it all seemed so right. When I saw your mother's face—! And what *will* King Henry do to us, and Roxy and Raven, too? Our decision wasn't theirs, but our marriage prevents them from complying with Henry's edict. Surely the king will blame them as well. 'Tisn't fair!"

He crooked a finger beneath Pamela's chin, tipping her face up to his. "You told me, sweetling, that Roxanne was far from keen on becoming my bride. And Raven cannot see himself as husband to any woman. I don't believe Henry will hold them accountable for our disobedience, and because we've spared them marriages they dreaded, I'd say we've done them both a favor."

Pamela did not agree. Her silence and the set of her chin conveyed that message to her husband.

"What is it? Is there something you've not told me?"

With a quick jerk of her head, she turned away and hid her face with her hair. "Aye. Nay. I don't know!"

"Tell me," he urged gently. "We must have no secrets from each other, now that we're man and wife."

Sighing raggedly, Pamela brought up her knees and clutched them with her arms. " 'Tis true my cousin was distraught at being ordered to wed an Englishman. She'd always thought to marry our cousin, Balin." Apologetically, she peeked at Peter sidelong. "In Wales, we've not the strict rules England has against marriages between relations."

"Aye." He nodded encouragingly. "Go on."

"I let you think Roxanne ran off because she didn't want to marry you. But that's not why she left Fortengall Castle."

"Why did she leave?" Peter's voice was suddenly taut.

Pamela hesitated. "I should have told you straight away, but I'd no wish to come between you and Raven. If I had, if you'd known Roxy really thought highly of you, you might not have married me. You'd have waited for her to return!''

"God's wounds! It *was* my brother who sent her fleeing, wasn't it?''

She nodded. "He accused her of causing your fall, your injury, in an attempt to kill you. 'Twas just as you suspected. But, Peter, it was worse than that. Raven threatened her with death if she dared go through with the marriage. Thus, she was forced to leave here because she feared for her life!''

"You knew.''

"Yes. But Roxanne bade me keep her secret. Raven did, too, when he discovered I knew.''

"Did he threaten you also?'' Peter demanded.

"No! Truly, he did not. I kept Roxy's secret because we're blood kin. Besides, I . . . I was protecting you.''

"Me?'' Peter's dark brows met above his nose in a perplexed frown. "From what?''

"From more distress. You'd already suffered a grievous injury, and your betrothed had abandoned you. How could I disclose that your brother was behind her going? You and he are so close—I saw his face contort with pain the night they set your leg. You're like halves of a whole, and I couldn't bear being responsible for severing the ties that bind you.''

"You're not responsible,'' Peter said grimly, looking away from Pamela, staring hard at the opposite wall. "Raven is.''

"Peter.'' She watched him uneasily. "What do you plan?''

"I'm not certain. But by the time my brother returns, I'll have plotted my revenge against him.''

"Nay!'' she cried, tugging on his hand, forcing him to face her. "You know that whatever he's done, he did because he loves you. He truly believed Roxanne tried to kill you, so he thought he saved your life by frightening her away! And think on it,'' she added softly, reaching up to stroke his cheek. "If Roxy hadn't ridden off, if Raven hadn't gone after her—which neither would have done were it not for your brother's brash accusations—we'd never have fallen in love. Certainly we'd never have married!''

Peter's eyes slanted toward his wife's face. For a moment, he contemplated her features thoughtfully. Then, slowly, a smile quirked the corners of his mouth. "Are you suggesting, my lady, that I ought to thank Raven for what he's done?"

"Aye." She nodded. "I believe I am. He may have had no idea what events he set in motion. But if he'd not done as he did, you and I would not be together now, and married."

He shook his head bemusedly, but his smile broadened. "You're right, of course. I am grateful, and I pity Raven, too." Peter slipped his hand beneath the covers and cupped Pamela's sex with his palm. "For his stupidity cost him this, and made it mine forever."

None disturbed the newlywedded couple that whole morning long. As if they remained in purposeful seclusion, a meal to break their fast was set outside the door. Pamela didn't open the door to retrieve it 'til the sun was high, and at that moment, behind her, Peter cried out in pain.

She spun around, frightened to see her husband so suddenly pale and pitching forward, clutching his shoulder. Flinging the platter aside, she sprinted back to the bed. "What ails you, dearest?" she demanded. "Sweet *Jesu,* should I call for your mother?"

"Aye." Inhaling a deep breath, Peter dropped his hand to the mattress and met Pamela's gaze. No longer were his eyes glazed with pain. "When you find her," he gasped, "tell her Raven's been hurt."

CHAPTER 26

Peter and Pamela moved to a chamber in the gallery where a bed had been set up for them to sleep upon. With assistance, Peter could negotiate the short span of stairs between their room and the great hall below. It was there, in that cavernous chamber, that he preferred to spend his days in the company of not only his wife, but all those who bustled through the castle. It was there, too, he and the rest of his family waited, with growing impatience, for news of Raven and Roxanne.

On a particular spring afternoon, hope arose when a messenger arrived. But hopes were dashed when it proved to be Lucien's man, bringing word of the birth of his new sons.

" 'Tis good news, that Adrienne has been delivered of two healthy babes," Lucinda declared with an overly bright smile as she, Lord Ian, Peter, and Pamela sat together in the hall. "They were past due, instead of early."

"And the messenger was late in coming, because of his lame horse. But now we know they were born as you predicted, sweetling," Ian said. "A third pair of twin boys, Arnulf and Ranulf."

A silence fell. Everyone was thinking about another pair, about Raven and Roxanne.

The earl cleared his throat and declared gruffly, as though someone had previously mentioned them, "Very well. Methinks the time has come to search for your twin, Peter. And for Roxanne. I myself will lead a party to Bittenshire Keep in the Marches."

"Oh, Ian!" Lucinda's forehead puckered with a weary frown. "Peter is sure Raven's been hurt. Do you think harm's befallen them?"

"I cannot say, dearest. 'Tis a long, hard journey betwixt here and there. On the other hand, Raven's a seasoned knight and Roxanne is no helpless waif. She rides as well as any man—"

"Mother! Father!"

All eyes turned to the source of the shout. They discovered Hugh careening through the archway, his younger brothers in hot pursuit. Grinning, he exclaimed excitedly, "Raven's been thpied on the road! He thould be here thortly!"

"What?" Lucinda shot up out of her chair and took several steps toward her gap-toothed son. But before Hugh could repeat himself, one of Farleigh's guards strode into the hall, confirming the child's report.

Again, the adults fell still. But this time the quiet was thrumming with impatient expectation. And the tension grew as time stretched taut. Although everyone felt relief to know the couple was well and soon to be among them again, Peter and Pamela, in particular, dreaded their confession and the inevitable confrontation to follow.

When Raven appeared, brushing dust from his cape, all, including Peter, came to their feet. But only the littlest lads, who'd never ceased their activity, exclaimed happily.

"Raven, you're back!" Hugh squealed, hugging his elder

brother's leg. "Mother and Father worried that thomething had gone amith. But I knew you'd be well. You alwayth are."

"That's true enough, Hugh," Raven agreed, tousling the child's fair hair. "I'm glad you had faith in me."

"We did, too!" Jamie and John chorused.

"I'm sure you did." He winked at the boys. Then Raven surveyed those who stood, silent and still as statues. His smile faded, leaving no discernable expression behind. "Mother?"

She raced forward and embraced him. "God's tears," she muttered, "you were gone so long without word! I see your arm is bandaged—Peter knew you'd been wounded somehow. Is it bad?"

"Nay. Not bad at all."

"Where's Roxy?" Pamela demanded fretfully.

Raven searched her face as his mother stepped aside. Then he glanced at Peter, whose expression was as inscrutable as his own. Finally, he turned back toward the archway and said softly, "Roxanne."

Pamela's cousin appeared and took his outstretched hand. Together, she and Raven came forward. "Greetings," Roxanne said, sweeping everyone with her gaze, though it lingered at last on Pamela and Peter.

"Your timing was provident," the earl declared briskly. "I was about to organize a party to go in search of you. We feared, after all this time, you'd had a misadventure."

"We did," Raven confirmed with a nod. "We'll tell you all the details later. But first"—he looked to his twin—"first, there's something else we must tell you."

"Lads!" Lucinda spoke sharply to her youngest children. "Go back outside and continue playing, now."

"But Raven only juth got back!" Hugh complained.

"We want to stay!" John whined.

"Out!" the earl barked, and the boys, with long faces, promptly obeyed.

"Raven," Peter said, "before you begin your tale, I've something I must say to you also."

"Please, let me speak first," Raven begged. Then he asked Pamela, "Did you tell Peter that I forced Roxanne to leave here before they could wed?"

"Aye." She nodded. "But not until—"

"I'm glad," he interrupted. "Peter, I'm sorry for that. And then again, I'm not." Raven glanced at Roxanne and shared a smile with her.

Peter didn't seem to notice. "Raven, I ... we ... have confessions of our own. I beg you, hear me out."

"Nay." He tugged Roxanne closer to him, slipping one arm behind her waist and clasping her hand against his chest. "What I need say will only increase your anger with me. I'd rather bear the brunt of your full wrath all at once, Peter, than a little at a time."

Pamela spied Raven's signet ring on her cousin's finger. "You're married!" she exclaimed in surprise.

"What!" the earl and Lucinda gasped aloud together.

"Aye," Raven confirmed, nodding as he met Pamela's gaze again. He told her, "My lady, 'twas never my intent to hurt you or my twin. But it would have been much worse for you both, had we all wed as Henry ordered us to do. 'Twasn't meant to be."

"Jesu!" Lucinda muttered, collapsing into her chair.

"God's bones!" Ian cursed. But before he could utter anything more, a guard standing just beyond the archway caught his eye. Unnoticed, Ian slipped away and joined his man.

"Sweet Mother Mary," Pamela murmured, looking incredulously at her cousin as she reached out to grasp her own husband's arm. She was unsure that grinning now would be appropriate.

Only Peter failed to exclaim at the news of his brother's marriage to the Bittenshire lady. He chuckled, then laughed, and finally threw back his head, roaring his mirth up to the rafters.

"What? I can't believe—" Raven frowned at his twin suspiciously. "What's so damnably funny?"

"We're married, also. Pamela and I," he managed to explain through his laughter.

Before the lord of Stonelee could respond, his lady let out a high-pitched, girlish squeal. Throwing her arms open wide, she rushed to Pamela and embraced her.

"By the saints, 'tis too incredible! But I'm delighted," Roxanne whispered in her ear. "I thought from the first that Peter would make you a good husband. He has, hasn't he?"

"Aye. But Raven?" Pamela's brow furrowed in disbelief as she leaned back far enough to look into Roxanne's face. "He threatened to kill you! I believed you detested him, and that you still held hopes of wedding Balin!"

"He did, I did . . . !" She tossed her mane of silky curls and giggled. "But everything changed. I'll tell you all, later."

Her attention and Pamela's was drawn again to Raven at the sound of his surly voice. He had stalked up to Peter, and the brothers now stood eye to eye as he demanded, "You wed the lady pledged to me in marriage without waiting 'til we might first discuss it?"

"Aye. Precisely as you did with *my* betrothed," Peter returned, a smirk quirking the corner of his mouth.

"It's not the same! Roxy and I wouldn't have wed without first speaking to you and Pamela, were it not absolutely necessary. If you must know," he continued, dropping his voice as he glanced sidelong at Roxanne, "I compromised my lady. Thus, the marriage could not be delayed until we returned to Peter. But you!" His voice grew louder as he poked Peter's chest with his blunt fingertip. "What on God's earth could have forced you into marriage with such haste?"

Peter leaned most of his weight on one crutch, which forced his hip out at a jaunty angle. He grinned. "We're alike, you and I, in case you didn't notice. At least in some ways. True enough, I didn't compromise Pamela, but only because we pledged our troth in secrecy moments before the deed was done!''

"Moments before . . . !'' Raven sputtered.

And Roxanne trilled a laugh. "Oh, cease your righteous indignation, husband,'' she chided, tugging on his sleeve. "You are hardly an injured party. Be happy, as I am, that Pamela and your brother have found each other. Weren't we fretting all the way back from Angleford on how they'd receive the news of *our* marriage?'' She flashed Peter a sly smile. "I suspected you and my cousin would make a fine match. Since you have, 'twould seem our own worst fears were for naught.''

"I think not,'' the earl interjected dourly, reentering the great hall. "We've been having news all day—first that your brother, Lucien, has got himself new twin sons. Next that you, Raven, and Lady Roxanne had returned. Now this, from the king.'' He held out a sheet of rolled parchment.

"Where is he? What does he say?'' Lucinda asked anxiously, hurrying to her husband's side.

"He's at Basil of Hedgewick's lodge. He wonders at not having heard from any of you.'' Ian's glance darted among his stepsons and daughters-by-marriage. "He wants word of your circumstances. I presume that means he wishes to know you've obeyed his command and wed as he ordered.''

The gaiety of the moment soured as love's victories were overshadowed by the implication of a monarch's wrath.

The earl's family spoke for long hours about all that had transpired, until everyone was caught up on nearly all the details. The evening meal was served and cleared, Lady Lucinda went upstairs to put her youngest children down for the night, and Lord Ian retired. At last, the two pairs of newlyweds found themselves alone together.

Roxanne looked at her husband as he moved his chair closer to hers. "Here we are, all happily wed. Yet, now we must confront Henry. I suppose Curtmantle's pride will not allow him to go easy on us."

"Roxy, you not only have English blood in your veins, you're married to an English lord," Pamela pointed out. "You shouldn't call King Henry such a name. 'Tis disrespectful. And when one considers he's your—"

"Hush!" She scowled. "I'll not hear that silly tale again. It's quite impossible."

"What's impossible?" Peter inquired, but she ignored him.

"Methinks we should speak with the king immediately," Raven announced. "Hedgewick's lodge is not two days' ride from here, but with your injured leg, Peter, 'twill take us nearly three days to make the journey with a cart. I suggest you and I leave on the morrow. Should it not go well for us," he said, glancing sidelong at Roxanne, "Henry may have us hauled back to London, shackled and chained. Then, you two ladies will have to decide what you want to do. Lord Ian has promised to assist you."

"Raven of Stonelee," Roxanne ground out, "you vowed we'd flee together beyond the cur's reach, if need be!"

"Sweetling, what I pledged in the throes of passion may not be possible in fact."

"But you promised me the same!" Pamela cried in dismay, turning to Peter.

He took her hand and stroked the back with his thumb. "We're all anticipating the worst, but I'm sure the most Henry will do is to take back the lands he awarded to Raven and me. He'll leave us wed, because 'twould be too much trouble to try to undo our vows. I also disbelieve he'd truly want us dead or imprisoned."

"Our vows, Peter, were made without benefit of witnesses or clergy," Pamela reminded him. "If King Henry decides it's best to believe we never said them, he can proclaim it."

"Your lands?" Roxanne hissed, her eyes locked on Raven's. "Bittenshire can never be mine, and because you wed me instead of Pamela, Angleford will never be yours. Raven, if you lose Stonelee, what will you have? He *can't* take it from you!"

His eyes met his wife's, and he winked. "Better my fief than my life."

"I'd gladly give up Stoneweather to keep you," Peter assured Pamela. "So we will travel to Lord Basil's lodge posthaste, and hopefully placate His Majesty with apologies and reassurances. If the king insists we surrender our strongholds, we shall do so willingly. 'Tis only land, after all."

"How can you say that?" Roxanne demanded, leaping up from her chair and glaring down at Raven's brother. "Only land! By God, 'tis your home, and it should one day belong to your children, your grandchildren. Land is never 'only' if it is yours by right. You should love it, nurture it, die for it!"

"I don't want Peter dying for any cause, most especially because he took me to wife!" Pamela cried.

"I don't want Raven dying, either. Nor should he have to give up his keep to the monarch." Roxanne arched an eyebrow. "And to that end, I've an idea."

"Which is?"

Her glance included both her own husband and Pamela's. "You two look exactly alike. Can your Angevin king tell you apart?"

"What are you suggesting?" Peter asked. His expression and his tone made it obvious he already knew.

Yet Roxanne explained, "When the king addresses you, Peter, you could answer as Raven. He could do the same when your king speaks to him."

"That might work!" Pamela exclaimed excitedly. "If you pretend to be each other, King Henry might never be the wiser."

"You're suggesting Raven and I switch identities?" Peter asked his wife. "We'll go on to Angleford, where I'll rule as

Lord Raven, and my brother will remain in England with Roxy, affecting to be me?''

Pamela frowned. ''It seems preposterous when you put it that way. Quite impossible.''

''Nay, it's not!'' Roxanne protested. ''But it is too much to dwell on. Now, we must deal with your sovereign lord. Let us survive the royal audience. Afterward, we'll decide how to continue.''

''You're not coming with us,'' Raven declared forcefully. ''Whether or not we attempt the ruse, Peter and I will travel to Hedgewick's lodge alone. You shan't be there.''

''Oh, yes. Yes, we shall,'' Pamela insisted before Roxanne could utter a word. She spoke softly but raised her chin rebelliously. ''We all disobeyed the king's edict. Therefore, Roxy and I should be present when he decides what our fates shall be.''

''She has a point,'' her husband conceded.

And Roxanne added, ''Besides, I think a feminine presence will prove beneficial in and of itself. Even kings, I expect, are more easily beguiled when in the company of beautiful, young women.'' She flashed a grin at Pamela.

Raven inhaled several deep breaths and eyed his bride skeptically. ''You, Roxanne? You think to behave demurely in the presence of *our* English king, whose name you hate to utter?''

''Aye, milord.'' Smiling seductively, she ran her hand over Raven's broad chest. ''For you, I could be soft-spoken and docile.''

Raven grabbed a fistful of Roxanne's hair, tugged her close, and kissed her handily. When he released her, he sighed. ''I pray you can bewitch Henry as you do me.''

To the others, he announced, '' 'Tis agreed, then. We all shall leave on the morn.''

CHAPTER 27

Basil of Hedgewick's lodge was a rustic place built of rough-hewn timber and stone. Nestled within a small parcel of park-land surrounded by a great forest, it seemed inhabited almost exclusively by men.

"Where are the ladies?" Pamela whispered to her husband as they stood in the main hall, still in their traveling clothes, waiting to be announced to the king.

"Henry and his confederates come here to seek respite from the women in their lives."

"Or they're sent here, so the women in their lives have some respite from *them*," Roxanne muttered beneath her breath.

Raven grabbed her elbow, leaned toward her, and whispered severely, "My lady, you vowed you could be sweet and temperate. 'Tis the only reason you're here."

"Peter would neither speak nor handle me so roughly. Are you not Peter, Lord of Stoneweather?"

Raven scowled at Roxanne, who in turn smiled at the approaching royal steward.

"His Highness would see you immediately, milords, miladies." The man stepped away, heading to a door at the opposite end of the hall. Before anyone could follow, Raven grabbed his wife's elbow again and said to the others, "Methinks 'twould be best if you ladies did not join us after all."

"Why?" Pamela asked, her eyes wide with worry. In a furtive whisper, she said, "I thought we'd made our plans."

"Aye," Roxanne agreed, speaking to her husband. "Our futures are at stake here, so we shan't be changing our strategies at this late hour."

The group followed the steward, who ushered them through a doorway. "Your Majesty, Lord and Lady of Stoneweather and Lord and Lady of Stonelee," he intoned formally when they had all entered. As he exited the room, he added, "As you requested, sire, I shall send in food and wine for you and your guests."

The king turned to his visitors as he waved away a young boy who'd been standing near him. "Off with you, now, Henry," he said to his son. "I've matters to discuss with these, my most loyal of subjects." His words dripped with sarcasm.

When the prince quit the room, Henry smiled benignly. "I take it you've done as instructed, then? You, Roxy, and you, Pamela, have wed Lady Lucinda of Fortengall's sons, just as I bid you do?"

Both women blinked. Neither dared to nod, let alone speak.

Henry stepped toward a high-backed chair that faced four empty ones. As he sat, he urged, "All of you, sit. Especially you, Peter. This is no formal gathering; you must be weary, hobbling about on crutches with a broken leg."

Pamela gasped; Roxanne scowled. The king recognized the twins, giving them no opportunity to play out their ruse. Dismayed, they scurried to sit in the row of chairs, searching out each other's eyes to exchange meaningful glances before any of them faced Henry again.

Raven broke the silence by asking what they all wondered.

"How did you know 'twas Peter with the broken leg, Your Majesty?"

"And not you, do you mean?" He made a sound deep in his throat. It was impossible to discern whether the noise was mirthful or menacing. "I know everything I need to know, Raven. I know, for instance, 'twas Peter who fell from the wall at Fortengall Castle."

Another moment of silence hung dreadfully heavy in the chamber. The king regarded his subjects with narrowed eyes before commenting, "I must admit I know not why you, Lady Pamela, cling to Lord Peter, and your cousin, Roxy, to Lord Raven."

Pamela tried to speak, but before she could utter a sound, her husband explained, "Your Highness, our brother, Lucien of Eynsham, informed us of your wish that Raven and I wed these fatherless cousins from Wales. We obeyed your directive and took them as our wives. However"—he cleared his throat and glanced at Pamela, who lay her small hand encouragingly upon his thigh—"however, I, Peter of Stoneweather, wed Lady Pamela. My brother, Lord of Stonelee, married Lady Roxanne."

His confession prefaced another, prolonged silence. The two couples remained rigidly at attention until Henry said softly—ominously softly—"Oh?"

Pamela found herself unable even to breathe, but Roxanne leaped up and stepped forward. "Aye," she confirmed, tossing her hair, lifting her chin. " 'Tis true. I am Raven's wife, and my cousin, here, is Peter's. We are all rather pleased with the arrangement."

"We are most pleased, sire," Pamela added hurriedly as she found her feet again. "We thank you for choosing such fine, handsome, kindly knights to be our husbands."

"*Did* I choose them?"

"Nay, you did not, my lord." Peter pushed himself out of his chair and stood beside his wife. "Yet, we are hopeful 'tis of no concern to you that I took the bride you meant for Raven, and he took the bride you meant for me.''

''Of no concern?'' the king repeated, sounding incredulous as he looked up at the dark lord leaning on his crutches. Henry did not have to stand in order to loom over the others. He merely arched one eyebrow as he glared at Peter.

''Your Grace, I beg your leave to explain,'' he pleaded. ''At first, we fully intended to wed those you bade us to. But circumstances delayed the ceremonies, and in that time we all, we each—'' He glanced at Raven and Roxanne before looking back at the king. ''We fell in love with those we eventually married.''

''Love!'' Henry snorted, shaking his head. ''Love rarely has anything to do with noble marriages.''

''In this instance, it has everything to do with it.'' Raven insinuated himself between Roxanne and the king. ''We knew we risked your displeasure, sire, but we risked it willingly.''

''You did.'' It was not a question Henry posed.

''Excuse me, Your Majesty,'' a servant said from the doorway. He was accompanied by another. Between them they bore a platter of cheese, fruits, and breads, and a tray laden with wine and goblets. ''Shall we serve, Your Grace?''

''Out!'' Henry ordered, pointing toward the door. The servants hastily set down their burdens on the nearest table and nearly tripped over each other stumbling back through the portal.

''Aye, we did,'' Roxanne assured the king, resuming the conversation as though there had been no interruption, as though Raven didn't stand between herself and the monarch. ''Marriage can last a long time, and we preferred not to spend it in misery. We did not believe you'd wish us to.''

''Sweet Mother Mary,'' Raven muttered. ''You're not aiding our cause, dearling.''

Henry harrumphed and shook his head. ''Roxy's not known ʳr holding her tongue, are you, milady?''

"I prefer truth over deceit, aye."

"I prefer obedience," Henry said sternly.

"Your Majesty, 'twas never our intent to disobey you. As Peter said, circumstances meddled with our best intentions. But what's been done cannot now be undone."

"Nay?"

"It shan't be." Roxanne stood on tiptoe, putting her chin on Raven's shoulder to better see the king. "There are no impediments to our marriages, and Pamela and I are of no mind to give our husbands up. Ow!"

Discreetly, Raven brought his heel down upon Roxanne's toes just long enough to silence her.

"Roxy, Roxy, Roxy." King Henry shook his head and spoke to her as though she were a recalcitrant child. " 'Twould appear you need a strong husband who can teach you obedience. I'm unsure Lord Raven is ready to make that effort."

"Though the wench may try me sorely, Your Grace, I've no wish for a subservient wife who does my bidding mindlessly."

"What do you mean, I try you sorely?" Roxanne demanded of her husband.

"Methinks we're straying from the matter at hand," Peter suggested. "Sire, Raven and I know well there shall be consequences to our actions. We're prepared to give up all we own if only you would approve our unions to these two ladies."

"All you own?" Henry peered at Peter curiously.

He nodded.

"Stonelee and Stoneweather? Angleford, too?" The king's gaze strayed to Pamela and remained there.

"Aye, Your Majesty," she said with a nod. "Only please, look kindly upon my marriage to Peter, and Roxanne's to Raven. Oh!"

Inadvertently, the toe of Pamela's shoe upset the tip of one of Peter's crutches. The brace skittered suddenly from beneath his arm, and she spun around to grab his middle, helping him balance so that he did not fall.

King Henry himself stepped forward, retrieved the toppled crutch, and set it surely under Peter's arm again. His look was thoughtful as he considered the pair before returning to stand in front of his chair.

"You can't mean to take Angleford from Pamela!" Roxanne gasped softly in disbelief. " 'Tis her home, her dowerland, her small piece of Cymru!"

"I don't care, Roxy." Pamela turned from her cousin to the king, begging, "Please, sire, let us leave with our heads and the clothes on our backs, and I'll gladly give over Angleford!"

"Stoneweather, too," Peter said.

"And Stonelee," Raven added.

"Stonelee?" Roxanne hissed, hanging on Raven's sleeve as she gaped at him incredulously. "How can you willingly give up what's yours without even a show of resistance? Sweet *Jesu,* I do not understand you English!"

"Roxanne, keep your mouth closed, or I shall be forced to hit you with my fist to silence you." Raven's dark eyes narrowed to slits as he ground out his threat.

Releasing his sleeve, she backed up a step. "You wouldn't dare."

"If you utter another word, I'll beg King Henry to dissolve our marriage so that I may keep Stonelee and be rid of you!"

"Mayhap *your* marriage, at least, *should* be annulled," Henry commented dryly.

Roxanne snapped her head around and stared at him, aghast. "Nay!"

"You do not seem to get on well, to me." He folded his arms nonchalantly across his chest.

"We do! Don't listen to my husband. He loves me even when he hates me!" She gave Raven a look that dared him to contradict her.

"Is that so?" Henry arched his eyebrows questioningly as he considered Lord Cedric's daughter. "Lady Pamela is willing give up her lands in Wales to keep her husband. Peter has also expressed his willingness to relinquish his stronghold to keep her as his bride. Your own husband says he'll sacrifice his claim to Stonelee, all for his love of you. But what of you, Roxy? Would you sacrifice lands in your cherished Wales to remain Raven's wife?''

"I've naught to give up," she grumbled petulantly, her lower lip protruding in a pout. "Bittenshire is Aggie and Thomas's, now. If aught happens to them, I've nephews and eight other sisters between us who would inherit that keep before it came to me. I've nothing to sacrifice for Raven."

"But if you did, Roxy?" Henry pressed.

And she lost her temper totally. The only thing that could have silenced her would have been her husband's fist. But he did not raise a hand against her despite his threat, and she shouted exasperatedly, "It matters not what I'd do if I had something, for I've nothing—no land, no keep! By taking this Englishman as my husband, I lost any chance to make some piece of Cymru my home again. And why, may I ask, do you keep calling me 'Roxy?' 'Tis a name only my family ever dares use!''

"Good God, Roxanne!" Exasperated, Raven grabbed both her arms, lifted her off her feet, and set her down some paces from the king. "Bite your tongue 'til it bleeds, will you?" he hissed. "How dare you question His Royal Highness? 'Tis his right to call you whatever he wishes!''

Spinning about to face Henry, Raven ducked his head respectfully. "I apologize, Your Grace. You are correct. I wonder myself if I'm the man to rein in this haridelle.''

"Please don't be angry with my cousin, sire," Pamela beseeched, folding her hands in supplication. "She's simply overwrought. We all are. But she doesn't hide her emotions well.''

"I know." A hint of a smile pulled up the corners of Henry's mouth. Again, he looked directly at Roxanne. " 'Tis a godfather's duty to know his godchild.''

"What!" She gasped.

The king's astonishing remark left even Raven confounded.

"You couldn't be," Roxanne insisted, shaking her head. "You'd have been a—a child at the time of my christening!"

"I assure you, my lady, I was a man—though in fact not old enough to be knighted. As my mother was already campaigning for my right to the English throne, and as your sire had no great love for Stephen of Blois nor his bastard son, Cedric became my ally and I, his last daughter's godfather."

Roxanne's mouth hung open another moment; suddenly, she clamped it shut.

Henry chuckled and smiled. "I see, Raven, I've managed to silence your bride, where you could not."

Raven approached his king slowly and canted his head to one side. "Can it be 'tis your will that she remain my bride, despite the fact she wasn't your choice for me?"

"Who said she was not?"

"Lucien said!" Peter answered the king. "When he brought the ladies to Stonelee Keep, he told us you wished me to wed Roxanne and Peter to wed Pamela."

"Aye," Raven confirmed. "He even brought scrolls bearing your royal edict."

"Did you read them?" Henry asked.

Raven blinked, searching his memory. When his eyes met their mirror image, he saw Peter shaking his head.

"Nay," Raven admitted. "We had a heated argument, and when Lucien brought us the documents to confirm he spoke true, I dared not rile him further. I accepted his word without even breaking the seal on your missive."

"So, too, did I," Peter added.

"A heated argument, you say?" Henry chuckled some more, and this time it threatened to become an outright laugh. "Somehow, I expected that. 'Tis why I spoke only with Lucien and had him escort my wards to your doors instead of demanding ˜ presence at Westminster. I had no wish to give you the opportunity to voice your displeasure in my presence. Had such occurred, the consequences for you both might have been dire.''

''But what are the consequences now?'' Peter asked.

''None.''

''None?''

Henry smiled, perching on the arm of his heavy chair. ''You've done naught to produce any consequences.''

''But you said you had Lucien convey your wishes to us so that we'd neither object nor defy you. Yet we did, Your Highness. Without malice, of course, we defied you by marrying ladies other than those you declared we must wed.''

The king shook his head. ''Nay, Peter. You took the bride I thought best suited to you, as did your brother.''

The twins looked askance at each other; so, too, did Roxanne and Pamela.

''I ... don't understand,'' Pamela confessed, her face pinched with confusion.

''And your husbands didn't read the missives I sent with their elder brother. Had they, Lords Peter and Raven would have learned I commanded them to wed two Welsh cousins—specifically, Lady Pamela of Angleford and Lady Roxanne of Bittenshire. But nowhere therein did I state that Peter should wed Roxanne, and Raven you.''

''You mean ... we were free to make our own choice between them?'' Peter asked softly.

Before King Henry could reply, Raven wondered aloud, ''How did you know we wouldn't read your missives?''

''Because, as well-acquainted with you as I am, Raven, I expected you to toss the parchment into the fire, declaring to any who'd listen that no man, not even your sovereign king, could force you into wedlock if you did not desire it.''

Raven's face ruddied.

''Then you really wanted me to wed Peter?'' Pamela ventured softly.

''Indeed, I did,'' Henry told her, ''though it was always to be your choice. I could, of course, have joined you and Peter together with naught but a simple word. These other two," Henry went on, motioning with a jerk of his bearded chin toward Raven and Roxanne, "I knew full well would resent my interference and, in the bargain, resent each other as much as their marriage. Thus, I misled Lucien of Eynsham into believing I wished Peter to wed Roxy and Raven to wed you." Henry glanced briefly at the other couple and then back again. "I suspected that somehow, someway, they'd find each other if they believed I wanted them apart—if only because of their well-known obstinacy."

Raven, wisely, ignored the insult to both himself and his bride, but could not refrain from asking, "How could you believe Roxy and I were well-suited?" His fingers flexed and unflexed as he made and unmade a fist with each hand. "I confess, Your Grace, that upon first meeting the wench, I thought her a sharp-tongued, shrewish bi—"

"Don't say it," she warned, interrupting.

This time, Henry really laughed. Throwing back his head, he let his mirth erupt.

"Admit it, Roxy," he urged, wiping a tear from the corner of his eye, "you thought no better of Raven at your first meeting."

"That's not true. It took me several meetings before I hated his rotten core."

"Yet, you came to love him, didn't you? Precisely as I believed you would."

"How did you know?" she demanded, hands on her hips.

"Because your father, my friend, kept in contact with me. As your godparent, and eventually as your king, Cedric knew your fate would fall to me if he passed before you took a husband. Since that Marcher Earl could find no man he considered suitable for his youngest, wildest, most headstrong daughter, he asked me to find one in his stead. Through the years,

'ric apprised me of your likes and dislikes, my lady, of your antics and your passions. I knew Raven of Stonelee would be your best match.''

She fell into stunned silence. Suddenly, Peter's chuckling dispelled the quiet in the room. ''Your Highness, are you saying we all did exactly as you wished us to, and that we need fear no punishment?''

''I am.'' Henry straightened his shoulders. ''You remain Lord of Stoneweather, and your brother Lord of Stonelee. But, Pamela, I must ask again if you are truly willing to give up Angleford.''

''What? Oh, aye, milord. If you wish it.''

He came to her and kissed her hand. When he raised his eyes, he glanced toward Peter and asked, ''Would you regret being denied the role of Marcher Earl of Angleford in addition to being Lord of Stoneweather?''

''Nay,'' he replied sincerely, resting a hand possessively on his wife's slim shoulder.

''Then, Pamela,'' Henry declared, ''I shall replace your dower with a cache of valuables I said would go to Roxanne. And, Roxy,'' he added, spinning on his heel to face her and Raven, ''I present Angleford to you and your new husband.''

She gasped and protested. ''Your Majesty, you cannot! Angleford should go to Pamela, not to me or to Raven!''

''I care not,'' Pamela insisted, rushing to her cousin. ''Remember once, long ago, I offered it to you? 'Twas your father who explained it wasn't mine to give to any save my husband. Unless,'' she added, ''the king decided otherwise. His highness has now decided. It shall be yours.''

''Roxanne, Lady of Stonelee,'' Henry said, reaching out to crook a finger beneath her chin and raise her face to his, ''I know you far better than you surmise. I'm aware of your abounding love of Wales and your need to live there—at least part of every year.'' He glanced at Raven briefly. ''Pamela will be content at Stoneweather with her husband and their children. Peter will also be content there, I'm sure. I've found he tends to occupy himself with his crops and his cattle, so much so, he has spent little time making merry with my court. Unlike his brother, your husband.

"You, sweetling, would fight any army with your own bow and broadsword, should your stronghold come under attack. I've been advised you have already done so. Angleford needs a lady in residence with your strength and courage, and I surmise that you need a place such as it."

Henry grinned as he moved his hand, placing it on Raven's shoulder. "This knight, who has already once saved Angleford from an attacking Welsh chieftain, needs such a place, also. Its defenses will keep him so busy, he'll have no time to idle away at court with the ladies who attend the queen."

"He'd not dare, even if he were a landless knight!" Roxanne vowed. She shot her husband a warning glance and then addressed the king. "But I thank you, sire, for your graciousness. And for—for being my godfather as well."

Tears in her eyes, she reached out impulsively and hugged Henry fiercely. For a moment, the others watched uneasily. Then they saw the king hug Roxanne in return, and he lifted her off her feet before finally releasing her. Everyone broke into happy—and relieved—smiles.

"You're a dusty lot, you are," Henry noted finally, looking from one to the other. "Go have a wash and change in to more suitable clothes. Upon your arrival, I ordered Basil to arrange a hearty feast in celebration of your weddings. I trust you'll want to look your best this eve."

Henry strolled jauntily toward the door, grabbing an apple off the tray of food as he passed. "By the way, I bid you stay here a few days. The hunting's fine, and we men would enjoy some female company since, unwisely, we left all our women behind. I'm confident you'll find no excuses to depart here swiftly because, to a one, you are all such obedient subjects."

king, he pulled open the door and left them.

"I cannot believe the king manipulated us all so deftly," Peter said softly. " 'Tis no wonder he's a great monarch!"

"You're not annoyed?" Pamela asked.

"Do I look annoyed?" He grinned at her, casually tossed aside one crutch, and clasped her to him before kissing her soundly.

"And you, Raven?" Roxanne peered up at her husband.

"God's tears, you know I am vexed with you. Thoroughly vexed. Righteously vexed!" He scowled at her darkly.

"You still despise Cymru so much?"

"Cymru, nay. I'm vexed by your behavior, Roxanne. You assured me you would lend demure gentility to this proceeding. When we realized our attempt to deceive Henry proved impossible, I did not expect you to shout and rail at the king!"

"Henry understood. He's my godfather, after all."

Raven snorted as the other pair blinked at Roxanne with amused expressions. "Henry, now, is it? Not 'your English king' or 'that damnable cur?' "

"Hush!" she warned, glancing at the portal through which Henry had so recently departed. "Someone might overhear and tell him what you said. Then he'd truly be angry. We mustn't rile our sovereign majesty."

Tilting his head back, Raven laughed and hugged Roxanne against his chest. "What? Are you claiming to be English now?"

"I *am* English. Married to an English lord. But he's also a Marcher Earl, and his children will be born on Cymry soil. Sweet Mother Mary," she whispered, snuggling against him, "but I'm a happy, contented Englishwoman."

Kissing her brow, Raven looked over Roxanne's head to ask his brother, "Are you satisfied, too, Peter? As Pamela's husband, Angleford should have come to you."

"I meant what I told Henry. I care no more about it than my lady wife does. Besides, with you gone to Wales much of every year, I'll have Stonelee to protect as well as Stoneweather.

And since you lost our wager, I shan't have to give up that pretty parcel of land near the border between our two demesnes. I'm pleased, indeed, still to call it my own.''

''What wager?'' Roxanne demanded.

''Never mind,'' her husband answered, dipping his head and kissing her soundly. ''Once, I was determined to win a particular prize. But the prize I won is a far better.''